THE ANNIHILATION SCORE

Ace Books by Charles Stross

SINGULARITY SKY

IRON SUNRISE

ACCELERANDO

THE ATROCITY ARCHIVES

GLASSHOUSE

HALTING STATE

SATURN'S CHILDREN

THE JENNIFER MORGUE

WIRELESS

THE FULLER MEMORANDUM

RULE 34

THE APOCALYPSE CODEX

NEPTUNE'S BROOD

THE RHESUS CHART

THE ANNIHILATION SCORE

THE
ANNIHILATION SCORE

CHARLES STROSS

ACE BOOKS, NEW YORK

ACE
An imprint of Penguin Random House LLC
375 Hudson Street, New York, New York 10014

This book is an original publication of Penguin Random House LLC.

Library of Congress Cataloging-in-Publication Data

Stross, Charles.
The annihilation score / Charles Stross.
pages ; cm. — (A laundry files novel ; 6)
ISBN 978-0-425-28117-8 (hardcover)
1. Howard, Bob (Fictitious character)—Fiction.   2. Intelligence service—Great Britain—Fiction.
3. Husband and wife—Fiction.   4. Women violinists—Fiction.   5. Demonology—Fiction.   I. Title.
PR6119.T79A85 2015
823'.92—dc23
2015002026

FIRST EDITION: July 2015

PRINTED IN THE UNITED STATES OF AMERICA

10 9 8 7 6 5 4 3 2 1

Cover illustration by Larry Rostant.
Cover design by Lesley Worrell.
Interior text design by Kristin del Rosario.

Penguin
Random
House

FOR MARTIN AND KIRSTY

ACHNOWLEDGMENTS

Novelists don't, surprisingly, work in a perfect vacuum, and when venturing out of our comfort zones we rely on the kindness and encouragement of others. As a boy growing up in Yorkshire in the 1970s, I lived in a Marvel- and DC Comics–devoid zone: aside from one memorable weekend's exposure to a stack of imported comics in a leisure center, my total experience of the American superhero tradition was limited to the Adam West *Batman* series on Saturday-morning TV and (later) to the Superman movies. (Which is a big part of why, when Marvel came calling in 2005 and asked if I wanted to write scripts for *Iron Man*, I ended up turning them down: Tony Stark just isn't my idea of a hero.) Yes, we had *2000 AD* and Judge Dredd: but the world of comics in 1970s Great Britain was *different*, and where American readers got *Wild Cards*, we got *Temps*.

Which is also why I'd like to thank the following people for their invaluable help and advice in kicking the tires on this novel when it was a work in progress, reassuring me when I was on target, and gently redirecting me when I was veering off track: Cat Valente, Seanan Maguire, Warren Ellis, John Rodgers, Aliette de Bodard, Jamais Cascio, Austin Grossman, Max Gladstone, Ben Aaronovitch, and (on the editorial side) Jenni Hill, Susan Allison, Caitlin Blasdell, and Marty Halpern.

I'd also like to thank my army of regular test-readers, including (but not limited to): Trey Palmer, Hugh Hancock, Phil Dyson, Soon Lee, Nelson Cunningham, Marcus Rowland, Beth Friedman, Andrew Adams, Dan Ritter, Stephen Harris, Tara Glover, Colette Bellingham, and Harry Payne.

Finally, I'd like to thank my previous editor at Ace Books in New York, Ginjer Buchanan, who retired in March 2013. She acquired my first novel, *Singularity Sky*, acquired back in 2001 and had edited my work ever since; and I'd like to thank my new editor, Susan Allison, for making the transition as smooth as possible.

PART 1

ORIGIN STORY

1.

PROLOGUE: THE INCORRIGIBLES

PLEASE ALLOW ME TO INTRODUCE MYSELF . . .

No. Strike that. Period stop backspace backspace bloody computer no stop that stop listening stop dictating end *end* oh I give up.

Will you stop doing that?

Starting *all over again* (typing this time: it's slower, but dam speech recognition and auto-defect to Heckmondwike):

MY HUSBAND IS SOMETIMES A BIT SLOW ON THE UPTAKE; YOU'D think that after ten years together he'd have realized that our relationship consisted of him, me, and a bone-white violin made for a Mad Scientist by a luthier-turned-necromancer. But no: the third party in our *ménage à trois* turns out to be a surprise to him after all these years, and he needs more time to think about it.

Bending over backwards to give him the benefit of the doubt, this has only become an issue since my husband acquired the ability to see

Lecter—that's what I call my violin when I argue with him*—for what he is. (He. She. It. *Whatever.*) Bob is very unusual in having lately developed this ability: it marks him as a member of a privileged elite, the select club of occult practitioners who can recognize what they're in the presence of and stand fast against it rather than fleeing screaming into the night. Like the Vampire Bitch from Human Resources, and what was *she* doing in the living room at five o'clock in the morning—?

Issues. Vampires, violins, and marital miscommunications. I'm going off-topic again, aren't I? Time out for tea!

TAKE THREE.

Hello.

My name is Mo; that's short for Dominique O'Brien. I'm forty-three years old, married to a man who calls himself Bob Howard, aged thirty-eight and a quarter. We are currently separated while we try to sort things out—things including, but not limited to: my relationship with my violin, his relationship with the Vampire Bitch from Human Resources, and the End Of The World As We Know It (which is an ongoing work-related headache).

This is my introduction to my work journal during OPERATION INCORRIGIBLE, and the period immediately before and after it. We're supposed to keep these journals in order to facilitate institutional knowledge retention in event of our death in the line of duty. And if you are reading it, you are probably a new Laundry recruit and I am probably not on hand to brief you in person because I'm dead.

Now, you might be wondering why this journal is so large. I could soft-soap you and claim that I just wanted to leave you with a full

---

* Lecter is not my violin's true name. I am not going to tell you its true name, because the aphorism "true names have power," while technically correct, is wildly misleading, and not in a good way. In the case of my violin, Lecter becomes aware of everyone who knows its true name, and sometimes takes an interest. And you *really* do not want Lecter to take an interest in you.

and balanced perspective on the events surrounding OPERATION INCORRIGIBLE—it's certainly a valid half-truth—but the real reason is that I've been under a lot of stress lately. Nervous breakdowns are a luxury item that we don't have time for right now, and anyway, all our security-cleared therapists are booked up eight months in advance: so the only psychotherapy I'm getting is the DIY kind, and pouring it all out into a private diary that's going to be classified up to its armpits and buried in a TOP SECRET vault guarded by security zombies until I'm too dead to be embarrassed by it seemed like a good compromise. So I wrote it this way, and I don't have the time (or inclination, frankly) to go back and take all the personal stuff out: duty calls, etcetera, and you'll just have to suck it up.

If I were Bob, this journal would probably claim to be written by "Sabine Braveheart" or some such nonsense, but after OPERATION INCORRIGIBLE my patience with silly pseudonyms is at an all-time low. So I'll use pseudonyms where necessary to protect high-clearance covert assets, and for people who insist on hiding under rocks—yes, Bob, if you're reading this I'm talking about you—but the rest of the time I'll call a spade a bloody shovel, not EARTHMOVER CRIMSON VORTEX.

Anyway, you got this far so let me finish the prelude to the intro by adding that if you can get past all the *Bridget Jones meets The Apocalypse* stuff you might pick up some useful workplace tips. (To say nothing of the juicy office gossip.)

NOW, TO THE SUBJECT MATTER AT HAND (FEEL FREE TO SKIP the rest of this foreword if you already know it all):[*]

Bob and I are operatives working for an obscure department of the British civil service, known to its inmates—of whom you are now one—as the Laundry. We're based in London. To family and friends, we're civil servants; Bob works in IT, while I have a part-time consul-

---

[*] Yes, there *will* be an exam afterwards.

tancy post and also teach theory and philosophy of music at Birkbeck College. In actual fact, Bob is a computational demonologist turned necromancer, and I am a combat epistemologist. (It's my job to study hostile philosophies, and disrupt them. Don't ask; it'll all become clear later.)

I also play the violin.

A brief recap: *magic* is the name given to the practice of manipulating the ultrastructure of reality by carrying out mathematical operations. We live in a multiverse, and certain operators trigger echoes in the Platonic realm of mathematical truth, echoes which can be amplified and fed back into our (and other) realities. Computers, being machines for executing mathematical operations at very high speed, are useful to us as occult engines. Likewise, some of us have the ability to carry out magical operations *in our own heads*, albeit at terrible cost.

Magic used to be rare and difficult and unsystematized. It became rather more common and easy and formal after Alan Turing put it on a sound theoretical footing at Bletchley Park during the war: for which sin, our predecessors had him bumped off during the 1950s. It was an act of epic stupidity; these days people who rediscover the core theorems are recruited and put to use by the organization.

Unfortunately, computers are *everywhere* these days—and so are hackers, to such an extent that we have a serious human resources problem, as in: too many people to keep track of. Worse: there are not only too many computers, but too many brains. The effect of all this thinking on the structure of spacetime is damaging—the more magic there is, the easier magic becomes, and the risk we run is that the increasing rate of thaum flux over time tends to infinity and we hit the magical singularity and ordinary people acquire godlike powers as spacetime breaks down, and then the ancient nightmares known as the Elder Gods come out to play. We in the Laundry refer to this apocalyptic situation as CASE NIGHTMARE GREEN, and it is the most immediate of the CASE NIGHTMARE RAINBOW scenarios— existential threats to the future survival of the human species. The bad news is, due to the population crisis we've been in the early stages of

CASE NIGHTMARE GREEN for the past few years, and we are unlikely to be safe again before the middle of the 22nd century.

And so it is that Bob and I live a curious double life—as boring middle-aged civil servants on the one hand, and as the nation's occult security service on the other.

Which brings me to the subject of OPERATION INCORRIGIBLE.

I'm supposed to give you a full and frank account of OPERATION INCORRIGIBLE. The trouble is, my experience of it was colored by certain events of a personal nature, and although I recognize that it's highly unprofessional to bring one's private life into the office, not to mention potentially offensive and a violation of HR guidelines on respect for diversity and sexual misconduct, *I can't let it pass.*

Bluntly: Bob started it, and I really can't see any way to explain what went wrong with OPERATION INCORRIGIBLE without reference to the Vampire Bitch from HR, not to mention Her With The Gills. Or the Mayor, the nude sculpture on the Fourth Plinth, and how I blew my cover. Also: the plague of superheroes, what it's like to have to set up a government agency from scratch during a crisis, and the truth about what it was like to be a member of the official Home Office superhero team. And finally, the truth about my relationship with Officer Friendly.

So, Bob—Bob? I know you're reading this—you'd better tell HR to get on the phone to RELATE and find us a marriage guidance counselor with a security clearance.

Because this is what happened, really and truly.

2.

MORNING AFTER

BUSINESS TRIPS: I HATE THEM.

Actually, *hatred* is too mild an emotion to encapsulate how I feel about my usual run-of-the-mill off-site work-related travel. *Fear and loathing* comes closer; I only ever get sent places when things have gotten so out of control that they need a troubleshooter. Or trouble-violinist. My typical business trips are traumatic and horrible, and leave me with nightmares and a tendency to startle at loud noises for weeks afterwards, not to mention an aversion to newspapers and TV reports on horrible incidents in far-off places. Bob is used to this. He does a wonderful job of keeping the home fires burning, providing warm cocoa and iced Scotch on demand, and over the years he's even learned to pretend to listen. (He's not very *good* at it, mind, but the gesture counts. And, to be fair, he has his own demons to wrestle with.)

But anyway: not long ago, for the first time in at least two years, I got sent on a job that didn't require me to confront *oh God, please make them stop eating the babies' faces* but instead required me to attend committee meetings in nice offices, and even a couple of diplomatic receptions. So I went shopping for a little black dress and matching shoes and accessories. Then I splashed out on a new suit I could also use for work after I got back. And then I got to do the whole cocktail-hour-at-the-embassy thing for real.

Cocktail hour at the embassy consisted of lots of charming men and women in suits and LBDs drinking Buck's Fizz and being friendly to one another, and *so what* if half of them had gill slits and dorsal fins under the tailoring, and the embassy smelled of seaweed because it was on an officially derelict oil rig in the middle of the North Sea, and the Other Side has the technical capability to exterminate every human being within two hundred kilometers of a coastline if they think we've violated the Benthic Treaty? It was *fun*. It was an officially sanctioned *party*. I was not there because my employers thought someone or something vile might need killing: I was there to add a discreet hint of muscle under the satin frock at a diplomatic reception in honor of the renewal of the non-aggression treaty between Her Majesty's Government and Our Friends The Deep Ones (also known as BLUE HADES).

The accommodation deck was a little utilitarian of course, even though they'd refitted it to make the Foreign Office Xenobiology staffers feel a bit more at home. And there was a baby grand piano in the hospitality suite, although nobody was playing it (which was a good thing because it meant nobody asked me if I'd like to accompany the pianist on violin, so I didn't have to explain that Lecter was indisposed because he was sleeping off a heavy blood meal in the locker under my bed).

In fact, now that I think about it, the entire week on the rig was almost entirely news-free and music-free.

And I didn't have any nightmares.

I'm still a bit worried about just why I got this plum of a job at such short notice, mind you. Gerry said he needed me to stand in for Julie Warren, who has somehow contracted pneumonia and is *hors de combat* thereby. But with 20/20 hindsight, my nasty suspicious mind suggests that maybe Strings Were Pulled. The charitable interpreta-

tion is that someone in HR noticed that I was a little overwrought—
Bob left them in no doubt about *that* after the Iranian business, bless
his little drama-bunny socks—but the uncharitable interpretation . . .
well, I'll get to that in a bit. Let's just say that if I'd known I was going
to run into Ramona, I might have had second thoughts about coming.

So, let's zoom in on the action, shall we?

It was Wednesday evening. We flew out to the embassy on Tuesday,
and spent the following day sitting around tables in breakout groups
discussing fisheries quotas, responsibility for mitigating leaks from
deep-sea oil drilling sites, leasing terms for right-of-way for suboce-
anic cables, and liaison protocols for resolving disputes over inadver-
tent territorial incursions by ignorant TV production crews in midget
submarines—I'm not making that bit up, you wouldn't believe how
close James Cameron came to provoking World War Three. We were
due to spend Thursday in more sessions and present our consensus
reports on ongoing future negotiations to the ambassadors on Friday
morning, before the ministers flew in to shake flippers and sign steles
on the current renewal round. But on Wednesday we wrapped up at
five. Our schedule gave us a couple hours to decompress and freshen
up, and then there was to be a cocktail reception hosted by His Scal-
iness, the Ambassador to the United Kingdom from BLUE HADES.*

These negotiations weren't just a UK/BH affair; the UK was leading an EU delegation, so we had a sprinkling of diplomats from just
about everywhere west of the Urals. (Except Switzerland, of course.)
It was really a professional mixer, a meet-and-greet for the two sides.
And that's what I was there for.

I'm not really a diplomat, except in the sense of the term understood by General von Clausewitz. I don't really know anything about
fisheries quotas or liaison protocols. What I was there to do was show

---

* The UK rates a BLUE HADES embassy by virtue of historic precedent; having once been
the world's pre-eminent naval power, we are now the subject of their ongoing interest. And
wish we weren't.

off my pretty face in a nice frock under the nose of the BLUE HADES cultural attaché, who would then recognize me and understand the significance of External Assets detaching me from my regular circuit of *fuck I didn't know they exploded like water balloons is that green stuff blood* to attend a polite soirée.

But drinking dilute bubbly and partying, for middle-aged values of partying (as Bob would put it), is a pleasant change of pace: I could get used to it. So picture me standing by the piano with a tall drink, listening to a really rather charming Chief Superintendent (on detached duty with the fisheries folks, out of uniform) spin sardonic stories about the problems he's having telling honest trawlermen from Russian smugglers and Portuguese fisheries pirates, when I suddenly realize I'm *enjoying* myself, if you ignore the spot on the back of my right ankle where my shoe is rubbing—picture me totally *relaxed*, in the moment right before reality sandbags me.

"Mo?" I hear, in a musical, almost liquid mezzo-soprano, rising on a note of excitement: "Is that really *you*?"

I begin to turn because something about the voice is tantalizingly familiar if unwelcome, and I manage to fix my face in a welcoming smile just in time because the speaker *is* familiar. "Ramona?" It's been seven years. I keep smiling. "Long time no see!" At this moment I'd be happier if it was fourteen years. Or twenty-one.

"Mo, it *is* you! You look wonderful," she enthuses.

"Hey, you're looking good yourself," I respond on autopilot while I try to get my pulse back under control. And it's true, because she *is* looking splendid. She's wearing a backless, gold lamé fishtail number that clings in all the right places to emphasize her supermodel-grade bone structure and make me feel underdressed and dowdy. That she's got ten years on me doesn't hurt either. Eyes of blue, lips with just the right amount of femme fatale gloss, hair in an elaborate chignon: she's trying for the mermaid look, I see. How appropriate. There's just a hint of gray to her skin, and—of course—the sharklike gill slits betwixt collar bones and throat, to give away the fact that it's not just a fashion statement. That, and the sky-high thaum field she's giving off: she's working a class four glamour, or I'll eat my corsage.* "I heard you were transitioning?"

She waves it off with a swish of a white kidskin opera glove. "We have ways of arresting or delaying the change. I can still function up here for a while. But within another two years I'll need a walker or a wheelchair all the time, and I can't pass in public anymore." Her eyebrows furrow minutely, telegraphing irritation. I peer at her. (Are those tiny translucent scales?) "So I decided to take this opportunity for a last visit." She takes a tiny step, swaying side-to-side as if she's wearing seven-inch stilettos: but of course she isn't, and where the train of her dress pools on the floor it conceals something other than feet. "How have you been? I haven't heard anything from you or Bob for ages."

For a brief moment she looks wistful, fey, and just very slightly vulnerable. I remind myself that I've got nothing against her: really, my instinctive aversion is just a side effect of the overwhelming intimidatory power of her glamour, which in turn is a cosmetic rendered necessary by her unfortunate medical condition. To find yourself trapped in a body with the wrong gender must be hard to bear: How much harsher to discover, at age thirty, that you're the wrong species?

"Life goes on," I say, with a light shrug. I glance at Mr. Fisheries Policeman to invite him to stick around, but he nods affably and slithers away in search of canapés and a refill for his glass of bubbly. "In the past month Bob has acquired a cat, a promotion, and a committee." (A committee where he's being run ragged by the Vampire Bitch from Human Resources, a long-ago girlfriend-from-hell who has returned from the dead seemingly for the sole purpose of making his life miserable.) "As for me, I'm enjoying myself here. Slumming it among the upper classes." I catch myself babbling and throw on the brakes. "Taking life easy."

"I hear things," Ramona says sympathetically. "The joint defense coordination committee passes stuff on. I have a—what passes for

---

* Not that I'm wearing one. Little Ms. Dowdy, like I said.

a—desk. It'd all be very familiar to you, I think, once you got used to my people. They're very—" She pauses. "I was going to say *human*, but that's not exactly the right word, is it? They're very *personable*. Cold-blooded and benthic, but they metabolize oxygen and generate memoranda all the same, just like any other bureaucratic life form. After a while you stop noticing the scales and tentacles and just relate to them as folks. But anyway: we hear things. About the Sleeper in the Pyramid and the Ancient of Days and the game of nightmares in Highgate Cemetery. And you have my deepest sympathy, for what it's worth. *Prosit.*" She raises her champagne flute in salute.

"Cheers." I take a sip of Buck's Fizz and focus on not displaying my ignorance. I am aware of the Sleeper and the Ancient, but . . . "Highgate Cemetery?"

"Oops." Fingers pressed to lips, her perfectly penciled eyebrows describe an arch: "Pretend you didn't hear that? Your people have it in hand, I'm sure you'll be briefed on it in due course." Well, perhaps I will be: but my skin is crawling. Ramona knows too much for my peace of mind, and she's too professional for this to be an accidental disclosure: she's letting it all hang out on purpose. *Why?* "Listen, you really ought to come and visit some time. My ma—people—are open to proposals for collaboration, you know. 'The time is right,' so to speak. For collaboration. With humans, or at least their agencies."

The thing about Ramona is, she's a professional in the same line of work as me and thee. She's an old hand: formerly an OCCINT asset enchained by the Black Chamber, now cut loose and reunited with the distaff side of her family tree—the inhuman one. She is proven by her presence here this evening to be a player in the game of spies, squishy-versus-scaly subplot, sufficiently trusted by BLUE HADES that they're willing to parade her around in public. She must have given them extraordinarily good reasons to trust her, such excellent reasons that I am now beginning to think that uninviting her to my wedding all those years ago was a strategic mistake. Time to rebuild damaged bridges, I think.

"Yes, we really ought to do lunch some time soon," I say. "We could talk about, oh, joint fisheries policy or something."

"Yes, that. Or maybe cabbages and kings, and why there are so many superheroes in the news this week?"

"Movies?" My turn to raise an eyebrow: "I know they were all the rage in Hollywood—"

She frowns, and I suddenly realize I've missed an important cue. "Don't be obtuse, Mo." She takes another carefully measured sip of champagne: I have to admire her control, even if I don't much like being around her because of what her presence reminds me of. "Three new outbreaks last week: one in London, one in Manchester, and one in Merthyr Tydfil. That last one would be Cap'n Coal, who, let me see, 'wears a hard hat and tunnels underground to pop up under the feet of dog-walkers who let their pooches foul the pavement.'" She smacks her lips with fishy amusement. "And then there was the bonded warehouse robbery at Heathrow that was stopped by Officer Friendly." I blink, taken aback.

"I haven't been following the news," I admit. "I spent the past few weeks getting over jet lag." *Jet lag* is a euphemism, like an actor's *resting* between theatrical engagements.

"Was that your business trip to Vakilabad?"

Her eyes widen as I grab her wrist. "Stop. *Right now.*" Her pupils are not circular; they're vertical figure eights, an infinity symbol stood on end. I feel as if I'm falling into them, and the ward on my discreet silver necklace flares hot. My grip tightens.

"I'm sorry, Mo," she says, quite sincerely, the ward cooling. She looks shaken. Maybe she got a bit of a soul-gaze in before my firewall kicked her out of my head.

"Where did you hear about Vakilabad?" I need to know: there's talking shop at a reception, and then there's this, this *brazen*—

"Weekly briefing report from Callista Soames in External Liaison," she says quietly. "I'm the equivalent, um, desk officer, for Downstairs. We share, too."

"Sharing." I lick my suddenly dry lips and raise my glass: "Here's to sharing." I do not, you will note, propose a toast to *over*-sharing. Or choose to share with her the details of the Vakilabad job, requested by the Iranian occult intelligence people, or the week-long sleeping-pills-and-whisky aftermath it hit me with because *bodies floating in the air, nooses dangling limply between their necks and the beam of the gallows, glowing eyes casting emerald shadows as dead throats chanted paeans of praise to an unborn nightmare*—I shudder and accidentally knock back half my glass in a single gulp.

"Are you all right?" she asks, allowing her perfect forehead to wrinkle very slightly in a show of concern.

"*Of course* I'm not all right," I grump. There's no point denying what she can see for herself. "Having a bit of a low-grade crisis, actually, hence someone penciling me in for the cocktail circuit by way of a change of pace."

"Trouble at home?" She gives me her best sympathetic look, and I stifle the urge to swear and dump the dregs of my glass over her perfect décolletage.

"None. Of. Your. Business," I say through gritted teeth.

"I'm sorry." She looks genuinely chastened. Worse, my ward tells me that she *is* genuinely sorry. It can detect intentional lies as well as actual threats, and it's been inert throughout our conversation. I feel as if I've just kicked a puppy. All right: an extremely fishy benthic puppy *who did* not *have sex with my husband* seven years ago when they were destiny-entangled and sent on an insane mission to the Caribbean to smoke out a mad billionaire who was trying to take over the world on behalf of his fluffy white cat. "It's just, he was so happy to be with you, you know?"

"We are *so* not going to fail the Bechdel test in public at a diplomatic reception, dear," I tell her. "That would be embarrassing." I take her elbow: "I think both our glasses are defective. Must be leaking, or their contents are evaporating or something." She lets me steer her towards one of the ubiquitous silent waiters, who tops us off. Her gait is unsteady, mincing. Almost as if she's hobbled or her legs are partially fused all the way down to her ankles. She's transitioning, slowly, into the obligate aquatic stage of her kind's life cycle. I feel a pang of misplaced pity for her: needing an ever-increasingly powerful glamour to pass for human, losing the ability to walk, internal organs rearranging themselves into new and unfamiliar structures. Why did I feel threatened by her? *Oh yes, that.* Spending a week destiny-entangled with someone—in and out of their head telepathically, among other things—is supposed to be like spending a year married to them. And Ramona *was* thoroughly entangled with Bob for a while. But that was most of a decade ago, and people change, and it's all water that flowed under the bridge before I married him, and I don't like to think of myself as an obsessive/intransigent bitch, and Mermaid Ramona probably isn't even anatomically *stop thinking about that* compatible anymore. "Let's go and find a tub you can curl up in while we swap war stories."

"Yes, let's," she agrees, and leans on my arm for balance. "You can tell me all about the bright lights in the big city—I haven't been further inland than Aberdeen harbor in years—and I can fill you in on what the fishwraps have been pushing. The vigilantes would be funny if they weren't so sad . . ."

THE ACCOMMODATION ON THIS FORMER OIL RIG HAS, AS I'VE mentioned, been heavily tailored towards its new function. Ramona and I make our way out through a couple of utilitarian-looking steel bulkhead doors, onto the walkway that surrounds the upper level of the reception area like a horseshoe-shaped verandah. The ubiquitous "they" have drilled holes in the deck and installed generously proportioned whirlpool spa tubs, with adjacent dry seating and poolside tables for those of us with an aversion to horrifying dry cleaning bills. And there's a transparent perspex screen to protect us from the worst of the wind.

I help Ramona into one of the tubs—her dress is, unsurprisingly, water-resistant—then collapse upon a strategically positioned chaise alongside. It's a near-cloudless spring evening on the North Sea and we're fifty meters above the wave crests: the view of the sunset is amazing, astonishing, adjectivally exhausting. I run out of superlatives halfway through my second glass. Ramona, it turns out, is a well-informed meteorology nerd. She points out cloud structures to me and explains about the North Atlantic thermohaline circulation and frontal weather systems. We get quietly, pleasantly drunk together, and by the end of the third drink a number of hatchets have been picked up, collaboratively discussed, and permanently re-interred in lead-lined coffins. It's easy to forget that I've harbored an unacknowledged grudge against her for years: hard to remember how long it's been since I last had any kind of heart-to-heart with a girlfriend who understands what it is that I do.

Unfortunately I now need to curtail this account of our discussion because, drunk or not, diplomatic or not, some of the subjects we touched on are so far above your pay grade that it isn't funny. However, I think it is safe to say that BLUE HADES are concerned about CASE NIGHTMARE GREEN and are positioning their human-compatible assets—including Ramona—to keep a closer eye on our activities. They are (whisper this) *actively cooperating*, and you may see more joint liaison committees meeting in the next year than in the previous six decades combined. So it would behoove you to *pay attention* to whatever you're told in diversity awareness training courses about dealing with folks with gray, scaly skin and an affinity for outfits featuring high, opaque necklines. Beyond that, however, my lips are sealed.

I'M IN MY NARROW OIL RIGGER'S BUNK BED BY MIDNIGHT, LIGHTS out and head spinning pleasantly from the fizz and the craic. For the first time in weeks I am relaxed. There is congenial company, a job to do which involves nothing more onerous than staying awake during committee meetings, sedate middle-aged partying in the evenings, and zero possibility whatsoever that I will be hauled out of bed by a dead-of-night phone call in order to go and fight nightmares. What more can a girl ask for?

(Well, the bed could be wider for one thing, and half-occupied by a sleeping husband for another. That would be an improvement, as long as he isn't stressing out about committee meetings and co-workers and things that go bump in the night. (We both do it, and sometimes we actually make each other worse.) But anyway: that's a trade-off— blessed peace and anxiety-free quiet against the security blanket effect of being able to reach out in the night and connect. And right now, peace and quiet is winning by a hair's breadth.)

Lecter is tucked away in his case, which in turn is locked inside the not-insubstantial gun cabinet that I found in my room when I arrived. I can feel his dreams, tickling at the back of my head: disturbing but muted echoes of Vakilabad. I feel slightly guilty that I haven't taken him out for practice in—is it really two days? Two days without tuning up? It seems like an eternity. But he's quiescent right now, even glutted, as if in a food coma. That's good. It means I can ignore his hunger for a while.

So I doze off to sleep. And I dream.

Did you know that keeping a work journal like this—only to be read after one's demise—can be therapeutic?

Let me tell you about my fucking dreams.

Lecter talks to me in my dreams. Like this one:

I'm dancing and it's black and white and it's a waltz, the last waltz at the Vienna Opera Ball—spot the stack of clichés, my internal critic snarks. My partner and I have the floor to ourselves, and we are lit by a lighting rig infinitely high above us that casts a spot as pitiless and harsh as the supernova glare of a dying star. My partner is a full head taller than me, so I'm eye-to-eye with the ivory knot of his tie—yes, white tie and tails, very 1890s. I'm wearing an elaborate gown that probably came out of a glass cabinet at the V&A, fit for a long-dead Archduke's mistress. I can't see his face and he's clearly not Bob (Bob has two left feet) for he leads me in graceful loops, holding me in a grip as strong as spring steel. I let him lead, feeling passive, head whirling (or is that the Buck's Fizz I put away earlier?), positively recumbent as he glides around the floor. It's a two-step in 3/4 time, rather old-fashioned and easy enough to keep up with, but I can't place the composition: it reminds me of von Weber, only . . . not. As we twirl briefly close to the edge of the stage, I glance into the umbral shadows of the orchestra pit, past my partner's occlusive shoulder. There are gaps in the orchestra, like teeth missing from a skull. A faint aroma of musty compost, overlaid with a graveyard tang. The musicians are dead and largely decomposed, swaying in the grip of their instruments, retaining only such body parts as the performance requires. The lead violin's seat gapes empty.

We haven't played today, Lecter whispers inside my head.

"I know." I lean my chin against his shoulder as he holds me tight, spinning before the empty eye sockets of the bone orchestra. It's easy to melt into his grip: he's a wonderful dancer and his iron embrace locks me in like my antique gown's stays.

You shall join the orchestra eventually. It's your destiny. He means the orchestra of his victims, the musicians he has twisted and killed over the decades since his grisly genesis in Erich Zahn's workshop in 1931. He was created at the behest of one Professor Doktor Mabuse. Mabuse the Gambler was a monster, and Zahn his enabler—but Lecter has outlasted and surpassed both of them.

"Not *this* time." I spare another glance for the shades beyond the stage. We have, it seems, an audience consisting only of the dead and drained. I squint: I have a feeling I should recognize some of them.

No, my dear. This is not your destination; this is merely the vestibule.

My dance partner pulls me into a slightly tighter embrace. I lean against him and he breaks with the dance, lowering his grip to my waist, lifting me from the floor to whirl around in helpless orbit.

"What are you *doing*?" I cling to him for dear life. He's overpowering and gorgeous, and despite the charnel horrors around us I find him exciting and exhilarating. Blood is pounding in my ears, and I flush, wanting him—this is silly—as if he's a human lover. Which is crazy talk and unimaginably dangerous and anyway I'm married, but *faceless strong stranger whirling me away in a romantic whirlwind race to nowhere* is an incredibly strong cultural trope to deconstruct when you're so turned-on you're desperately trying not to hump his leg and *get a grip on yourself Mo, this is* not *good*—

"Get the *fuck* out of my head," I snarl, and awaken to find myself lying stone-cold sober in a tangle of sheets saturated with ice-cold sweat, my crotch hot and throbbing, while the cobwebby echoes of Lecter's dream lover giggle and chitter and bounce around the corners of my skull like so many Hallowe'en bat toys.

Bitch, Lecter mocks. ***You know you want me.***

"Fuck you."

Touch me, sex me, feed me.

"Fuck you."

I'm on my feet, fumbling with the key to the gun locker. It contains no guns: just a scuffed white violin case that sports a dog-eared sticker reading THIS MACHINE KILLS DEMONS. Other, more subtle wards engraved between the laminated layers of the case bind the contents in an approximation of safety, much like the sarcophagus around the Number Two reactor at Chernobyl; the instrument itself is considerably deadlier than an assault rifle. I lean against the wall as I lift the case out and lay it on the damp bedsheets, then flick the clasps and lift the coffin-like lid.

Lecter gleams within, old bone in the moonlight shining through the cabin's porthole. I touch his neck and draw my fingers slowly down it, across his body towards the saddle. (Is it my imagination, or does his fingerboard shudder in anticipation?) I reach into the lid with my other hand and pick up the bow. A brief measure from the Diabelli Variations, perhaps? What could be the harm (other than the risk of disturbing my neighbors, who in any case are sleeping in the accommodation deck of a former oil rig, which was presumably designed with soundproofing in mind)?

I wrap my hand around his bridge and lift him gently, then raise his rigid body to my shoulder and rest my cheek against his rest. For an instant I have a disturbing hallucination, that I'm holding something that doesn't resemble a violin so much as an unearthly bone-scaled lizard, f-hole shaped fistulae in its shell flashing me a glimpse of pulsing coils of blood-engorged viscera within—but it passes, and he is once again my instrument, almost an extension of my fingertips. I purse my lips and focus, lower the bow to touch his strings as delicately as *don't think of that*, begin to draw it back, and feel for his pitch—

Then my phone rings.

Play me! Lecter snarls, but the moment has passed.

My phone shrills again as I lower bow and body to the bed and rummage under my discarded dress for the evening clutch. I get to the phone by the fourth ring and answer it. It's a blocked number, but that doesn't mean anything. "Mo speaking. Who is it?"

"Duty Officer, Agent Candid. Please confirm your ID?" He gives me a password and I respond. Then: "We have a Code Red, repeat, a Code Red, Code Red at Dansey House. The Major Incident Contingency Plan has been activated. You are on the B-list; a Coast Guard helicopter is on its way out from Stornoway and will transport you directly to London. Your fallback coordinator is Vikram Choudhury, secondary supervisor is Colonel Lockhart. Report to them upon your arrival. Over and out."

I drop the phone and stare at Lecter. "You knew about this, didn't you?"

But the violin remains stubbornly silent. And when I re-inter him in his velvet-lined coffin, he seems to throb with sullen, frustrated desire.

I DON'T LIKE HELICOPTERS.

They are incredibly noisy, vibrate like a badly balanced tumble drier, and smell faintly of cat piss. (Actually, that latter is probably a function of my sense of smell being a little off—jet fuel smells odd to me—but even so, knowing what it is doesn't help when you're locked in one for the best part of four hours.) The worst thing about them, though, is that *they don't make sense.* They hang from the sky by invisible hooks, and as if that's not bad enough, when you look at a diagram of how they're supposed to work, it turns out that the food processor up top is connected to the people shaker underneath using a component called the Jesus Nut. It's called that because, if it breaks, that's your last word. Bob rabbits on about single points of failure and coffin corners and whatnot, but for me the most undesirable aspect of helicopters can be encapsulated by their dependence on messiah testicles.

This particular chopper is bright yellow, the size of a double-decker bus, and it's older than I am. (And *I'm* old enough that if I'd given it the old school try in my late teens, I could be a grandmother by now.) I gather it's an ancient RAF war horse, long since pensioned off to a life of rescuing lost yachtsmen and annoying trawler captains. It's held together by layers of paint and about sixty thousand rivets, and it rattles the fillings loose from my teeth as it roars and claws its way southwest towards the coast somewhere north of Newcastle. I get about ten minutes' respite when we land at a heliport, but there's barely time to get my sense of balance back before they finish pouring *eau de tomcat* into the fuel tanks and it's time to go juddering up and onwards towards the M25 and the skyscrapers beyond.

By the time the Sea King bounces to a wheezing halt on a police helipad near Hendon, I'm vibrating with exhaustion and stress. Violin case in one hand and suitcase in the other, I clamber down from the chopper and duck-walk under its swinging blades to the Police Armed Response car at the edge of the pad. There are a pair of uniforms waiting beside it, big solid constables who loom over me with the curiously condescending deference police display towards those they've been assured are On Their Side but who nevertheless suffer the existential handicap of not being sworn officers of the law. "Ms. O'Brien?"

"Dr. O'Brien," I correct him automatically. "I've been out of the loop for two hours. Any developments?"

"We're to take you to the incident site, Doctor. Um." He glances at the violin case. "Medical?"

"The other type," I tell him as I slide into the back seat. "I need to make a call."

They drive while my phone rings. On about the sixth attempt I get through to the switchboard. "Duty Officer. Identify yourself, please." We do the challenge/response tap dance. "Where are you?"

"I'm in the back of a police car, on my way through . . ." I look for road signs. "I've been out of touch since pickup at zero one twenty hours. I'll be with you in approximately forty minutes. What do I need to know?"

Already I can feel my guts clenching in anticipation, the awful bowel-watering apprehension that I'm on another of those jobs that will end with a solo virtuoso performance, blood leaking from my fingertips to lubricate Lecter's fretboard and summon his peculiar power.

"The Code Red has been resolved." The DO sounds tired and emotional, and I suddenly realize that he's not the same DO that I spoke to earlier. "We have casualties but the situation has come under control and the alert status is cancelled. You should go—"

"Casualties?" I interrupt. A sense of dread wraps itself around my shoulders. "Is Agent Howard involved?"

"I'm sorry, I can't—" The DO pauses. "Excuse me, handing you over now."

There's a crackle as someone else takes the line, and for a second or so the sense of dread becomes a choking certainty, then: "Dr. O'Brien, I presume? Your husband is safe." It's the Senior Auditor, and I feel a stab of guilt about having diverted his attention, even momentarily, from whatever he's dealing with. "I sent him home half an hour ago. He's physically unharmed but has had a very bad time, I'm afraid, so I'd be grateful if you'd follow him and report back to this line if there are any problems. I'm mopping up and will be handing over to Gerry Lockhart in an hour; you can report to him and join the clean-up crew tomorrow."

"Thank you," I say, adding *I think* under my breath before I hang up. "Change of destination," I announce to the driver, then give him my home address.

"That's a—" He pauses. "Is that one of your department's offices?" he asks.

"I've been told to check up on one of our people," I tell him, then shut my trap.

"Is it an emergency?"

"It could be." I cross my arms and stare at the back of his neck until he hits a button and I see the blue and red reflections in the windows to either side. It's probably—almost certainly—a misuse of authority, but they've already blown the annual budget by getting the Coast Guard to haul me five hundred miles by helicopter, and if the Senior Auditor thinks that Bob needs checking up on, *well . . .*

I close my eyes and try to compose myself for whatever I'm going to find at the other end as we screech through the rainy predawn London streetscape, lurching and bouncing across road pillows and swaying through traffic-calming chicanes.

The past twelve hours have rattled me, taking me very far from my stable center: hopefully Bob will be all right and we can use each other for support. He tends to bounce back, bless him, almost as if he's too dim to see the horrors clearly. (I used to think he's one of life's innocents, although there have been times recently, especially since the business in Brookwood Cemetery a year ago, when I've been pretty sure *he's* hiding nightmares from *me*. Certainly Gerry and Angleton have begun to take a keen interest in his professional development, and he's started running high-level errands for External Assets. This latest business with the PHANGs—Photogolic Hemophagic Anagathic Neurotropic Guys, that's bureaucratese for "vampire" to me or thee—has certainly demonstrated a growing talent for shit-stirring on his part. Almost as if he's finally showing signs of growing up.) I keep my eyes closed, and systematically dismiss the worries, counting them off my list one by one and consigning them to my mental rubbish bin. It's a little ritual I use from time to time when things are piling up and threatening to overwhelm me: usually it works brilliantly.

The car slows, turns, slows further, and comes to a halt. I open my eyes to see a familiar street in the predawn gloom. "Miss?" It's the driver. "Would you mind signing here, here, and here?"

A clipboard is thrust under my nose. The London Met are probably the most expensive taxi firm in the city; they're definitely the most rule-bound and paperwork-ridden. I sign off on the ride, then find the door handle doesn't work. "Let me out, please?" I ask.

"Certainly, miss." There's a click as the door springs open. "Have a good day!"

"You, too," I say, then park my violin and suitcase on the front doorstep while I fumble with my keys.

Bob and I live in an inter-war London semi which, frankly, we couldn't afford to rent or buy—but it's owned by the Crown Estates, and we qualify as essential personnel and get it for a peppercorn rent in return for providing periodic out-of-hours cover. Because it's an official safe house, it's also kitted out with various security systems and occult wards—protective circuits configured to repel most magical manifestations. I'm exhausted from a sleepless night, the alarms and wards are all showing green for safety, the Code Red has been cancelled, and I'm not expecting trouble. That's the only excuse I can offer for what happens next.

The key turns in the lock, and I pick up my violin case with my left hand as I push the door open with my right. The door swings ajar, opening onto the darkness of our front hall. The living room door opens to my right, which is likewise open and dark. "Hi, honey, I'm home!" I call as I pull the key out of the lock, hold the door open with my left foot, and swing my suitcase over the threshold with my right hand.

I set my right foot forward as Bob calls from upstairs: "Hi? I'm up here."

Then something pale moves in the living room doorway.

I drop my suitcase and keys and raise my right hand. My left index finger clenches on a protruding button on the inside of the handle of my violin case—a motion I've practiced until it's pure autonomic reflex. I do not normally open Lecter's case using the quick-release button, because it's held in place with powerful springs and reassembling it after I push the button is a fiddly nuisance: but if I need it, I need it *badly*. When I squeeze the button, the front and back of the case eject, leaving me holding a handle at one end of a frame that grips the violin by the c-ribs. The frame is hinged, and the other end holds the bow by a clip. With my right hand, I grasp the scroll and raise the violin to my shoulder, then I let go of the handle, reach around, and take the fiddle. The violin is ready and eager, and I feel a thrill of power rush through my fingertips as I bring the instrument to bear on the doorway to the living room and draw back a quavering, screeching, utterly non-euphonious note of challenge.

All of which takes a *lot* longer to write—or to read—than to do; I can release and raise my instrument in the time it takes you to draw and aim a pistol. And I'm trained for this. No, seriously. *My instrument kills demons.* And there's one in my sights right now, sprawled halfway through the living room doorway, bone-thin arms raised towards me and fangs bared.

Yesss!!! Lecter snarls triumphantly as I draw back the bow and channel my attention into the sigil carved on the osseous scrollwork at the top of his neck. My fingertips burn as if I've rubbed chili oil into them, and the strings fluoresce, glowing first green, then shining blue as I strike up a note, and another note, and begin to search for the right chord to draw the soul out through the ears and eyes of the half-dressed blonde bitch baring her oversized canines at me.

She's young and sharp-featured and hungry for blood, filled with an appetite that suggests a natural chord in the key of Lecter—oh yes, he knows what to do with her—with *Mhari*, that's her name, isn't it? Bob's bunny-boiler ex from hell, long since banished, latterly returned triumphant to the organization with an MBA and a little coterie of blood-sucking merchant banker IT minions.

I put it all together in a single instant, and it's enough to make my skull pop with rage even as my heart freezes over. Code Red, Bob damaged, and I get home to find this manipulative bitch in my home, half-dressed—bare feet, black mini-dress, disheveled as if she's just *don't go there*—I adjust my grip, tense my fingers, summoning up the killing rage as I prepare to let Lecter off his leash.

"Stand down!"

It's Bob. As I stare at Mhari I experience a strange shift in perspective, as if I'm staring at a Rubin vase: the meaning of what I'm seeing inverts. She crouches before me on her knees, looking up at me like a puppy that's just shit its owner's bed and doesn't know what to do. Her face is a snarl—no, a *smile*—of terror. I'm older than she is, and since becoming a PHANG she looks younger than her years, barely out of her teens: she's baring her teeth ingratiatingly, the way pretty girls are trained to. As if you can talk your way out of any situation, however bad, with a pretty smile and a simper.

The wards are intact. *Bob must have invited her in.*

I am so stricken by the implicit betrayal that I stand frozen, pointing Lecter at her like a dummy until Bob throws himself across my line of fire. He's wearing his threadbare dressing gown and his hair is tousled. He gasps out nonsense phrases that don't signify anything: "We had an internal threat! I told her she could stay here! The threat situation was resolved about three hours ago at the New Annex! She's about to leave."

"It's true," she whines, panic driving her words at me: "there was an elder inside the Laundry—he was sending a vampire hunter to murder all the PHANGs—Bob said he must have access to the personnel records—this would be the last place a vampire hunter would look for me—I've been sleeping in the living room—I'll just get my stuff and be going—"

She's contemptible. But there's someone else here, isn't there? I make eye contact with Bob. "Is. This. True?" *Did you really bring her back here? Is this really what it looks like?*

Bob seems to make his mind up about something. "Yes," he says crisply.

I stare at him, trying to understand what's happened. The bitch scrambles backwards, into the living room and out of sight: I ignore her. She's a vampire and she could be gearing up to re-plumb my jugular for all I know, but I find that I simply don't give a fuck. The enormity of Bob's betrayal is a Berlin Wall between us, standing like a vast slab of irrefrangible concrete, impossible to bridge.

"You didn't email," I tell him. *Why didn't you email?*

"I thought you were on a—" His eyes track towards the living room door. Every momentary saccade is like a coil of barbed wire tightening around my heart. "Out of contact."

"That's not the point," I say. "You invited that—*thing*—into our house." I gesture, carelessly swinging Lecter to bear on the living room doorway. The vampire whimpers quietly. *Good.*

"She's a member of non-operational staff who has contracted an unfortunate but controllable medical condition, Mo. We have a duty to look after our own."

His hypocrisy is breathtaking. "Yes well, I can see *exactly* how important that is to you." The thing in the living room is moving around, doing something. I lean around the doorway. "You," I call.

It can't hear you, Lecter tells me. ***You can only get her attention in one way. Allow me?***

I rest the bow lightly across the bridge and tweak gently, between two fingers. Lecter obliges, singing a soul into torment. "Keep away from him, you bitch," I call through the doorway.

The vampire moans.

"Stop hurting her," someone is saying.

I keep moving the bow. It's not something I can control: the notes want to flow.

"*Stop!*" Bob sounds upset.

"I can't—" The bow drags my fingers along behind it, burning them. I'm bleeding. The strings are glowing and the vampire is scream-ing in pain.

I try to lock my wrist in place but the bow is fighting me. I try to open my fingers, to drop the bow. "It won't let me!"

You want me to do this, Lecter assures me. His voice is an echo of my father (dead for many years), kindly, avuncular, control-ling. ***This is simply what you want.***

"**Stop**," says Bob, in a tongue and a voice I have never felt from him before. He grabs my right elbow and pinches hard: pain stabs up my arm. There's a rattling crash from the living room as the Vampire Bitch from Human Resources legs it through the bay window and runs screaming into the predawn light.

Mistress, you *will* obey, hisses Lecter, and there's a cramp in my side as he forces me to turn, raising his body and bringing it to bear on my husband in a moment of horror—

"**Stop**," Bob repeats. He's speaking Old Enochian; not a language I thought he was fluent in. There's something very weird and unpleas-antly familiar about his accent.

I shake my head. "You're hurting me."

"I'm sorry." He loosens his grip on my elbow but doesn't let go. Something inside me feels broken.

"Did you have sex with her?" I have to ask, God help me.

"No."

I drop the bow. My fingers tingle and throb and don't want to work properly. They feel wet. I'm bleeding. I finally manage to unkink my elbow and put down the violin. Blood is trickling along its neck, threatening to stain the scrimshaw.

"You're bleeding." Bob sounds shocked. "Let me get you a towel."

He vanishes up the hall corridor and I manage to bend down and lay the violin on top of its case. I don't trust myself to think or to speak or to feel. I'm numb. Is he telling the truth? He denies it. But is he? Isn't he? My ward should tell me, but right now it's mute.

A sharp realization hits me: regardless of what Bob may or may not have been up to, Lecter wants me to think the worst of him.

Bob hands me a roll of kitchen towels, and I tear a bunch off and wrap them around my hand. "Kitchen," I say faintly. I don't trust myself to speak in any sentence longer than a single word.

We get to the kitchen. I sit down quietly, holding the bloody wedge of tissue to my fingertips. I look around. It seems so normal, doesn't it? Not like a disaster scene. Bob just hangs around with a stupid, stunned expression on his face.

"She's a vampire," I say numbly.

"So is *that*." He nods in the direction of the hall door, pointing at Lecter and his quick-release carapace.

"That's . . . different." I don't know why I should feel defensive. Lecter wanted to kill Bob, didn't he? First he wanted to kill Mhari, then . . . Bob.

"The difference is, now it wants me dead." Bob looks at me. He's tired and careworn, and there's something else. "You know that, don't you?"

"When it turned on you, it was horrible." I shudder. I can't seem to stop shaking. The paranoia, the suspicion: they say there's no smoke without fire, but what if an enemy is laying a smoke screen to justify terrible acts? "Oh God, that was awful." *You should be dead, Bob,* something whispers at the back of my mind. Lecter is too powerful. "Bob, how did you stop it? You shouldn't have been able to . . ."

"Angleton's dead."

"*What?*"

"The Code Red last night. The intruder was a, an ancient PHANG. He killed Angleton."

"Oh my God. Oh my God."

I lose the plot completely for a few seconds. Stupid me. I reach for him across the infinite gulf of the kitchen table and he's still there, only different. He takes my hand. "You're *him* now." Angleton is another of our ancient monsters, the mortal vessel of the Eater of Souls. One of the night haunts upon whose shoulders the Laundry rests. For years he's used Bob as a footstool, dropping tidbits of lore in front of him, sharing abilities, but over these past two years, Bob's become something more: the ritual at Brookwood, where the Brotherhood of the Black Pharaoh tried to sacrifice him, changed something in him. Now he's different. The way he managed to break through Lecter's siren song . . .

"Not really," he demurs. I feel a flicker of sullen resentment: his talent for self-deprecation borders on willful blindness. "But I have access to a lot of, of—" He falls silent. "Stuff."

Unpalatable facts:

Bob and I have come this far together by treating life as a three-legged race, relying on one another to keep us sane when we simply can't face up to what we're doing anymore. I've come to count on our relationship working like this, but in the space of a couple of hours the rug has been pulled from under my feet.

This is a new and unfamiliar Bob. Whether he's lying or not, whether he was hosting an innocent sleepover in a safe house or carrying on an affair in my own bed while I was away, pales into insignificance compared to the unwelcome realization that he isn't just Bob anymore, but Bob with eldritch necromantic strings attached. He's finally stepped across a threshold I passed long ago, realized that he has responsibilities larger than his own life. And it means we're into terra incognita.

"What are you going to do?" I ask him.

"I should destroy that thing." His expression as he looks at the hall doorway is venomous, but I can tell from the set of his shoulders that he knows how futile the suggestion is. I feel a pang of mild resentment. I'd like to be rid of the violin, too; what does he think carrying it does to me?

"They won't let you. The organization needs it. It's all I can do to keep squashing the proposals to make more of them."

"Yes, but if I don't it's going to try and kill me again," he points out.

I try to plot a way out of the cleft stick we find ourselves in. Of course, there isn't one. "I can't let go of it." I chew my lip. "If I let go of it—return it to Supplies, convince them I can't carry it anymore—they'll just give it to someone else. Someone inexperienced. It was inactive for years before they gave it to me. Starving and in hibernation. It's awake now. And the stars are right."

This is why I have to keep calm and carry Lecter. Until someone better qualified comes along, I'm where the buck stops. And the chances of someone coming along who is more able than I—an agent with eight years' experience of holding my course and not being swayed by the blandishments of the bone violin—are slim. I hope Bob can understand this. It's not really any different from the Eater of Souls thing: now that Angleton's gone, Bob's next in the firing line.

"What are we going to do? It wants me dead," he says dolefully.

I talk myself through to the bitter end, as much for my own benefit as for his. "If I let go of it a lot of other people will die, Bob. I'm the only thing holding it back. Do you want that? Do you really want to take responsibility for letting it off the leash with an inexperienced handler?"

I meet his gaze. My heart breaks as he says the inevitable words.

"I'm going to have to move out."

3.

THE FOURTH WALL

I REASSEMBLE THE VIOLIN CASE ON THE KITCHEN TABLE WHILE Bob moves around upstairs, assembling his go-bag and adding an extra supply of necessities. His footsteps are heavy and drag as if he's drunk. My hands are shaking and I have to sortie to the bathroom for sticking plasters a couple of times, but I finally succeed in fitting the case back together again. I retrieve the bow and violin, then fetch the cleaning kit: then I focus on the fingerboard so intently that the sound of the front door closing takes me by surprise. I realize with a start that my husband has left me without saying good-bye.

I shut the case and leave it on the kitchen table. To my mild surprise, I feel numb and distant. It feels *wrong*: I should be angry, bitter and burning and full of rage and resentment. I ought to be furious with the violin, which is sleeping smug and satiated in its bone-white coffin-case, having finally gotten its way. I should be pissed off at Mhari for having injected herself back into Bob's life like some kind of vile parasitic worm. (At least Ramona has the decency to stay away and lead a life of her own.) I should be having a screaming jealousy fit at my husband for fucking that bitch, or worse, for *not* fucking her and for being so oblivious to the possibility and to what it might mean to me that he didn't realize offering her crash space in our living room while I was away *without telling me* might be open to misinterpretation. I should be mourning Angleton, the scary old coffin-dodger. I should be having a screaming breakdown fit right now, shouting imprecations at the setting moon and throwing toiletries out of the window. But I'm not; I'm just icily over-controlled, methodically going through the motions.

How very *grown-up* of me.

Around six o'clock I realize I'm yawning uncontrollably. My emotional state is freewheeling downhill with burned-out brakes: I'll be unable to put up a fight if Lecter tries to romance me in my dreams. Also, my mobile phone is down to about 30 percent of battery charge—which is bad, if I'm even potentially on-call. So I take precautions. I lock and bolt the front door, arm the burglar alarm, check and then power up the protective grids on all the windows, and prepare for a siege. (The living room window, it turns out, is both intact and closed: Bob must have seen to it on his way out. Damn him for his consideration.)

I pick up the violin case and carry it upstairs. We have a big old wardrobe in the bedroom, and there's a lock on its door. I bed Lecter down between Bob's mothballed funeral suit and a random selection of dresses left over from the last decade of wedding invitations, lock the wardrobe, carefully draw a basic containment ward around the lock using my conductive Sharpie, then take the key downstairs and put it inside the ceramic jar of pre-ground coffee. Bob carefully left an old crowbar under the bed some years ago, just in case, so in event of a *real* emergency I can get to the violin without going downstairs . . . but I'd rather not make it too easy. I'm not a sleepwalker, but there's always a first time. Finally, I use the bathroom, then lock myself in the bedroom, plug in my phone, and set an alarm for noon.

And so to bed, perchance to sleep like a log. And, by some miracle, Lecter leaves me alone.

*   *   *

UNFORTUNATELY I DO NOT GET MY FULL LIE-IN.

I vaguely register confused sensations of a furry face pushing against my head, but I grew up in a house with cats and I can ignore Spooky ruthlessly, even in my sleep. But an hour before my alarm call—at about ten to eleven—my ears register the distant ringing of the work telephone in the kitchen. I'm asleep when it rings the first time, but by the second I am on my feet, and by the third I walk straight into the closed-and-locked bedroom door. Swearing ensues.

It takes me eleven rings—six more than usual—to get to the phone, and I pick it up bleary-eyed and panting. "Yes?" I gasp, certain that something is *wrong*—then I realize what it is: Bob would normally have answered the phone because he sleeps on the side of the bed nearest the door.

"Ops desk. Is that Agent Candid?"

Two calls in twelve hours. "Yes," I admit, and authenticate myself. "What is it?"

"Sorry to bother you after last night, but we have a"—the DO sounds reticent, which is just plain *wrong*—"peculiar situation emerging. How soon can you get to Trafalgar Square? With your instrument?"

"What for?"

"We want you to busk."

Flummoxed is my middle name. "You want me to busk why, precisely? In Trafalgar Square? Don't you need a license to—"

"The police will cover for you. Um, it would be best if you dressed casual—a mature student out having fun, something like that."

My mouth flaps uselessly as I try to process this vexing—not to say patronizing—instruction. I don't know how to explain to the DO that most music students aren't in their early forties: Maybe I just look young for my age? I sigh. "I'll give it a try. What's the plan?"

"There's a developing situation on the Fourth Plinth, and we need someone to keep an eye on it who isn't going to draw attention and who is equipped to intervene if it escalates. All our reserves are committed after last night, so, um, I know this sounds bad, but when I say we're scraping the barrel I mean we're totally overcommitted and running on 120 percent and we didn't want to disturb you but we're entirely out of unobtrusive assets . . ."

Suddenly it clicks. "You want me because I'm socially invisible."

"You could put it like that: personally I'd rather not, but Colonel Lockhart said you'd understand?" He ends on a whimper blue-shifting into a whine, and so he should. The landline phone is a 1940s-era Bakelite-and-steel assembly. If it was made of flimsy modern plastics my death-grip would be crumbling it to splinters at this point.

"I'll be there in an hour," I snarl, then slam the receiver down so hard that it bounces.

The Laundry is, regrettably, top-heavy with men of a certain age. Institutional culture propagates down the decades, and however much we may want change, change takes time. As it happens, the Laundry is a lot better today than it was when I was sucked into the machinery a decade ago. We're part of the civil service, and we're required to follow anti-discrimination law to the letter: and for the most part we do an okay job. But as with all organizations, shit trickles down from the top, and if the assholes at the top hold antediluvian attitudes formed in previous decades, you're going to have to keep practicing your shit-eating grin until they retire.

In this particular case I am forced to admit that Lockhart has a valid point. Women over a certain age become socially invisible: people just *ignore* us. I'm close enough to the tipping point that if I don't take care of my appearance, I can fall foul of it. It's a very strange experience, being the invisible middle-aged woman. You can walk into a shop or restaurant or a bar and eyeballs just seem to slide past you as if you aren't there. When you're trying to get served, it's infuriating, sometimes to the point of being humiliating as well, but in our line of work . . .

. . . Sometimes having a passive cloak of invisibility that doesn't set off every thaum detector within a kilometer comes in handy.

Okay, Mo, you can do this. One step at a time. Treat it as an exercise in street theater, you can do that, can't you? I grumble to myself as I refill the cat's bowl, retrieve my instrument, run a brush through my hair (which is lank from the seaside air and subsequent helicopter ride: slept in sufficiently that it's probably on the edge of becoming a des res for upwardly mobile dormice), and hunt out casualwear I'd ordinarily have relegated to housework-only use. I pick out: jeans, a chunky cable-knit sweater, what used to be a nice flying jacket of Bob's, a comfy but worn pair of DMs, and by way of accessories a Liberty scarf and a black beret that have both seen better days. *Yeah, that's my boho mature student persona, baby.* For a moment I contemplate going hipster instead, but that might stand out. A smear of lipstick and a battered leather handbag and I'm ready to serenade the one-legged pigeons of London.

I collect my instrument, head for the end of the street, and flag down a cab, trying not to spook at odd-looking low-slung black cars or random passers-by. Taxis are expensive, but I'm going to take a "how soon can you" call by the DO as carte blanche to run up a tab. "I need to get to Charing Cross," I tell the driver. She nods, drops the apocryphal fifth wheel that allows the black cab to pivot in place, then floors the accelerator.

London traffic is its normal self, which is to say composed entirely of nose-to-tail black cabs, red buses, and confused delivery drivers. Bike couriers weave in and out of the intermittently stationary vehicles without once demonstrating their possession of a survival instinct; I cringe at a couple of near misses and hunker down in the back, wishing the windows were tinted. I feel *way* too exposed out here: exposed and trapped simultaneously. A killer on a stolen motorbike could come up behind us while we're stopped at traffic lights and put two bullets in the back of my head and I wouldn't even see them approaching . . . *try not to think about it.* There are commuters on bicycles, and numerous tourists pedaling along gamely on bright blue Boris Bikes. Maybe I should have rented one instead of paying the cabbie? Tried to blend in with the anonymous hordes? It might even have been faster.

She drops me precisely outside the nearest entrance to Charing Cross tube station. I thank her and head towards the confused mass of pedestrian crossings on the Strand. It takes me a minute or two to make it to the edge of the Square, where I pause beneath the supercilious gaze of the one-eyed admiral, mentally tug my middle-aged invisibility cloak tight around my shoulders, and take stock of my surroundings.

In the middle of the square: the fountains, fronted by Nelson's Column. At each corner: the four plinths, three of them surmounted by pompous Victorian triumphalist statues—General Sir Henry Havelock, General Sir Charles James Napier, and His Nobby Nob-ness, King George the Fourth. (Who was not even remotely as pompous as his statue suggests.) Over to the left at the back, there's the infamously empty Fourth Plinth, subject of the Duty Officer's scrutiny.

And the instant I clap eyes on it, I realize that we have a problem. No, make that a *problem*.

The Fourth Plinth is one of those British affectations which we love to parade around in public as a sign of our broad-minded tolerance and love of eccentricity. It's actually just another classical stone plinth, originally intended to support an equestrian statue. It's been empty for about a hundred and fifty years because nobody could agree who to put on it. Then around the turn of the millennium, the Royal Society of Arts said, "Oi, can we borrow the spare plinth? It's an Art thing." And since then it's been occupied by an ever-changing succession of arts projects: sometimes a statue, sometimes an abstract sculpture, sometimes a random member of the public reciting poetry or narrating Shakespeare in semaphore.

Today there appears to be a human pyramid on the plinth. Or maybe it's a rugby scrum? Or a public orgy, or a sponsored die-in? I'm not sure, because I'm at the other side of the square and there are a lot of people between me and the plinth. But in any case, there's what looks like a pile of naked human bodies up there. Here and there, a leg or arm flops limply over the side. *Hmm.*

I sit on one of the steps and open the violin case. Pigeons rattle and flap their way across the flagstones; I force myself not to let them distract me, even though they remind me too damn much of the seagulls swirling around the oil rig. At the far side of the square I spot a van with a satellite uplink dish on its roof and an open door, a journalist with cameraman in tow. They seem to be looking up at the plinth. I lift Lecter and his bow out, latch the case closed, and sling it across my shoulder. Standing, violin in hand, I scan for police. There's always a car or two, or a van, drawn up around the edge. Today I spot three vans and four cars, one with the distinctive markings of an Armed Response vehicle. They're all parked along the west side of the square. A handful of bobbies in stabbies are dispersed among the crowd, which is no thinner or thicker than I'd expect for a weekday in one of the nation's most prominent tourist attractions. No sign of anything particularly unusual, though, except—

"Whoa!" I'm so startled by what I see that I speak aloud. Nobody pays me any attention, though, because everyone else who sees it responds the same way.

A woman floats into the air in front of the plinth. She's a yummy-mummy type, modishly dressed, with a matchingly accessorized baby in a buggy the size of a Range Rover. She's waving her arms and legs like an upside-down beetle, clinging on to the pushchair—which is also airborne—for grim death. I can just about hear her desperate screams for help above the traffic noise and the hum of the crowd as she levitates alongside the four-meter-tall slab of marble. The push-chair tilts sideways and sheds its load: a rain of baby bottles and nappies splatter to the ground. The woman screams again and loses her grip on the buggy. It drops for a moment, then swoops, and kisses the ground in a controlled landing. Its securely strapped-in passenger laughs and claps appreciatively. She, however, is not so lucky: what-ever force holds her airborne raises her higher, then slides her over the pile of bodies on the plinth. Then invisible hands start to undress her in mid-air.

I look around. Police are dotted around the plinth, but they seem reluctant to approach it. I look closer, and see they're putting down cones and unrolling incident tape. *Shit.*

The woman is naked now. Suddenly she stops thrashing, as if par-alyzed or stunned. Her invisible assailant floats her slowly over the plinth, then lowers her atop the mound of bodies. *Oh shit. I hope she's not dead.* I stand up and start to walk towards the middle of the square. This isn't a gumshoe job anymore.

"Sorry, miss, you can't go there. Turn around and go back. Stop right there!"

I stop, because there's not much point trying to walk right through the two-meter-tall slab of London's finest who has just stepped in front of me. Looking past his shoulder I spot another couple of vans pulling up, cops in riot gear climbing out and forming a line facing outwards around the plinth, like a kettling in reverse.

I pull out my warrant card and hold it where he can't ignore it: "Take me to your incident controller."

"You can't—" He goes cross-eyed as the warrant card grabs his undivided attention and digs in.* "Er. You want Detective Chief Inspector Sullivan, boss, she's over there." He gestures. "Follow me."

A BIG NAVY BLUE MOBILE COMMAND CENTER IS BUSILY SHOE-horning itself into a parking spot just round the corner in Pall Mall, and my guide leads me straight towards it. I've got my hands full with my instrument right now, which is a problem: I think I need to call in my own mobile support team. We approach the bus just as a knot of police officers converge on it. A short woman with a no-nonsense attitude is giving them marching orders. I'm about to raise my warrant card when she turns and stares at me and I recognize her. "Oh good," says Josephine, "is this *your* mess?"

"I don't know, I only just got here." I shrug, bow and fiddle in either hand. I feel calmer now that I've got a professional to work with. "Got a call an hour ago. When did it kick off?"

"Wait." She turns to her posse. "Peeps, this is Dr. O'Brien. She works with us: give her what she asks for. Any questions, bring them to me. Now get moving." If I were the praying kind, I'd think my

---

* Laundry warrant cards have this power: in addition to identifying the holder, they carry a powerful geas that enables the holder—as long as they're on official business—to convince any other servant of Her Majesty's Government that you're a superior.†

† Don't try this on the Prime Minister. Or the Queen.

wishes were answered. Jo Sullivan is one of our direct contacts within the Met; she's worked with us, on and off, for longer than I've been doing field work. In fact, last time I saw her she was working for our Internal Affairs people. I suppose it was inevitable she'd rotate back into the regular force, given the number of paranormal events they must be handling these days. Anyway, if I'd been asked to name the cop I wanted to see in charge of this, she'd be at the top of my list.

She turns back to me. "Seventy-eight minutes ago, body number one goes flying up to situationist art-show heaven. Male Australian backpacker, mid-twenties, best we can tell. Infrared camera on the chopper says they're still warm and breathing but they're not moving and whatever's doing it likes its bananas peeled." She glances at her tablet: "We're up to a count of twelve bodies now, but nobody has any idea who or what is responsible. We sent up the bat-signal for Officer Friendly, but he's not answering."

"Officer Friendly?"

She raises an eyebrow: "Haven't met him yet? He's one of ours: nominally he's with ACPO, but they're stretched too thin. Probably still tangled up in paperwork and witness statements from his last big call-out." Her frustration is palpable: "I don't want to have to cordon off Trafalgar Square, but if we can't find the perp—"

"Well. Let me put my kit down and I'll see if the office knows anything." We're standing next to a van with open doors: I put Lecter and his bow on the front seat while I pull out my phone and dial. "Duty desk? O'Brien here. Can you put me through to whoever thought it was a good idea to send me over to Trafalgar Square without a plan?"

"Yes, Dr. O'Brien. Transferring you now . . ."

"Good morning, Mo." I recognize Gerry Lockhart's gravelly voice. "What's going on?"

I resist the urge to roll my eyes. "We have a major incident going on in Trafalgar Square and you're asking *me*? Something is stripping tourists naked and building a pile of bodies on the Fourth Plinth. Paralyzing them, too. The police have no idea and they're on the edge of—" Sudden shouting distracts me: I hunch my head over to hold my phone against my shoulder and turn to see what's going on. "Oh *fuck* it just escalated. Got to go, I'll call you back."

Another body is floating upwards. He's hanging on to his trademark bicycle by the handlebars, legs pedaling furiously in mid-air. Portly, his suit rumpled and his mass of unkempt hair flopping across his forehead, he is instantly recognizable as the Mayor of London.

"Oh dear fucking Christ on a crutch," mouths Josephine, her eyes round with horror. I wince and nod in sympathy. *"Get him!"* she shouts.

Cops are already converging on the levitating Mayor like a pack of hounds in pursuit of a fox—the unspeakable in full pursuit of the uneatable. He floats above them, calling for help. One of them jumps high enough to grab the rear wheel of the bike, but dangles for barely a second before it slips from the Mayor's grip. He lands with a crash and the Mayor floats higher.

I ring off, then fumble through the phone's confusing mass of icons until I get into the OFCUT suite—occult sensors and countermeasures, yes, we do indeed have an app for that. I raise the phone, and slowly pan it across the square. The Mayor's struggles are limned in green, the contours of the thaum field outlined by the phone's modified camera chip. The bodies atop the plinth also glow . . .

Aha!

I tap Josephine's shoulder to get her attention. She whirls: "Yes?" she demands.

"Don't be too obvious about it," I say, keeping my voice quiet and conversational, "but our merry prankster appears to be human." (Which is a huge relief because human problems, however exotic, usually have human solutions. The alternatives are all much, much worse.) "He's chilling out on the northeast plinth, between the legs of the horse." His silhouette is lit up like a laser-backlit emerald in my phone's display, but when I try to look at him with my mark one peepers, they just don't seem to want to see him—it's far too easy to focus on the horse's head or the stone plinth beneath it. "He's got some kind of invisibility field, but he's definitely responsible." Shimmering green contrails link his swooping hands to the body of his current victim.

"Charming." She grins savagely. "Let's lift him—"

"No." I slide my phone back into my jacket pocket, then collect Lecter from the van. "We have no idea of his full capabilities. So far he's given us telekinesis, paralysis, and observation-avoidance. That's quite a hat trick, isn't it? But we don't know it's all he's capable of. And there are his victims to consider." Her smile vanishes. "If we take him down, does the paralysis suddenly wear off? If so, they're lying naked on top of a four-meter-high platform above flagstones. Someone *is* going to fall and break something if they start moving."

"Damn. And there's the motivation issue to consider."

"Yes." I pause. "Do you have any ideas?"

Above the plinth, the Mayor of London is twirling around his long axis like a plucked chicken on a rotisserie. His coat has taken flight and is flapping around the top of Nelson's Column like a demented raven; his shoes pop off like champagne corks as our prankster prepares to debag the old Etonian. Beneath him, that damned TV camera is presumably getting the lead item for tonight's news channels.

"Public safety comes first. I need to get a couple of squads ready to rush in air bags," Josephine decides. "Then someone to disable him, on my word." She takes a deep breath, then her eyes flicker towards the Mayor: "I don't want to authorize lethal force, but I may have to, if he escalates further. All of that's going to take time and I'd rather not go there. Can you distract him, at least? Or immobilize him?"

I look around the square. It's actually busier, if anything, except for the area immediately around the plinth that the police have got cordoned off. "I can distract him and I can probably disable him." Unlike Jo I don't need to go up a level to authorize force: I answer to my oath, my conscience, and the Auditors. "Give me a minute to report in, then I'll go and make a song and dance under his nose. If he gives me grief, I'll take him down; you could help by having some bodies standing by to bag him. Starting in, uh"—I check my watch—"five minutes?"

"You've got three. If we don't nail him fast, someone's going to get hurt." She heads for the steps of the mobile incident room.

I WALK ACROSS THE CROWDED PLAZA, GAZE DOWNCAST TO avoid eye contact with the people I'm using for cover. Anything to keep from standing out until I'm in position. The police are clearing the northwest corner of the square by forming a line, elbow to elbow, and expanding it: Josephine's obviously told them to keep it low-key and friendly because there's a marked lack of jostling and riot shields. They are having to work at it, though, because if there is one thing guaranteed to attract the attention of tourists and locals alike, it's the sight of a levitating semi-naked Mayor. The square is stippled with the diamante glitter of camera fill-in flashes.

I have to shimmy to avoid the elbows and backpacks of oblivious non-natives stopping dead to peer at their tourist guides. My line of sight on George the Fourth is tenuous, and in any case I can't be too obvious about keeping an eye on him and remain invisible. Rather than heading directly towards the joker, I stroll in a wide curve around the outside of the square, violin at my shoulder and bow poised. Finally I find a reasonable pitch. It's nothing special, just a patch of flagstones beside a low wall that isn't already occupied by a tour group or another musical hopeful. But it's about fifty meters away from Georgie and his unseen passenger, and I've got a sight-line on the police around the Fourth Plinth and, past them, the mobile incident command vehicle.

I unsling the empty violin case and lay it open at my feet, just like every other busker. Then I flex my fingers.

Lecter is sleepy and reluctant to rise to full awareness. *Good.* While he's in this state he's little more than a regular instrument. I check the pickups and switch off the small pre-amp built into his lower bout.

What are you doing?

I ignore him and start to tune up. The strings are just about right: the damp sea air didn't have a chance to affect them. *Excellent.* I check my watch: it's time. I launch into the Ciaccona from Bach's Partita in D minor because I can do it in my sleep while reserving 90 percent of my attention for keeping track of developments and, more importantly, Lecter is used to me using it as a basic exercise rather than the prelude to an attack.

What are you *doing?* he whines. I let him see the statue through my eyes, complete with the disturbing blind spot between the front legs of the horse. ***Ah.***

I turn slowly to gaze in the direction of the plinth. The Mayor twirls slowly, stripped back to a pair of polka-dotted navy boxers. As I watch, they begin to slide south. He grabs them: for a moment he keeps his grip, but then the fabric rips and they fly away. "Oh my," I mouth, nearly losing my fingering. The spangle and flicker of camera flashes rises to a manic intensity: I know *exactly* what's going to be on the front page of all the newspapers tomorrow. Then I turn back towards my target.

"*Lend me your vision,*" I instruct Lecter as I stare across the bridge of my instrument. My vision grays out for a moment and then returns. Some colors are emphasized: there's a strange lambency to the air between the horse's hooves, and it slowly resolves into the shape of a seated human figure.

Can I eat him?

"*No,*" I convey through the tension of my fingertips. "*Mine, not yours.*"

Hungry!

"*Nevertheless.*" I tighten my grip and draw on the violin's power. Bach, I decide, is inappropriate. This calls for something more contemporary. I segue into a different form, a more rhythmic, sinister melody wrapped around an implicit beat: "Bela Lugosi's Dead," for solo improv violin values of mortality. "*Now . . .*"

I relax my grip on Lecter's appetite and he strains forward eagerly, sucking on the energy source in front of him. The blind spot twists and twitches slightly, then begins to shrink. Arms and legs slide into view. Hands move, agitated: Laughing Boy has finally begun to realize that something is wrong.

Out of the corner of my eye I spot the Mayor standing on top of the pile of naked bodies on the other plinth; he's waving and gesticulating in my direction. *Is he a sensitive? Shit.* There's nothing to be done about it if he is: I press on. Raising the bow for a second I flip the switch on my violin's pre-amp. It's not an audio amplifier, and those aren't electronic pickups. I started subtle, but now it's time to party. *The bats have left the belfry—*

—And I'm almost airborne. *Whoops.* My ward buzzes angrily and I hastily squirt juice into it, juice sucked from the joker on the plinth who has taken aim at me. I land with a painful jolt but manage to absorb the drop with my knees. I'll feel them tomorrow but I'm rooted to the ground for now. I increase both volume and tempo, whirling into a screaming blur as the song rises: the strings begin to glow and now I reach out with Lecter's power and wrap my will around my target. *The victims have been bled—*

Got you.

He struggles as I lift him into the air, stabbing at me with pulses of near-solid air that would rupture eardrums and break bones if I didn't have a ward in place, drawing on the near-infinite depths of the violin's power. I stare at him as he screams obscenities and lashes out at me: for a moment I wonder if I've caught a giant frog. Then I realize he's just a little overweight—beer guts and Lycra body stockings really don't play well together.

"Put me down you motherfucking hippie bitch! Put me down or I will rape you so hard you'll walk bow-legged for a month!"

I tighten my grip on him and he shuts up, unable to draw breath. I see red: heart pounding and head throbbing in time to the beat I'm imagining. Laughing Boy likes to strip the clothes off young women in public as he adds them to the pornographic sculpture he's building on the empty plinth? Laughing Boy thinks rape jokes are funny?

Laughing Boy thinks it's all fun and games until a motherfucking hippie bitch turns his own mojo back on him, does he? *I'll show him, I'll squeeze him until his guts explode—*

"*Stop that,*" I tell Lecter. Laughing Boy is turning blue in the face, eyes bulging as I dangle him above the heads of the crowd. Almost like the bodies on the giant gallows in Vakilabad—

I let him down gently, in the middle of a knot of riot police, then stop the music dead and lower my instrument. "Oh God oh God oh God," I mumble. The residual power surge warms the protective ward at the base of my throat. I feel sick. I nearly hanged a man with a noose of air. *But he threatened to* that's disproportionate *rape you* he's just a sad middle-aged man with no life who has suddenly acquired superpowers *and* then decided to have some fun and *sexually abuse random passers-by in public* and I believe we should have a little word with Jo Sullivan, and *stop arguing with yourself*, yes?

I put my instrument away, pick up the case, and begin to walk towards the mobile incident command vehicle.

And that's when I see the other TV uplink van that was parked behind me, and the BBC news crew with the camera tracking me for my reaction shot when I realize they broadcast the entire magical duel live on News 24.

NOW, IT IS A FACT UNIVERSALLY ACKNOWLEDGED BY THE MODern intelligence agent that whoever said lies could travel halfway around the world while the truth was still getting its running shoes on clearly lived in a YouTube-free bubble.

I am a professional. I do not blog, I do not leak, I am discreet, I do not tweet. I *do* have a Facebook page, because not having one would mark me out as a freak of nature in this disclosure-obsessed age, but it's monitored by Human Resources and I don't talk about work or politics and I don't friend my colleagues.

When a BBC camera crew shoves a microphone under my nose and a vaguely familiar face with an expensive hairdo and a fashionable suit starts asking me pointed questions, I politely redirect their enquiries towards the nearest uniformed police superintendent, then walk away (mouthing *"get me out of here"* in Jo Sullivan's direction).

Which is how I get my second ride home in a jam sandwich with flashing blues and twos in just under twelve hours, cringing in the back seat every time I notice a random bystander who looks like a journalist or a van that resembles the TV news crew's uplink vehicle. The neighbors are going to think I'm some kind of criminal mastermind at this rate, aren't they?

I'm in the kitchen, brewing up a cafetière of Kenyan on autopilot as Spooky rubs against my ankles in hope of attention, when the landline from HQ rings. It's Vikram. "You made quite a splash." His tone is surprisingly mild.

"I didn't mean to: the second camera crew arrived while I was already engaged." I shudder convulsively and bite down on my instinctive urge to start apologizing. It's undignified for one thing, and for another, if I start I don't know if I'll be able to stop. "What happens next?"

"We're meeting at three to discuss damage control policy. The Auditors are calling the shots on this one, I'm afraid. Um, we're using room 4102 in Admiralty House, just off the Spring Gardens entrance; the New Annex is inaccessible today."

"The New Annex is *what*?"

"Last night's Code Red left quite a mess." Vik isn't normally quite this taciturn; he must be badly rattled. "We're activating the emergency migration plan while the clean-up proceeds."

"I see." Stiff upper lips appear to be the order of the day. Well, my workplace calendar is clear—I was supposed to be stuck in the middle of the North Sea for the rest of the week—so it's not as if I'm expected in the office, apart from this new meeting. But the sense of hollow dread and loss gnawing at my guts won't go away. "How bad is the public exposure?"

"Bad." He pauses. "Chin up, and see you in a few hours."

Whoops.

I set the timer on my phone to give me a countdown alarm, sit down at the kitchen table, and allow the tears to flow. It's not hard, and the therapeutic effect of a good cry shouldn't be underestimated: you secrete endorphins in your tears, and there's a good chunk of research showing that it really *does* relieve stress. Trial and error experimentation has taught me that an eight-minute session followed by seven minutes of deep breathing and meditation is the minimum I can get away with to rebalance myself when I'm in danger of losing my shit completely. (It used to be four minutes, back when I started practicing it a couple of years ago. It's been creeping up on me for some time now.) If I follow it with a brief session of calming meditation, it sets me right as rain, for a while.

Fifteen-minute interval over (and feeling a lot better for it) I haul my suitcase upstairs and shower, then wash and blow-dry my hair. Opening the bag, I haul out the black trouser suit I bought for the deep-sea negotiations. Add a cream blouse, heels, and just enough makeup and earrings to soften the look slightly, and it'll be just about right for what's coming up this afternoon, which is inevitably going to be suspension followed by a formal enquiry with the authority to recommend disciplinary sanctions. I hadn't thought things could get any worse after Bob left, but this . . . this is *ridiculous*.

No. Wrong word. Try *disastrous* on for size instead.

I DO NOT OVER-SHARE ON FACEBOOK. UNFORTUNATELY, I HAVE an idiot sister who thinks Facebook is the internet, and that the internet is the right way to keep in touch with her friends.

Twelve percent of all the photographs ever taken in human history have been taken in the last twelve months. And 40 percent of them are on Facebook. Many of these photographs are taken at family social gatherings, and the people who upload them tag them with the names of their relatives and friends. Which means that unless you are a paranoid recluse who has been hiding in a cave since the early 1980s, there is almost certainly a photograph of your face tagged with your name and public profile in Facebook's database.

An hour ago I took down an angry white guy with occult powers in the middle of Trafalgar Square. I don't think I had any alternative:

he was holding the Mayor of London hostage—the man most likely to be our next Prime Minister—not to mention a dozen innocent bystanders.

Unfortunately I did so right in front of a TV news crew and about a thousand tourists armed with DSLRs and SD cards that automatically upload everything they see to the internet via wireless.

Back in the prehistoric era of the 1980s, we could stop this shit dead in its tracks. The TV and newspaper crews could be silenced by means of a quaint instrument called a D-Notice, a formal warning that publication would put them in breach of the Official Secrets Act and result in prosecution. The ordinary witnesses carried cameras full of film that could be confiscated, and which in any case couldn't be tagged and matched and searched on the internet.

But today . . . Let's just say Sis is in for a *real* surprise the next time she checks in on Facebook.

I get dressed, put my hair up, apply foundation, eyeliner, and lipstick, then go downstairs. With a growing sense of dread, I fire up the laptop and start poking at dusty news sites. I've got about half an hour before it'll be time to set off—time to see if I need to keep my head down.

It's not looking good:

- I am squarely in the frame of the photograph that accompanies the lead news item on the BBC News website. Recognizably me, even in casual mufti with a rat's nest under my beret.
- The same video clip is on YouTube. It has been viewed 223,195 times already. (Make that 223,196.)
- There are links to six more videos of the incident, from different angles. One of them was taken by a Korean tourist whose funky high-def camera had some sort of bizarre polarizing filter that is sensitive to thaum fields; bolts of psychedelic lightning zig and zag across the concourse, roughly connecting Lecter to Laughing Boy, who shows up in luminous green.
- There's an interview with the Mayor, from his hospital bed, breathlessly expressing his gratitude and admiration to "the redhead with

the violin" who took down Strip Jack Spratt, as the supervillain man-
qué apparently calls himself. (Alias Dougal Slaithwaite, age 52, un-
employed, of no fixed abode: now facing charges of kidnapping,
indecent assault, and threatening behavior.)

- There are linked news items—human interest color, I gather—about
  other superhero outbreaks. *Who* ordered *that?* Apparently my media
  habit is sufficiently out of the mainstream that I've been missing out
  on the summer's big story.
- There are more than seventy messages waiting for me in my Facebook
  inbox. I delete them all. Another one appears almost immediately. (I
  log out.)

I don't bother checking the newspapers. Instead, I repack my
suitcase, adding my second-best suit in place of the one I'm wearing.
It may be some time before I can come home without running a
gauntlet of journalists. The first of them may already be on their
way, depending on how good they are at image manipulation and
social engineering. As I said, Sis is in for a real surprise next time she
checks in . . .

But for me, it's time to face the music.

I PHONE FOR A CAB, AND THEY PICK ME UP AT MY FRONT DOOR.
My skin's crawling as I do the perp walk out to the curb, but there
are no tabloid reporters or paparazzi waiting in the bushes yet: it's a
lucky escape that I can't count on repeating. I feel nauseous as I contemplate what's coming up next. An auto-da-fé if I'm lucky; utter
shame otherwise.

Of course the cabbie turns out to be the talkative kind. "Did you
'ear about the mess in Trafalgar Square?" he asks. "I'm going to 'ave
to loop around to drop you on Pall Mall, that end's all blocked off.
One of those supervillains went off 'is trolley and kidnapped the
Mayor! Then some girl with a magic guitar took 'im down, right in
front of Nelson's Column! The news is saying she works for a *secret
government agency*," he confides with a knowing look.

"I'm sure she does." I cross my arms and peer out of the window, feigning boredom. I'm certain he can hear my pulse pounding over the noise of the lorry we're nose-to-tail with.

"Stands to reason, the government must have some kind of plan for dealing with them, right?" He sounds worried.

"Them?"

"Yeah, the crazies with superpowers."

"Crazies with—" I catch his eye in the mirror, looking at me as if he's wondering what planet I'm from.

"Yeah, crazies. Like the bloke wot tore up that community center in Tooting last week, with 'is bare 'ands. It's anarchy, that's wot it is, even with all these crime-fighters in pervert suits coming out of the woodwork."

"Pervert suits?" I ask, caught by his phrasing.

"Yeah, it's like there's some kind of law or something: ordinary bloke acquires the power to turn his 'ead into a teapot, he has to start poncing around in Lycra and fishnets. Like something from the *Rocky Horror*, innit? You know what? That sort of thing turns my stomach. There ought to be a law against it."

"What, turning your head into a teapot?"

"No, the pervy suits. I mean, no offense, if a fit bird with super-powers wants to wear a skimpy dress and thigh-high boots I've got no problem, knowworramean? But some of these blokes, they're a bit past their sell-by. There oughta be a law about it, right? They should make all the fat supervillains wear burkas. But they ain't doing any-thing about *any* of it right now, looks like. It's a crime! The police should do something."

And so on and on and on, for approximately twenty-five minutes. By the time we arrive at the Admiralty my cheek is twitching and, if I had my choice of superpowers, I would cheerfully sell my soul for the ability to turn my driver's head into a cafetière.

I'm so tense by the time we arrive that I forget to ask for a receipt when I pay. But swearing won't help and I don't feel like running after the taxi, so I make my way stiffly to the front desk, where a splendidly uniformed doorman waits behind a desk carved from the timbers of an eighteenth-century man-o-war. I present my warrant card: "Dr. O'Brien. I'm here for a meeting in room 4102."

It sounds so much better than *disciplinary hearing*.

"If you'd care to sign here, ma'am . . . now stare into the camera, just for a second." It's one of the ubiquitous eyeball-on-a-stalk web-cams, disquietingly like something I once met in a hotel hallway in Amsterdam. I try to will the lens to crack, but I'm not quite ugly enough. "Jolly good, now I'm just going to print you out a badge. Remember to wear it at all times and return it when you leave. I'm afraid you'll have to leave those bags here. You can check them into the cloak room, but I'm afraid we'll have to scan them—"

"You can take the suitcase, but the violin has to stay with me." I put it on the desk. "You're welcome to inspect it right here, but I can't let it out of my possession. It's rather valuable." I tense up, anticipating a fight.

"Really?" He smiles over gilt-framed half-moon glasses. "Well, if you insist, I can hand search it." Bless the Corps of Commissionaires: they're ex-military enough to know when to bend the rules.

We deposit my suitcase, I show him Lecter and let him hand-check the sides and back of the case, then I take my badge and go in search of the borrowed conference room.

It's funny how the mere anticipation of a verbal confrontation can be worse than life-and-death combat: my stomach is hollow and chest a little fluttery. The floors in this building are paved in Italian marble, uncarpeted, utterly lethal if you slip, and liable to cause permanent hearing damage if you walk on them for too long in heels. It's enough to make me long for the beige institutional carpet of the New Annex—

And then I'm standing in front of a pair of imposing black double doors framed by Corinthian columns, surmounted by an arch with painted putti blowing on the sails of ships of the line. I take a deep breath and knock, twice.

Vikram opens the door; he looks nearly as nervous as I feel. "Oh good, we were getting worried," he says. *Worried?*

"Is there a problem?" I ask cautiously.

"Yes, we've been running interference from upstairs, but . . ." He steps backwards. "Come on in. We have coffee and refreshments."

I follow him into the room. It's about the size of an aircraft carrier's hangar deck, with baroque gilt-encrusted benches and side-tables drawn up against wood-paneled walls that have fossilized under the weight of their decorative plasterwork. The floor-to-ceiling windows admit a waterfall of golden afternoon light that floods the room and washes across a hand-woven Persian carpet that must have cost a prince's ransom.

"Ah, Dr. O'Brien." I nearly jump out of my skin: It's Dr. Michael (never a Mike) Armstrong, the Senior Auditor. He smiles like a tired crocodile. "What a relief. Are you well?"

I manage not to stagger under the weight of his regard: he actually looks *concerned*. "Have you spoken to Bob this morning?" I ask.

"Yes—wait, not since the early hours." His left eyebrow wrinkles. "Is something the matter?"

"Um." I glance round. He's brought a couple of admin bodies I don't know, but some faces I expected to see are absent. "Yes, but I'm not sure it's relevant to the matter in hand. Where's Judith?"

"Dead."

"*What?*"

Armstrong clasps his hands behind his back, as sober as a funeral director. "Last night, during the Code Red. We were attacked at the New Annex."

"I knew that, but—*Judith?*" Dr. Carroll was the second ranking Auditor who dealt with our department. I was expecting her to chair this session. She wasn't exactly a friend, but I was certain I'd get a fair hearing from her, and to learn that she's dead so recently comes like a punch in the guts.

He looks at me, his expression deceptively mild. "We lost others."

"Oh my God."

"Andrew Newstrom. Doris Goodman. James Angleton."

"Oh my—" My knees nearly give way. Everything's a blur. The next thing I know, the Senior Auditor has my arm—he's almost holding me up—and is leading me towards a chair. "—God." It's not that it's entirely news to me: I knew we'd lost Angleton. But the scale of it hits me hard. And Andy was a friend: not a close one, but a friend nonetheless.

"God won't help you, I'm afraid," the SA murmurs sympathetically. More loudly: "I'm sorry, you should have been kept informed."

"But—Andy?"

"Yes." I feel the hard edge of a chair butt up against my legs: I allow myself to collapse onto it. "Your husband is picking up the pieces."

"But he's—" My lips don't seem to want to work properly: I take a few seconds to get them back under control. "This is a catastrophe."

"Yes," he agrees.

It puts everything that's happened to me in the past twenty-four hours in a new perspective. Tilt-shift mode on a shiny new digital camera: all of a sudden, your larger-than-life problems look like a miniature diorama. "Oh God. Bob and I had a huge row. If I'd known—"

"Not to worry," Dr. Armstrong murmurs gently. He sits down beside me. "I'm sure allowances will be made, accommodations can be reached. But that's not what we're here for, is it?"

Oh, that. "No," I agree.

"You know what's coming next." It's a statement, not a question.

"Give me a couple of seconds, please? This is all a bit of a shock." I reach for the empty chair on my other side, and lay Lecter's case there. I try to relax, even though every instinct tells me to tense up. What's coming next is one of the scariest nonviolent experiences you can undergo—and if you work for the Laundry, you *will* undergo it, sooner or later. "I'm ready now." I turn my head and stare into his eyes, which are deep and brown and have unusually long lashes.

"All right. Sabbath. Claymore. Diamond. Rocket. Execute Sitrep One."

My tongue feels like a lump of wood: my eyes do not belong to me. Something inside my head uses my larynx to make its report:

"Subjective integrity is maintained. Subjective continuity of experience is maintained. Subject observes no tampering."

"Good." The Senior Auditor smiles warmly. "Execute Sitrep Two."

"Subjective operational readiness state: green. Subjective background state: amber, trending to red."

"Hmm." His smile slips. "Exit supervision." A brief pause: "Mo, before we get to the main business of this meeting, in your own words—how was your trip going, before you were recalled? Was there a message for us?"

The unseen narrator using my vocal cords goes back to sleep. I clear my throat as I regain control of my own mind. "Ramona invited me to come visit some time. We had a lengthy gossip sesh. But that's all. Nothing substantial."

"Nice to know the neighbors are steady." The set of his shoulders relaxes slightly. "So. Tell me what happened in Trafalgar Square . . ."

My shoulders tense. "Total screw-up, I'm afraid. I went in under-informed and under-equipped and didn't even notice the news crew until it was way too late. Also, um, I'd like to report that I had some self-control issues. Nearly took out my personal frustration on the idiot who caused the scene. Utterly unconscionable, and I was able to stop myself, but. But. You need to know—"

He raises a hand and I manage to stop myself before I begin to babble. Then he speaks, his voice low and soothing: "You dealt with a crisis while sleep-deprived and in the wake of a major domestic argument, and you dealt with it effectively. Did you rough him up? If not, I see no problem here except that perhaps the DO should have looked a little further before assigning assets to deal with what appeared at first to be a trivial distraction. That you feel the need to confess that you were tempted is creditable but, under the circumstances, unnecessary: we do not punish people for thoughtcrime, Dr. O'Brien." He pauses. "And in any event, we would have encountered this particular crisis sooner or later, regardless of who had to deal with the feckless Mr. Spratt. It was just bad luck that it happened to you rather than to someone else."

"What crisis?" I pause long enough to lick my lips. "The Code Red?"

"Dealt with," he says, with a dismissive wave of the hand. "The PHANGs are locked down tight, the external and internal threats have been neutralized"—for a moment there's a flicker of fire in his eyes—"and damage control is in hand. No, this isn't the disciplinary hearing you were expecting: we have another crisis to deal with." He gestures at the boardroom table at the far end of the room. "So, whenever you're ready . . ."

4.

BRIEFINGS

IT TAKES A FEW MINUTES, BUT EVENTUALLY EVERYBODY IS seated around the table. I'm about to go to the foot of it, but the SA shakes his head and directs me towards a seat immediately to his left—and he's chairing it. "Mr. Choudhury, if you'd like to start the briefing?"

Vikram clears his throat. He looks worried. "Do we have time?" he asks. "She's due in front of the CO subcommittee in Conference Room A at five, and they don't like to be kept waiting—"

"They'll wait for us." The SA is imperturbable. "She needs to be fully briefed, Vikram. *Fully* briefed."

"Fully—" Vik shakes his head. "We could be here all week. Is she cleared?"

"She is now." Dr. Armstrong looks at me. So does everyone else: I try not to shrink into a puddle in my seat. We have Jez Wilson and Gerry Lockhart, both with bags under their eyes. Jez manages Support and Liaison Ops, a euphemism that covers our friends from the Artists' Rifles in Hereford; Gerry is in charge of External Assets, which, if this were a Bond movie, would be the double-0 section. There's a woman I don't know by name but associate with Audit Ops, kindly face, twinset and pearls; an elderly fellow with a halo of flyaway hair and a bushy Einsteinian mustache; and Emma MacDougal from HR. The point is, everyone I recognize here deals with Mahogany Row— the organization's elite tier of semiautonomous practitioners—on a daily basis: some of them even have offices there. Which makes this a worryingly high-powered meeting.

"Dominique, welcome to the INCORRIGIBLE working group, whose deliberations you are now on the approved list for. We're missing a few faces today—Angleton and Judith are terrible losses—so I'm afraid we're going to have to improvise a bit. Mr. Choudhury?"

Vikram clears his throat. "You have probably noticed we have a growing problem with paranormal vigilantes," he begins, then stops and shrugs. "And hooligans, like this morning's miscreant. I'm sorry. If not for last night's emergency, you wouldn't have been in the firing line . . . but what's done is done, and the genie is out of the bottle."

The genie? Paranormal vigilantes? INCORRIGIBLE working group? What is this? I shake my head.

"Allow me to recap." Vik walks over to a trolley with a laptop and overhead projector mounted on it. There's a screen situated in front of the wall that I hadn't paid any attention to before. He fidgets with the laptop for a moment, then brings up a graph. "CASE NIGHT-MARE GREEN began, let's see, nineteen months ago." A vertical dotted line appears near the left of the time line. "We're here." Another dotted line marches up the screen near the right-hand edge of the graph. "Here's one of the side effects: the frequency curve for paranormal incidents. Defined as ordinary people who wake up one morning and discover they have acquired a talent for summonings and bindings, ritual magic—which they mistake for superpowers."

Oh dear. It's your classic growth curve, starting low and staying low until about three months ago. Then it begins to double. And double again, rising fast, until it hits the dateline. Either the first quartile of a sigmoid curve, or—don't go there—an exponential.

"Until recently we were seeing perhaps two or three incidents per ten million people per month. But we're now up to one per million and climbing. If we extrapolate forward, we get to here," says Vik.

Another graph, with the first one shrunk down to occupy the left hand side of the screen. "If the growth rate doesn't show signs of slackening soon, if we're looking at a genuine exponential, it tends towards infinity in another four months. At which point we hit the, um, superhero singularity."

I can't seem to help myself: I know it's bad form, but I interrupt. "Wait. Can you characterize these incidents? How serious are they?"

"Ah, *that*." Vikram smiles ruefully. "It's a bit difficult. There seems to be a power law function covering the spread of abilities. Next slide . . ." He brings it on-screen and, yes, it shows a classic bell curve—a Gaussian distribution—with the left side cut off around the eightieth percentile. "Here we are. Really minor anomalies don't show up at all: I mean, we've got no way of identifying a four-year-old whose puppy always comes when she calls it, have we? Or a trawler-man who can call fishes, but is over quota and landing them illegally on the black market in Portugal. Now, a fifteen-year-old with the ability to control animals is a bit more obvious, especially if they attract attention by making a passing police horse tap-dance for their friends. And at the other end of the bell curve they stick out like a sore thumb: there was that business in Walthamstow last week, the, ah, 'crazy cat lady.'"

I don't remember hearing about a crazy cat lady in Walthamstow last week, but I've been a bit too busy to bother with the newspapers or TV news for the past few months. Judging by the winces around the table I must have missed out on something really extraordinarily noteworthy. I nod politely.

"More disturbingly, there are the negative powers. PHANG syndrome you know about. There are others. Being able to transform bits of your body into other objects might sound like a superpower until you get it wrong—there's been an uptick in some really bizarre teratomas—cancers that look like fully developed organs in inappropriate places. Human Torches who lose self-control for even a second end up with a coroner delivering a narrative verdict of Spontaneous Human Combustion. And there seems to be an association, as one would expect, between people with abilities to the right of the normal distribution and, um, Krantzberg syndrome. We're already seeing the first rapid-onset dementia cases, some as young as thirteen."

Oh good grief, I think again.

K syndrome is an unpleasant side effect of practicing ritual magic. If you solve the right theorems in your head, you can invoke various interesting extradimensional entities and make them *do things.* But there's a cost. Microscopic Eaters phase in and out of our universe in response to the thaum fields generated in this way. And sometimes, some of them pause for long enough to take a microscopic bite out of your gray matter until you go "insane on the brane" as Bob puts it. Once they get started they tend to come back to the buffet: K syndrome is progressive, and the only way to stop it progressing is to *stop practicing magic.*

"We believe the superpowers are a direct side effect of unconstrained background cognitive bandwidth processing. Bluntly, random people are thinking themselves into modes where they attract Actor/Agent entities and acquire various . . . abilities. It's not yet obvious whether this is a true exponential, or just a step-function that will stabilize soon, but in the worst case, in another few months, almost everyone will be above the minimum threshold for ritual activation."

"Oh *dear,*" Emma MacDougal says faintly, and fans herself with a notepad. "That's *really* going to complicate our recruitment process." I couldn't put it better myself.

"I do not believe it is going to go that far," Dr. Armstrong says calmly. "Professor Ford is preparing a report. Although he isn't willing to release it until he's triple-checked everything, he says that the step-function model is most likely to hold true, and that the rate of increase will taper off shortly. Something about there being no true singularities in nature, outside of a black hole."

I take a deep breath and let it go slowly. If Mike Ford says it's so, then there's *some* reason for hope: he's our resident expert on CASE NIGHTMARE GREEN, the conjunction of stellar drift, the dreaming monkey population spike, and the computational singularity that is responsible for the surge in magic. If he's right, it's not the end of the world as we know it, just a very annoying new problem to deal with. He's been known to be wrong from time to time, but if he is, the prospect of everyone on the planet suddenly acquiring superpowers simply doesn't bear thinking about.

"Yes, well. One may hope he's right again." Vikram taps a key on the laptop. "Let me give you some examples. Annie Smith, from Leicester, aged twenty-two, works in a Poundland store. Last Friday robbers broke in through the loading bay as the manager was cashing up. They knew where the alarm cable run was located—the police are sure there was an inside accomplice—and they were attempting to make off with the previous three days' takings when Annie knocked them unconscious by bouncing them off the ceiling. Not the false ceiling, mind you, but the concrete ceiling one and a half meters above the suspended tiles. Annie is a hundred and forty-five centimeters tall—four feet and nine inches in old money—and weighs fifty kilos: they outweighed her four to one. Then there's Geraldine Fawcett, eighty-two, of Oakshott, who has taken to wearing fishnet hose and a merry widow, and fights late night noise nuisances by—"

He goes on for another couple of increasingly surreal, not to say implausible, minutes before the SA clears his throat pointedly.

"Yes?"

"As you have already noted, we have limited time. Can I suggest we proceed to the psychological/media profile problem next?"

"If you insist." Vikram pauses for long enough to take a mouthful of water from the glass in front of his place setting. "The reason we are seeing such a surge in Lycra futures is that ordinary people who know nothing about our business interpret their new abilities in terms of their pre-existing cognitive biases. A century ago it would have been framed in terms of miracles and angels and devils: witchcraft, in other words. But this is the twenty-first century in Britain, where the most rapidly growing religious demographic is 'none of the above.' And for the past few decades we've lived in a media environment where a particular fictional genre has been growing in popularity. I refer, of course, to the American superhero movie—"

"What about comics?" asks the fellow with the flyaway hair. He seems enthused. "Surely Marvel and DC are somewhat to blame? I remember when they first arrived on these shores in the 1960s . . ."

"Yes, comics too, I suppose, but movies reach a bigger audience," Vikram says wearily. He looks as if he's been back and forth over this ground until it's churned into mud. "Superman, Iron Man, Batman"— Flyaway Hair winces visibly—"you name it. Rich, powerful, white alpha males who dress up in gimp suits and beat up ethnically diverse lower-class criminals. Reprehensible lawless vigilantes! It would be so much easier if we had Greek or Roman gods and demigods to deal with instead . . . ACPO are spitting blood." (ACPO is the Association of Chief Police Officers, the not-a-trade-union for supercops that handles a lot of outsourced high-level policing policy work on behalf of the Home Office.) "The Home Office hates vigilantes in Lycra fancy-dress outfits almost as much as they hate lawbreakers. You see, superheroes don't follow the rules of evidence. They take procedural shortcuts, assault criminals, mess up crime scenes, and generally make it almost impossible to secure a conviction. Not to mention committing a basket-load of offenses in their own right: aggravated trespass, assault, violating controlled airspace and flying without a license, breaking and entering, criminal damage . . ."

Oh. *Oh.* I finger a simple chord on my blotter, then realize that Gerry Lockhart is staring at my hand with an expression of deep distaste, and force myself to stop fidgeting. *John* bloody *Williams.* Why do I have to be earwormed by the first violin's theme from *Superman* right now?

"Are any of them attributing it to magic?" I ask.

"Yes, some." Vikram frowns. "But it's currently running at less than twenty percent. Superhero is the dominant paradigm, and new fish tend to swim with the school. Why do you ask?"

"Well, let's see. Am I right in thinking that the nature of the IN-CORRIGIBLE problem is that we are dealing with a plague of untrained occult practitioners who are interpreting their somewhat random skills as superhero abilities?"

Vikram nods, but the Senior Auditor takes it upon himself to reply. "Essentially yes, you've nailed it. But there's more to it than that. Jez?"

Vikram takes his seat as Jez Wilson nods and picks up the thread. "The real problem isn't just identification and suppression, Dr. O'Brien. The real problem is that it's *too public*. It caught us on the hop, and now the news media are sensitized so they're picking it up everywhere. The usual press chorus, *something must be done*, is already tuning up. The business this morning is just the latest and worst case, and your showing up on camera may actually be a blessing in disguise, because we need to find a way to get in front of the situation and take overt action to bring the paranormally enhanced under control—otherwise we're going to be run ragged dealing with this nonsense rather than focusing on the organization's core mission."

There is a chirp from the SA's suit pocket, then another chirp: the discreet mating call of the mobile phone. That the Senior Auditor carries a mobile phone at all, let alone that he doesn't silence it in meetings, is so extraordinary a revelation that I stare, but then something even stranger happens: he pulls it out (a rather ancient Blackberry, plastic edges polished to a shine by constant use) and *answers* it, right in front of our shocked faces. In, as I said, a highly sensitive meeting.

"Hello? I'm in the INCORRIGIBLE session, didn't I say I wasn't to be— Oh. I see." (A pause.) "He insists, does he? Damn. Damn. Yes, I'll tell them."

He puts his phone away and frowns.

"I'm afraid I'm going to have to cut this short, ladies and gentlemen: they've brought the meeting forward an hour. Dr. O'Brien, Agent CANDID." He nods at me. "As you can see, our organization has been dragged into dangerously close proximity to the public sphere by the INCORRIGIBLE problem. In particular, Mahogany Row are desperately keen to stay out of the limelight. So in order to avoid compromising our core mission, we need to generate a semi-classified proxy to deal with the superhero problem.

"Dominique." I tense: his use of my first name is unusual enough to put my adrenal glands on fight-or-flee alert. "The narrative we are developing is that there is a secret department within the Security Service"—better known to members of the public as MI5—"which deals with superpowered threats to the realm. As your cover has been comprehensively blown by this morning's events, I have decided that it is necessary to place Agent CANDID on indefinite furlough."

I'm afraid I gasp involuntarily: I manage to suppress the flinch reflex. Agent CANDID is my operational designation. Worse, it has framed my working life for the past several years. Part-time academic by day, part-time Laundry researcher and active service operative by night—and occasional on-call executioner.

The Senior Auditor rolls on, pretending not to notice my lapse: "Meanwhile, we want you—that is, Dr. Dominique O'Brien—to become the semi-public face of OPERATION INCORRIGIBLE. Semi-public in this context means that you will interact directly with other government agencies. Your cover story is that you are a senior member of the aforementioned secret department of MI5, answering to the Home Office, where you will recruit and operate an, ah, 'Superhero Team' to, um, 'fight crime.' You will appear to report to the regular Security Service authorities, and your department will identify and execute suitable responses to the anomalous power threat.

"Fighting crime is the cover story for the BBC and national news media. The internal narrative within other civil service departments, and for open dissemination within MI5 and the Police, is that your primary objective is to put the frighteners on the pervert suits. Compliant ones will be recruited and corralled in a safe organizational framework that provides them with plenty of opportunities for make-believe superhero work; noncompliant ones can be taken down in public if necessary, without compromising the operational security of designated national security agencies. We anticipate full and enthusiastic support for this goal from the Police and the Security Service, because this strategy feeds into their operational goals and all they're required to do is to claim credit for your hard work.

"But those are merely your tertiary and secondary tasks. Your *primary* objective is to insulate the Laundry from public exposure and consequential political meddling by directing media attention away from us and towards the antics of the official government superhero team, working for this fictional department within the Security Service." His smile is terrifying. "In other words, think of yourself as James Bond's M—if Bond had a cape."

"But no such organization exists!" I protest, horrified. *I've got to battle supervillains in public?* Worse: *I'm working for the Home Office?* The Laundry is part of the security services, answerable to the Ministry of Defense, while the Home Office is all about law enforcement. "Two cultures" doesn't even *begin* to describe the scale of the divide.

"The organization you will be in charge of exists as of now, at least on paper." The SA's smile is fey. "Mrs. MacDougal, the dossier, if you please . . . ?"

Emma gives me a sympathetic look as she slides a ten-centimeter-thick dossier across the table towards me. "Sorry dear," she says: "I'm afraid you're promoted—sideways."

"Better read quickly," the Senior Auditor adds. "Because that phone call was the Chief Secretary to the Cabinet Office. They're expecting you in Cabinet Office Briefing Room A in forty-two minutes precisely. Just in time to update the Deputy Prime Minister on your new assignment."

I THOUGHT I'D HIT ROCK BOTTOM ON MY WAY INTO THE ADMI-ralty building: little did I suspect how much further there was to sink!

Emma's dossier is a doozie. If it's to be believed, I have been promoted three whole grades in a single bound. I am now attached to the org chart of the sprawling bureaucratic empire popularly misidentified as MI5, about three management tiers down from the top and so far off to one side that I'm teetering on the edge of a virtual cliff, with dotted lines leading off the edge of the paper in the direction of the iceberg labelled Home Office. And what a view this cliff overlooks! I have no less than five subdepartments under me, and something like forty staff. But it's a skeleton crew for now. Their niches on the org chart are all blank for the time being, a tabula rasa labelled INSERT RECRUIT HERE; half of them are tagged SUPERHERO. I have a budget of three million a year, an open requisition for a Secret Bunker and a Team

Headquarters (subject to authorization, approval, and planning permission), and an entire back story to memorize for my decades-old career as some kind of high-level counter-espionage expert.

It's *utterly humiliating*, that's what it is.

What I really wanted and expected was to receive my entirely justified bollocking behind closed doors, then to go home and take a month of garden leave and several sessions with a security-cleared therapist and maybe a talk with a marriage guidance counselor. Not to mention a discreet word with Emma about commencing the search for a suitable candidate to take over a certain bone-white cross that I bear. (It's a long shot but it just *might* work, although the search might take a while to bear fruit.)

Instead, they seem to think they're *doing me a favor* by promoting me, dumping a huge load of unfamiliar management responsibilities on my shoulders, and putting me in charge of my very own department (in another organization, to boot).

Once my speed-reading session with the dossier runs out of time, they form a protective phalanx around me and march me in bureaucratic lockstep down marble corridors and the pavement alongside Whitehall, past the Scotland Office, unto the front steps of the Cabinet Office building. Or maybe they're just making sure I have no opportunity to escape before the ritual feeding of the newly commissioned departmental director to the ministers.

As I climb the steps and present my ID to the policemen on duty, all I can think of is a silly book that Bob told me he was reading a couple of years ago, by some dead famous author, who came up with a clever neologism, what was it . . . an out of concept problem? No: an out of *context* problem. Something which organizations or cultures encounter in very much the same way that a sentence encounters a full stop.

I can't shake the sense that today is my very own hyper-personalized out of context problem. I talk to my violin in the privacy of my own head: fine. When my violin talks back and tries to use me as a puppet to murder my husband, that's not so fine. When I go on to nearly kill a man in the middle of Trafalgar Square live on network TV, that's even less fine. But then there's *this*.

What should I expect next, if the day continues to go downhill at this rate? An invading army of elves for after-dinner amusement?

I'm so wrapped up in myself that I nearly walk into a familiar-looking man in a rumpled suit clutching a battered red leather file box under one arm. I flinch violently and nearly push Lecter's quick-release button by accident: "Whoops, sorry," I say, trying to force my heart back down into my chest where it belongs.

"Not to—" He does a double take, noticing my violin case. "Ah! You must be the star of the show." He offers me a handshake: I accept it instinctively. "Jolly good. See you later, must dash." And with that, the Justice Minister—number five in the Cabinet—deftly sidesteps around me, body-swerves between Vik and the Senior Auditor, and barrels down the front steps.

Oh dear God, I've fallen into "The Thick of It."

"Was that . . . ?" Vikram asks faintly.

"Stiff upper lip," murmurs Dr. Armstrong. "Yes, it was. If you'd like to go in, Dr. O'Brien, they'll be expecting you. We'll be back to pick you up at six, when the meeting's over."

I will not *show fear.* I smile at him, baring my teeth like a good little girl. "Looking forward to it." Then I enter the dragon's den.

COBRA IS CABINET OFFICE BRIEFING ROOM A, ON THE FIRST floor of the Cabinet Office building on Whitehall. Contrary to media folklore, there is no such thing as "the COBRA committee." That implies an implausible level of permanence. COBRA is simply the place where ministers and senior civil servants meet to be briefed on, assess, and respond to civil and military emergencies.

It may be on the first floor rather than in a reinforced bunker, but there are no windows in COBRA's reinforced walls, and the whole section of the building is surrounded by not one, but two Faraday cages and an airlock tunnel lined with metal detectors and other sensors. Naturally, there are discreet security checkpoints that make your typical airport boarding experience look like it's run by Larry, Moe, and Curly, and the whole building is contained within the security cordon that embraces Downing Street, much of Whitehall, and the Houses of Parliament.

On my way in to COBRA they take my handbag and phone. They don't take my earrings or necklace, but they check them over with handheld emission detectors. As for Lecter . . . he's just going to have to get used to the hand searches. The quick-release springs in his case worry them, but in the end we reach a tense compromise: after they X-ray and manually examine him, I leave him in a security locker (along with my handbag and phone), but they let me take both the keys to the locker.

It's funny: I'm fully dressed but I feel naked without my violin.

The Briefing Room itself is nearly filled by a thoroughly modern bleached pine boardroom table. One wall is a solid slab of TV screens, and there are charge points for laptops and tablets on the table—internet, too, I gather, but not for the likes of me: requests for access have to be cleared in advance by CESG. Today's session is chaired by the Deputy Prime Minister, a last-minute substitution due to the Big Cheese himself being distracted by an opportunity to be seen rubbing snouts with his frenemy the Mayor by whatever proportion of the populace still bother watching the News at Nine. Also in attendance are Barry Jennings, the avuncular Justice Minister I nearly ran down earlier, and Jessica Greene, the Home Secretary, Lady High Executioner, and pin-up girl for the hanging's-too-good-for-them electoral demographic.*

---

* Actually, such tabloid caricatures are rather poor representations of the reality; they're all charming, personable, extremely sharp individuals who are terrifyingly well-informed about the workings of their departments. You don't get to the top table of a government—any government—without being an overachiever. This doesn't mean I'd vote (or not vote) for them; as ministers it's their duty to toe the line with respect to the governing party's policy platform, and I'm not the kind of girl who'll vote for a friendly dude I'd like to share a beer with if I happen to suspect that he'd quite like to invade Poland. But I find it faintly reassuring to confirm that, however misguided I might privately think some of our government's policies might be, at least they are being executed with enthusiasm and zeal by first-class overachievers. Because it beats the alternative.

In addition to the political heavies, there's a small coterie of lower-level drones and minor flappers: the Commissioner of Police (London's copper-in-chief), a female Assistant Commissioner attending on behalf of ACPO (the Association of Chief Police Officers), the Chief Secretary to the Cabinet Office, representatives from the Prison Service, and so on. It's all a bit intimidating: I feel like a secondary school football coach who's been summoned to a meeting of the Premier League chairmen. Who are, of course, very busy men (and want you to know it).

"Dr. O'Brien." The Deputy PM starts up smoothly without any social lubrication: "Can you tell us exactly what happened in Trafalgar Square this morning?"

I stand up, and deliver the cover story that the INCORRIGIBLE committee sweated their skulls over for me while I was heading home for a quick change and shower at lunchtime.

I am used to giving lectures: this is no different, I tell myself. I can't be suffering from stage fright, can I? I've done this thousands of times before—just to different audiences. I recall a trick I used to use at unfamiliar academic conferences, where I pretend I'm addressing a room full of sapient cauliflowers from Arcturus. It's less nerve-wracking than lecturing some of the most powerful civil servants and policy-makers in the land, so I do that. It does indeed make everything easier, except for a slight tendency to get distracted (Bob *really* doesn't like brassicas—even the smell upsets him—which leads to a hypnagogic vision of my husband choking as he tries to eat the Deputy Prison Minister's head).

High points:

- I run a very small, very new department within MI5 which keeps tabs on superheroes and supervillains.
- Sometimes the two are easy to tell apart; sometimes they're indistinguishable.
- The number of them crawling out of the woodwork is increasing.
- I, myself, have some small talent in that direction.

- I happened to be in town on my day off when the Trafalgar Square incident kicked off.
- Yes, my department works with the Metropolitan Police. Together, we fight crime.

I am at the end of my canned spiel, congratulating myself on a message well-delivered, when the Home Secretary herself fixes me with a brooding, brown-eyed stare.

"Dr. O'Brien, what you've outlined to us is a purely reactive stance. But this incident isn't an isolated event. We can't afford to be on the back foot: the terrorism implications are dreadful. Where's your strategy to get ahead of the problem?"

"It's coming." I swallow. "With all due respect, I was called to this briefing at short notice. My department is in fact working overtime on a broad strategy for managing the superpowered. Unfortunately we currently have neither the budget nor the enabling legislative framework to implement the plan, but—"

"You'll have it on my desk by nine a.m. sharp next Monday morning." She doesn't smile: Jessica Greene only opens wide to swallow her prey. "You will personally brief my staff later that day, subject to scheduling."

"Yes, ma'am," I say automatically. I don't *think* a heel-click would be appreciated, but—"Is there anything else?"

"No," she says dismissively: "I think we've heard all we—"

The red telephone next to the Deputy PM's elbow trills for attention.

"Yah?" Deputy Prime Minister Dennis Baker—at age forty-one the head of the junior party in the coalition, and one of the most powerful politicians in the country—actually *yahs*. He does it with the indolent, satisfied smirk of the utterly entitled; then something odd happens. He stiffens, an expression of sudden urgency wiping the grin from his features. "Oh dear. How unfortun— *What?*" (Another pause, during which all of us try to pretend we're not holding our breath in hope of learning what could set Golden Boy's face in such a severe rictus of dismay.) "Oh dear, that's really rather serious, isn't

it? Yes, I can see why you felt it necessary to interrupt—yes, I'll tell
them. Keep me informed of any developments. Yes. Bye."

He puts the phone down, then leans forward and plants his hands
palm-down on either side of his blotter for a moment. For a moment
he struggles visibly for words.

"*Where* is Officer Friendly when you need him?" he finally bursts
out. Then he takes a deep breath and uses the moment to get a grip
on himself. "I apologize, ladies and gentlemen. It appears that the
incident in Trafalgar Square may have been a diversion."

"What?" (That's my contribution to the sudden uproar.)

"While Dr. O'Brien was defending our friend the Mayor from
Strip Jack Spratt in front of the cameras around the Fourth Plinth,
somebody broke into the Bank of England."

"THEY BROKE INTO THE BANK OF ENGLAND VAULTS," I REPEAT
later that evening, "crowbarred their way into one of the secure terminals, and downloaded the private keys to the currency serialization
printer."

Vikram: "Who are 'they'?"

Emma: "What's a currency serialization printer?"

We're in a private room at the Civil Service Club, a couple of
blocks away from the Cabinet Office. Our booking on the room in
Admiralty House ran out, and the New Annex is still out of service,
so the Senior Auditor personally signed us into the club and agreed to
a subsistence claim. Which is a good thing, because I am shaky and
ravenous with hunger—I haven't eaten properly since before last
night's reception on the oil rig.

I push my hair back (isolated strands are making individual bids
for freedom from the knot I imposed on them after I showered) and
wet my lips before I reply. It's a really nice Beaujolais: the SA has
good taste in wine. "Nobody knows who 'they' are, which is in itself
highly suspicious," I explain. "The cameras saw nothing. Literally,
nothing. The recording isn't blank, it just shows what you'd expect
to see in a room with nobody there, until suddenly there's an explo-

sion and bits of computer and broken glass and ceiling tiles all over the floor."

"Do go on." Dr. Armstrong's spectacles twinkle: reflections from the candles in the middle of the table.

"They broke into the vault where they keep the secure computer system the bank uses to generate the numbers on banknotes. It's an anti-forgery measure: the serial numbers aren't purely sequential, and they aren't random. They're actually a sequence number and a cryptographic hash function generated by a *very* private key indeed. Banks can use a copy of the B of E's public key to verify that high-denomination notes aren't forgeries. It's a back-stop: even if an enterprising crook can get hold of a supply of the right paper and ink, beg borrow or steal a secure hologram-capable intaglio printer, and manufacture currency plates, they still have to get the number right."

"I thought they used RFID chips these days?" says Jez Wilson. "And DNA?"

"The DNA tagging hasn't been rolled out yet; when it is, it can be sampled and amplified by PCR to authenticate the new banknotes. RFID chips—not for anything small, they're too expensive. Euro zone issuers use RFID chips in fifty-euro notes and up, but the Bank of England doesn't do that yet. The key security measure is still the cryptographic checksum in the machine-readable number."

"So they stole what, the private key?"

"Not known." I take another sip of wine. "What we *do* know is that they ran off a couple of tapes full of signed serialized numbers. At least, that's what the Treasury people are saying they think happened. All the room contains is a terminal and a pair of minicomputers, old enough to vote and with all but two of their i/o ports soldered shut. They generate sequences and dump them onto magnetic tape, which is then transported under guard to a secure banknote printing site, loaded onto the printing station that adds the serial numbers, and then degaussed on the spot to prevent the tape being reused."

"How do they know the tapes were taken?"

"There's a mechanical rev counter inside the tape drive they use— not visible if you're looking at the front panel. It's all very old-school:

they open it up every week and write down the number of tapes that have been written in a ledger. Apparently someone ran off a couple of reels of twenty-pound notes. Each tape can store a million valid currency numbers, so they're good for twenty million pounds of perfect forgeries per cartridge. Then they left behind an EMP bomb—a shaped implosion charge wrapped around a small electromagnetic coil. It made a mess of the room, and more importantly fried every chip, hard drive, tape, and floppy disk within twenty meters." That's when the security guards noticed: there was a bone-rattling thump from the basement and their mobile phones died.

"Charming," murmurs the SA. "So they've got no idea who did it, except that the culprits knew exactly what they were doing, could bamboozle TV cameras, and got away with a couple of incredibly portable items that are worth twenty million pounds each. What makes them think it's connected with Strip Jack Spratt's song-and-dance session?"

"Well, there are two clues to work on." *This calls for another sip of wine.* "Firstly, as near as we can tell, the break-in happened at exactly the same time that Jack started building his pornographic sculpture on the Fourth Plinth. It might be a pure coincidence, but what are the odds? And secondly"—I pause for another sip—"the thief left a calling card."

The SA winces almost imperceptibly. "What did it say?" he asks, clearly nerving himself for bad news.

"It said, 'The World Shall Hear From Me Again! Tremble, Fools, Before It Is Too Late!—Professor Freudstein.'

"And it was printed in Comic Sans."

So. First we have an outbreak of superpowers . . . and now we have a *soi-disant* Mad Scientist with *really bad* typographic taste on our hands.

How could things possibly get any worse?

5.

THE OFFICE

THE NEXT DAY I AWAKEN EARLY, WITH A MILD HANGOVER AND A bad case of *oh dear God did I really say that to the Senior Auditor?* I roll over and reach out, meaning to ask Bob's opinion, and hit cold air on the other side of an unfamiliar hotel bed. Everything crashes down on me at once and I sit bolt upright. Then reflex takes over: I reach for my laptop.

I have email, lots of email. Temporary office space has been assigned in one of our outlying buildings just south of the river, under the shadow of the glittering green glass block-pile that is Legoland, the Secret Intelligence Service headquarters building. (That's MI6 to you.) A memo from Emma MacDougal: she's going to spend the morning trawling for available staff to assign to my department and she'll send them across as soon as possible. *Damn, I'll have to get in to the new office early to head them off at the pass.* Another email, this time from the secure Metropolitan Police intranet: Jo Sullivan wants to talk to me. Well, that's good to know, because *I* want to talk to *her.* The shortest route to an arrested villain in an interview room is through his arresting officer's boss, and Strip Jack Spratt is currently the only lead I've got on this Freudstein character.

Of course I'm not totally naive, so I google Freudstein before I even think about going downstairs and seeing if my room tariff includes breakfast. First hit: an EBM/techno band from Brighton. Second hit: the villain in an obscure Italian cult horror movie from 1981. Somehow neither of these seem like promising candidates for the sort of lunatic who'd break into the Bank of England. I rub my forehead and groan. Usually when I go to sleep, all the crises of the day look better—or at least more distant—the next morning. This is that rare and unwelcome exception: a day when I wake up to find that yesterday's bad news is still rumbling downhill, gathering momentum like a giant snowball.

Despair, dismay, disorientation, and delusion: the four horsemen of the bureaucratic apocalypse are coming my way. I want to crawl back under the covers and hide from the world, but somehow I don't think the world is going to let me escape so easily. So I roll sideways out of bed (a day older and a day creakier) and shuffle towards the compact hotel bathroom.

Someone has been kind enough to send my suitcase over. I raid it for a change of underwear, then dress in my work weeds and head downstairs. I discover that I am set up for breakfast. Unfortunately the hotel buffet is pretty much wall-to-wall fried meat and carbs. I manage to choke down a bowl of muesli and some diabolically bad coffee before giving up and retreating back to my room. A quick call to the front desk confirms that I've got the room for two more nights, thanks to the SA: bless his little cotton socks for thinking it through. (By Friday the tabloids will begin to lose interest, and by Saturday I might be able to sneak back into my own home through the kitchen window without being mugged by paparazzi.) So I collect my violin case, shoehorn my laptop into my handbag, and head for the nearest tube station. It's time to go to work.

Work turns out to be a rented office suite in a refurbished warehouse in Hoxton, an odd survivor left over from the Silicon Roundabout boom. (The local council helpfully kicked out all the startups to make room for student flats: apparently rented accommodation is better for the post-housing boom economy than creating new businesses.)

I get there a whisker before ten o'clock. There's an anonymous-looking steel door with an entryphone system and reinforced bolts; behind it there's a security desk, two unlabelled doorways with complex locks on them, and a blue-suiter who failed to hop on the G4S gravy train when it rolled past. "Dr. O'Brien," I introduce myself, showing my warrant card. "I gather I have an office here."

The security officer stirs himself for long enough to look at my card, then does a double take. "I'm sorry, ma'am—Director—let me sign you in." He takes my card and scans it, then unlocks a drawer and hands the card back to me, along with a lanyard and badge. I freeze for a moment, eyeball-to-eyeball with a glassy-eyed version of me who looks as if she's just swallowed a frog. "Please come this way."

We go through the left door (which unlocks when you hold your ID badge against the sensor and face a camera at eye level). Behind it, the guard ushers me along a narrow windowless corridor, up the elevator to the fourth floor, and out into a stairwell with a glass-fronted interior reception area beyond it. "All yours, ma'am. I'd better get back to the front desk."

All mine? It feels very strange. There's a bog-standard bleached-pine desk in the lobby area, but no PC or chair yet. A pile of flat-pack furniture boxes stacked up behind it appear to have been abandoned by the previous occupants. There are the usual false floor and ceiling tiles, beige carpet for the one and off-white polystyrene for the other. I use my badge to let myself into the offices beyond, noting that the door might be made of glass but it's more than two centimeters thick and the copper-and-wire-mesh gasket of a Faraday cage is visible in the door frame, a security precaution intended to block wireless emissions.

A completely empty office suite is more than a little eerie. I walk a circuit of the rectangular corridor, noting office doors, toilets, cafeteria. The cafeteria is bare, cupboard doors hanging open like hungry mouths. The only office with any distinguishing features at all is at the far corner: there's a discreet plaque on the door that says DIRECTOR.

I go in.

As Director, I apparently rate a spacious, airy corner office with thick pile carpet and tinted windows that overlook the high street. More than that: before I get to it I have to run the gauntlet of a medium-sized outer office that is clearly intended for the director's personal assistant. My offices are bigger than the top floor of my house. Alas, the effect is slightly spoiled by the profound lack of any visible furniture. Raised floor panels show where the phones and network cables will be plumbed in: but I suppose they think I'm such an elevated personage that I can just levitate in lotus position until such time as someone delivers my desk and chair.

I pull out my phone to call Facilities back at the New Annex, but just as I'm about to dial, it vibrates to announce an incoming call. (So much for the Faraday cage.) There's a familiar face on the screen and for a heart-stabbing moment I consider not answering: but no, that's not an option.

"Bob?"

"Mo? How are you? I heard about the news—"

"Where are you? Where are you staying? I haven't been back home since yesterday lunchtime—"

Our words collide and overlap in a birefringent sheen of ripples: or perhaps that's just my eyes. I stop and listen, clinging to the phone as if it's a life-saver.

"I'm in the New Annex, Mo. It's a real mess here; the fire extinguishers were triggered, there's water damage and other stuff. Second floor's utterly inaccessible while the crime scene folks work it over. I'm crashing on my office floor: I've got a sleeping bag. They want me to disarm all the traps in Angleton's office and get into the Memex. It could take some time. How about you?"

I twirl in place, very slowly. Is he sleeping in the office to avoid me, or avoid Lecter? That's the question. "They've given me a corner office. Great view, shame about the furniture. Emma said she'd start sending people over this afternoon but unless Facilities get here first I've got nowhere to put them." I realize dismally that we're talking about work. Retreating into the routine to avoid dealing with the uncanny rift that's opened up between us. "I need moral support. Can we meet up somewhere?"

"Yes, but you said you haven't been home—"

"Paparazzi, dear."

"Did you feed Spooky?"

Oh snap, I *knew* I'd forgotten something. Horrid little fleabag. "Yes, but that was yesterday and you were going to clean the litter tray and I can't go home, I'm horribly busy and the journalists will doorstep me—"

"Just stop it, Mo." He sounds weary. "I'll go round there as soon as I can get away from here, find a cattery or something. Park her in my office if not. It's not fair to leave her alone in an empty house."

"I'll be—" I take a deep breath. "I can go home on Saturday. The SA reckons the tabloids will lose interest after seventy-two hours." I realize how stupid this is the moment I say it: I'm going to give a bored cat the free run of the house and bedroom, and ample time to demonstrate its diabolically inventive (not to say fragrant) displeasure? I may not like cats, but that's only because I understand the way their twisty little minds work. "If you can find time to pick her up some time today, I'd be ever so." I dangle a concession in front of him: "You can even bring her home to stay once I'm able to move back in."

"Okay, I'll do that. We still need to talk—"

My phone vibrates again. "Uh oh, I've got an incoming. Looks like it's Emma. Can we continue this later? Great, bye—*smooches*," I add, but he's already hung up. So by the time I utter the last word I'm speaking to Mrs. MacDougal from Human Resources. "Oops, that was meant for my husband. How are you this morning, Emma?"

"*I'm* fine." There's a rather odd emphasis in her voice, as if to imply *but you aren't*: but maybe that's just my paranoia speaking. "I was calling to give you your initial personnel assignments; as you probably gathered, things are a little hectic today? But I've found four warm bodies for your team and we can fill in from there as the week goes on. I've got names for group tech support, two analyst/planners, and of course your deputy director—"

"That's great," I say, and I mean it, "but where am I going to put them? There's no furniture here, Emma! Not even chairs. Has anyone told Facilities?"

"Oh hell, Moira was supposed to get onto that first thing. I told her to send six employee kits over—"

"Would they be flat packs, by any chance?" I stalk towards the lobby area.

"Yes, six desks, six chairs, six individual bookcases, and a supply cupboard—"

"Bingo." The teetering pile of boxes stares me. "Could you maybe send someone round with a screwdriver, no, make that a full toolbox? And half a dozen six-way mains extension bars." My notebook is weighing my handbag down. "I don't think we've got any network access here, so I'll email you a bullet list of everything else I can think of that we're going to need in the next twenty-four hours. We're going to be running on laptops and external security discipline for a while."

"You do that," Emma says warmly. "Anything else I can do for you?"

"Yes; just tell anyone who asks that we're not open for business today. Tomorrow is another matter."

"Okay, bye."

"Bye."

I put my phone away and head back to my enormous, empty office. I park Lecter's case in the corner between the two windows, sit cross-legged in the middle of the carpet, and start typing furiously on my laptop. Because tomorrow may belong to me, but the day after tomorrow belongs to the Home Secretary: and if I'm not ready to deliver a dog-and-pony show by Monday, the presence or absence of our departmental coffee percolator will be the least of my worries.

THE DAY PASSES IN A BLUR. IF YOU'VE EVER MOVED HOUSE, you'll have some inkling of what it's like to bootstrap an empty office suite from scratch. I spend the first hour writing want lists for Emma to throw at her minions. Then the front door buzzer beeps for attention. It's a bloke from Facilities, with toolbox, as requested. "One employee desk and chair set needs to go in each of those offices"—I point—"starting with the Director's corner office and the receptionist's room. Um. If there's a separate management-grade kit, give it to the Director. And the stores cupboard can go in there." I wave vaguely at the empty windowless room next to the kitchen.

"Sure and I can be doing that." He grins cheerily. "I'll have you somewhere to sit in a jiffy."

"You get started." I nod. "I'm nipping out. Back in an hour."

It turns out that there's a Café Nero around the corner with free wifi and comfy leather sofas—they're playing tag with Starbucks for the migratory worker base—so I take self plus violin there, and plant myself behind a laptop screen and a venti mocha with a double shot and a good view of the door and windows. Then I start hammering the keys: it turns out that HR have a canned departmental starter-kit on file, and there are a *lot* of forms to fill out. (Yes, we've all had the security talk about open wireless networks. I've also had the weekly special en-clueing from my dear husband. We have a VPN, and firewalls, and you do not want to mess with them because the design spec for the Laundry's firewall software is not to keep intruders out, but to make them undergo spontaneous combustion when they get in: as Bob puts it, it's the only way to be sure.)

After an hour in the cafe I drift furtively back to my office suite. There is now a sign on the glass lobby door: TRANSHUMAN POL-ICY COORDINATION UNIT. It strikes me as indiscreet at first, but then I think it through: given that I'm running a Potemkin village, indiscretion had better be my middle name from now on. Just as long as it's *planned* indiscretion.

Back in my office, things are looking up: it contains a Desk and a Chair, both so grand that they really demand capitalization. The Desk is a very fine desk indeed—my laptop sits adrift in the middle of its empty bleached woodgrain ocean, looking lost. The Director's throne is a high-end piece of Herman Miller sculpture: all resin and chrome, it looks as if it was designed by H. R. Giger. I check it carefully for teeth and ovipositors before I dare to sit on it. Once adjusted to my height and seating position, it is, indeed, indecently comfortable: I feel as if I'm levitating. Then I look at my laptop's battery status and swear.

Martin from Facilities sticks his head around the door while I'm crawling around on my hands and knees, plugging the computer's power supply into the socket under the desk. "Miss? There's someone at the front desk who says he's been sent over to see you."

I scoot backwards and sit up, barely managing not to bang my head on the underside of the desk. "Send him in." So much for directorial dignity. Bob did this for a living, for years on end, crawling under desks with one end of a cable clutched between his teeth? No wonder he went mad and volunteered for active ops.

I'm back on my throne by the time the door opens. "Hello?" A hipsterish head—mid-twenties male, owlish black horn-rimmed spectacles and highly ironic beard—oozes round the door frame, followed shortly thereafter by a hipsterish body. "Dr. O'Brien? I'm Samuel Jennings. Emma MacDougal sent me."

"She did, did she?" I look at him for a while, until he swallows. There's probably a personnel file clogging up my inbox, but I like to get an unvarnished look at people before I resort to the funhouse mirror of HR's misconceptions. (The next personnel file I read that describes its subject accurately will be the first: at best they're misleadingly out of date, and at worst they're just plain misleading.) "As you can see, things are a bit sparse around here right now—sorry there's no visitor's chair yet! Your file hasn't caught up with you. So, Samuel—or is it Sam? What do you do?"

"What—" He shifts gears with an almost audible *clunk*. "Oh, *that*. Senior analyst, level two. Background in abstract theoretical xenobiology with application to endogenous evolved neurocomputing architecture." The beard twitches in a self-deprecatingly ironic smile. "I think I'm here because I got caught moonlighting a year ago and HR carpeted me for it."

"Moonlighting?" I do a double take. *Is that even* possible? *This is* the Laundry. *We have an oath of office that fries us from the inside out if we do anything remotely dodgy!* I lean forward: "What were you doing?"

"I have an, er, hobby. Scriptwriting comics. I'm a so-so illustrator but after doing some indy work I landed a gig writing for a second-tier Titan property."

Right. "So. And this qualifies you to work for Transhuman Policy Coordination, how?"

"Beats me, but HR seem to think that writing about intelligent alien insect invaders from Sirius qualifies me as an expert on the paranormally enhanced." He shrugs. "My office got trashed the day before yesterday so I'm temporarily homeless, and there's the xenotech neurocomputing specialty to consider, and I'm an analyst, so I got this call from Moira in HR, and she said, 'You're the superhero expert, go analyze!' So here I am."

"Cool. You'll have to tell me all about the comics business some day." I stand up. "Let's go find you an office. Got laptop?"

"Got laptop." He pats a carnivorous-looking Crumpler messenger bag.

"Let's get you going then. Hmm. As you can see, we've barely begun moving in. You can start by drawing up a wish list for equipment and I'll forward it to Facilities—anything you expect you'll need to get an analysis and reporting office for four up and running within the next month. You can also answer the door and send anyone new who shows up through to me. That's just for today, mind. Tomorrow, we'll hold an all-hands at two o'clock sharp. Clear?"

"Absolutely." His head bobs: he looks at me with an expression that makes me feel very strange for a few seconds until I realize what it signifies. I've mostly seen it in research students up 'til now. It's the look you give your new and terrifyingly efficient and impressive boss on your way out their office door the first time you meet them, when you realize that you've survived the encounter and you don't even need a change of underwear.

Am I *that* kind of office dragon?

It'll be fun finding out.

BY SIX O'CLOCK I'M ABOUT READY TO CALL IT A WRAP FOR THE day. It's threatening to get dark outside: the shadows are lengthening in the canyon-like street below my window, and the traffic is hitting its rush-hour peak. In addition to Sam, I have acquired another analyst (Nick: mid-thirties, serious male-pattern baldness on top, wiry build that hints at alarmingly athletic exercise preferences, specializes in traffic analysis, owns a huge DVD collection and identifies himself as a sad fan who goes to conventions for fun—almost as if it's an ethnicity or a calling), and a techie (Sara: I vaguely know her, she used to work for Bob a couple of years ago). Sara gets a phone installed on every desk by five o'clock, promises to plumb us into the intranet tomorrow morning, and even finds me a visitor's chair from somewhere. She seems a bit shy and diffident, but then again, I'm fifteen years her senior and the sign on my door says DIRECTOR.

So Sam, Nick, and Sara have gone home and at half past six I'm all alone in the office, finishing up my PowerPoint slides for tomorrow's all-hands, when there's a knock on the door. "Come in," I say, not looking up.

"Hi, I'm your new deputy director—oh *shit*."

I look up, and freeze.

"*You*," we both say at the same time.

The door swings shut behind my new deputy director with a solid *click*.

I stare at her, calculating angles and distances. It doesn't look good: Lecter is about three meters behind my chair, leaning against the corner between the windows. I don't have a gun or a knife, Facilities haven't installed the security wards in this room yet, and there's no panic button. Even if I had a hotline to the blue-suiters on the front desk, I very much doubt they could get here in time to help.

"What's that on your face?"

"Theatrical makeup." Her glare could curdle milk. "Nobody mentioned I'd be working for *you*. What a fucking mess."

"Take a seat," I say, heart pounding and the small of my back suddenly prickling-hot and slick with sweat.

"No thanks, I'd rather stand."

Mhari stares at me: I stare back at her.

She's a willowy blonde with a figure fit to send vapid twenty-something non-supermodels into paroxysms of jealousy. Her only flaw is that her face is pancaked with theatrical quantities of makeup.

She does the severe-office-power-suit thing way better than I do: everything's black except for her high-collared red silk blouse. She looks like the walking human incarnation of a venomous spider. It takes me an extra moment to notice that she's wearing opaque black hosiery and gloves: the only skin on display is her face. "Nice outfit. Sun getting to you?"

"It's a workaround." She reaches into her handbag and produces a pair of mirrored aviator shades. "A sub-optimal one." She twirls them lazily between left index finger and thumb, like an Old West gunslinger.

I need to get control of this situation. *Fast.* "I'll give you a choice. You can go out the door, go back to whatever box they put you in, and I'll tell Emma to roll the dice again. Without prejudice. Or you can sit down"—I point at the chair—"*right now* and we will work this out."

My heart is going about a hundred and fifty beats a minute, and I'm so keyed up that my hand is shaking: I lower it hastily, in case she notices. Coldsweat terror claws at the back of my neck.

"Promise you won't try to kill me with that *thing*." I note her gaze tracking towards the corner between the windows. My perspective flips, in another of those dizzying Rubin vase moments: Is *she* afraid of *me*?

"Don't be silly, killing one's staff is workplace harassment. Definitely gross misconduct: I think it's a sacking offense." (It's also murder, and the Black Assizes take a very dim view of it, but I don't bring that up: I don't want her to feel too comfortable.) I pause. "Sit down and let's talk things over like grown-ups."

She sits, but she's wound up like a watch spring: back straight, knees together, oversized black leather handbag clenched on her lap. "Is this some kind of sick joke?"

I consider the idea. "Very possibly." But if so, who is the joke aimed at? And where's the joker?

"Emma told me this is a new departmental start-up, a public front to deflect attention from the Laundry. Also an attempt to contain the pervert suit problem."

Very succinct. "Yes."

"You're directing it, why? Is this something to do with yesterday's headlines?"

Kid, you have no *idea.* I nod, stiffly. "I've been reallocated. My old job became nonviable the, the instant the TV cameras locked on."

"*Oh.*" I recognize that expression from somewhere. I wish I didn't: I don't need her sympathy, however grudging. "Right."

I lace my fingers together in front of me to stop my hands from shaking with the effort of not fidgeting as I stare back at her: "Why do you think Emma thought you were suited for the role of deputy director of this unit?" I see her hesitate, so I add, "If it helps, try to imagine you're talking to someone else. Animal, vegetable, sentient cauliflower from Arcturus: it doesn't matter, just as long as they're not me."

"I don't need egg-sucking lessons." Her lip curls, momentarily supercilious, then she realizes what she's doing and hides it behind an instantly raised hand. Anything to avoid slipping me a flash of the old ivory gnashers. "Really, it's not hard. I spent three years in HR, back in the day. Then I transferred to the deactivation list and was outplaced into the second-largest investment bank in Europe. While I was working there I did a part-time MBA and worked in a variety of roles, most recently as the operations manager for an internal business unit with a turnover of roughly two hundred million pounds a year." She squares her shoulders and sticks her chest out: "I am also a blood-sucking fiend, *out* and *proud*. Superpowers: I have them. What do *you* bring to the table, Mrs. Howard?"

I grin and bare my teeth at her: "That's Dr. O'Brien to you, Ms. Murphy."

I glance over my shoulder at Lecter: his case is the right way round to display the sticker on its side. THIS MACHINE KILLS DEMONS.

"That facetious bumper-sticker sums up what I used to do for our organization—our *real* organization, that is. I destroy emergent threats. When I'm not doing field work, I have a PhD in philosophy of mathematics, lecture part-time in music theory at Birkbeck, and specialize in the application of fast Fourier transforms to psychoacoustic summoning systems. And I appear to be your designated line manager."

Superpowers I do *not* have, but I've got five years on this highly annoying person, and age and guile trump youth and enthusiasm—or so they say. I must remember to bear in mind that I've *only* got five years on her: she may be able to pass for her early twenties but she's roughly Bob's age. Unfortunately, in addition to the butterflies that come of knowing I'm unarmed and in the presence of a potentially immortal and superstrong obligate carnivore, I've got a curious sinking sensation in my stomach. It comes from the realization that, on paper at least, Mhari is *impressively* well-qualified to be my executive officer.

"Right," she says crisply. "So. The job of this unit is to generate and then execute a strategy for containing and mitigating the superhero nuisance. We've got office space, two analysts, and a target—?" She raises a latex-smeared eyebrow and I nod, very slightly. "And all that's holding us back is a marked lack of trust between the designated director and their executive assistant."

I nod again.

She leans forward as she speaks, loudly and clearly: "I did *not* fuck your husband."

I nod once more, feeling cornered despite all the empty space behind my chair.

Mezzo forte: "I didn't even drink his blood!"

The only way to respond is fortissimo: "So *that* makes everything all right?"

(I swear at myself: she's clearly trying to build bridges, why am I trying to knock them down?)

She rises to a crescendo: "*Can we agree* that he should probably have let you know I was staying over?"

If pauses can be pregnant, this one's on the run from a fertility clinic. A drop of sweat trickles down the small of my back. *Reevaluate. Re-evaluate. Prioritize.* On Monday morning I have to stand up in front of the Home Secretary and deliver a cogent, achievable plan for getting Her Majesty's Government out in front of the paranormal power-assisted pervert suit menace, *stat*. This woman, who I *dislike intensely*, who seriously fucked up Bob before I met him and spent a couple of years working through his neuroses about the opposite sex, this woman *who I trust as far as I can throw her*, this Vampire Bitch from Human Resources *who nearly triggers panic attacks when I see her*, also happens to be exactly the strong right arm that I need to get the job done.

And besides, she's got a point. Even if it falls perilously close to blaming the one person who isn't present at the meeting.

"Yes."

"Fine!" She switches on a smile so manic that I'm certain the last pixie dream girl she mugged is in need of a face transplant. "Does that mean you agree that the potential exists for us to construct and maintain an arm's-length business relationship based on team values, mutual esteem, and peer-to-peer respect for our complementary abilities? One that's free from any incursion of bedroom politics and green-eyed jealousy?"

Oh for fuck's sake. If I could mend fences with Ramona I ought at least *try* to get along with Mhari without sucking her soul out through her eyeballs with my violin. As long as she keeps her fangs out of my neck and Bob out of her bed, I can probably do this. "Jealousy is such a nasty word," I say. Then I narrow my eyes. "But I have a question for you. Why are *you* so keen to work with *me*?"

Mhari rolls her eyes. "Because, in business terms, you just parachuted straight into the CEO's seat of an entrepreneurial startup that bypassed the incubator and angel rounds and went straight to a juicy Series A term sheet." Some of the tension has leached out of her shoulders: the handbag sits limp on her lap, her knees aren't clenched as tightly, she no longer looks—*good Lord, she was* terrified!

"You probably think I'm an ambitious greasy-pole climber. If so, you'd be absolutely right. You might just have noticed that I have special dietary needs: *expensive* ones. The Laundry will find a way to feed me, no questions asked, as long as I make myself useful. *You* might be a workaholic who lives for the job, but if *I* don't work, I don't get to live. Not dying is a wonderful motivating factor, don't you think? So I need to make myself indispensable, or at least too useful to put down."

She relaxes infinitesimally as she gets into her pitch, but her expression remains intense. I have the uneasy sense that I'm getting a window on the real Mhari's soul, one that she doesn't draw back the curtains on very often.

"In business, the fastest way to the top is to join a new organization in the early days and make it grow under you. If you join an established company, you have to fight your way up through all the accumulated dead wood. Unfortunately, new banking start-ups don't come along very often. The Scrum was going to be my ticket to the boardroom, but then PHANG happened. So, anyway, speaking as an ambitious management bitch, my plan is simple: get on board a new org chart early, push for growth, Series B, Series C. There is no IPO when you're part of a government agency—the usual breakout in the age of privatization is to be spun off as a GovCo, then sold to one of the big service corporations—but there *is* a plateau of stability when the growth curve stabilizes, at which point the executives can run out the gangway and waltz back over to rejoin their parent organizations at a *much* higher level than they were at when they left, a comparatively short time ago. Take you, for example: if this works, your new department won't last forever—but if you go back to the Laundry, you'll take your new grade with you."

Wow. If this was a marketing presentation, it would be standing ovation time. Her intensity is terrifying: it makes me want to pin a notice on her power suit saying FRONT TOWARDS ENEMY. An idea for how to harness her dangerous energy begins to percolate up from the depths of my subconscious. I keep a lid on it for now—the interview isn't over yet—but it bears exploration, just as soon as I've cleared up some loose ends.

"Okay, I hear where you're coming from. I have a couple of follow-on questions, though. Does your condition mean you'll have difficulty keeping regular office hours or appearing in public? And what are you doing about, um, eating in the short term?"

"My condition is *my* problem," she says tartly. "You might want

to bear in mind the civil service policy guidelines on respect for disabilities in the workplace before you ask such questions. But, since
you ask: in the absolute worst case, a full traditional *hijab* and *niqab*
will keep me from frying, and in overcast and twilight conditions I
can get away with theatrical face paint and sunglasses. So yes, I can
be on hand during core office hours, although I'll need to have blackout blinds fitted in my office. Point *deux*: I still mostly eat normal
food. The question of how to provide a regular supply of my special
dietary supplement is being dealt with by a committee chaired by Dr.
Wills." For an instant I see a flicker of something that might almost
be grief cross her face, but the pancake of latex and foundation she's
wearing makes it hard to read micro-expressions. "Again, may I remind you of our policy on disabilities? Other people have equally
distasteful needs. It's only relatively recently that individuals with
growth hormone deficiency gained a source of somatotropin that
wasn't harvested from cadaver brains, for example."

"I—I—I—" I restart: "You've made your point."

I stand up, slowly, and warily make my way around my desk—and
she stands up, her posture defensive. *Fight or flee?* I suppress a panic-
shudder and stop a meter away from her, just outside her personal
space. Then I force myself to raise my right hand.

"Welcome aboard," I say. After a second, she raises her hand, too.
We shake, very gingerly. Her nylon-sheathed fingers are slippery and
cool.

"No back-stabbing," she says. Maybe it's an offer.

"No annoying personal shit," I counter-offer. "Let's keep it one
hundred percent professional."

She nods, unsmiling. "All right. Now what?"

I exhale slowly, still shuddery-shaky from my initial reaction to her.
"Tomorrow, at two o'clock, I'm holding an all-hands. I'm supposed to
deliver a briefing, with concrete proposals, to the Home Secretary on
Monday morning. *Everything* is secondary to that. We're going to be
working in crunch mode until then—we've got a looming first dead-
line, and if we don't make it, we are dead in the water. So dead there
won't be a hole deep enough to bury us in. So it's going to be sixteen-

hour days and working all weekend if necessary. Unfortunately I've *also* got some off-site stuff to do—stuff that is so time-critical it can't wait, because it may feed into the HomeSec's briefing—so I need you to keep an eye on the analysts and manage the new intake of staff while I'm out of the office."

She bites her lower lip, still keeping her canines discreetly out of sight. "Do you have a strategy?"

"I do indeed." I reach over to the desk and spin the notebook round so that we can both see the screen. "Let me talk you through it . . ."

6.

AN EXCITABLE BOY

I STUMBLE THROUGH MY HOTEL ROOM'S DOORWAY JUST AFTER eleven o'clock, bone-tired and shaky from the post-adrenaline crash. I'm still only half-certain there's a chance that my paper plane will leave the runway. Mhari and I put in nearly four hours on the key strategy proposal and my presentation, and she kicked the tires *very* thoroughly before she handed me the metaphorical air hose. If she can be trusted to hold up her end of the deal, we might be able to make it fly. If. *If.* Ah well. I may not trust her personally—actually, I can barely hold back my fight/flight impulse in her presence—but I can't fault her motivation.

If I can learn not to break out in a hot flush (or get the shudders or random stabs of ossified reflexive jealousy) when she walks in the door—and if she can learn not to jump out of her skin when I pick up my violin case (as she did when we were leaving, and then she tried to make a shaky-voiced joke of it)—we can make policy faster than a speeding bullet and leap tall buildings full of paperwork.

But it's going to take practice and a lot of patience.

Once I crawl between the sheets, I go out like a lamp. Sleep is dreamless at first, but some time in the small hours I awaken just enough to do the bathroom sleepwalk shuffle—and when I go back to bed I start to dream. I'm on that monochrome dance floor again, whirling in the arms of my white-clad faceless lover. This time it's no waltz; I'm gothed up like my mid-teenaged self's vision of her aspirational adult persona—all rather jejune, with way too much black lace: what can I say, it was a phase I was going through—as we dance to a New Romantic/eighties synthpop beat. There's a band between the columns of speakers, faceless men in suits surrounded by a wall of ancient Korg and Yamaha kit. "The Damned Don't Cry," "Enola Gay": as we whirl to the dance floor beat I feel like a machine, as soulless as my partner.

Who leans towards my face and whispers, ***You could have taken her soul.***

"You say that like you think I should want it." His voice is autumn leaves blowing through the doorway of an open crypt; mine is toneless.

He pulls me closer. ***You *should* have taken her. She lied to you.***

"I can't kill people just because they lie to me. Or because I don't like them."

He laughs and whirls me in a tight circle. I lean backwards, relying on his arms around me for support. ***You've killed people you didn't like before. Firouz the Pasdaran lieutenant, in Vakilabad. The nest of idiot goat-worshipers in Amstelveen. Your—***

"Shut up and dance." It's not a very goth dance, it's *far* too intimate. I break out of his grip, sway sidelong away, then catch the rhythm: grab the bat, hug the bat, drop the bat. *Work* those hips, raise your arms: big box, little box, big box, little box. Back to swaying on the spot: grab the bat, hug the bat, drop the bat, kick the bat across the dancefloor. Then I grab the bat again and suddenly find my arms filled by my dance partner, his arms wrapped around me like the steel bars of an impossible cage.

Love is all you need, he whispers breathily in my ear, and runs his tongue down the side of my neck to the base of my throat.

The rasp of his flinty tongue strikes a spark that sets me on fire. I wrap my arms around him and play intimate chords of power on the fingerboard of his spine. He shivers eerily and lifts me, and I wrap my knees around his hips, then—the logic of dreams holds no brief for zippers, underwear, or hook-and-eye fasteners—his teeth are locked around my painfully taut right nipple as he lowers me onto his sound post.

I become one with the sound as we whirl around the dance floor in a frenzy of pleasure, pulses rippling through me as we "Fade to Grey."

I COME TO MY SENSES IN A PILE OF COLD, SWEAT-DRENCHED sheets, shuddering in the receding wake of the most powerful orgasm I've had since *no, stop, that's* far *too long ago.* I try to roll over—*no, too soon.* According to the alarm radio it's a quarter to seven. *Not fair.* I reach for the light switch and glare bleary-eyed at the violin case on the hotel room desk. Why does it seem to look smug?

"Bastard," I mutter as I try to sit up. I feel obscurely guilty. It was just an erotic dream: I don't cheat on my husband. At least, I don't think I do . . . do imaginary violins count? To my sleep-clouded eyes, Lecter's case seems slightly flaccid, slowly pulsing. Or maybe it's just the arteries in the back of my eyeballs.

I take a long shower, mainly because I crave the sensation of washing ghostly adulterous fingertips off my skin. I have to lean against the wall, my knees are so weak: it was positively tectonic. I close my eyes under the warm rain and wish Bob was here to hold me in the afterglow.

I dress in my second-best work suit, the houndstooth check Jaeger one. It's a bit frumpy, if I'm perfectly honest with myself, maybe *too* frumpy—but even though my work wardrobe needs an overhaul in light of my new job, I am damned if I'm going to get into a sartorial arms race with Mhari. Before she became a PHANG she was merely pretty; now she could take up modeling, if it wasn't for the slight bursting-into-flames-when-exposed-to-bright-lights problem. I go with the lowest heels and the least office makeup I can get away with:

I've got a lot of walking to do today. I don't bother with the vile hotel breakfast. Instead, I collect Lecter and I'm out the door by eight thirty, straight into the comfortingly anonymous rush-hour crowd and on my way to the first appointment of the day.

Nobody sane drives in London: I take the bus. By the time I get to my destination I've lost most of my early-mover time, but I've had a chance to come fully awake, meditate for a few minutes, and go over my agenda three or four times in search of holes. I can't spot any. I fend off flashbacks as I walk back along a stretch of pavement that rings under my heels with echoes of the other day's walk-to-the-scaffold experience. I'm reasonably centered again, back in my professional sweet spot, and more importantly I know what to expect today. So I am feeling reasonably confident when I march up to the front desk of Belgravia Police Station and say, "Dominique O'Brien to see Chief Inspector Sullivan. I have an appointment."

For a moment I'm afraid the desk sergeant is going to succumb to my middle-aged invisibility field, but then his roving eyeballs land on my warrant card and his pupils dilate slightly as it snags the surface of his mind. "Yes, ma'am." He doesn't exactly snap to attention—his attitude is more like one of suppressed annoyance at having his routine interrupted by the urgent need to perform hand-holding duties for a senior officer who ought to know better—but suddenly he's all over the switchboard. "DCI Sullivan, please: a Dr. O'Brien is waiting for you . . . Where? . . . I'll send her over right away, ma'am." He looks back at me. "She's in the custody suite, ma'am. The special one. Is that where you're expecting to find her?"

I nod. "Which way is it?"

He grabs a constable who is hurrying past: "Julie, would you be a dear and show the superintendent here to the special custody suite? DCI Sullivan is waiting on her."

Julie, suffering the be-a-dear in professional silence, leads me through the badger's sett that is the back side of the police station—scuffed white paint, flickering overhead tubes, and a pervasive smell of stale coffee—and then down a concrete stairwell to a heavy steel door overlooked by half a dozen cameras in armored enclosures.

"This is the old custody suite, ma'am. The main one's on the other side of the building—we were using this to store the riot kit until they repurposed it for the differently empowered three months ago. Have they filled you in on that? The special handling requirements?"

"I'm here to see Jo Sullivan about it," I reassure her. "She'll fill me in."

"Great. May I go? I was on my way to a briefing when—"

"Go on"—pause—"and thanks," I call after her rapidly receding back. Then I turn to the heavy steel door, the like of which one normally only finds in bank vaults and other places that store stuff that really shouldn't be allowed to escape. There is a very prosaic white plastic doorbell stapled inexpertly to the wall next to it. I push the button.

A minute later, there is a squeal of inadequately lubricated gears as the door slides open a crack. "Dominique? Good to see you again."

I cross the threshold and shake hands with Jo. (The threshold is about ten centimeters thick and cross-hatched with yellow stripes and warning stickers showing the grisly things that will happen to you if you happen to be standing in the doorway when the powered door closes.) "So this is the superhero lock-up?"

"Yeah. One of them." Jo takes a step backwards and gestures me in. As I follow her the huge vault-type door whines shut behind me. It closes a lot more smoothly than it opens: there's a *thunk* of steel bolts sliding home, then I notice the background hum of the air conditioners. "The interview suites are over there, that corridor leads to three cells, that one leads to Facilities, staff restrooms, custody officer's room, and a ready room. They're only Cat-B secure—we can't store über-villains here—but it's the best we can do this close to the center of town, at least until the CrossRail TBMs come available to dig the deep London lock-up they've been talking about. How about a coffee while we discuss your request?"

Uh-oh. "A coffee would be great, thanks," I say, and she leads me to the ready room. It does not escape my attention that the entire underground custody suite seems to be embedded in reinforced concrete and has its own air supply. "What is this, a former nuclear bunker?"

"Yes, that's exactly what it used to be." She switches on the battered kettle. "Most of the central London police stations built before 1970 have them. Anyone trying to use them for shelter probably didn't stand a prayer, but they'd still be structurally sound after the rubble stopped bouncing, unlike most of the other buildings, and we'd have needed somewhere for the surviving officers to use as a station. The cells were to be used as dormitories and arms lockers."

"Why? Wouldn't you have needed them as, well, cells?"

Jo shakes her head. "Not after a nuclear war, Mo. Think martial law and firing squads." She grabs two chipped mugs from the cupboard and sloshes coffee and milk into them. "Be glad it never happened."

I fear that we might yet end up going that way if we can't get a handle on CASE NIGHTMARE GREEN. I take my mug and sit down. "Has he coughed yet?"

She's a stand-and-pace type. "Alas, yes. Unfortunately our little canary has gone Section 2 on us. He's absolutely Upney;* halfway to Dagenham, in fact. We're keeping him here because he's not deemed a hazard to himself, but so far he's confessed to assassinating Margaret Thatcher—"

"But Maggie died of natural causes—"

"Yes, exactly. He's also confessed to conspiracy to rob the Bank of England, which is flat-out impossible because he was in custody right here at the time he says he did it. He's delusional about other subjects as well. The duty psychiatrist spent some time assessing him yesterday and thinks he's unfit to stand trial; he's raving about conspiracies and Mad Scientists trying to take over the world and radio receivers in his head. We did some background legwork and found he was diagnosed paranoid schizophrenic four years ago. Looks like he'd been off his meds for some time and was already going downhill fast—he was Sectioned twice in the past nine months—when he came down with an acute attack of superpower-itis."

"Oh dear." I take a mouthful of coffee. It is, if anything, even

---

* The next stop out from Barking on the District Line: as in, Barking Mad.

worse than the hotel buffet brew. When my eyes uncross I take another gulp: the last thing I need is a caffeine headache. "Well, since I've come this far I suppose I ought to interview him anyway . . ."

"You'll be lucky to get anything out of him. Listen, I've talked to more than my fair share of paranoid schizophrenics over the years, and you get a handle on them after a while. Most of them are lovely people, they just can't stop *hearing* things. And they get mood swings and medication side effects and obsessive-compulsive tics. Spratt's different. His powers mean he expresses his delusions, sometimes violently, on whoever's around him. And something about him doesn't feel *right*. If I was a shrink, I'd say he's under the influence of something else—but the duty doc took bloods and he's clean."

"So what you're saying is, you don't expect me to get anything out of him?"

"Yes. Also, about that: you know we're going to have to do the rules of evidence tap dance and haul the duty solicitor in if Laughing Boy so much as looks like he wants representation?"

"Oh hell." I take another mouthful. "Well, my cover can't get any more blown than it is already, and I'm not held to the same rules of evidence as—"

"Yes, you are!" Jo's expression is fierce: "As long as you're in this nick, you're on *my* turf, and we play by the rules here. No spook head-games permitted. Jack's going down one way or the other: maybe he'll pull a long stretch in prison, but more likely he's due to check in for the Broadmoor rest cure. Where he ends up is for the judge and the psychiatrists to figure out, and if your people *really* want to take him off my hands, that's another option, but as long as he's in my custody I am *not* going to permit you to waltz in and jeopardize his conviction—"

I raise my hands: "I surrender."

"—By messing up his inter— Okay. Sorry, Mo, didn't mean to blow up at you. I've been butting heads with too damn many cowboys and would-be vigilantes recently. Not to mention the tabloid hang 'em and flog 'em brigade and a steady stream of superhero-obsessed liqui-bullshit raining down from the top of the pyramid. The

Home Office are screaming, and whenever they get a bee in their bonnet we all get stung sooner or later." She begins to calm down and sips on her coffee, then pulls a face. "This is *disgusting*."

"Really? I'd never have guessed." I push my mug away. "I just want to run some names past him."

"What names?"

"Something I found in a box of cereal. Sorry, Jo, I won't know for sure unless he bites. And, um, national security. Suppose I say I want to rule him out of the Thatcher assassination enquiry that doesn't officially exist?"

She shakes her head. "That's just peachy. Look, I'm pretty sure you won't get anything out of him, but if you insist, I'll set you up. Interview Room 2, ten minutes' time, okay?"

I nod. "Okay."

She disappears, and I finish my vile coffee. (The third mouthful stuns my taste buds enough to let the rest slip down without too much pain.) I hope this isn't going to turn out to be a wild goose chase . . .

TWENTY MINUTES LATER A PLACID-LOOKING CUSTODY SERGEANT fetches me from the break room (where I have forced down a second mug of the stuff festering in the bottom of the filter machine jug) and escorts me to Interview Room 2. "The Chief's already in there with your customer, ma'am. He's a little excitable so we don't want to leave him alone."

"Excitable?"

"Positively bouncing off the walls and ceiling."

The interview rooms in the superhero lock-up are as nonstandard as the Police and Criminal Evidence Act (1984) permits. For one thing, there are two doors—one opening onto the cell block, the other into the office area. For another thing, the room is split in two by a giant sheet of extremely thick toughened glass. Someone has etched a gigantic containment ward into the glass and grounded the hell out of it, just in case. Finally, there's a CCTV camera pointed at the wall.

It's all admissible evidence, and if a villain with hitherto-unplumbed occult superpowers does something terminally stupid, it might save the lives of the next interview team.

On our side of the glass wall, we've got chairs and a desk that supports a DVD recording machine, a box of disks, and sealable envelopes to stash the confessions in. On his side of the wall, Strip Jack Spratt has got five thoroughly padded surfaces—walls, ceiling, floor, even the door is padded—and I'm pretty sure if they had transparent padding for bulletproof glass, they'd have added it to the window. There are wards stenciled on the padding and on every available non-transparent surface. Someone is *really* worried about stray thaum currents in there.

And then there's Strip Jack Spratt himself.

"Have a seat—" Jo winces in time to a meaty thud. "I wish he'd stop doing that."

Strip Jack Spratt is totally naked. It's impossible to ignore: the thud was the noise he made plastering himself across the glass wall, upside down. He's right in front of us with one foot in contact with the ceiling and his arms spread wide across the glass in best Spiderman tradition, which means his pasty-skinned gut bucket and equally pallid wedding tackle are approximately at eye level. He's about fifty, BMI just on the high side of clinically obese, totally bald and hairless, and he has eyes like red-rimmed piss-holes in the snow. Also, he's gurning like a mad clown.

"When Sergeant Jackson said he was bouncing off the walls and ceiling, I didn't realize he was speaking literally."

"Brian's very literal," says Josephine. "Hey, there he goes again."

Spratt, who has been mouthing at us like a catfish, arches his back in an implausible belly-wobbling backflip, then careens across the room and bounces off the rear wall, tumbles to the floor, then falls upwards until his back is plastered to the ceiling. He screams, proving that the glass isn't impervious to sound. It's not a scream of pain: more like a warbling war cry. Or glossolalia.

"Better start recording," I say. "This looks messy."

"If you insist." Jo pushes a button on the recording deck's panel.

"Interview requested by Dr. Dominique O'Brien, Security Service, with Chief Inspector Sullivan present, zero nine forty-six . . ." She reels off the date and other mandatory notices, then raises her voice to read Spratt his rights under questioning. Spratt ignores her throughout. "All right, Dr. O'Brien, he's all yours."

Where to begin? "Good morning, Jack," I try.

He ignores me, other than to cease his gurgling scream and fall silent.

"Jack, I want to ask you some questions."

He ignores me. Lying on the ceiling, perfectly recumbent, he looks ready to compete at Ignoring Intelligence Officers for Britain in the Olympics.

"Jack, you're not helping yourself."

Jo spares me a sidelong, pitying look. Spratt continues to practice Ignoring Intelligence Officers.

I sigh. *Okay, he won't listen to me. How about . . . ?* I pick up my violin case and plant it on the table. No response. I unlatch the case, open the lid, and remove the bow. Then I pick up Lecter.

Sullivan grabs my left arm. "Doctor, I hope you're not planning to—"

"No, I'm not. I'd just like to play him a straight melody, with no extras: see if it gets his attention. Look at the shielding around him, he's safe from anything I can do short of taking a sledgehammer to the window. Is that permissible?"

She gives me a hard look. "Music only."

"If I had a practice violin, I'd use it instead of this one," I assure her. "This one's valuable. May I?"

Spratt closes his eyes. After a few seconds he begins to snore. *We'll see about that,* someone thinks—I'm not sure whether it's Lecter or me.

I push my chair back, stand up, and begin to play the same improvisation on "Bela Lugosi's Dead" that I took him down with the other day, minus the eerie harmonics from the Hilbert-space pickups. He takes it for about three seconds. Then he stops ignoring me.

The violent flailing is boring. The bouncing off the walls, floor, ceiling, and window like a self-propelled middle-aged sex doll is mildly disturbing. But then he thumps into the glass face-first less than a meter away from me, so hard that his nose begins to bleed, a snarl of existential hatred plastered across his face. "Motherfucker!" he screams. "Bitch fuck cunt piss-flaps sicksicksick eat my shit!"

Oh goody, we have contact. Even if it's bringing out his Tourette's. I raise the bow. "Would you like me to play something else?" I ask.

Jo, I notice, is leaning back very slightly, face set in a deadpan mask of concentration.

"No!" he snaps petulantly. "Kill it kill it kill it with fire!"

"Kill what?" I ask.

"It! It! It! It! It!" He points at me. After a moment I realize he's trying to indicate the violin.

"Why should I?"

"He wants it! He does! The King in Yellow! The Professor in Emerald! The Gambling Doctor! He put the computer in my brain that says to do what he wants and he wants it and he'll have it and dance to the ditty that destroys the world! The Queen in Red and the King in Yellow! Ia! Ia! Hurts, it hurts!" He clutches his head: "Worst headache ever!"

Well, fuck. I put my violin down and make eye contact with Jo, then give a tiny shake of the head: she nods. *Useless.* Computers-in-brains aside, he's hopelessly contaminated with Lovecraft. One last try. "Who is the professor?" I ask. "Are you talking about Freudstein?"

Spratt stops ranting and looks at me. "What?" he asks, abruptly lucid. "Head aches—"

"Are you talking about Professor Freudstein?" I ask.

An expression of abject terror crosses his face. "Not allowed! Computer says No! Hurts!"

"What's not allowed?"

"Not allowed! Pain!"

"Are you forbidden to talk about Professor Freudstein?" I ask, slowly and clearly.

"*No—*" Spratt wails, then abruptly drops to the floor like a puppet whose strings have been cut. There is nothing theatrical or contrived about it: I've seen sacks of potatoes with more muscular control. So, by her reaction, has Jo: she spares me a horrified glance, swears, and is out the door so fast she knocks her chair halfway across the room. I stay just long enough to put Lecter back in his case and am about to hurry after Jo and find out where they keep the emergency resuscitation kit when I glance back at Spratt.

He's lying on his back with his feet against the glass, legs slightly spread and one arm twisted behind his back. His left cheek is twitching, the heel of his left foot banging on the floor: but to all appearances, my chief suspect has just suffered a massive stroke.

I DO NOT GET TO LEAVE THE POLICE STATION FOR SOME TIME. I am, as they say, unavoidably detained. Not as unavoidably as the late Mr. Spratt, who is pronounced dead at the scene by the on-call doctor. But DCI Sullivan isn't going to let me escape until she's taken me aside for a very free and frank exchange of opinions.

"Spill it," she demands, leaning in my face.

"I was testing a hypothesis." I hunch my shoulders. I feel dreadful: too exposed, in need of some safe space to retreat into while I get my head centered again. *Did I kill Spratt?* No, of course not. *But I asked him the fatal question . . .* "Did you hear about the Bank of England case?" I ask, more to distract myself than to inform Jo.

"The *what?*" The penny drops, instantly.

"Okay, so they're locking the lid down tight on it." That makes this easier. "Listen, Jack may not have been as out-of-it as your shrink thought. While he was busy doing his thing with the Mayor, somebody did something *really bad* that you haven't been told about and don't want to stick your nose in."

"Shit. That's not just a major crime, that's the kind that . . ."

"Yes, *that*." We share a moment's conspiratorial silence. "Think in terms of the Northern Bank robbery and you'll be on the right track. You'll hear about it after they've completed the emergency damage control. Until then, keep your trap shut."

"Jesus wept." She's gone all clipped and stiff-upper-lip on me: utterly aghast. Good, she's got the message.

Let me give you a brief rundown: the Northern Bank Robbery of 2004 was the biggest bank robbery in Northern Irish history. Hell, it was one of the biggest bank robberies anywhere, ever. The robbers, using an MO that is eerily familiar to anyone who had dealings with the happy fun guys from the Provisional IRA back in the bad old days, took two bank managers' families hostage to guarantee their cooperation, then hit the bank's cash center. They were spectacularly successful and got away with a truckload of banknotes. In fact they were *too* successful. Northern Bank is an issuing bank—one of the four banks licensed by the Bank of England to print Northern Irish currency. Northern Ireland isn't very large: the robbers stole nearly a tenth of *all* the banknotes that institution had in circulation. In fact, they stole so much that the bank issued a total currency recall, printed new currency, and hastily took the old ones out of circulation, thereby turning the entire truckload of stolen lucre into high-quality toilet paper (because it's just a little bit difficult to launder 10 percent of an entire currency in a couple of months).

"The, ah, naughty person, left a calling card," I tell her. "It was signed 'Professor Freudstein.'"

"Jesus . . ." She takes a deep breath. "You think our man was an accomplice or a diversion?"

"Did he or did he not babble about that name? And about the bank? And kinda-sorta confess to being involved in a real crime you didn't know about at the time?"

Jo looks as if she's sucking on a lemon. "I don't know what to think. But he's dead. Stroked out when you asked that question, didn't he?"

I nod jerkily, trying to hold myself together. "It was a stroke for sure." And a massive one: by the time the duty medic got to him, it was all over bar the autopsy.

"Any idea what could have done that?"

Jo looks at me sharply. I could speculate about K syndrome and untrained superpowers overclocking the firmware until they get holes nibbled all through their gray matter and blow a gasket in the Circle of Willis, but I'm not sure she's cleared for it—and anyway, I might be wrong. I confine myself to a pained expression and a shake of the head. "Didn't like him. But. He deserved better."

"Don't we all." She punches me lightly on my left arm. "You have no idea of the shitpile of paperwork that's about to descend on my head, Mo. You have *no idea*. People are not supposed to die in custody cells anymore, not unless it's a shitty medical emergency and the duty medic fucks up. And the duty medic wasn't present. Incoming IPCC investigation at six o'clock high. I'll be lucky not to get suspended over this, you know?"

"I'm"—I swallow—"due in front of the Home Secretary's desk on Monday at nine o'clock sharp. If I'm not dog food by ten thirty, if it's remotely possible to do so, I'll put in a word."

Jo doesn't look relieved. She's not naive enough to think that a *good word* will save an honest cop from being hung out to dry for Madam Executioner's public relations convenience; the HomeSec clearly has her sights set on Number Ten, and she's a member of the hardline wing of a party who eat their weak with gusto because it makes the survivors stronger. "Just promise me that you'll nail the bastard. Or call me so *I* can nail him. Whoever this Freudstein guy is."

"You know I will," I assure her.

AFTER WHICH, THE REST OF THE WEEK DRAINS AWAY DOWNHILL like floodwater.

I steel myself and head across to the New Annex, to report developments in person to the INCORRIGIBLE committee. Then, before I head back to the TPCU office, I sneak around to Emma's office and politely request a list of all her other nominations for my team, just in case. I am wound up like an over-tightened spring, but Bob, the object of my angst, is apparently busy disarming traps in Angleton's office and has his phone set to do-not-disturb. I can't bring myself to check his own office, so I chicken out and text him a carefully worded query as to Spooky's state of health.

Back in the TPCU, everything is running swimmingly. Martin from Facilities is hammering and power-screwing furniture together like a one-man IKEA assault team; Sara is swearing over a glass-fronted equipment cabinet full of flickering LEDs and patch cables; Sam and Nick the analysts are installed in an office with two desks, hammering away at tasks assigned to them by Mhari (insert token shudder here) who is tucked away in the office adjacent to mine, working on the corner (well, 50 percent share) of the Roadmap that I handed her yesterday evening.

So I retreat into my office and work until it's time for the all-hands.

Which goes something like this:

"HELLO, EVERYBODY," I BEGIN.

We don't have a boardroom yet—Martin is still bolting chairs together—so we're all standing in the lobby area behind the glass wall. It's all a little stiff, but at least it's an incentive to keep this short.

"I'm going to keep this as short as possible. On Monday"—today being Friday—"at nine o'clock in the morning I have to be ready to walk into the Home Secretary's office and deliver a presentation articulating our goals, our strategic plan for achieving those goals, the enabling regulations or primary legislation we need in order to reach those goals in a lawful manner, our required budget, a roadmap for implementation, metrics for assessing our performance on an ongoing basis, and the moon on a stick."

I see eyes going wide. Also some silently mouthed rude words, which I pretend to ignore.

"Let me emphasize that I do not intend to run this organization in continuous crunch mode. Crunch mode is bad for morale, worse for productivity, and does terrible things to the shelf life of the milk in the break room fridge. I don't like being on the receiving end of it, and neither do you. But. *But.* We got set up too late to fit this all in during our regular nine-'til-five core hours, and there's no way to pull in any more bodies and get them bedded down in time to help. Our next intake isn't due to turn up until Monday afternoon, and our job is to ensure that we're still in business when it's time to receive them. So I'm hoping everybody is able to stay late tonight, and to be in and working tomorrow and Sunday as well." I pause. "Keep track of your hours, and once we're fully staffed and stable, I'll sign you all off for time-and-a-half in lieu to make up for it." I pause again. "Does anyone have a real problem with that? Hospital appointments, elderly parents or infants, or some other immovable obstacle?"

Nick's hand rises, hesitantly. I don't wait for him to speak, don't want to risk embarrassing him in front of everybody else. "Email me or see me in my office. If I can help out—if it's something I *can* help out with—I'll move heaven and earth to do so. If not, you're off the hook: we'll figure something out."

I have a bottle of water: I take a swig. "Now, as to the strategy and the plan . . . our job is to get out in front of the superhero/supervillain/ superpower problem. I don't believe in one-size-fits-all solutions, so we're going to go wide, not deep. One task will be analysis and forward intelligence." Nick and Sam *both* perk up at that. "A second task will be Police and Home Office liaison and support—it's no good for us to know all about the problem if we don't tell anybody, and approaching it from the opposite direction, if we can get the Home Office on board, they can be a huge force multiplier for us. The third task is public relations: we need to generate a message about how the government wants the newly superpowered to behave, and we need to get it out through all available media. Our fourth and final task— really, a subsidiary of the third—is to go after the high-end threats ourselves. And that means we need a framework for managing superpowers directly."

That creates a stir. *Good.* Let them think about it for a while. Mhari smirks knowingly and taps the toe of one glossy black pump as if she's impatient to give the game away. I make eye contact briefly and the smirk vanishes. She nods, imperceptibly. *You're a deputy director: bloody act like it.*

"That's all for now," I add. "I sent out new task assignments five minutes ago, they should be in your inboxes by the time you get back to your desks. Finish up what you're working on today, and let me know what your obstacles are. My door's open."

And that, I realize with a start, *is* everything I needed to say. Because there's nothing left but a dismal weekend of sixteen-hour work-days in the office, followed by a visit to the Lion's Den on Monday.

And then, if we're really lucky, we will get the green light of approval for my master plan . . .

It's a crazy scheme but it just *might* work.

PART 2

THE SORTING ALGORITHM
OF EVIL

7.

OFFICER FRIENDLY

THAT FRIDAY, I CHECKED OUT OF THE HOTEL AND WALKED MY
suitcase to the office by way of an express dry cleaning outfit. At
lunchtime I followed Bob's example and nipped out for just long
enough to buy a sleeping bag and a camping mattress. It turned out
there was a staff shower room on the ground floor for the cyclists.
From experience I knew that I could get by without going home for
a while, just as long as I stuck to the rules: four hours' sleep, two
square meals, and one shower every day. Although on Sunday I began
to realize that people were looking at me oddly—working nearly
sixty hours in three days will do that.

Okay, so for three days *I had no life* except for PowerPoint,
MS Project, Excel, and a bunch of PRINCE2 worksheets. But after a
while I got into a soothing routine of deep focus, meal breaks, an
hour off to run chores, then back to a different task that required
my attention. I was so preoccupied that I forgot to twitch when I
ran into Mhari in the corridor, or to shudder when the engine note
of a passing truck outside my window triggered a flashback to a
Green Zone suicide bomber. It's amazing how much work you can

get done in three days if you hold a blowtorch to each end of the candle.

But around 2 a.m. on Monday morning, I finally had to admit that I was right down to the wire. It's good to have the world's most polished business plan or financial projection, but if you fall asleep in the middle of delivering it, the message will get mangled. So I dialed in a four-hour timer on my phone, locked the office door, crawled into my sleeping bag, and curled up next to my violin case.

Blink.

And now it's six in the morning, my pillow is vibrating alarmingly, and it's time to get up, shower, caffeinate my bloodstream, and prep myself for round two with the lioness in her Home Office den. Even though I'm much too old for this lifestyle.

Blink again.

And it's eight in the morning. I am awake, hair brushed, face painted, booted and suited. Laptop fully charged: check. Presentation loaded and ready at the first slide: check. Violin—

Oh *damn.* I whimper faintly. Here's the thing: I am meant to be the sober and suitable director of a small but significant department of a government agency, tasked with dealing with the transhuman menace. And I am about to walk into a briefing session so close to the apex of government that mere civil servants need oxygen masks to function there. I do *not* want to look like some sort of eccentric. As a part-time lecturer in music theory, carrying a violin everywhere I go is perfectly normal—*and I need to email Danny about my tutorial schedule next semester as we're going to have to find a stand-in quick: damn, I should probably resign from faculty, or at least take a sabbatical, if this turns out to be ongoing*—and in the Laundry they only look at you twice if you've got a nonstandard number of heads. But out in the rest of the civil service violins are definitely *not* normal uniform accessories for executives.

But I can't leave Lecter alone, can I? I just *can't.* It's not possible.

Oh, wait.

I carried him into a COBRA meeting last week. The HomeSec's

already seen him. She's seen him on the news on TV, for crying out loud: she knows he's a paranormal instrument. What's nagging me—

Oh. *The sticker.* No, that definitely won't do. I can wing the rest, tell them just enough of the truth to satisfy them about the violin, but the sticker's got to go. Damn, I *like* that sticker. It's been a constant reminder for the past eight years. But it looks unprofessional: I'll have to cover it up.

Five minutes later, Lecter's case is discreetly updated with a strip of duct tape—just another musical instrument, rather than a thing that KILLS DEMONS. And I'm ready to go.

I HAIL A CAB AND TELL THE DRIVER TO DROP ME ON HORSE-ferry Road, round the corner from the shiny new Home Office building on Marsham Street. Actually, it's not just a single building, but a campus of three glass-and-steel blocks connected by a four-story-high bridge. I head for the Peel building,* present my credentials, receive a visitor's pass, collect Lecter from the far end of the X-ray belt, and am given directions to a briefing room on the sixth floor.

People are already arriving for the Home Secretary's regular Monday morning session, and there's a coffee urn in the vestibule outside—so far, it's turning out to be so much like a regular conference lecture theater that I feel a momentary stab of déjà vu. But students don't generally wear formal business attire, much less dress in police commissioners' uniforms. A pleasant-mannered senior something-or-other in a suit intercepts me once I've filled a coffee cup, with nary a glance at my violin case: "Dr. O'Brien? Good morning, hope you found it easy to find us. You haven't attended one of these sessions before, so I should warn you that we have a tight agenda to stick to for this

---

* Named for Sir Robert Peel, who laid down the principles of modern policing by consent and founded the Metropolitan Police.

morning's meeting, and everything will go so much more easily if I can remind you to keep to your sixteen-minute slot? There is an open-ended Q&A after the last of the presentations, around eleven fifteen, when the ministers may call you back to the podium to clarify any points, so you'll need to stick around until then . . ."

He hands me an agenda, shows me where to plug my laptop in, reassures me that it will all go swimmingly, and vanishes in search of his next target.

The seats are all assigned by name. It's an invitation-only meeting, which is why I'm here on my own (although, given our personal chemistry, bringing my deputy director along for moral support might have been a bit counterproductive). I make my way to my chair and stash the violin case under it. I'm four rows back, at the side of the aisle where they've parked the presenters for easy access. Very efficient. I am, it appears, speaker number seven: Dr. D. O'Brien, Security Service, Subject: "Introducing the Transhuman Policy Coordination Unit strategy roadmap." Bleary-eyed and tired, I notice the empty seats to my right just as a looming uniform to my left clears its throat. "Excuse me, ma'am . . ."

"Uh, hi, sure." I shuffle sideways to let him through. I'm no expert on police insignia, but judging from the shoulder boards and the amount of braid on his tunic I think he's got to be a superintendent or above. He sits down next to me and I try not to stare too obviously: there's something familiar about him.

"Ah, Dr. O'Brien! We meet again." He smiles and offers me a hand.

I smile and shake, racking my memory. He *does* look familiar, but where . . .

"Jim Grey. I was boring you last week with bafflegab about fisheries when you were snatched from under my nose by a mermaid."

"Oh yes!" My eyes widen infinitesimally. *"That."*

"Yes." He nods, a twinkle of complicity in the corner of one eye. "I'm one of your organization's intimates."

"Ah." I relax slightly. He's another insider, like Jo. Not all senior police officers know about us, but if he was on that oil rig, he's in on

BLUE HADES at the very least.* "Which stakeholder are you representing today?"

"Not fisheries: that's done and dusted as of last Thursday. No, I'm supposed to be back on my regular secondment with ACPO, monitoring developments relating to the steaming pile of crap that got unloaded on you last week. For which, you have my deepest sympathy."

"By steaming pile of etcetera am I right in assuming you mean the transhuman problem . . . ?"

"That's—" He sits up slightly and looks round. "Ah, looks like we're nearly ready to start."

A procession is winding its way up the middle of the aisle. Jessica Greene is in the lead, murmuring forehead-to-forehead with a distinguished-looking fellow who I take to be the Permanent Secretary to the Home Office. They are followed, in strict pecking order, by three Ministers of State, two Parliamentary Undersecretaries of State, and four more terribly distinguished senior civil servants. They spread out and occupy the front row, and then my meeter-and-greeter walks up to the podium and starts things rolling.

"Good morning, ladies and gentlemen, and welcome to the weekly briefing. First, I note that the committee are present. Secondly, apologies. I'd like to draw your attention to item four on the agenda, reporting on the progress on the antisocial behavior reduction initiative: Mr. McBride sends his apologies, but he has been unavoidably delayed by circumstances beyond his control—there's been a major RTA on the A40 and he's stuck in the tailback. Other than that, the agenda

---

* The Laundry operates in a gray area, but some parts of the regular government machinery have to be directly aware of us—bits of the Ministry of Defense, some police officers, units within the Home Office. And others have to be pre-vetted so that in event of a crisis they can be briefed immediately. Normally, anyone who doesn't have need to know is kept in the dark, unless and until their NTK status changes. We do *not*, for example, generally stand up and give briefings in front of Commons Select Committees or the assembled Home Office Ministers. But any politician who makes it to the rank of Secretary of State for the Home Department is cleared before they get there, because they may suddenly develop need to know at very short notice. As Jessica Greene is about to learn . . .

as printed at eight thirty this morning is complete. So, moving swiftly on, item three: presentations. I'd like to introduce our first speaker . . ."

God, I am *so* glad I'm not the first course on the menu. The Ministerial lions' ears prick up, they lash their tails angrily. The gazelle at the focus of their amber gaze is here to report on progress in fixing shortcomings in a cluster of private-sector-outsourced immigration-processing facilities, and *oh dear it's definitely going to be* Bambi tartare *for dinner*. He stumbles a couple of times under the weight of the Home Secretary's unblinking medusoid stare. This is a woman who models herself on Margaret Thatcher, only without the warmth and compassion. The room is silent but for the scritching of pens on paper, writing death sentences for the poor underachiever's career.

Moving swiftly on.

In what seems like no time at all, it's my turn to take my place in the ring. Luckily for me the lions have already nibbled on their prey and are feeling distinctly post-prandial. I am, it seems, destined merely for after-dinner amusement. Lions are a little too intimidating for comfort, so I mentally replace them with the good old sapient cauliflowers from Arcturus as I rattle through my presentation.

"Good morning. My unit has been tasked with developing a strategy initiative for reducing and containing the increase in transhuman-related crime. The full proposal is in your red box this morning. To summarize: we propose to pursue four distinct channels: analysis and intelligence, liaison and support for the police and security services, public information campaigns to get the government's message across, and finally, active co-option and deployment of the more amenable superpowered. Let me tackle these in order . . ."

I have to scramble to get my last proposal in under the descending curtain, but I make it *just* in time. I return to my seat with my pulse hammering and my blouse stuck to the small of my back; the trouble with sapient cauliflowers is that it's impossible to read their expressions. They're great for distraction-avoidance during a presentation, not so great if you're looking for clues as to how it's being received.

I drop in my seat just as speaker #8 stands up. Jim leans towards me, confidingly: "Great show, excellent proposal," he says quietly. "Well thought out."

"You think so?" I'm stunned.

"Yes, but it's anybody's guess whether their right honorable selves will swallow it. That last one is bound to stretch their credulity, even if you and I know it makes sense."

Oh *hell*. I subside into the puddle of funk in the middle of my chair that I was afraid I'd end up in at the COBRA session. The next three presentations whizz through at high speed. And then . . .

"Thank you, and that's all the presentations. We will now break for ten minutes before opening to questions from the front bench," says the fellow with the agenda. I sigh and try to stand on knees that are abruptly wobbly.

Jim offers me a hand. "Are you all right?" he asks.

"A bit stressed," I admit. I haul out a tissue and dab at my forehead. "I was up until two this morning, working on that." Sixty hours of sweat distilled down to sixteen minutes of concentrated stage fright.

"Coffee?" he asks. "If you need to powder your nose, I'll fetch one for you. How do you take it?"

"White, no sugar," I say gratefully, then grab Lecter and flee in search of the bathroom.

When I get back to my seat—there was a queue for the ladies, would you believe, in a building commissioned in the twenty-first century—I find Jim waiting for me with a cup of coffee. Bless him: a man after my own heart. Not to mention that he's a restful sight for sore eyes: he's well built without being muscle-bound, moves lightly despite his height. I smile gratefully, stow Lecter under my seat, and accept the offered beverage: "Thanks."

"Happy to be of service. I remember what it was like when I first got on the list for these sessions: two hours of boredom interrupted by fifteen minutes of terror."

"That's about—" I begin to reply, when there's a ripple of silence and our moderator stands up to open the round of sudden-death questions.

"Dr. O'Brien, please." I recognize the Home Secretary's icily polite diction. "We have some questions for you."

I leave my coffee untouched and march, stiff-legged, straight back to the podium. I'm too surprised for fear: I thought they were going to go after the illegal immigrant processing guy first?

I find myself facing an audience which consists of about a tenth of the Cabinet, fronting a phalanx of about fifty Home Office executives any one of whom is senior—on paper, anyway—to the Senior Auditor. They run an organization with sub-agencies whose combined budget is bigger than Google or Microsoft, if you want to put it in multinational terms (as Mhari did), directing a couple of hundred thousand staff and contractors. And they're looking at me as if I have a nonstandard number of heads or a violin case strapped to my back.

"Dr. O'Brien," the Home Secretary begins, surprisingly tentatively, "I'd like to thank you for giving the most creative proposal we've heard in this room in, hmm, two or three years. Very imaginative, forward-looking. *Daring*, one might even say." Her tone is light, just this side of mocking. "How did you come to the conclusion that the Home Office needs a *superhero team*?"

Oh you bitch. I keep my face carefully composed. "I did not come to that conclusion on my own, or rapidly. As the Secretary of State is aware, my organization has been tracking this phenomenon with increasing concern for a number of years, although it is only in the past three months that it has become apparent that the frequency of outbreaks is increasing exponentially. I'd like to stress that this proposal emerged by consensus after extensive monitoring and analysis. We believe that ninety-five percent of the problems we've been having can be addressed by providing a role model for good citizenship: the superpowered are just ordinary people who have, randomly and inexplicably, found themselves *enhanced*. Most normal people are law-abiding citizens and do not represent a problem. Our headache is the outliers: the criminally insane and the plain criminal. We also have a secondary problem with the vigilante role model provided by the popular entertainment media: some of the more excitable law-abiding citizens think they can help us by taking the law into their own hands. We need to discourage that. So it seems reasonable to co-opt the popular cultural superhero model and use it to keep the good citizens in line, while suppressing the rare outbreaks of superpowered criminality.

"There are a handful of police officers who have acquired miraculous powers"—I am *not* going to mention the enigma wrapped in a mystery that is Officer Friendly at a Home Office briefing—"and my department proposes to use them as a cadre to work with suitably vetted individuals with superpowers, training them as Police Auxiliaries or Special Constables and providing suitable oversight and discipline. They will *not* be vigilantes in capes and tights, they will be entirely under the control of the police services, and their job will be to conduct operations against individuals with superpowers who have been identified as suspects in the course of regular police intelligence operations. And . . ."

I pause to swallow, then realize it's so quiet I could hear a pin drop.

"This *also* feeds into the question of public education. If we have a fully managed government superhero team, we can give TV and media crews access to them—subject to careful control of their public profiles. The message we will put across is that vigilantism is *not* the solution to crime, and we will deal even-handedly with all lawbreakers—including misguided volunteers. People with special abilities who wish to combat criminal activity should volunteer to become SPCs, so that they can operate within a clearly established legal framework. Eccentrics who think a Lycra body stocking and the power of flight entitle them to beat up bank chairmen in the street need to realize that their antics are illegal and counterproductive, and that the official government superhero squad will come down on them as hard as on any bank-vault-robbing mole-man. In this way, we propose to take our current problem and extract from it the seeds of its own solution."

Applause. *Applause.* I blink. The Home Secretary is leading the applause: not enthusiastically, but just slightly faster than a slow clap. She's actually *smiling*, although I've seen a warmer expression on a rattlesnake at the zoo.

After about thirty seconds the applause dies down. "I'd like to thank Dr. O'Brien for her excellent and creative proposal, which I believe deserves further consideration," says the Home Secretary. "My right honorable colleagues and I will discuss it and respond within the next week, Dr. O'Brien, thank you very much for your time. Now, moving swiftly on to a much more mundane topic, the question of how to deal with our underperforming immigrant processing centers—seeing it's impossible to issue our contractors with capes and superpowers, perhaps Mr. Jennings would like to return to the podium . . . ?"

I make my retreat, carefully keeping my face impassive. I pass the immigration department gazelle on my way to my seat: he looks just as bad going out as I feel coming back.

MY NEIGHBOR FROM ACPO INTERCEPTS ME BEFORE I HAVE A chance to sit back down. "Back of the room, *now*," he whispers. I shakily grab for my violin case and shuffle towards the back; he follows me as discreetly as a nearly two-meter-tall man of steel in a uniform held together with silver braid and medal ribbons can manage. He cracks the door open and gestures me through it, then follows me out into the atrium.

"That went surprisingly well," he says. "You knocked 'em cold." He looks at me, appraising, thoughtful.

"I thought it was terrible," I admit. "She was all but *laughing* at me at the end."

"Really? I don't think so."

"Hmm?" I stare back at him, mildly annoyed that I'm not wearing heels high enough to look him in the eye. I'm quite a bit taller than average, but he's built like Superman: I'd need six-inch platforms to be level with him, and those aren't suitable business dress, at least not in my world. "What makes you say that?"

"You were talking to an audience of senior politicians from the law-and-order side of their party. You don't get to that position unless you're an instinctive authoritarian who likes to put everyone in a neat little box. The Home Office top brass have only really become aware of the paranormal in the past few months, and they don't like to have to think about it because it upsets their stack of Tupperware. Jessica Greene is at least *trying* to come to terms with the new reality—she may be an authoritarian, but she's also terribly bright, and ambitious enough to believe six impossible things before breakfast if that's what it takes to get to the top. However, I think she still finds it threatening to her model of the natural order of things. Laughter is her way of handling cognitive dissonance; the fact that you got a chuckle out of her is very positive. A negative response would be some sort of belittling dismissal or outright denial or even a very public meltdown and tantrum. I'd say you came out ahead by provoking the mildest reaction. Next time the subject comes up, she'll think of you with amused tolerance rather than denial or fear."

"That's a very interesting analysis," I slowly say. (Officer Grey has clearly been studying social psychology.) "But what do *you* want?"

He begins to walk slowly back towards the central Street that connects the three buildings. After a moment I scurry to catch up. "I think there's a cafe around here somewhere. Can I buy you a flat white in return for a few minutes of your time? I've got an idea I'd like to run past you."

I can tell a setup when I smell one. "Who are you, *really*?"

"Really?" His smile is crooked. "I could tell you, but then I'd have to kill you—no, not really. All right, I confess: I attended that briefing because when word that you'd be presenting crossed my boss's desk, she sent me along. I'm only a chief superintendent, far too low down the totem pole to make policy. But then again, *you're* far too low down the totem pole to be making policy, under normal circumstances. So it's a good thing that circumstances aren't normal, isn't it?"

"I couldn't possibly comment." If I wasn't carrying a violin and a handbag, I'd cross my arms defensively. "So how did the agenda of that particular meeting end up on your desk?" *And are you a scary stalker with a security clearance or an ally?*

"Well." We walk past a shuttered shop front in the side of the Street; just past it, there's an open awning and a Costa's sign. He swerves towards the entrance. "I'm nominally with the Met, but for the past three years I've been on semi-permanent loan to ACPO. And I've been liaising with your people."

I stop. "Who do you believe my people are?" I demand.

"Mahogany Row. SOE Q Division." So he knows about the Laundry. "You take it white, no sugar, yes?" There's that twinkle in his eye again.

"Nope: this time mine's a tall mocha, no cream, one extra shot."

"Capital. Find a table and I'll be right over."

I select a table with upright armchairs and pick the one where I can keep my back to the wall and watch the passers-by in the Street. I have a very peculiar feeling about this dashing officer of the law. He's far too good to be true. A year or two older than me, athletic, handsome, self-assured, friendly, shows signs of having a sense of humor and several decades more insight into human psychology than Bob has ever developed while I've known him—Why am I even making that comparison? It's silly and pointless. I feel obscurely guilty as I watch him return from the counter bearing a tray with two large cups. Then I feel suspicious. Just why is a chief superintendent who works for the Association of Chief Police Officers soft-soaping me? What does he want?

"I was tipped off about you by Tim Whitehead, Jo Sullivan's guvnor. Not to mention the rolling coverage you stirred up on News 24. 'Paranormal Violinist's Virtuoso Performance Swats Human Fly' as the tabloids put it." He pours a thin stream of brown sugar into his coffee and stirs it thoughtfully. "So I asked Gerry Lockhart, and he suggested talking to you directly."

I'm all ears, and on edge. "What exactly do you do for ACPO?"

"This and that—most recently, discuss fisheries patrols with our scaly friends. And other things that I don't think you need to know about. ACPO has fingers in a lot of pies, and paranormal issues are just one of them. We handle the stuff that would fall through the cracks if we left it to the regional police forces, but which needs horizontal networking rather than top-down policy directives from the Home Office: inter-force cooperation, professional standards, intelligence gathering, anything that needs tackling on a national level and isn't so important that the right honorable members will pass enabling legislation and approve a budget for a new national-level special police force."

"Special police force?"

"Civil Nuclear Constabulary, British Transport Police." He shrugs. "A problem normally has got to be so big that it's glaringly obvious that the locals can't handle it, and need at least a thousand full-time bodies, before they'll approve a new organization. Supervillains aren't there yet, but they're a highly specialized problem and they cut across force boundaries so we got asked to carry the can."

"So what is it you want?" I ask. "You think ACPO should run the official government superhero team?"

"God, no!" He looks shocked. "The risk of blowback is enormous. In fact, we're backing out of direct policing support everywhere we can. The scandal over the NPOIU—the National Public Order Intelligence Unit—a few years ago forced a major rethink. We'd gotten ourselves—ACPO—into a wag-the-dog situation: a subsidiary task came far too close for comfort to taking over the entire organization and turning it into a de facto secret police agency, getting up to all sorts of unsavory activities. Sleeping with suspects, framing people, supplying bombs. It was unethical, illegal, and could have compromised our ability to do our core job, which is to coordinate between police forces."

"Really?" I ask brightly. This is *fascinating*. After the past few days it's wonderful to meet someone whose problems are even bigger than mine.

"But," he continues, as I take a mouthful of mocha, "as you know, at least one of the newly superpowered is, in fact, a police officer. And there may be others. I believe I can use ACPO channels to find them and point them your way. I also know who to go to within the Met to help you set up a special operations unit as a posting for them. You're going to need to coordinate with us sooner or later. The way I see it working, you—in your guise as, ahem, a department of the Security Service—will be handling the intelligence, policy, liaison, outreach, public relations, and technical operations side of the team you proposed forming. But if you're serious about them operating lawfully as sworn police officers, you really need to go through a force. The Met is the biggest police force in the UK, and I'm upper middle-management there. Which is the second reason why you want me on board."

I smile at him pleasantly and put my cup down. Okay, so he's a player and he wants something: probably the obvious, to grab my unit and turn it into a new leaf on their org tree. *Here comes the pitch.* "What's the first reason?" I ask.

He flashes me a quick grin: "I'm Officer Friendly."

I GIVE HIM MY BEST VACANT STARE. "IS THAT SUPPOSED TO mean something to me?" *Jo said something about Officer Friendly, didn't she? And come to think of it, Ramona . . .* "I haven't been following the news much," I admit.

He chuckles. He doesn't sound offended, which is a relief. "That's all right. Officer Friendly hasn't been out there 'fighting crime' for very long. Um. This is in confidence, you understand, because you *do* have need to know, but I'd rather my secret identity didn't get noised around needlessly."

"I feel your pain," I say fervently. "Been there, done that, I won't drop you in it. But who exactly is Officer Friendly, when he's not wearing Chief Superintendent Grey's uniform?"

"I'm still finding out." He flashes me a grin that takes twenty years off his age. "I woke up with a terrible headache about nine months ago. Thought I was having a stroke, so I got out of bed to call an ambulance—and just keeled over. Fainted dead. When I woke up I stumbled to the bathroom, didn't realize at the time that the electricity was out and it was pitch black—I could see just fine. It wasn't until I ripped the towel rail off the wall drying my hands that I realized I had acquired super-strength as well as night vision. I tried to push the rail back, and it just *bent*. Like warm toffee, not chromed steel tubing."

He picks up his coffee cup delicately and blows on it. "The other powers took a while to show up. For instance, it took me about two weeks to realize I could fly and a month or two after that to fully debug it. I'm afraid I scared the crap out of the police free-fall club in the process: it confuses them if they follow you out of the plane and you meet them in the clubhouse afterwards with your parachute still in its pack."

"That must give you an interesting perspective," I say cautiously. "So you fight crime?"

"Actually, that's an oversimplification." He shows me that grin again: "I uphold my oath to enforce the law by carrying out my assigned duties. *Fighting* is sloppy rhetoric: How do you fight an abstraction, like crime? I just happen to have unusual abilities that enable me to support my fellow officers in unconventional situations. Being Officer Friendly is actually a nuisance: it gets in the way of my real job, and I wish I could delegate it to someone else. I'm a super, I direct operations at divisional level, I'm not supposed to be out on the beat nicking petty offenders. Doesn't matter whether or not they can fly, brainwash people into falling asleep, or teleport the contents of a jeweler's window display into their backpack, they're still individual criminals."

I take another mouthful of mocha. I suddenly feel ravenously hungry, and realize it's nearly noon and I skipped breakfast. "That hadn't occurred to me," I admit. "It's an unusual drawback."

"Yeah. The last thing you want is for your superpowers to be concentrated at the top of the pyramid instead of the bottom. On the other hand, it has its compensations. Officer Friendly dropping in to lend a hand during an armed siege is good for morale. It's fun to get out of the office a couple times a week. And"—his forehead wrinkles ruefully—"I suppose it gives me slightly more insight into supervillain psychology than most officers have. On top of the crim. psych. degree."

"So you think you'd be a good fit to lead Transhuman Policy Coordination's superhero team?"

He shakes his head. "Not lead, exactly, no. But once you've staffed it, you're going to need a big stick to keep the egos in line. Correct me

if I'm wrong, but *that*"—he points at my violin case with his spoon—
"is more of a sawn-off shotgun than a side-arm baton? You need
someone who can handle the police procedural aspect of the operation, but who your team know isn't just a paper pusher."

"You make a cogent case." I make a show of checking my watch,
then drain my mug. "Listen, I'm due in another meeting in half an
hour and I'm running late, but I really want to take this further. Do
you have a card?" He nods, and we do the business-card-swapping
thing. "Great. Got to run. See you later!"

And I'm out of there before he can work his way any further into
my confidences. He's smooth. *Wow*, is he smooth: he's almost too
good to be true. And I did not get this job by taking anything at face
value—even straight-arrow superheroes in police uniforms.

Memo to self: as soon as I get a chance to check my email, send a
request for information up the line. *Because if you've been lying to
me, Officer Friendly, you are* so *screwed.*

PICTURE THE SCENE LATER THAT EVENING: IT'S NINE O'CLOCK
at night in the O'Brien/Howard household, currently reduced to just
me, my violin, and my husband's cat. I got home a couple of hours
ago, showered, changed into jeans and a sweater to remind myself I
wasn't working and am supposed to decompress while off-duty, and
made myself a lonely supper for one: M&S prepackaged salad (ugh)
and the remains of a chicken I've been working on.

I've started to tackle the washing-up and I'm about to perform
triage on the fridge contents—it's astonishing how quickly food goes
off when you downsize your family by 50 percent—when my mobile
trills for attention.

I grab it with soapy hands and nearly drop it when I see it's Mhari
calling. "Yes?" I demand, tensing in anticipation of bad news.

"Boss, we just got a Code Blue—"

The landline from work rings. "Hang on," I tell her, and dash into
the front hall to grab the ancient Bakelite handset. "O'Brien here, DO.
Is this a Code Blue for my team?"

I have the unique pleasure of hearing surprise in the Duty Officer's voice. "Yes, Doctor, I have an all-hands call out for the Transhuman Policy Coordination team. Incident on Euston Road—"

"Please hold," I tell him. To the phone in my other hand: "Mhari, are you getting this? Euston?"

"Yes, I'm on my way out the door."

"Okay, I'll meet you there. Notify the analysts, I'll handle the DO."

She hangs up and I focus on one thing at a time: "Sitrep please."

"Freudstein just hit the British Library . . ."

It takes me twenty-two minutes to get to Euston Road, most of them spent trying not to throw up all over the floor of a police car whose driver is in a *real* hurry. My mobile is ringing almost constantly throughout the trip, adding to my nausea with a constant diet of dismaying information. This time Freudstein didn't make it in and out before we got the news: there's still a chance he's on the scene, so every second counts. Mhari is on her way, and so are about half of SCO19, the specialist firearms command. Everybody is very excited and keyed up, which is exactly what we don't need right now because it's the perfect recipe for a blue-on-blue clusterfuck.

My driver screeches to a halt at one end of a pileup of patrol cars, dog vans, and firearms units that stretches halfway from Euston to St Pancras. Sirens and the strobing of many light bars turn the night to hell. It's raining lightly and a pall of smoke hangs on the air. I bail out, look around for the nearest body who looks as if they're directing traffic—the cops are sending the buses and taxis that normally clog this stretch of road linking three of London's biggest railway terminals on a magical mystery tour to keep them out of stray bullet range—and walk towards him, holding up my warrant card.

"Stop right there, miss! Don't move!"

The constable who gets in my face this time is much less friendly than the ones in Trafalgar Square, even before you get to the semi-automatic carbine he's carrying—a submachine gun by any other name. I freeze, but raise my voice, keeping the card where he can see it: "O'Brien, Transhuman Policy Coordination, Security Service, responding to control request for specialist backup. Take me to—"

"Stand down!" The stentorian roar seems to come from about a meter above and behind my left ear. *"Stand down!"*

I can't help myself: I jump halfway out of my skin as I turn and look.

You've seen TV news broadcasts and newspaper reports and maybe even thinly fictionalized movies, but nothing can prepare you for your first superhero.

Officer Friendly looms behind me, silhouetted against the red-brick wall surrounding the library campus by the flickering light bars of vans and fire engines—one of which I now see is wedged in the crumpled and bent steel vehicle gates opening onto the piazza, stopping them from closing. He hovers a meter above the street and I can see a faint shimmering beneath the ridged soles of his steel boots. His suit is blue, somewhere between cobalt and dull gunmetal in shade, a thing of interlocking slabs of metal that is more like a deep-sea diver's hardshell or a space suit than mediaeval armor. There's an elaborate equipment belt, of course, and a Tetra radio handset incongruously clipped to his left pauldron, screen glowing pale gray. His face is a steel glacis pierced by narrow, dark vision slots beneath an armored copy of the regular policeman's custodian helmet. The light beacon on top pulses lazily, flaring blue against the night.

"Doctor O'Brien, this way please." Officer Friendly descends from the sky and steps onto the pavement with a ponderous thud, boots clomping like the armored treads of a main battle tank. The firearms officer takes a step back and waves me past, then starts speaking into his radio headset.

"Is Freudstein still inside the building?" I ask, hurrying beside him: Officer Friendly appears to move at a slow walk, but it's only slow if you're not trying to keep up.

Jim cranks his megaphone down to a merely human volume level, for my ears only: "We don't know. SCO19 have secured the perimeter and evacuated the admin block. Two security guards are unaccounted for."

"Is it on fire?"

We reach the stretch of curb that fronts the library's huge air conditioning outlet gratings, now silent. "We don't know." A group of armed officers are crouched behind the rear of the fire engine. "Freudstein's minions hit the fire station up the street. They TDA'd two pumps at gunpoint just as a visitor in the library tripped the fire alarm. When the library gate guard saw fire engines with lights, he opened the gate at which point pump number one drove in and ram-raided the library shop front window. They rammed the other pump into the gate to block it." (The gate opens into a piazza with sculptures, benches, a fountain, and the usual service/access entrances; viewed from ground level on the outside, the library is a windowless slab of red brick that sprawls across almost as much land as King's Cross or St Pancras stations.) "The first responding officer attempted to gain entry but retreated when shots were fired. Since then there's been no sign of anyone leaving, so we've got a potential hostage situation with the missing guards, not to mention the contents of the library."

I shudder: losing the library would be a catastrophe. The British Library is the second largest research library in the world, with over 150 million items in its catalog and about two hundred kilometers of shelves occupied by everything from a copy of every newspaper and book published in the UK to originals of the Magna Carta, the Codex Sinaiticus, and several collections of priceless ancient manuscripts. "You're sure it's Freudstein?" If he's here, he's probably after something important.

Officer Friendly reaches into an armored pocket on one giant thigh and produces an evidence baggie. There's a familiar-looking business card in it. "Found balanced on the steering wheel of the pump wedged in the gate." Well, that tears it: so far Freudstein's existence isn't public knowledge. But that's not going to last—it suggests we're dealing with someone who's hungry for fame.

We're level with the huddle of armed officers near the entrance. A couple of higher-ups are approaching on foot, winkled out of their offices in Scotland Yard by what promises to be the major incident of the decade. I see another familiar figure approaching. "She's with me." I point at Mhari and a minute later she's with us, standing in the lee of the pump, looking like either an upwardly mobile plain-clothes detective inspector or an out-of-place banker.

"J— Officer Friendly, this is my deputy director, Mhari Murphy. Mhari, this is Officer Friendly. I gather as a chief superintendent he's the ranking officer here." Mhari ducks her head and I see that some time after I left the office she scrubbed off the layered war-paint she uses as sunblock. She looks younger without it, and almost colorless.

There's a burst of radio chatter from the armed police, followed by some shifting around. One of them gets down and begins to worm his way under the crashed fire engine, pushing an assault rifle kitted out with night vision sights before him. Two others climb into the rear cab through the open door then disappear from view.

"What's going—"

"Wait here," Officer Friendly says tersely. Then he gathers himself and *jumps*. I'm expecting him to come back down with a jaw-rattling thud, but he soars up and over the wall and the fire engine and vanishes from view. A couple of seconds later there is indeed a loud thump as he lands on the far side of the obstacle, then a succession of shouted orders as half a dozen specialist firearms officers pour through the open doors of the fire engine and into the piazza beyond it.

"I hate this," Mhari says vehemently. "Who does he think we are?"

I slide the violin's case around and rest my hand on the handle. "Civilians who aren't equipped for a shootout."

"Right." Mhari unfastens her jacket, and that's when I realize she's wearing a discreet shoulder holster. Standard issue Glock 17, by the look of it. "What are we waiting for again?"

I flick the catch on Lecter's case and lift him out, then close the case and sling it over my shoulder. Mhari tenses. "Ever been part of a blue-on-blue incident?" I ask, and she pauses momentarily before she shakes her head. Very tactful of her. "Trust me, you don't want to be." Even more tactfully, I don't ask if she's been certificated to carry that popgun. Anyway it's not as if she needs it.

I hear more radio chatter from the two cops who've remained behind. One of them turns to us, his face pale in the gloom. "Ma'am, the super says they've secured the piazza and established a security cordon inside the lobby and library shop. If you'd care to—"

Mhari doesn't wait: she jumps for the back of the wedged fire engine and scrambles up and over it terrifyingly fast. I swear quietly and take the low road, through the back of the cab and over the seatbacks and then slither down through the front door: I don't want to be silhouetted against the sky, and besides, I'm carrying.

The smell of wood or paper smoke is much stronger inside the piazza, along with an acrid note that reminds me of Bonfire Night fireworks. My heart sinks. Whatever we find inside, it won't be good: the bad guys' black-clad minions have had half an hour to ram-raid a repository of the nation's most precious treasures and set fire to the rest by way of a diversion. Police officers run past us and disperse to prearranged points close to the fire exits that open onto the piazza as we leg it towards the second fire engine, which is embedded in the shattered brick-and-plate-glass front of the institution's bookshop. "How did they expect to escape?" Mhari asks quietly, echoing my own thoughts.

"I don't—"

There's a crackle of automatic gunfire from the direction of the elevator tower that overlooks the piazza, followed rapidly by *really loud* return fire from the specialist under the fire engine, about ten meters behind us. "Cover!" I shout, and Mhari blurs into motion, vanishing into the shattered front of the library lobby, pistol in hand. I don't hang around either: if I could see the shooter, I could light him up with Lecter, but we're exposed on the piazza and it's just turned into a killing ground, as witness the AFOs all scuttling for cover like heavily armed cockroaches—

We make it into the darkened lobby and go to ground behind the receptionist's podium. The fire alarms are shrilling and there's glass everywhere on the mosaic-inlaid floor. The central atrium of the library stretches up above us, but something is badly wrong: it takes me a second to realize that the five-story-high display cabinet full of rare manuscripts is leaning sideways, ripped away from its upper-floor supports and glass front smashed, in an act of calculated vandalism.

"They're still in here," Mhari says quietly, leaning close to me. Her nostrils flare; her pupils are very wide, black holes in a paper-pale face.

I shift my grip on Lecter. For a miracle, he's obedient, waiting on my command: he shows no sign of thirsting after my executive officer. "Yes, and in a moment I'm going to locate them. Don't be alarmed." I raise the violin, flick on the pickups, and finger the strings as I lean back and point the pegboard up into the darkness of the mezzanine level. Mhari holds her breath and tenses but doesn't flee. Meanwhile—

Where are they? I ask, opening myself to the feeling of fingers on my bony spine—an indescribable sensation.

Where are who? My instrument sounds lazily amused.

Don't fuck with me, Lecter. You know who I want.

He doesn't reply, but shows me. Pale dots in the twilight: blue figures determinedly moving between cover as they push further into the building at ground level. Further away, carmine drops of glowing blood pierce the night like a vampire's kiss. They're down below, in the archival stores under the public spaces of the library. Typical: Officer Friendly and his folks are storming the wrong floor.

I open my eyes. "Follow me," I tell Mhari. She nods, pointing her gun at the floor, then follows as I crawl out from the desk and scuttle towards an unmarked door with no handle—an emergency exit from the staff-only spaces of the institution. It's secured by an electronic combination lock, but Lecter makes short work of it.

Lecter barely gives me any warning at all when a group of cops converge on us from a side corridor. I get an inkling—then a man's voice shouts, "You, stop right there!" And suddenly we're covered by the wobbly red dots of laser sights, like hungry bedbugs only much less friendly.

Mhari hisses. I stop and turn just in time to see Mhari raise her warrant card, glowing a nacreous silver in the darkness as she bares her fangs at the nearest cop—the one who's talking, not the half-dozen others who are aiming. "Stand down! Stand down!"

"Who the fuck are you?" he demands.

"Transhuman Policy Coordination," Mhari says crisply enough. "Security Service."

"Get Officer Friendly here," I add, raising my own warrant card, "he's chasing the bad guys' decoy. Their real target is down here in the stacks. Follow me, I'll take you to them and you can do the forced entry."

About thirty seconds later we're on course for the emergency stairwell down to the second basement level, this time with half a dozen AFOs in tow, their eyes slightly glazed by the impact of two Laundry warrant cards demanding their obedience. They're all dressed in their best stabbies and armed to the teeth with a librarian's nightmare of high-energy paper punches manufactured by Messrs Heckler & Koch. I'd be a lot happier if I was at the head of a proper OCCULUS team from the Territorial SAS, but needs must. "They came here to steal a rare manuscript," I explain, showcasing my elite powers of deduction, "and they're all over the controlled environment archive along—"

I stop. We're at a crossroads, facing a corridor. Most of the lights are out except for the emergency exit illumination, but the doors to either side feature round portholes and warnings about Halon discharge fire suppression systems. The basements are all climate and humidity controlled. I blink, and Lecter shows me a clump of rubies in the night, just beyond the next door. "They're in here," I whisper to Mhari, who nods, and relays the word back to our escort. I squint at the sign. RARE MANUSCRIPT SCORES 7612/A. Scores? Musical scores? I turn back to the cops. "You have three targets in this room," I tell them; "one about three meters to your left as you go through the door, two others among the shelves five meters over to your right and about ten meters away, near the back of the room—"

I'm about to step back and hand over the forced entry to the cops (if necessary dragging Mhari with me because, let's face it, neither of us are trained or equipped for close-quarter arrests: too much risk of us accidentally killing someone) when the door flips open and everything goes to shit.

There is a bang, so loud that it's more like having my head slammed in a door than anything I can call a noise. There is also a blinding flash of light. I fall over, clutching Lecter as I go down, and a couple of pairs of size fifty hobnailed boots run past my shoulder. Through the cotton wool haze in my head I hear shouting, a piercing scream, and the flat bang of pistol fire. *"Stop! Police! You're under arrest!"* booms a voice the size of an aircraft carrier. *Oh great,* I think, dazedly, *Officer Friendly saves the day.* For my part I'm trying to stay out of the way because I'm on the ground and I'll get myself damaged if I get in the way of the ruck that's just thundered past me into the document store—

A hand grabs my shoulder. "Dr. O'Brien! Are you all right?"

I open my eyes and see Mhari leaning over me. She looks extremely pissed off. Maybe thirty seconds have passed, but it feels like an hour.

"Flash-bang?" I ask haltingly. My ears are ringing and purple-green after-images dance in front of my eyes.

"Yes." She stands, then grabs me by one hand and hauls me onto my feet. I manage to lean against the wall as I unwrap myself from around Lecter. I'll have new bruises tomorrow, but I kept him safe. "You're late," she says coldly to somebody standing out of view behind my shoulder. I use the seconds to try and pull myself together.

"You shouldn't be here." Officer Friendly dials his voice back down to normal: "There are shooters at large."

"Yes, well." I force myself to stand on my own feet, albeit unsteadily. "What they came for is in here."

"How do you"—the blank metal face turns to me—"know?"

I raise Lecter. ***Come on, if you think you're hard enough,*** the violin taunts him silently: I don't give voice to the words.

"Jim, we're from *the Laundry,* it's our *job* to know." Because we're an intelligence agency, and how much intelligence do you need to figure out that if a Mad Scientist sends their minions to rob a library, they're more likely to be going after a rare manuscript than last month's issue of *Homes and Gardens.* The shouting and banging has moved away: Lecter shows me a cluster of dots, dimming as they disappear down another corridor that opens onto the far side of this archive room because, silly me, *of course* you'd design more than one exit onto a conservation store full of priceless and potentially combustible manuscripts. And if you think the police are coming in through the front, you throw a flash-bang at them by way of distraction before you leg it out through the back. "They're getting away," I add.

"I don't see how," Officer Friendly says tersely, then clams up, obviously sucked into another round of radio comms with his colleagues. "Oh. Follow me, at the double; it's kicking off upstairs again."

He doesn't wait but pounds away back the way we came like a baby tyrannosaur in cast-iron clogs. Mhari and I trail along in his stompy wake, followed by a forlorn gaggle of officers who couldn't keep up with the escaping furball as Freudstein's minions beat a fighting retreat from the archives.

As we arrive in the lobby a deafeningly loud helicopter roars overhead, so low that it almost scrapes the steeply pitched upper roof and elevator tower of the museum. It's big and fast, and as it circles to hover over the flat roof of the Center for Conservation, tiny figures scramble through the windows overlooking the flat deck and rush towards it.

"Shit." I shouldn't swear in front of employees but right now I find I don't care about setting a good example. Besides, everybody else is thinking it.

"The roof won't take it!" Mhari exclaims excitedly. It's almost as if she *wants* to see a disaster.

"I don't think they're planning on staying for a picnic," I tell her. Officer Friendly dashes through the lobby and lifts off like a rocket, then circles around the helicopter: but for some reason he keeps his distance. A moment later I hear more gunfire and flinch. *They're shooting at Jim!* For some reason this makes me much angrier than the flash-bang earlier or the unaimed fire when the police gained entrance—almost as angry as the desecration of the national institution we're approaching.

The smell of smoke is strong. We keep well back behind the police line, but the awning over the building blocks off our view of the drama unfolding on the rooftop as the pitch of the helicopter's engine winds up. *Where are they?* I ask Lecter.

They? You mean your prey? He still sounds mildly amused.

Yes, them—

He shows me: pale red dots now, visible through the glassy outline of the walls as they scramble roofwards. ***Mine,*** he says eagerly.

Not yours.

Not them, fool: what they took.

Wait, what— I clamp down on it. Some questions are best not asked in the presence of the pale violin. Whatever Freudstein wanted, he's got: I'll learn what's missing tomorrow, when Lecter is safely back in his box and the staff have had time to comb through the wreckage. I hold the violin at the ready, braced against my shoulder, and line up on the rooftop: then I shiver in the grip of an adrenaline-driven cold sweat as I realize that I could take down the chopper—but then what?

Decisions. At least six heavily armed bad guys just stole a national treasure, and they're getting away. ***I can take them,*** Lecter tells me, chillingly assured.

Yes, but then the chopper would crash. And I have this vision of four or five tons of metal and jet fuel raining down on the national library of record's rare document collection, of the deaths of everybody on board—at least six people—and possibly of officers on the ground, and the loss of whatever they stole besides. It just doesn't bear thinking about. I can't force the chopper down and resolve the situation safely: all Agent CANDID can do is destroy everybody on board and escalate a clusterfuck into a catastrophe. *Stand down.*

I shakily force myself to lower Lecter, then unsling the violin case and re-inter him. He buzzes his frustration in the key of a million flies as I latch the lid. Then I watch from the shadows of the broken building frontage as the chopper hovers over the rooftop and the robbers climb aboard.

I've got a bad feeling about this whole situation: it stinks. Jim might be able to track the chopper—more likely it's a job for Air Traffic Control and an RAF fighter will already be inbound to intercept it. But if this *is* Freudstein, we're talking about the criminal mastermind who robbed the Bank of England. He'll have contingency plans in hand. He'll have anticipated the prompt dispatch of a pair of Typhoons, and if I gambled I'd bet serious money that by the time they scream in from the QRA line at RAF Coningsby in Lincolnshire—which is ten minutes away, because they're unable to go supersonic on full afterburner without breaking half the windows in North London—the helicopter will be nowhere to be found.

The chopper turns and thunders away, the pounding of its blades setting up a matching echo in my skull, which is still aching from the flash-bang and the mental exertion of keeping Lecter from going on a killing spree. Once it's out of sight I shuffle back into the atrium, to look at the gigantic display cabinet and the other cases where documents of national significance are laid before the public. The lighting in here is dim even in daytime, to avoid damaging the delicate treasures stored under glass in humidity-controlled cabinets. The main display may be badly damaged but the cabinet on the mezzanine landing is intact, and I take a shuddering breath of relief as I look at one of the two surviving copies of the Magna Carta on public view, the eight-hundred-year-old foundational document of our system of government. Someone clears their throat. I glance sideways: it's Mhari.

"Look," she says, pointing (with a finger that I am gratified to see is wobbling just a little: I'm not the only one who's outside her comfort zone tonight). Then I follow her direction and my stomach clenches.

The glass is intact and the precious manuscript is undamaged. But, positioned proudly on top of it like a brash intrusion from another era, is another of Freudstein's calling cards. He's thumbing his nose at us now: *Look what I could have taken if I'd wanted it!*

This is going to be a very long night . . .

8.

UNAVOIDABLE CONSEQUENCES

THE NEXT MORNING I HEAD FOR THE OFFICE EARLY—STILL yawning: I was up past midnight being checked out by paramedics, then filling out incident reports—then pull my emergency meeting suit out of its carrier and head round to the New Annex. I've been summoned by the Auditors: happy joy. It's not just the SA, in his capacity as chair of the INCORRIGIBLE committee, but the Auditors as a committee, sitting *en banc*. The report on Agent CANDID's encounter with Strip Jack Spratt has collided with a copy of the fatal accident report that is climbing its way up the Independent Police Complaints Commission's in tray and butted heads with yesterday's fracas at the library. We still don't have a complete list of what went stolen or missing in the raid—Freudstein's people made a comprehensive mess out of the main display in the atrium and did a real number on several archives, and were working over the rare music manuscripts when I interrupted them—but the Auditors want to hear from me *in person* even in the absence of a full report. This is quite worrying because it suggests the organization as a whole may be going into damage-control mode.

They've cleared one of the larger offices on the top floor—one of the Mahogany Row offices—and rolled out the resonant carpet. I wait in the receptionist's office until I'm summoned, trying not to succumb to anticipatory collywobbles. I've been so busy lately that this almost seemed like a trivial irritation at first; certainly, after being carpeted by the COBRA subcommittee and then the Home Secretary, I'm becoming inured to high-level grilling. But you can't ignore the Auditors. They're the front line of our operational oversight system: if you run an organization that gives people like me extraordinary (and lethal) occult powers, you need investigators with similar skills to keep them on the straight and narrow. And their powers to compel and control are themselves extraordinary, and potentially lethal.

"Dr. O'Brien, if you'd please come in?" The secretary to the Audit Committee sticks her head round the door and gives me a sympathetic smile.

I stand up and enter. There are five of them, sitting behind a table with seating for six. The empty chair is telling. *Judith*, I think, with a pang.

"Good morning," says Dr. Armstrong. His colleagues nod affably.

"Hello," I say, somewhat nervously.

"If you'd like to take a seat?" asks the man to the SA's right. His accent has a faintly musical lilt: not one I recognize. He's a distinguished looking fellow in late middle-age, possibly with Jamaican ancestry; his beard is bushy and mostly white.

"Um." There's a wooden chair in the middle of the grid woven into the carpet. "Thanks." I walk across to it and sit down. My buttocks tense as if I'm taking a seat in Old Sparky.

"Let's keep this simple, shall we?" asks the woman sitting to the left of Judith's empty chair. Middle-aged, mousy and inoffensive, she's probably capable of zapping me into a pile of smoldering cinders if she takes a dislike to me. "Dr. O'Brien"—she looks at me, and as I meet her gaze and fall into her infinitely dark pupils I lose contact with my body—"did you deliberately kill Strip Jack Spratt, also known as Dougal Slaithwaite, in the cells under Belgravia Police Station last Thursday?"

"No." My tongue is chokingly large and made of dry leather, dusty as the tomb. I can no more stop it wagging than I can stop my heart beating. "I was unaware of the significance of his medical condition until it was too late."

My interrogator nods. The SA looks relaxed as he asks the next question: "Do you believe he was working for Professor Freudstein?"

"That seems probable—although I believe Mr. Slaithwaite might not have fully understood what he was doing."

The auditors glance at each other. "Told you so," murmurs the man on the SA's right.

More questions follow, as they piece together a detailed time line of the events in Trafalgar Square—then probe my awareness of the unpleasantness at the Bank of England, and finally walk me through my recollection of yesterday's events at the British Library. Then: "Do you have any other suspicions?" asks Dr. Armstrong.

"M-maybe." My traitor tongue is *hesitant*? In front of the Auditors? I nearly go cross-eyed in disbelief, despite the powerful geas that alienates me from control of my own body.

"What do you mean *maybe*?" The woman sitting at the far right end of the table leans forward intently. She's nearly as striking as Mhari, but entirely human. She has long black hair and is somewhat Middle-Eastern looking, seemingly younger than I am—although you can never be certain among the DSSs of Mahogany Row. "What do you—"

"Wait, Seph," says the other woman. "Let her—"

I somehow manage to lick my dry lips. "I'm not sure and I don't want to prejudice your investigations. Suspicions not related to the killing. No obvious causal chain. But there's something odd about the staff assignments to the Transhuman Policy Coordination Unit. Something smells funny."

Dr. Armstrong smiles. "*Good*," he says. "If you'll excuse me"—he turns to his colleagues—"we have addressed the core concern, have we not? If you don't mind, I would like to discuss Dr. O'Brien's other concerns with her under her own volition rather than under compulsion, in my capacity as operational oversight supervisor for the INCORRIGIBLE committee."

"Why don't you want us to—" Seph seems to want to grill me further, but the SA won't let her. He turns positively waspish, in fact.

"You know perfectly well that once you start digging for information under compulsion, trying to find evidence to support a hypothesis, you will find it every time! Even if it's the wrong hypothesis in the first place. I would prefer to rely on Dr. O'Brien's freely given cooperation." His smile vanishes. "Why don't you, Persephone? Don't you trust her?"

She crosses her arms. "Very well, have it your own way." She's obviously annoyed with him about something but I have no idea what, and it's perilously far above my pay grade to speculate. Chalk it up to hitherto unexplained politics among the Auditors, throw salt over your shoulder, and move on.

"End testimony," incants the mousy-looking woman. Directly, to me: "You may leave the grid now, Dr. O'Brien."

I feel as if invisible fetters have just evaporated from my hands and feet. I take a deep breath, as I stand up: "Thank you."

"Don't thank us." She nods affably. "Your oath of office simply verified that you cleared yourself."

The SA stands up and walks across the room: he holds the door open for me. I emerge blinking into the daylight, feeling shaky and a little numb. More formerly solid pieces of my life are crumbling into fragments. Everything is spinning out of control. It is not a sensation I am remotely at ease with.

AFTER MY SESSION WITH THE AUDIT COMMITTEE I TAKE A LONG lunch break while I pull myself together, then head over to a police station to give a statement about last night's excitement, then back to the office to chip away at the paperwork mountain. And I'm still there at seven o'clock in the evening when my desk phone rings.

"You've got to come home," says Bob: "Spooky needs you."

"But I don't need Spooky."

It's seven o'clock and everyone but me and Mhari have gone home. I told them all not to bother coming in before noon tomorrow unless they feel like it. They're still catching their breath from the weekend madness, and I'm playing catch-up from the weekend, the Home Office grilling, *and* an exciting visit to the library. It feels as if I'm drowning in work, but it can't wait. Right now I'm paging through a list of rare music manuscripts that are missing from a certain archive, trying to figure out if there's anything here that might give us a handle on Freudstein's goals or interests—

Bob sounds distressed: "They're sending me away tomorrow!"

"What?" *Does not compute.* Suddenly I find myself paying complete attention to the phone call. "What do you mean?"

"I have to go up to Dunwich. Angleton ran a lab there for dangerous experiments of some kind and they need me to defuse the defensive wards. It might be an overnight trip, but having seen what he did to his office, it could easily take me the rest of the week."

Work *can* wait. "Where are you now?" I ask.

"In the kitchen."

Oh damn. "This long-distance telephone tag is no good," I tell him. I hit "save" on the laptop, leaving the list of stolen manuscripts for later. (Judging by what his minions took, Freudstein must *really* like obscure nineteenth-century violin pieces.) "How about I come round? Do you want to call for a carry-out?" Hope begins to rise. "I know you're scared of L—the violin, but I figured out a way to secure it overnight."

"Let's do that," he says after a pause. "Make a formal date of it?"

A date? In my own home, with my own husband? How strange: something about his offer makes me shiver, but in a nice way. "Yes, let's do that."

"Love you," he says, as if he needs reassurance.

"Love you, too, dear. I'll be about an hour."

IT TAKES ME TEN MINUTES TO PREPARE MY SUITCASE, GRAB MY violin, and lock up the office. Mhari looks up as I pass her open door. "What's up?" she asks.

I show her some teeth: "I've got a home to go to. See you to-morrow."

She wrinkles her nose. "Don't you want to see the list of what Freudstein grabbed?" She looks affronted. "I pulled in favors to get this report, Mo—"

"Oh." *Wait.* "Is that the same list I got three hours ago? Because if—"

"Nope." She turns her laptop so that the screen points my way. "This is what Officer Friendly sent round fifteen minutes ago. They eliminated duplicates and struck off a lot of items that got thrown on the floor when Freudstein went through, and we're down to about fifty possible primary targets and maybe two hundred other items. *But.*" She flashes me a feral grin: "I asked the archivists at Dansey House to cross-reference them against our classification index."

Oh. "Good thinking," I admit. I lean Lecter's case in the doorway and cross over to her desk. She can probably hear my heart thumping involuntarily but she gives no sign of it as she pointedly turns back to her computer. "Did they find anything?"

"Not much," she admits. "But there's a lot of weird-ass shit—that's their term, by the way, not mine—in the BL stacks, and some of it is possibly interesting. Did you know they had the score to a rock opera composed by Charles Manson on file?" Her brow wrinkles: "It's a bit shit," she admits. "But that's not all. A whole bunch of esotericists dabbled in musicology over the past couple of centuries. Freudstein stole an organ piece by Aleister Crowley, to be performed in Coventry Cathedral—the old one, before it got bombed during the war—during a thunderstorm to summon the Great Salamander of Galvanism, whatever that means. Bloody show-off. Then there's Delia Derbyshire's symphony for fixed-disk storage systems that requires about two million pounds' worth of 1970-vintage IBM 370-series mainframe: apparently if you move the disk drive read/write heads fast enough they make screeching sounds at set frequencies. And there was an operetta of *The King in Yellow*, scored as a violin concerto. It's all rare stuff, but it's hard to put a cash value on it—it's not like the Bank of England heist. Maybe Freudstein's trying to steal the sound track to a low-budget horror movie?"

I sigh. What kind of sense do any of Freudstein's activities make? We've got a no-shit Mad Scientist on our hands and no idea what on Earth he's trying to achieve; in terms of profiling him (or her) we're a complete bust right now. "You done good," I assure her. "But I really have to be going: domestic emergency." *Bob wants the cat tray cleaned.* "Can you email it to me for tomorrow? I mean, unless there's something so time-critical that it really can't wait for morning . . ."

"Sure." She sounds slightly disappointed. "No, nothing that can't wait. Probably." She pushes her own chair back. "I could be going, too," she says quietly, as if trying to convince herself.

Knowing we've at least got a handle on the extent of the robbery salves the pain very slightly. Which I need because the long hours have finally gotten to me. The adrenaline surge from my grilling by the Auditors has long since worn off and I feel, not to put it too crudely, like a used dish-rag.

I catch a bus most of the way home, then walk the last half kilometer. The suitcase seems to gain an extra kilo with every step: by the time I get to the front door I'm almost staggering, so I lean close enough to push the doorbell with my nose, and wait.

Seconds pass. Then the door suddenly opens and I fall into the welcome arms of my husband. "Mo—" I drop my suitcase. "Ouch!" It lands on his foot.

"Sorry," I murmur in his ear. I have a double armful of husband. World's best teddy bear/security blanket, combining intimacy and sex. What *was* I thinking, letting go of him? *Oh. Right.* The violin case I'm holding behind his back suddenly weighs a ton. I reluctantly relax my grip on him: "Let me in, I've got stuff to put down."

"Food can be ready whenever you want," he says, taking a step back. He looks me up and down with evident concern: whether for my well-being, or because he's worried I'm about to explode, isn't immediately obvious. "Come in, Mo. Make yourself"—a sad little chuckle—"at home."

I step across the threshold, shove the door closed, and look at him.

Same old Bob, maybe beginning to go a little thin on top. Are those new worry lines etched around his eyes? He's wearing the Hugo Boss suit I made him buy for meetings, albeit tieless, which is ultra-formal in Bob terms—I am acutely aware that I look like I've been dragged through a hedge backwards. "Will dinner keep? Because I want to hit the bathroom first. I've been living out of a suitcase for days."

"That makes two of us," he says. "Don't worry about the food, I can heat it up." *Now* he looks obscurely disappointed.

"You look great." Which is a little white lie—Bob never looks unreservedly great unless I put some effort into his turnout—but I want to build bridges, not burn them, and he seems to want to make an effort. The past week has been the cinematic trailer for *Divorce: The High-Budget Remake*, and it's not a movie I plan on buying a ticket to: I don't even want it on cut-price DVD, thanks. I put the violin case down, then close in on my man for a hug and a kiss. I was hoping for something more than a peck on his sandpaper cheek: disappointment stabs briefly. "Sore at me?"

"A little," he admits.

I make a second attempt, and we smooch like awkward teenagers for a few seconds. Not only is it unsatisfying, one or both of us has morning breath. I pull back: "I really need the bathroom?" I say. "Freshen up and a quick change—then I've got a surprise for you, if you're still serious about us dating. Half an hour?"

He thinks for a moment, then nods. "I'll feed Spooky and lay the table. She likes to sleep on a full stomach." He looks at me, and I shiver pleasantly and raise an eyebrow, and he twitches back, and suddenly I know we're on converging courses again. We've been together long enough that we can read each other's signals.

"Deferred gratification," I warn him, then grab my suitcase and violin and flee upstairs.

HOW DO YOU PREPARE FOR A DATE WHEN YOU'RE WORRIED you've irreparably damaged your marriage?

I shove my violin case in the wardrobe again, lock it, and check the ward I put there last week is still working. Then I make sure the damn cat isn't hiding in the bedroom, strip off, and head for the shower. It's not actually as good as the one at the office (we have no booster pump at home, just traditional British plumbing that predates the last ice age) but it's mine, in my own home. That makes up for all defects. Also I've got a shower cap, which shaves half an hour off the process.

I raid the bedroom closet for my special underwear, then slither into the other dress I bought for the diplomatic junket and didn't get to wear. It's not so much cocktail hour as black tie: a black silk number that I knew at the time was a bit too daring, but couldn't resist. Floor-length skirt slit as high as my stocking tops, lace bodice with short sleeves. At the back of the shoe rail I have a pair of five-inch heels I shouldn't have bought in the first place, so high I can't descend a staircase in them without a handrail—then I add lipstick and eyeliner. *This is silly,* I think. *It's bedroom cosplay.* I wouldn't dare wear this combination in public: but in my own house, with my own husband, who isn't terribly good at doing subtle . . .

"How's the food, dear?" I call down the stairs.

"Are you hungry?" he replies from below. In the living room, I think. "Because I can have it ready in fifteen minutes."

He'd better not: I have other plans. "I'll be right with you!"

I manage to descend the stairs safely, then mince into the living room and strike a pose. Bob is sitting on the sofa with a half-empty glass of red wine in one hand, reading something on his tablet and looking morose. I notice he's actually wearing a tie—a piece of fabric to which he's just about allergic. For Bob this is more than smart: he's making a weddings-and-funeral-grade effort. I'm touched. The moment lasts almost a second, then he notices me. He drops the tablet and puts the wine glass down and stands up hastily, looking dazzled. "Do you like this?" I ask.

"I, um—" He licks his lips. "Wow! You said you wanted a date, I didn't think you meant a night at the opera—"

"I didn't." His pupils dilate. I look into his eyes and see my own need mirrored there. I step close to him and take hold of the end of his tie. I tug, gently. "Come here, husband." He makes an unfamiliar growling noise and zombie-shuffles closer, then remembers to wrap his arms around me and pull me close. My bedroom-only heels are so high that I'm actually looking down into his upturned, wondering face. My great big teddy bear doesn't do subtle: you have to tell him what you need very clearly. "It's not the opera, dear. I just want you to fuck my brains out." God, I've missed that side of things.

"What, right now—" I silence him with a kiss and reach for his fly. His brain might be stuck at deer-in-the-headlights, but below the belt he's getting the message. He kisses me back with increasing urgency, finally realizing that I'm serious and he's not hallucinating. I crouch down and open his fly and lick, then suck, until the taste of his skin fills my mouth and I can feel his fingers tangling in my hair and he begins to make a noise like a stovetop kettle's whistle. "Oh God, Mo," he moans, and I shiver. I give him a last kiss and stand up.

"Do me," I tell him. "*Right now.*" He picks me up and carries me to the over-padded sofa, where he lays me down, carefully parts my legs with his hands, and sets fire to me with his tongue. I close my eyes and fantasize my faceless dream lover in his place, and I begin to shudder. Then, when he's sure I'm as desperate as he is, he climbs on top of me and we mate like frenzied forty-year-old mammals who know it might be their last time ever.

WE MAKE IT TO THE KITCHEN EVENTUALLY—IN MY CASE BY WAY of a diversion to the bathroom to undo some of the worst of the damage. I confront myself in the mirror. My hair is back to being a nest fit for crows, my lipstick and eyeliner are smeared, one lace stocking is slightly laddered, I left my shoes and best knickers on the living room carpet, and my fortune cookie says there will be a big dry cleaning bill in my future, so why is my reflection glowing? Sounds carry much too well in this house, and I can hear Bob whistling as he putters about the kitchen. I ache pleasantly and I'm hungry and he's about to feed me. Life is suddenly more than good: it's wonderful.

I fix what I can fix, bounce downstairs, and ease my feet back into my bedroom shoes because I want to serve notice on Bob that we aren't done yet. Then I tiptoe through into the kitchen, where pleasant smells are wafting from the fan-assisted oven.

"Nearly ready!" he says cheerfully, pulling back one of the kitchen chairs for me. He has actually unearthed the linen tablecloth, a wedding present that sees the light of day less than once a year. There are lit candles and a bottle of overpriced pinot noir, and he's laid out the silver-plated cutlery set my grandmother left me. "Cheers!"

"To us!" I say, raising my wine glass. His is nearly empty: I can see I have some catching up to do.

"To that," he echoes as the kitchen timer goes off, then he hurries to unload the oven.

The food is nothing special, but it's after ten o'clock and I've worked up an appetite, and Bob knows how to spice up a Chinese takeaway enough to bring it up to overworked-busy-restaurant standard. I force myself to leave a third of my food unfinished; Bob is still eating so I stretch my leg out and play footsie with the inside of his calf. I'm still extremely hungry, but not for food.

"Bob," I begin to say.

He sighs. "We can't both stay the night."

"What?" *I do not need this right now.*

"There's—" He puts his chopsticks down and swallows. "Still the problem." He is crestfallen.

Oh, that. "What if I've got a solution?"

That gets his immediate attention. "What kind of solution?"

I tell him about the ward on the wardrobe. And the key. "Here it is." I slide it across the top of the table. "Put it somewhere safe and don't tell me where. That way I can't accidentally get my hands on the violin in my sleep. If there's an emergency and you can't retrieve the key, there's always the crowbar under the bed."

"Which will . . ." He looks at me so hopefully it's almost heartbreaking. "You're sure you can live with being parted from it that way?"

"Proximity works. I don't need to hold him—it—the whole time." I shake my head. "He just has to be within reach. The wardrobe by the bed will do, and you've got the key."

He looks at me, still concerned. "You tried this."

"Yes. And it was still in the wardrobe the next morning."

He licks his lips nervously as I force myself to wait, patiently, for him to see sense. *Sex or safety, which will win?* His face relaxes slightly, cheeks drooping just a bit. "You want us both to stay the night."

"When did we last have sex like that?" I ask rhetorically. We share a knowing glance. *Yup, sex is winning.* We're at or past the ten-year mark: things have calmed down to a weekly tempo, subject to work-related travel and other irritations. But things haven't been going so well since the Iran business, and then we just had a week of enforced separation. What we just did in the living room is unprecedented in recent years. It's why I married him in the first place, and just sharing that sly look of complicity with him has set me tingling again. "Have you eaten enough?"

He looks at his bowl. Then he looks at me. His smile is luminous. "Food can wait. I suppose you want the main course now?"

I ease my chair back and stand, then tiptoe around the table towards him. He meets me halfway. "In the bedroom this time," I murmur into his ear. "Nice and slowly. It's not as if one of us has to rush for the last tube."

WE GO UPSTAIRS AFTER DINNER AND THIS TIME WE TAKE THE time to undress one another—at least, he wants me to undress him— he likes me to keep some of my underwear on. We make love until we're both sore and exhausted and it's more painful than ecstatic, and then I make him fuck me a little more because I have an aching Bob-shaped emptiness that I want to fill. He falls asleep sprawled half on top of me, an hour after midnight, slowly withdrawing. *World's biggest teddy bear*: a comforting weight, almost suffocatingly heavy. I shift around until I can breathe comfortably, then spend so long thinking wistful middle-aged thoughts about the bathroom that I, too, fall asleep.

Unfortunately my sleep is not dreamless. I'm on the black and white dancefloor again, whirling in the arms of my faceless white-clad partner—early twentieth-century ballroom, not Viennese opera or New Romantic gothic clubland—this time wearing a long white debutante gown and flat pumps. ***You disappoint me,*** he says, in my father's borrowed tones: ***I thought you were Daddy's girl.***

I realize that I got the scene wrong; it's not early twentieth-century ballroom, but early twenty-first-century Promise Keepers, father-and-daughter religious freaks dancing to century-old melodies. Outrage and anger squeezes scatology from my lips: *"Fuck this shit!"* I scream, words I don't use much in waking life. I try to stop and stand my ground, but he won't let me—I stumble and he whirls me onwards on resisting feet. *"My father never abused me! You're* lying! *Stop trying to gaslight me! You're pushing a button that doesn't exist!"*

My partner chuckles, then answers: not in Daddy's long-dead voice, for which I am grateful. ***Of course not. You can't blame me for trying, though, can you? It only works around ten percent of the time, but when it works, it's *very* effective.*** He lifts me bodily from the floor and swings me around him, forcing me to cling to his arms for dear life. ***But if you won't cooperate of your free will, I'm afraid I'll have to compel you.***

"Wait what—"

And I'm somewhere else but still trapped in the claustrophobic dream, still spotlit but now seated: in an orchestra pit, wearing concert black with Lecter at my shoulder and his bow between my fingers. There is a music stand with a score positioned just where it belongs. The other violinists of the ensemble sit motionless to my right and left. I'm afraid to glance sideways: there's something uncannily gaunt about them as they wait, utterly still, like a bone sculpture garden at midnight. I sight-read the visible pages of the piece, feeling increasingly doubtful as I go along. It's an operatic composition with a vaguely familiar name: *The King in Yellow*. Wait, isn't this one of the stolen manuscripts that Mhari crosschecked in the Laundry archive index? It seems to be a solo piece for first violin from Act I, Scene 2: "Cassilda's Song." It's a pleasant if somewhat naively conventional melody, although the lyrics for the soprano who I am to accompany fill me with a vague sense of dread.

Play me, urges the thing in my hands—white and polished bone and, simultaneously, bloated and visceral and filled with rotting blood, ***it is the price you must pay.***

"No," I try to say, the skin-crawling sense of wrongness intensifying, as the bow tries to drag itself across the strings, my fingers in thrall to it. "No!"

I am choking. I can't breathe. I try to stand up or to move but I'm being held down by something and it's so heavy and I can't *breathe*, and when I try to inhale there's a hideous charnel house smell and something sharp stabs at my forehead—

—And I'm awake in bed with Bob sprawled across me and the fucking cat is standing on my forehead with her claws out, hissing like a teakettle that's about to explode—

I manage to vent a shuddering wordless cry of unease and aversion: "Waaugh!"

Spooky stops hissing, hunkers down, and leaps—using my head as an extremely painful springboard—right onto the small of Bob's back, nearly driving the wind out of both of us. Bob raises his head, and phosphorescent green pinworms coil and whirl behind his eyelids—

Blink.

I'm crouched on the landing at the top of the staircase, naked except for one wrinkled and laddered stocking and a couple of bruises that will be impressive by morning. I'm pulling the bedroom door closed and I've got a crowbar in my hand and the thing in Bob's body is slowly sitting up in the middle of the bed, raising zombie hands towards its face. A black furry shadow zips through the narrowing gap with a squawk of protest, leaps over my legs, and bolts downstairs. *Clever puss.* The revenant is between me and the wardrobe, and the bedroom door only locks on the inside and I am so fucked that it isn't funny—

Blink.

"Mo? Are you all right?"

The next thing I am aware of is that I am lying on the upstairs landing carpet, staring at the light bulb swinging overhead at the end of its tether. Bob is lowering himself to crouch by my side, a look of deep concern on his face. I startle and try to slither sideways away from him, but I run into the wall before I can go anywhere and then I realize that his eyes are perfectly normal. "You—you—" I raise my right hand and point at him: *"Feeders!"*

"What?" he asks, very intelligently.

I'm beginning to wake up, and the questions cluttering up my head distract me so that I only notice after a few seconds that he's stroking my knee in what he evidently believes is a reassuring manner. I close my eyes and try not to cry. *I'm not dying.* The green glowing worms in the eyes are a sign of possession by the feeders in the night, which are contagious and lethal if you're not warded. Oddly, I don't wear a ward in bed with my husband. I am clearly losing the plot. I sniff, then sniff again, and begin to weep piteously. After a minute I feel the comforting warmth of his arms around my shoulders.

"What scared you?" he asks after a while. "Can I get you anything?"

I just weep harder, from sheer frustration as much as anything else. Stupid lachrymatory reflex. What can I say? *I thought you'd died in the night and were possessed by a feeder? I was going to stick this crowbar through your chest?* None of it works; all of those sentences lead to broken futures.

"The cat," I finally manage through my sniffles. "Is she all right?"

"Is she—I don't know. Do you want me to go and look?"

I try to nod. "Yes. She ran downstairs." *She saved my life. Or maybe yours.* If she hadn't woken both of us in time . . .

I sniff again and take a deep breath. We're both grown-ups, aren't we? Bob thinks, with some justification, that my violin is a danger to his life. Well, I'm sure we can find a way to work around that. But what if *Bob* is a danger to *me?* I think back to something he said last week. *I have access to a lot of stuff.* Angleton's *stuff.* Angleton was possessed by—or superpowered by: take your pick—an ancient and powerful alien intelligence from another universe. Bob was accidentally cross-linked to it a couple years ago when a cult of murderous idiots tried to sacrifice him in order to invoke and incarnate the Eater of Souls. Now Angleton is dead, Bob is the only mortal vessel for the Eater of Souls to walk the Earth. And one of the first skills Angleton taught him was the control and summoning of the lesser feeders.

I take another deep breath that ends in a bubbly snuffle. I shuffle back against the wall and then push myself creakily to my feet. I stumble to the bathroom: I'm a sight fit to frighten babies. I blow my nose, then, hands shaking, I pull out a couple of makeup remover pads. Sleeping in eyeliner and lipstick: *ick*. The ritual of removal gives me time to calm down and center myself, and I manage not to jump out of my skin when the floorboards outside the bathroom door creak under the weight of Bob's tread.

I turn and look at my husband. He's standing there completely naked except for the black furry comma cradled in his arms. Spooky blinks at me dim-wittedly, then purrs as Bob scritches along the edge of her jaw. Stupid self-centered animal! I straighten up and extend a tentative finger for the cat to sniff. All I can manage for Bob is my most fragile smile: one suitable for weddings, funerals, and being woken up in the middle of the night by demons. "Thanks," I say.

"Thanks for what?" He looks puzzled.

"Thanks for not being dead." I can't help myself: I nearly lose it again.

When I come back to myself, he's not holding Spooky anymore, but he still looks puzzled. "What happened?" he asks.

I take a deep breath. "I'm not sure we can make this work."

"Oh, Mo—"

"It's not just Lecter. Your eyes: Did you know they glow in the dark?"

"Wait—what?"

"You've become the fucking *Eater of Souls*." I cross my arms. "Pardon my French. You, you, I can't *stand* this!"

A couple of seconds later I'm shivering and weeping on his shoulder. He stands still, holding me. He periodically tries to pat my shoulder, ineffectually offering reassurance.

"Are you undead?" I ask anxiously between sobs.

"I don't think so," he says after a while. "I don't *feel* as if I died. At least, not recently."

"But your eyes did the glowing thing. If Spooky hadn't woken you up—"

"Do you really think I'd willingly harm a hair on your head?"

"Not *you*." I'm shaking. "*It*. The thing you carry around with you all the time now. Your new passenger." The irony of what I'm saying isn't lost on me. "I don't know what it wants, but it frightens me." Another little white lie: I'm afraid that it is aware of Lecter and sees the violin and its bearer as a threat. I've been steering my own course for most of a decade, despite being burdened with a monstrous payload. I know how hard it can be to know your own mind, to separate your desire from the subtle blandishments of an insidious intruder. How hard is it going to be for Bob? He doesn't have my experience. I grab his waist and try to bury my chin in his shoulder. The shaking intensifies. I feel cold.

"I think"—I hear his voice as if it comes from far away—"we can still live together. If it's only sleeping that's the issue, we just need another bedroom, locks and wards on the doors—"

I pull back for just long enough to punch his arm. "In London. *Stupid*. Might as well ask for a lottery win." We live in a key worker's house we rent from the Laundry at a price based on what it was worth thirty years ago. London's current overheated bubble market has been running for decades and the average two-bedroom apartment with cardboard walls in a bad part of suburbia costs around half a million pounds. We're civil servants. While we're not badly paid, we'd need a hundred thousand in cash just to put down a deposit. We don't have that kind of money.

"If only a life of crime was an option."

"I'd have gotten away with it, too, if it wasn't for you meddling kids."

He chuckles sadly. "Go back to bed, Mo. Lock the bedroom door. I'll grab the spare duvet and use the living room sofa."

"But tomorrow—"

"Tomorrow I've got to go down to Dunwich. We can talk about it while I'm gone, can't we? We'll figure something out."

"Yes, we will," I reply.

But I'm increasingly scared that we won't.

9.

TEAM OF CHAMPIONS

I WAKE UP HOURS LATER THAN I MEANT TO. A SMALL BLACK CAT is curled up against my head, weighing down my hair. Her purr is deafening, but what pulls me out of a deep and dreamless sleep is the indescribable sensation of having my eyebrows licked. "Urgh!" I growl. Spooky chirrups in satisfaction and walks across the pillow, pulling my hair painfully, then applying her surprisingly heavy paws to various parts of my anatomy through the duvet. She migrates to my belly, sits down—and starts to massage my bladder.

"Ow. Okay, I get the message." I sit up, grab her behind her shoulders, and pour her onto the floor. Then I go to the bathroom. When I get back, she's washing herself with evident unconcern, right in the middle of the bed. Clearly determined to wake me up. *Typical.*

I rattle the wardrobe door for a minute before I remember giving the key to Bob. "Bob?" I call. There's no reply, so I stumble downstairs and peer round the living room door. The spare duvet is neatly folded on the sofa with a white envelope sitting neatly on top of it like a cherry on a pudding. I pick it up and the key falls out. So does a sheet of paper.

Dear Mo—

Had to leave early to get the train. You're right but I don't like it.

Will try to figure out how to rob a bank without breaking the law.

Love, Bob

I sigh. *Bob, you incurable fool.* No, he doesn't like it. Neither do I, but I went through a divorce once before, some years before I met him. Neither of us want it to happen but that doesn't mean it's not going to. Yesterday I thought it was just a matter of finding someone else to carry Lecter. Now it looks infinitely bleaker.

I go upstairs and unlock the wardrobe, pull out the violin case, and sort out a work outfit: slacks, top, regular jacket. Then I pick out a severe suit and blouse, suitable for emergency meetings with ministers, and fold them into an old carry-on bag. It can go live in the office: I'm not planning on dressing like an undertaker every day, just on the off chance that I will come to the attention of important people.

"Mrrow?" I glance down as Spooky weaves between my legs, tail high, eyes big and pleading.

"Oh, you." I take my kit back down to the kitchen, then hunt around until I figure out what Bob's been feeding her. I top up her bowl and then—this is icky—look in the cellar. *Oh dear.* Well, at least Bob cleaned the litter tray before he left. Spooky follows me in and, seeing a pristine field, determines that *this cannot be.* I turn my back and flee while she goes about her business.

I see from the kitchen clock that it's nearly ten o'clock. I swear softly. Bob must have left an hour or two ago. Dismay sweeps across me like a frontal weather system, deepening and darkening as it comes. This is silly: We have phones, don't we? Suddenly the kitchen feels claustrophobic and stifling: everything in here reminds me of our life together, piling weight atop the feeling that we're sliding out of control towards the edge of a cliff. I've lived with Bob for half my adult life, nearly a quarter of my entire existence: *I can't stand this,* I realize. I set up the cafetière with shaking hands, boil the kettle, and carefully make myself a coffee. I pull my laptop out and plug it in to check my email, then find I can't read the subject lines because my eyes are watering all the time.

I ache, physically and mentally.

When I pull myself together and finish snivelling, I wipe my eyes and try again. The first message is from the SA. "Good grief," it reads, "what did you tell them at the Home Office briefing? HomeSec reported to have said it's the funniest thing she's seen since the remake of *Yes, Minister*. PS: Scuttlebutt is that they're taking yr. pitch seriously. Budget likely to be approved, subject to enhanced performance metrics and a ten percent haircut."

I blink with surprise. No plan survives contact with the enemy, so I'd assumed they'd approve a fraction of what I was pitching for. To get 90 percent is unexpected, to say the least.

It is against my personal policy to answer any email message short of a declaration of war within an hour of waking up, or before finishing my morning coffee. So I don't reply, but move on to the next. And the next. I'm just about certain it's all trivia when I run across a missive from Internal Security. "With regard to your enquiry about Chief Superintendent James Grey, I can confirm that he has cleared background checks and has signed Section Three. Chief Superintendent Grey is an approved liaison officer for Laundry operations requiring a Command Level or lower London Metropolitan Police contact. Chief Superintendent Grey reports to Deputy Assistant Commissioner Smedly of the Metropolitan Police Service, is assigned to the Special Operations Directorate led by Assistant Commissioner Stanwick, and is currently on semi-permanent secondment to ACPO. He is an approved liaison officer for Laundry operations requiring a Command Level or lower contact to coordinate with any Territorial or Special Police Force."

So Jim is on the up-and-up? I speed-read the rest of the (detailed) reply. Then I double-check my assumptions and go look for a description of a Chief Super's role and responsibilities. He's one step below chief officer rank—that makes him the equivalent of an Army colonel. The secondment to ACPO . . . think in terms of a colonel working for the General Staff of an army: he's clearly riding the "up" escalator. In other words, he's a high-flyer. Which in turn means that he's quite possibly more ambitious than Mhari. Now *that's* a scary thought.

I file it away for later while I check the rest of my inbox, which is overflowing with mundanity. Mhari has, of course, sent over a full list of the confirmed-missing manuscripts. Following a hunch I double-check, and yes, the score to an unperformed operetta of *The King in Yellow* is on the list, along with an index number in the Dansey House stacks. I keep on reading. Something about the business at the British Library is nagging at me, something that feels *wrong*, even in the context of a Mad Scientist with a horror music obsession: but it doesn't quite gel, so I lose myself in the pile of routine correspondence. Nothing else demands my immediate attention until I get to a missive from Mhari, time-stamped half an hour ago. "Help! HR are threatening to send us a liaison from [REDACTED BY FIREWALL FILTER]! I don't know what to do!"

A *what*? Damn. This calls for a reply—she's clearly in a tizzy, and anything coming out of HR that is capable of wrong-footing my bureaucratic tightrope–walking MBA vampire is definite cause for concern. Especially as Emma told me to expect a second wave of staff to show up this week. I fire back: "Hold the fort, I'll be in by noon. PS: The firewall ate your key facts."

I finish my coffee, descend into the cellar, and hold my nose while I wield the slotted scoop of shame on behalf of Spooky. Then I pack my bags and head for the office.

I arrive around half eleven and climb the stairs, cursing my aching knees, not to mention last night's intimate aches and strains. Sara is busy with the equipment rack behind the front desk; she nods as I go past. The analysts, Sam and Nick, are at their desks, but they look as if they only just got there: I give them what I hope is a sufficiently knowing smile as I walk by. I dump my violin and the overnight bag in the corner of my office, and I'm just about to head next door when Mhari pops her head round the corner. I manage not to hiss and jump backwards as she recoils dramatically into the corridor. "What is it?" I ask.

"The windows—"

"Oh. Wait one." I dive back across my office and pull down the Venetian blinds. "That better?"

"Yes, thank you," she says, sounding slightly shaken as she sidles into the room. She's back to her anti-sunlight warpaint, but less of it this morning: she's probably afraid it's insufficient to avoid sunburn. She's also dialed back on the office formalwear a notch. "It's that HR thing, I'm afraid, I don't know what to do about—"

"Wait." I offer her the visitor's chair. "You'll need to explain it all over again; the firewall ate the middle of your message."

"The firewall *what*?" It almost comes out in a wail. She grabs the armrests and digs her fingers in. "You didn't get it?"

"Get *what*?"

"Emma's trying to be helpful!" Mhari bursts out.

"What's wrong with—? Oh. Yes, that *could* be a problem if she makes a habit of it, I'll have to dissuade her discreetly." I pause. "So she's sending us some kind of liaison person? Is it Jim Grey?"

Mhari looks at me blankly. "No. Who?"

"Officer Friendly, in his real-life disguise as a senior cop from ACPO. Okay, so it's not him. He's on the list, though, I expect him to be parachuted in just to keep an eye on what we're up to, and there are no grounds to keep him out. Who—"

"A deep one!" she bursts out. My stomach flip-flops. *Tell me this isn't who I think it is?* I nod at Mhari encouragingly, hoping my pallid smile doesn't look too sickeningly stunned. She takes a deep breath: "They're *actively liaising with surface dwellers*, according to Emma. It's all terribly new—since last month—but they say they want to *help* us and lend us resources for dealing with the random superpower problem! Emma says we can't afford not to take what's on offer for fear of offending the, the BLUE HADES, so it looks like whether we like it or not we're going to get lumbered with this fish-fucker—"

"Ms. Murphy!" I snap, suddenly angry.

"What?" She looks at me wide-eyed.

"May I remind you of the existence of our diversity and discrimination policies?" I ask, trying to keep my voice sweet: "The selfsame policies you had cause to remind me of last Thursday? And of our duties under the Disability Discrimination Act (2010)?"

"Ooh." She purses her lips, astonished, then leans back in her chair, relaxing in a thoughtful pose. "Yes. You're right and I'm wrong. Sorry. Won't happen again." She nods. "You're the boss."

I somehow manage to keep a straight face. "Is this liaison from BLUE HADES by any chance—" My desk phone rings. "Sorry, got to answer." I pick up the call while Mhari waits. "Hello?"

"Ma'am?" It's the security guard on reception. "There's a lady here who says Emma MacDougal in HR sent her. But she doesn't have a warrant card and her ID smells of seaweed—"

I roll my eyes at Mhari. She nods, expression grim: PHANG super-senses for the win. There's no need for a speakerphone when my deputy can hear a pin drop at five hundred meters. "Is she in a wheel-chair?" I ask. "And what's her name?"

"Yes, how did you know about the chair? She, um, I know this sounds odd, but she says she's called Ramona Random. Does that—"

"Oh yes, send her right up, I've been expecting her," I say, trying to keep a straight face as I savor Mhari's surprise. Then I put the phone down. "This is a setup," I tell her, keeping my tone even. "Someone upstairs from Emma is deliberately stacking the manage-ment deck, so unsubtly they don't care if I know. I'm going to make it my business to find out why, but first, we've got to find her a desk."

"Why? Who is she?"

Well, I never—but of course. Mhari left before Bob got sent to Saint Martin on that joint operation with the Black Chamber, didn't she?

"Let's just say, she's a friend of Bob's." I am not blind to the way she twitches microscopically at any mention of my husband's name. I stand up: "Come on, it's time for you to meet your first mermaid."

THE NEXT FEW DAYS GO AS SMOOTHLY AS CAN BE EXPECTED. Let me summarize rapidly so we can get to the next significant hap-pening:

I briefed Mhari about Ramona on our way to reception. I couldn't resist explaining the business on Saint Martin: I told her all about Ramona's destiny entanglement with Bob and her regrettable dietary needs while she was under the thumb of the Black Chamber. It was cruel of me, but really fucking *amusing*. Ahem.

For her part, Ramona arrives by elevator because that's how she rolls these days. She rides in a motorized wheelchair, using a rug or a long skirt to hide her deformed lower limbs. Her glamour is more effective by far than my makeup or Mhari's PHANG-enhanced appearance, but she makes up for it by being disarmingly friendly and charming as well as supernaturally pretty. At first Mhari circles her like a suspicious cat, tail raised and bristling, unsure whether to attack or roll over, but Ramona can deal with Mhari in her sleep. I put Ramona in charge of Human Resources, with a remit to ride herd on Emma MacDougal's more madcap misapprehensions about the personnel requirements of the Transhuman Policy Coordination Unit. It works swimmingly, and by Thursday M. and R. are practically joined at the hip, drawing up a skills matrix for evaluating the core competencies of candidates for the embryonic Transhuman Law Enforcement Assistance Force.* On Friday I come in to find them preparing briefings for freelance comic scriptwriters—to help us to flesh out the image of the Home Office superteam in the public eye—and I mentally pat myself on the back. Teamwork: we have it.

Once I've given my statements and written up all the reports arising from the British Library business, it's back to the real job. With people and processes covered, I'm free to focus on long-range policy and work out how to bluff my way through the executive vision thing. Which is as it should be.

I steal an hour a day to go down to the basement storeroom, hang out a DO NOT DISTURB sign, lock the door securely, and tune up my violin. Practice: we need it. Initially Lecter sulks. He's baffled and

---

* We're British, dammit, we have an ISO-standard national sense of humor. Some jobsworth will doubtless change the organization's title when it goes before a Home Office subcommittee for approval, but in the meantime, we brew up strong.

frustrated by my failure to feed him my husband's soul, and resentful at my recent neglect of his needs. At first his timbre is lifeless and rough. But the exigencies of practice slowly reach him, and after an hour or so the old magic flows. So does blood from the ears of the security guard when he hears something and comes to listen through the door; so on subsequent practices I not only lock the basement storeroom, but have his replacement wedge the fire door giving access to the basement stairwell shut. I'm much less likely to die in a fire down there than I am to suck the soul from an unwitting intruder. As for the guard, I make sure to send him a card in hospital.

I work late most evenings, doing my reading and writing up reports to a background of BBC Radio 3 or Classic FM on a portable radio I brought into my office. It's my one guilty pleasure: I turn it on only after everyone else has left. When I go home I sleep in my own bed. There are no recurrences of the horrid dancing dreams, much less of sight-reading the score from "Cassilda's Song." (I don't even know if it's a real part of the missing score: Mhari's probing determines that the BL held the only known copy of *The King in Yellow*, which has never had an actual no-shit performance in public and was written in the 1920s by an over-impressionable disciple of Schoenberg's, Austin Osman Spare, who ended up in Broadmoor Hospital.)

Spooky takes to waking me in the morning by wrapping herself, purring, around my head: she sleeps cuddled up against my side and sits in my lap when I check my email on the sofa after dinner. This would be wonderfully endearing if she wasn't also prone to waking up howling in the middle of the night and running lengths of the house. She also stalks my toes if I accidentally stick them out from under the duvet, and yells at me when the litter tray isn't cleaned to her scrupulous standards. Endearing, my ass.

Bob emails me once a day, from a secure terminal. I email him back. Sweet nothings, miss you, wish you were here. We kick the can down the road: I can't be sure, but I'm very much afraid it's a highway, destination signposted to nowhere.

On Wednesday morning I get dragged over to the Home Office for a much less intimidating meeting, chaired by an Undersecretary and his staff. They go over my strategy proposal point by point, ironing out any ambiguities and nailing down assumptions. We spend a couple of hours on it and part amicably. I go over to the New Annex, which is now mostly up and running again, and attend the weekly Special Projects briefing. SpecProj is a security-cleared meet-and-greet intended to ensure that everyone with a stake in one or another of our R&D streams is at least vaguely aware of what else is going on—at least, about the stuff they're cleared for that they might need to use. We hear a report from the subcommittee on occult artifacts (such as Lecter); also a report on capabilities and threat postures presented by foreign government OCCINT agencies, a backgrounder on the latest updates to the Benthic Treaties (as signed by the various ambassadors last Friday, although they've been in the works for years), and finally a presentation on the population dynamics of superpower distribution.

"The growth curve *is* showing signs of slackening, as of last week," says the earnest young man from Epidemiology. "It's still too early to be sure—the error bars are quite wide—but we are reasonably optimistic that by this time next month we'll be able to plot a curve and see where things are going to within a five percent confidence interval. We're also refining the power distribution curve. Stripping out the hard stats: if the growth curve is the sigmoid we *think* we're looking at, then when it levels off, about one person per million in the general population will have high-level superpowers, five-sigma stuff. The main body of the normal distribution, one sigma either side of the norm, is one in a thousand, and we can't detect anything more than a single sigma to the left of the median."

There are some dismayed noises when the audience realizes the implication—sixty thousand people in the UK can expect to receive "normal" levels of superpowers—but he goes on to pour reassuringly cold water on their fears. "Normal one-sigma powers aren't much to worry about. We're talking about powers like the unerring ability to stand on a tube platform right where the doors of the train will open, every time. Or to call pigeons. That's single-sigma stuff: it's nothing you can't match with careful training or a bag of stale bread crumbs.

In fact, half the people in this room are practitioners with powers equal to or exceeding a three-sigma superhero or supervillain—if you have the advance notice and equipment to set it up."

I raise my hand. "Tell me about the four and five sigmas."

"I can't." He's blunt but looks apologetic. "The four sigmas are typically stronger than a locomotive and faster than a speeding bullet—until air friction burns their face off. There's a wide range of abilities, often stacked in multiples. Strip Jack Spratt"—I wince—"was probably a three- to four-sigma super-whacko. A four sigma is probably able to equal the capabilities of a DSS, if they had the training and self-discipline." A DSS is a Detached Special Secretary, in Laundry speak—unofficially, a Deeply Scary Sorcerer. (Mahogany Row members are all at that level or above: but most of the Laundry doesn't know or isn't cleared for or doesn't understand Mahogany Row.) "A five sigma would be something we haven't met yet, and a walking disaster if they turn out to be malevolent. We're talking superheroes or supervillains out of Marvel or DC Comics here. Superfast, superstrong, pretty much invincible. If they turned out bad, our only hope would be to outwit them or rely on superior logistics and organizational capabilities to wear them down."

I raise my hand again. People are beginning to look at me oddly. "What about Officer Friendly? Or Professor Freudstein?"

Our tame epidemiologist frowns. "Officer Friendly is probably a three- to four-sigma case. Super-strength, flight, night vision. Plus there's that armor of his. He has to have a tech support backup—possibly a four-sigma tinker, or maybe it's outsourced to BAe Systems." (I've been asking myself questions. Like: Officer Friendly flies around wearing blue body armor, complete with a piece of protective headgear modeled on the classic British bobby's custodian helmet, with a flashing beacon light on top. So who made it for him?) "I could venture some speculations, but I'd rather not. He only seems to turn up when the Police need him; let's leave it at that."

"And Freudstein?" I repeat.

"Professor—" He glances round the room. "At first glance he looks like a five-sigma super-intelligence. But there's something about it that smells funny. I have some ideas, but nothing concrete," he says abruptly. "See me later."

But I don't get a chance to do that.

DR. MICHAEL ARMSTRONG, THE SENIOR AUDITOR, HAS AN OFFICE in the New Annex. And on Wednesday, after my Home Office meeting, I visit him in his office.

If you walk the length of the plushly carpeted corridor called Mahogany Row, you may or may not notice a discreetly paneled door. It depends on whether or not its occupant wants you to see it. The office behind it overflows the bounding-box described by the architectural plans for the New Annex: it's about five meters longer and two meters wider than it can be and still fit within the walls. Also, it's on the fourth floor, but I am told the window looks out on a vista from ground level. As you can imagine, some people find that sort of thing disturbing.

"Come in, Mo," he says, surprisingly informally. "Make yourself at home."

I would think his den was invitingly collegiate if I didn't know exactly what he does for a living. The SA was, until a week ago, Angleton's supervisor: his hall monitor, sanity check, what-have-you. The SA isn't himself an unhuman entity like the Eater of Souls, but you don't put someone in charge of Angleton unless they have the power to bind and release demons from the depths of the dungeon dimensions, and more besides.

Two decades ago Dr. Armstrong was one of the most powerful members of the Invisible College (as Mahogany Row is sometimes still known by the oldest of old-timers). Today, he largely works in a supervisory role. They relied too much on ritual magic back in the day: Krantzberg syndrome was an ever-present risk. So they thought it best to retire at the peak of their abilities, to a position where their experience (and their insight into the temptations and corruptions a practitioner can fall victim to) was still of use to the organization.

He's still an extremely powerful sorcerer—it's just that if he makes much use of his skills, he stands to lose them in the most unpleasant manner imaginable.

As I enter his office I look around. The interior is dominated by floor-to-ceiling bookcases on three sides. One wall is interrupted by an archaic cast-iron radiator set beneath a sash window, the view through which is concealed by curtains. As it's the outer wall of his office, but the inner wall is barely inside the building, I am not terribly keen to see the landscape it opens onto. Michael's desk is pretty much what you'd expect, although most of its top is covered by a beautiful Victorian escritoire, a leather-topped writing slope. The other half supports an ancient green-screen computer terminal, the variety that uses a cathode ray tube to display wavering little monospaced characters and can't do graphics at all. Angleton might have disapproved, but I find the SA's reliance on such intermediate technology rather charming, like a penchant for 1970s sports cars or a complete collection of Grateful Dead bootlegs.

"You wanted to talk to me."

"Yes, I wanted to talk to you." His silence is thoughtful.

He gestures at a battered-looking sofa next to the window. As I walk over to it he drags his office chair out from behind his desk—it's an antique banker's swivel chair, an oak-and-leather forerunner to the Herman Miller monstrosity in my own office—and sits down in it so that the desk doesn't separate us. The sofa tries to swallow me. Escape may be difficult.

"You shut down the enquiry rather fast."

"Yes, I did." His pensive stare is directed at a bookshelf about a meter to the right of my shoulder, for which I am grateful.

"Why?" I ask bluntly. "Is the Audit Commission compromised?"

After a disturbingly long pause he replied: "I don't *think* so."

Oh dear. Oh dear. Oh dear. "Then what?"

"Tell me about your suspicions." He smiles. It's the avuncular smile of an executioner shaking his client's hand and reassuring him that this won't hurt at all.

I swallow. "I trust Emma MacDougal implicitly," I say. "But her staff selections are a little bit too selective for it to be a coincidence, don't you think?"

"Which selections?" He raises an eyebrow. "No, wait: you look a little fraught. Hmm. You have no more meetings scheduled until after lunchtime." (I'm not sure how he knows that: the only thing in this office that's capable of talking to the departmental calendar server is my phone.) "Let me offer you an aperitif. And a little something else." He reaches around the side of his desk and opens a drawer, from which he takes two cut glass tumblers and a dark green bottle.

"Um." I stare at the bottle. "Organization policy on drinking in the workplace says—"

"I predate it, and I outrank it. I do not propose to get you drunk, merely slightly relaxed, with a lunch break in which to recover your composure before you return to your office."

"But what if—" I begin to frame another objection.

"Dr. O'Brien." There is a steely glint in his eye as he breaks the seal on a bottle of single malt that is not only older than I am but probably costs more than I earn in a week. "This organization *trusts you to carry a certain violin.*" I instinctively reach for the case that sits at my feet. "As for me, I spent six years with that instrument singing to me in my dreams. You are *still alive.* I believe that you have demonstrated sufficient willpower that you can withstand a single measure of the water of life."

He hands me a tumbler. I accept it in stunned silence, and inhale the nose. The whisky is amazing: smoky, peaty, with a lingering slightly sweet after-note. I hold it until he raises his glass in a toast: "To your success."

"My what?"

"You've carried him—I used to call him Dracula—for the third longest time that anybody has managed. In fact, you're a week away from making it into second place. That's very impressive, Doctor, but it can't go on forever."

"It can't?" I sip the whisky. "Of course not, but I mean, *you* carried him?"

"Yes, for a number of years before he passed into your hands." Dr. Armstrong examines me coolly. He reaches into his desk drawer and pulls out a small packet. "I think you should take this. You can use it to call on me at any time if you think you can't cope anymore. Hopefully it's an unnecessary precaution, just in case. There was a gap between I and my successor, you know. I'm afraid I could only handle him for six years and two months before he hospitalized me."

He takes another sip. I notice that the skin on the backs of his hands is wrinkled with age, and liver-spotted: they are shaking slightly, and I realize that not once has he looked directly at Lecter's case. I open the packet and shake a silver chain and a small bangle into my hand.

"What happened?" I ask, running the chain through my fingers.

"That's a story for another time," he says. "For now, just hang on to that. When you can't bear it anymore, call me and I'll come. But that's not why I invited you here today: what I really want is for you to tell me about your suspicions. What do you think is wrong?"

I take a deep breath and try to relax. It's the wrong move: I shudder, transfixed by a sudden irrational fear that we're being listened in on by Mhari. "It, it's the staff assignments coming from HR." I take a mouthful of raw spirit, disrespectfully fast, choke on it, and start to cough. He says nothing but simply waits me out. He recognizes a delaying tactic when he sees one, damn it. "I have a problem with the violin."

He nods encouragement.

I laugh, shakily. "Bob is convinced it wants to eat him."

Armstrong looks understanding. "Yes, I can understand that."

I shiver. "Bob and I are, are living apart. While we sort things out. There've been incidents. Problems. You know he's the Eater of Souls now. The violin and the hungry ghost do not see eye-to-eye."

A pause, then: "I understand." He speaks in the distant, respectful tones of an undertaker.

"Emma MacDougal sent me a brilliantly qualified deputy director. On paper, she's absolutely the best possible pick. Management fast-track, MBA, extremely ambitious and motivated, a real self-starter. Only she, she, she's Mhari Murphy."

"Do you have a problem with Ms. Murphy?" Armstrong asks sympathetically.

"She's Bob's ex! And she's a PHANG, and the last time we met before she was assigned to me, she was sleeping in my living room—Bob had invited her, it was the night of the Code Red and he said she needed a safe house to stay where nobody would think to look for her—and we, we—" I swallow. "Lecter tried to murder her."

"Lecter." He raises an eyebrow. "Also known as Dracula?"

I nod.

"Well then, I can see why you might have a problem," he says soothingly. "But she's still on your organization chart? Have you . . . ?"

"No." I swallow. "As I said, she's superbly suited for the job: it'd be a disaster to lose her over something so, so stupid. So we came to a working agreement. I don't know if it'll hold." I take another sip of whisky. "I trust her as far as I can throw her. She's a vampire and an ambitious bitch besides, and I still get panic attacks when she comes up behind me. But she's scared of me, too. Or she's scared of Lecter. Balance of terror in the boardroom: what an innovative and ingenious way to run a department, got to keep the directors on their toes . . ." I stop, because I'm babbling again.

"Aside from Ms. Murphy, who as you note is superbly qualified for the job, do you have any other problems?" he asks.

"Yes! Emma sent me a personnel manager who shouldn't even be in the organization *at all*! Do you know the background to JENNIFER MORGUE?" He nods. "BLUE HADES have come over all helpful. Two weeks ago, at the treaty birds-of-a-feather, I ran into Ramona Random. *Purely* at random, of course, except it *wasn't* and you can't convince me it's any kind of accident that *they* sent *her* to *us* as a liaison body and HR sent her to *me* to babysit. Tell me, what kind of circus are we running that a rival firm can inject a known operative into our organization and we're expected to babysit them? It's worse than crazy, it's against OPSEC doctrine! Hell, it's a *photographic negative* of OPSEC doctrine!" I realize my voice has risen to a shrill whine when he winces, and I shut it down quick.

"Well, that's a very interesting coincidence indeed," he says knowingly. (Which is when I realize I've been set up.) "Is there anything else you want me to know about?"

I roll my eyes. "What, like a certain Chief Superintendent of Police who works for the Association of Chief Police Officers, who *just happens* to be cleared to work with us? And who in another life *just happens* to also be a four-sigma superhero, Officer Friendly? And who *just happened* to turn up in time for the Freudstein debacle at the library a couple of days ago, and who is due to turn up in my office tomorrow to discuss how he's going to run the official government superhero team for me? And speaking of Freudstein, did you know he's been stealing *violin scores*?"

"Hmm. That all sounds *extremely* interesting," the SA says brightly. I take another sip of whisky as he continues: "What a fascinating barrage of coincidences! It must be amazingly convenient for you to have such a high-powered team to work with."

I cough whisky halfway across the room. "You're kidding," I croak.

"Not at all." He smiles beatifically. "I see you're off to a flying start."

I put my empty tumbler down on the edge of his desk, hoping he won't move to refill it. "Wh-what?"

"Dr. O'Brien." He leans back and rests one ankle atop the other. "Your brief is to operate the official Government superhero team."

"Yes?"

"So. Look at it from our point of view." He takes another sip of whisky and looks contemplative. "In the next few days you will receive confirmation that your funding is in the pipeline and the Home-Sec has approved your Phase One mission goals. Your next job will be to recruit and train a team of superpowers. Three- or four-sigma superheroes, to be precise. Volunteers who have the right attitude—supporters of law and order. Which, in this context, means you're going to be overrun by *Daily Mail* readers who can hurl lightning bolts and grow tentacles."

"Wait—"

I must look horrified because he gives an avuncular little chuckle as he twinkles at me. "What sort of fool goes out and buys a Lycra body stocking and cape, then beats up on bank robbers for their jollies? They're not like you and I. 'Normal for Norfolk,' maybe, but not likely to pass our background checks and personality profiling under regular conditions. They're also going to be three- or four-sigma types who are already visible to the public. A certain level of narcissistic personality disorder goes with the territory, as does a predisposition towards authoritarianism, and a naive belief in playing cops and robbers. *Charming* people. So we need someone to keep them in line, and that someone is you."

"Oh hell." I'm doomed. *Utterly* doomed. His logic is completely, unassailably right. We're going to be inundated with numbskulls who have acquired the power to vent their existential rage on a complex multicultural society that they don't understand. We're going to end up with UKIP in a pervert suit. "But we're going to have to comply with gender, ethnicity, and disability non-discrimination law—"

He shakes his head. "I'm sorry, but the official Home Office superhero team is going to have to conform to public expectations of what a superhero team should look like, or it's not really going to work terribly well. There's room for one person of color, one female or LGBT, and one disability in a core team of four—if you push it beyond that ratio it'll lose credibility with the crucial sixteen to twenty-four male target demographic, by deviating too far from their expectations. Remember, *reasonable* people who acquire superpowers are not our target. This is a propaganda operation aimed at the unreasonable ones: disturbed hero-worshiping nerd-bigots who, if they accidentally acquire superpowers, will go on a *Macht Recht* spree unless they're held in check by firm guidance and a role model to channel them in less destructive directions."

"But, but, you're telling me I'm going to be managing a team of four-sigma assholes in capes! How am I supposed to keep them in line?" The SA smiles again, and now I realize that he's taking delight in my dismay. "That's impossible!"

"No it isn't, Dr. O'Brien." He sits up and leans towards me, confidingly: "You see, *I* was the one who instructed Emma to send you the people you're talking about."

"You—*what*?"

"For the *real* Home Office superhero team, Dr. O'Brien, the *management* superhero team. The ones who will stay discreetly in the background and organize the paperwork and the logistics and do all the heavy lifting, while the Incorrigibles arrest supervillains and take credit for everything and preen in front of the television cameras. For the *real* team who will yank the Incorrigibles' choke chain if they get out of hand. The team I've very carefully spent the past month recruiting and assembling for you." He begins raising fingers: "First, the Met offered us the use of Officer Friendly, who, as a four-sigma superhero in his own right, *also* happens to be one of the three highest-ranking police officers cleared for Laundry liaison operations. Abilities: super-strength, flight, night vision, powers of arrest and paperwork, and a master's degree in criminal psychology. We'd be idiots to turn him down, even if *they* think he's there to keep his line managers fully informed of our activities: he's a perfect fit for the team.

"Secondly: *I* asked BLUE HADES if we could borrow Ramona Random. She's a retired occult clandestine operations officer and a highly experienced intelligence analyst. She can operate underwater, in which environment she has unparalleled flexibility; you might also have noticed that she is able to project an extremely powerful glamour. She's a rather powerful necromancer as well, thanks to a not-dissimilar entanglement process to the one that gifted your husband with the powers of the Eater of Souls. Oh, and BLUE HADES kindly agreed to loan us—and train her in operating—a rather interesting piece of high-technology equipment that will come in handy when you need to move the team around. Think of her as your Science backup." He pauses to pick up the bottle of Scotch and tips a finger into my glass.

"Thirdly: we come to Ms. Mhari Murphy. Who needs no introduction, except to say, she's a PHANG: a person of hemophagous anagathic neurodegeneracy. Otherwise known as a vampire, complete with super-strength, mind control, inability to see herself in mirrors, and a tendency to catch fire in sunlight. The usual, in other words. Yes, she's a blood-sucking fiend. But she's also a superbly competent administrator and has an MBA which I think you'll agree makes up for a lot of sins: speaking of which, you *do* remember that she and your husband were over practically before you met him? High-level managers often have to work with highly competent officers who they do not like, but do so in a professional and even-handed manner. Think of it as a test of your resilience, if you want.

"And finally, there's *you*, Doctor. Combat epistemologist, lecturer in paradimensional harmonic summonings, highly competent magus, and entangled with—sorry, *bearer of*—the Pale Violin."

I watch, horrified, as he reaches for the decanter once more: "Together," he declares as he wraps my nerveless fingers around the refilled tumbler, "you *will* fight crime!"

IT IS ONLY ON MY WAY BACK TO MY DESK AFTER LUNCH—THE SA insists on taking me to his club for a celebratory meal—that I realize I never got to discuss the vexatious Professor Freudstein and his curious musicological obsession with him.

WHEN I FINALLY GET BACK TO MY OFFICE I AM RATTLED TO FIND Officer Friendly cooling his heels in the lobby, just as Dr. Armstrong promised. He's in mufti—wearing a suit, not a Police uniform—but everything about him screams cop.

I manage to fake a smile, even though my stomach is leaden and acid indigestion threatens. "Good afternoon, Chief Superintendent. Are you a Jim or a James?"

He rises. "Jim is fine," he purrs. We shake hands: his grip is reassuringly solid. "I gather you've been in a meeting with the, ah, Senior Auditor—"

"Dr. Armstrong, yes. He told me to expect you." I hold up a finger. "Let's talk in my office."

Office furniture conveys relative status: I park myself on my throne and Jim responds adroitly by moving his seat off to one side so the desk isn't between us. "My grand-boss put him in touch with me a month ago," he says, sounding utterly unapologetic. "He told me not to tip you the wink prematurely."

Jesus, how high up does this go? "Well. Welcome aboard. I guess you're our official Police liaison, coming at this from the SS side of the table." I shrug. "Where are you desking on the Police side?"

"In a Portakabin in the car park round the back of Belgravia nick." He looks crestfallen. "We're ridiculously short on office space in central London these days, since they sold the old Yard off because they thought that moving everybody over to hot desking and smartphones would save floor space. On the other hand, all I need on that side is an analyst and a pair of bodies to handle contacts and paperwork until we've got a team ready to deploy. About which . . ." He glances at the doorway expectantly.

"Yes, that. Wait one." I pick up my phone and make a couple of brief calls. By the time I put the handset down, the first invitee is slipping in the door. "Mhari? I'd like you to meet Chief Superintendent Jim Grey, from the Met. Jim is on secondment to ACPO, and he's going to be our point of contact with the Police. You've already met his alter-ego."

"How do you do." Mhari shakes hands with Jim and peers into his eyes. They both flinch: "Ouch!"

"Charmed." Jim smiles thinly.

Mhari frowns and tucks her gloved hand behind her. "Pleased to meet you, too," she says darkly.

I try to make sense of this as the door opens and Ramona wheels in. "Gang's all here," I announce. "Jim, this is Ramona . . ." More introductions: this time nobody tries for a psychic beat-down. "If you'd like to grab chairs and gather round?"

"Yes, well, what's"—Mhari's eyes slide towards Jim—"this all about?"

"We've been set up!" I announce cheerily. "The culprit confessed, which is the good news."

"What *kind* of setup?" Mhari's eyes narrow.

"A logical one." I nod at Officer Friendly. "Jim is the final corner of our tent. It's all Dr. Armstrong's fault: he decided to assemble a team without telling its prospective members, which is why I've been looking over my shoulder this whole time. I'm supposed to set strategy. Mhari, you're on execution of policy. Ramona, you're in charge of human resources and logistics. And Jim, you're here for liaison and forward intelligence. It was *absolutely* a setup, but our puppet master believes in giving his proxies enough free will to tangle up their own strings."

"Oh hell—" Mhari begins, just as Jim tries to say something. "What?"

"It's Thursday afternoon," I tell them. "So, the SA tells me that next Monday HR are going to send round our third wave of recruits. We've got tomorrow to read résumés and filter out the obvious no-hopers; next week we get to interview the survivors. Our job is to pick four of them and mold them into a *public* superhero team, complete with uniforms, origin stories, the whole Marvel/DC public relations package." I glance round the room. "Sort of like us, actually, only younger, more photogenic, and willing to get beaten up by supervillains on BBC News 24. We just have to handle the paperwork and run the office. Nothing, really."

That gets a chuckle, except from Jim, who has presumably spent so many years collaring miscreants that the joke's worn thin.

"Great," says Ramona. "That explains the rumbling from HR about a pile of CVs they're going to drop on us this evening."

"Can you all clear tomorrow afternoon from your calendars, so we can go over them together?" I ask.

"I've got a meeting at two with my Divisional Commander," says Jim. "It's to sign off on the resources I need for this project, so it really can't wait."

"But can you be over here by five?" I ask. He hesitates for a moment, then nods. "Great. Well then, the rest of us will get stuck in beforehand. And then, well, I was thinking about adjourning for a team-building exercise at seven."

"What do you have in mind?" asks Mhari.

"Any cuisine we all like, as long as it doesn't include calamari."
I keep an eye on Ramona, but she doesn't even twitch.

"I know a decent trattoria that's not far away," Jim volunteers.
"Want me to make a reservation?"

"That would be great." I stand. "I should have laid in some bubbly
for this, shouldn't I? Anyway, here's to teamwork!" And for some
reason they all stand and we end up in some kind of four-way handshake, and for a moment I have a very odd feeling that an invisible
caped figure larger than any of us is looming over all our shoulders
and nodding its approval.

10.

GREAT PAY AND BENEFITS! APPLY HERE!

IT IS MONDAY AFTERNOON. JIM AND I ARE IN MY OFFICE, IN-terviewing the third job applicant of the day, while Ramona and Mhari tackle candidate number four. It is not looking good.

"So, Mr., ah, Human," says Jim, "do you have any practical experience of community policing?"

The Human Cowboy snorts bullishly and paws the carpet with one cloven hoof. "Nope," he grunts. All his replies are monosyllables: I'm not sure he'd recognize a compound noun phrase if it tugged on his tail. He has impressive presence, not to mention gravitas—it's hard not to when you're two and a half meters tall, have the head of a bull, and your horns leave grooves in the ceiling tiles—but he's not going to go down a storm with interviewers. To be honest, he's not going down a storm with us, either, but at least he doesn't have a disqualifying prior unspent criminal conviction like applicant #1. (And the less said about applicant #2, the better.)

"Any experience of dealing with law enforcement issues at all?" Jim asks, overly optimistically in my opinion.

"*Mroooo-oo.* Nope."

"So, ah, what led you to apply for a job as a Police Auxiliary?" Jim coaxes. "Can you tell us what influenced your decision to respond to our advertisement?"

"JobCentre in Buslingthorpe said tha'd cut ma bennies if I di'n't."

Coming from the Human Cowboy this is a Shakespearean soliloquy, but it's not exactly the answer either of us were hoping for. Jim's forehead wrinkles. "Is that the only reason?"

"Tha' said ye'd give us a flyin' combine harvester." He stares at us with bovine patience. "Izzat true?"

"Yes, well." Jim sighs. "Maybe not."

I glance back at the skills matrix on my tablet. The Human Cowboy is superstrong and has an amazing sense of smell. Unfortunately his IQ seems to be off the scale, in the wrong direction. And there's nothing here about his educational attainments. *Nothing.* As if they've been redacted. "Mr. Human, the CV we were sent is missing a few details. Can you tell me which school you attended? What grades you left with? Any other educational qualifications?"

"Nope." He shuffles uneasily from side to side as if the question disturbs him.

"Why not?"

"Dun'remember."

"Why don't you remember?" Jim asks quietly.

"Was before tha' accident."

Oh. I share a glance with Jim. "Thank you very much for coming here, Mr. Human," I tell him. "We'll be sure to tell the JobCentre you attended the interview, and we'll be in touch within a week to let you know how you did and to reimburse your travel expenses." After all, he did come all the way from a farm in North Yorkshire by Megabus, just for this: I feel obscurely guilty. We stand up and I let Jim do the hand-shaking thing and show him out the door because, frankly, Minotaurs scare me.

"Well *that* went well," I say as Jim shuts the door. Exercising my real superpower: vinegar-dry sarcasm.

"Indeed." He sighs. "File under 'mostly harmless.' Poor bastard is probably unemployable. He's barely able to speak in grammatically formed sentences. What was the accident, I wonder? Was he bitten by a radioactive cow?"

"Not our department, but I *knew* letting HR publish a job advertisement and send it around every JobCentre in the country was a bad idea. 'Trust us,' said Emma. I am"—I glance at the next CV on my screen—"getting burned-out. We've got fifteen minutes until the next one arrives. Break for coffee?"

INTERVIEWING APPLICANTS FOR AN ILL-DEFINED JOB WITH NO obvious career-progression ladder that doesn't exist yet turns out to be a logistical nightmare, not to mention giving me headaches. I can see it's even beginning to get to Jim, who is used to dealing with bottom-dwelling criminal minds on a daily basis. "I think this was definitely a mistake," I tell him over coffee. "I know that as a non-secret organization—operating as part of the regular civil service—we're required to advertise all postings publicly and interview all applicants who meet the requirements regardless of background, but we're getting spammed senseless by recruitment agencies and the Job-Centres are using us as a soft touch for giving their no-hope clients the interviews they need to keep their Jobseekers' Allowance . . ."

I realize I'm trailing off. Blowing mental smoke rings. Jim is watching me expectantly.

"If we don't get anywhere in the next two days, I think we ought to take a leaf from the SA's book. Send out some discreet targeted invitations."

"I thought you'd already done that?" he says.

"You—" I stare. "Oh hell. Should I?"

He shrugs. "For what it's worth I think we're wasting our time interviewing random superpowers. Well, apart from building a dossier of new and exciting antisocial personality disorders, but we don't need to do that in person, do we? Why don't you delegate, Mo? Grab a couple of bods from HR and a couple of analysts, get Mhari to supervise, and let them do the donkey work. It's invaluable research, making our future surveillance targets come to us for a job interview—and you never know, if we accidentally trip over someone who isn't completely dysfunctional, we can even give them a job."

"You're right." A knot in my stomach that I've barely been aware of relaxes. "Hell, we could even invite Freudstein, couldn't we? But seriously, let's start at the top and work down. Who was that guy who rescued the woman who drove her car into an overflowing river the other day? We ought to look him up. Proactively identify the good citizens, filter out the ones with criminal records, and see if they're willing to play ball. Shove all this messing around with no-hopers onto—" My phone bleeps. "Damn, next candidate is due in five minutes." I blow on my coffee. "Too late to cancel at this point." At least he's the last for today. "Want to go over his CV?"

Jim picks up his tablet. His brows furrow. "Candidate number four Age: Twenty-two. Name: Fabian Everyman. Assumed superhero alias: 'The Mandate.' School: Attended Eton College, took five A-levels at grade A*. University: Oxford, Brasenose College, graduated with a distinguished first in Philosophy, Politics, and Economics. Also: Member of the Oxford Union, Debating Society team captain." His frown deepens.

Something in my subconscious is ringing alarm bells. "That's not a superhero CV, that's a *parliamentary*—" My phone trills. "Yes?" It's the front desk. "Right-o, send him up." I look at Jim. "Would you mind escorting Mr. Everyman from the lift?"

"I've got a bad feeling about this one," Jim murmurs.

"Me, too. Wait one." I've taken to wearing a basic Laundry-issue protective ward all the time, but I pull open my desk drawer. There, nestled in foam inserts, are a pair of heavy-duty bracelet wards, beside a tube of extremely unusual mascara. I pass Jim a bracelet. "Wear this," I suggest. I clasp the other one around my left wrist, then tap the mascara tube against the edge of my desk, hoping it hasn't dried up completely. Pale Grace™ Bright Eyes® products have been off the market for years, but in the course of wrapping up the Billington corporate empire we seized some of the more exotic ingredients, and if life hands your research department lemons and a recipe, you shouldn't be surprised if they make lemonade for you. Or, better still, anti-lemonade countermeasures.

The mascara turns out to be dry and crumbly with age. I manage to mess up one eye before I hear Jim's heavy tread again. *Damn.* I wipe it off as best I can, put the brush back in the tube and the tube in my jacket pocket, and am blinking irritably when the office door opens. Jim enters, followed by candidate #4.

How to describe the Mandate?

We asked all our applicants to change into character for their interview—they can use the shower room downstairs if they're too embarrassed to be seen on the street. But the Mandate could easily have marched up the pavement and in through our front door in his superpower persona without raising any eyebrows. He smiles, teeth gleaming like a toothpaste advert: "Dr. O'Brien! I'm so pleased to meet you at last. I've been hearing great things about your work." His handshake is warm, dry, and firm as a manifesto promise. "You, too, Chief Superintendent. Marvelous to see you."

He makes a superb first impression but I really couldn't tell you the color of his eyes. I can't tell you the color of his skin or his hair, either. His suit is impeccably cut, his shirt and tie immaculate, the whole turnout just a millisecond behind the leading edge of current fashion. He wears discreet cufflinks and mirror-polished Oxfords; he has a carefully rolled-up copy of the *Times* tucked under his left arm.

"Have a seat." I smile instinctively. Jim sits next to me, closer than normal—*Is he nervous?* "So, Mr. Everyman. You do understand that we're not a constituency party selection committee? We're actually recruiting for a superhero team who will work for the Home Office. What talents can you bring to the table?"

He smiles, and it's so contagious that I find myself grinning back at him involuntarily. "Well, you see," he says with boyish enthusiasm, "I can run it for you. From the top, that is: I know we're still fifteen months from the next election, but I'm going to be the next Home Secretary." He chuckles at his own joke, and it's so funny Jim and I join in, too, although I have a distracting shooting pain in my left wrist. "That's my ability, you see: I have unshakable faith in myself, and if I believe in something, everyone around me has to believe it, too." I nod along: that's a *very* useful ability. "And I believe that, a-ha, *tomorrow belongs to me.*" He smiles and whistles a familiar melody. *Cabaret.*

"Wonderful," Jim says with feeling. "But what about your other powers?"

"Oh, I don't need any." The Mandate's smile widens. I realize that he's absolutely correct: if you can make the people around you believe whatever you believe, why would you need super-strength or the ability to fly? He'll be a wonderful Home Secretary, right up until he graduates to Prime Minister. "I can make bank robbers hand themselves in and volunteer to return their ill-gotten goods. I can make orphans laugh and I can make wife-beaters beg their victims for mercy. If I was so inclined, I could sell you bridges that don't exist. I can *and will* bring peace to the Middle East. I can even do a Tony Blair impression." He has Jim in stitches with that one: it's true, he's got the charismatic former Prime Minister's mannerisms down perfectly—only he's better, more convincing.

I struggle to keep track of my interview checklist. I seem to have mild heartburn—no, my silly necklace is just overheating. I'm about to reach up and unfasten it, but the pain in my left wrist has turned into a burning itch like nettle-rash, spreading halfway to my elbow. I rub it with my right hand, and feel an unfamiliar restraint that seems to pulse in time with my heart. "Why do you want to, to work with, with our—"

His smile disappears, replaced by a tiny frown of concern. "Oh, I don't want to work *with* you, Dr. O'Brien! I'm sorry, you seem to be laboring under a misapprehension. I'm here because I want *you* to work for *me.*" I nod, encouraging him to continue with his explanation even though I'm squirming in my seat, driven half mad by the nagging itch in my left wrist.

"'Scuse me," I finally burst out. "Need to powder my nose—urgently. Back in a minute."

"Take your time," the Mandate says indulgently. "I'd be very grateful if you could fetch me a coffee on your way back? White, two sugars."

I scurry towards the door and dash for the ladies. I lean over the sink for a minute, gasping and trying not to throw up as I run my left wrist under the cold tap. The red welt left by the high-power defensive ward on the bracelet begins to fade. *Damn! That was close.* I shudder, skin crawling, and force myself to breathe slowly and deeply. I've seen heavy-duty glamours in action before, but *that* was something else. I try to remember his face, but there's just a smear of skin between hairline and chin, a vacant mask onto which it is altogether too tempting to project the kindly, caring features of an identikit best friend. *Hairline?* I can't remember. Then I realize he's still in the room with Jim and my violin case is parked under the desk and I swear softly.

I pull out the mascara tube and carefully brush more of it onto my lashes. It's crumbly and rubbish and as it moistens it begins to run— I'm going to have horrible raccoon eyes this evening—but I have a compact mirror, and I manage to get some of it to stick where it belongs. It stings a little, but when I finish blinking, everything is bleak and crystal-clear. I put the tube away, pull out my phone, and call Mhari's office line.

"Yes? I'm in with a candidate—"

"We have trouble," I interrupt. "Jim's in my office and we've got a problem, *our* candidate has a glamour, level six or higher, maybe even an eight. It's a full-blown you-gotta-believe-me field and I need backup to get the bastard out of the building. Put your candidate on hold and meet me at the front desk *right now*. Over."

I put the phone back in my pocket and head for the front. Mhari arrives a moment later, followed by Ramona. They seem to have caught my sense of urgency. "What?" asks Ramona, looking up from her wheelchair. I offer her the mascara tube. "Is this what I think it is?" I nod.

Mhari shakes her head. "Level six or higher, you say?" She takes my left wrist and I suppress a violent flinch as she touches the bracelet: "Like *that'll* do you a lot of good." She tries to look me in the eye. "Mo, stop that. Don't freak out on me now! Listen, are the blinds in your office down?"

"I—I—" I swallow. "Yes." I breathe deeply, trying to center myself again. "He sneaked in under the radar and he's got Jim's undivided attention, and worse: my violin's inaccessible. Under my desk."

Ramona pauses in the middle of applying the brush to her lashes. (*Ew, sharing mascara brushes,* part of me thinks, but it's not as if we've got spares: that stuff is worth at least three times its weight in gold, and they're not going to be manufacturing any more of it once the supply of ingredients runs out.) "You should be safe from him with this," she says. "It's pretty potent stuff."

"Right." Mhari taps her toes, waiting for Ramona to pass her the makeup tube. "So you want to get him out of the premises as fast as possible? Do you want him to leave via the window or the lift shaft?"

"I think he'll go willingly if he realizes we can see through him," I say. "The big problem is Jim. If he decides to stand his ground and tells Officer Friendly to neutralize us . . ."

Ramona glances at Mhari, who is now working on her own eyes. Our clumpy lashes make us look like a failed goth revival. "Right, so that's what we plan for. How about you and I distract Jim, while you"—she's looking at me—"go in, avoid engaging the target, retrieve your violin and order him to leave? *If* he doesn't leave—*then* we tackle him."

"Wait one," says Mhari. She hands me the mascara, then she disappears. I mean, she *literally* disappears: she dashes back towards her windowless cubbyhole of an office so fast that I can't track her. A couple of seconds later she comes screeching back, all but leaving scorch marks on the carpet. "You'll need these," she says, offering us a small, translucent box.

"What." I focus on it. "Earplugs? Good thinking." *Why does Mhari keep silicone earplugs in her office?* Ramona takes the box, extracts a pair, and passes it to me. I have second thoughts and pass it back to

Mhari: plugs will get in the way of me deploying Lecter. "You need these more than I do," I tell her. Then I beckon: "Follow me."

It all goes down in a matter of seconds. I open my office door and march directly to my desk. Mhari follows at my left shoulder, and Ramona wheels in behind her and zigzags to clear the doorway. I pay no attention to the two sapient cauliflowers from Arcturus but instead bend down, pick up my violin case, press the eject stud, and bring my instrument to bear on Fabian Everyman in one fluid movement.

"*Freeze,*" I say, glaring at him along the fretboard. Lecter hums under my fingertips: he seems edgy, even nervous. Mr. Everyman turns to look at me, and with my Pale Grace™-enhanced vision and my defensive wards cranked up to eleven I see him for what he is. The fine hairs on the back of my neck rise and I burst out in a cold sweat as Mhari and Ramona grab Jim and pull him out of the firing line, shoving him towards the door with *go, go, go!* urgency.

"Well, this *is* a surprise," says the Mandate. He grins widely. I'm not sure which is more disturbing: the gaping jaws crammed with pointy carnivorous ivory, the red-rimmed eyes, or the scaly green skin. "I really didn't think you had it in you, Dr. O'Brien. May I congratulate—"

"This interview is terminated," I announce. I draw my bow lightly across a string that shimmers as it vibrates, bringing a note into being that is so pure that it threatens to rip apart reality. Firmly: "Your application is rejected with prejudice. You will leave this building *right now* and never return. You have ten seconds to comply."

My target raises his arms in surrender—arms that end in green-skinned webbed hands, their fingers tipped with claws. I tense, nerving myself for the next note in the killing symphony, but he seems to mean it: "As you insist, I will depart peacefully. There's absolutely no need to be nasty about this! But please, I urge you, don't say anything you might regret after the next election?" His smile gapes wider, but thanks to the Bathory™ brand mascara I'm immune to his charms.

I track him, alert, bow at the ready. "Which party is going to select you as a candidate?" I demand, as he stands and turns to leave. "Not that it matters, but I want to know who to vote against."

"Which party?" The lizard-man spares me a saturnine grin from the doorway. "It doesn't really matter: I'll be running for whichever party wins the election. Toodle pip, dear girl. I expect to see you in my office sooner or later . . ."

LATE MORNING, THE DAY AFTER.

We're having a post-mortem on the interviews, and have reached a consensus that none of the applicants are even remotely suitable. Mhari and Ramona have just finished swearing about their last exploding clown-car of an interview with TV Channel Changing Boy. (He can fast-forward through advertising intermissions by snapping his fingers and pointing at the TiVo, crack the DRM on Blu-ray discs by squinting at them, and he's the Federation Against Copyright Theft's worst nightmare; Home Office superhero candidate, not so much.) "*Definitely* no more interviews with open applications," Mhari complains. "We had seven meetings with highly dysfunctional no-hopers and one plausible nightmare that was *entirely* too close for comfort."

Jim sits, hunched and uncharacteristically quiet. "Indeed," he says thoughtfully. "That was a teachable moment."

"Was he applying to be a superhero or a supervillain?" Ramona asks plaintively.

"It depends on whether he fills out his parliamentary expenses form right. Damn, we're *definitely* going to have to keep tabs on him. I have a feeling there was something else inside the lizard-skin . . ." I stop, convinced I'm jumping at shadows, but Ramona picks up on it.

"Yes, I think so, too," she says. "The super-politician front with the level seven glamour is just a cover—the first secret identity. When you got him to drop it, the lizard-man wasn't his real identity either—there was something even deeper going on. I wouldn't rule out the possibility that it's onion skins all the way down: just a vacuum wearing an empty suit."

Jim speaks up. "I think we may just have met our first genuine five-sigma superpower. The question of whether he's a superhero or supervillain is, at that level, strictly irrelevant."

"Irrelevant, why?" Mhari crosses her arms.

Jim leans back: he looks almost bored. "Crime isn't always black and white. It's easy enough to finger petty criminals, but the high-level ones get really complicated. Was the 2007 financial crisis a crime? Certainly there were criminal actions involved: it flushed out Mr. Madoff's pyramid scheme, for example. Over ten billion pounds were stolen. But that was just the ripple on the surface, as trillions of dollars of derivatives evaporated when the market lost confidence in their existence. Were *those* losses criminal? Were the naked short-sellers who gambled against the market and undermined confidence in it criminals? Or was something else going on? Sometimes bad stuff—crimes, even—happen, but there's nobody to blame. And sometimes you get people who commit criminal acts for what they consider to be good moral reasons."

"I don't think—" Mhari begins, and I'm about to interrupt because I don't want to get derailed into an argument over fraud between our super-cop and our former investment banker, but Jim rolls over her.

"Criminology," he announces, "is the study of criminal behavior and criminal psychology. But it has an Achilles heel"—*good grief, a cop who uses classical references and expects his audience to follow him*—"insofar as we can only study the criminals who, through happenstance or stupidity, manage to get themselves arrested. Designated or self-proclaimed supervillains are *idiots*. They're damaged narcissistic personalities acting out their needy cravings in the public gaze. They're creating the spectacle of the absurd, Warholian junkies searching for their fifteen minutes of fame. Supervillain teams are even worse: they get locked into group-think and end up with the same failure modes as the homicidal maniacs who fly packed airliners into skyscrapers. But *those are just the ones we know about*."

Suddenly Mhari focuses on him like a guided missile that's just locked onto a target. "Like vampire elders," she says thoughtfully.

Jim looks puzzled. "Elders?"

"Let me tell you the first law of vampire school." She stands up and paces across the office to stand against the wall, daringly close to the window blinds. "The first law of vampire school is, if I can tell you're a vampire, I must kill you. Because if *I* can tell, the sheeple—no offense, that's how the elders think of you—might also notice, and institute national noonday naked roll calls or something." She frowns at Jim. "Functional supervillains would be like vampire elders, staying out of the limelight, maybe even finding ways to dispose of the narcissists who risk drawing public wrath down upon the superpowered. Yes?"

"Possibly." He looks pensive. "But there *are* super-criminals—I'm sorry, that's unclear. I don't mean criminals with superpowers, I mean criminals who overachieve spectacularly and get away with it. They're so successful that they pass laws to legitimize their past actions: we don't call them criminals, we call them the Prime Minister of Italy or the President of the Russian Federation. 'Treason doth never prosper, what's the reason? For if it prosper, none dare call it Treason.' Add superpowers to *that* kind of super-criminal and they could plausibly go where you're pointing." He looks up at Mhari. "But the Mandate isn't a supervillain: he's not damaged enough. He's something *worse*."

I sigh and shove a stray wisp of hair out of the way. "I'm going to get Sam and Nick to open a file on him," I tell them. "I also need to seek advice from Legal—maybe even the DPP. We need guidance on how to handle political cases. The blowback could be immense if we start monitoring a candidate and it turns out he isn't guilty of anything. But this bears further investigation. Just in case we've got a two-meter-tall flesh-eating lizard running for Parliament."

"I really wouldn't take the reptile face seriously," Ramona chips in. Her smile is acid: "He's riffing off David Icke, the whole lizard royal family conspiracy thing. It's a double-blind to make anyone who sniffs him out look like a crank. I don't know for sure what he is, but you can be certain the truth will be much, *much* worse."

I start to shove my hair back into shape again, but end up clutching my forehead. A half-breed mermaid sent by the Deep Ones is telling me not to worry about shape-shifting lizards disguised as politicians? And a Chief Superintendent is telling me that there's an entire category of criminal he can't collar because they're so successful they end up running the country? What next?

Mhari grimaces, baring her canines. "Which brings me to the next topic. I need you to follow up the requests for Nick and Sam to get access to TEMPORA, Mo—it's been four days and we haven't heard back from CESG. And Jim, these PNC and SIS login authorizations you offered to sort out are becoming an urgent priority. Without those information systems they're not really able to pull their weight. Once they've got access I'd like to requisition at least two more analysts; we're going to need bodies to build up a general database of known three-sigma and up superpowers, and more bodies to weed out potential employment candidates and, from the other end, persons of interest to monitor. If we can get those authorizations sorted out by tomorrow, they should be rolling out reports by the back end of next week—"

My smartphone vibrates for attention and I grab it. It's Dr. Armstrong's office line. *Oh dear, this can't be good.* "Yes?" I say.

"Trouble," he says crisply. "You can expect a major incident call to reach you within half an hour. Assemble your team, you're going to have to deploy prematurely and at short notice."

"Wait, what—"

"Can't stay, got to run." He hangs up on me. Meanwhile, Jim is answering *his* phone. "Yes? Yes? I see, sir. Can you repeat that—" He pulls out a pocket notebook and begins to scribble furiously in it. "Yes, certainly, yes, we can do that. Give me your number—" More scribbling. "All right, on our way. I'll call you back once we're mobile."

He hangs up. "That was the Assistant Chief Constable for Greater Manchester. The GMP have got a major incident developing and they want our help *right now.*"

Well, fuck. We don't even have a proper superhero team to deploy, just a bunch of managers suffering from post-traumatic interview syndrome. "What can you do?" I ask Jim.

He stands up. "I'd better suit up. Be right back, don't go anywhere without me . . ."

I pick up Lecter and glance at the other two. "I know Jim can fly," I say, "but what about the rest of us?"

"Leave it to me," says Ramona. "Meet me in the subbasement car park in ten minutes; I've got to file a flight plan first . . ."

11.

BATTLE WITHOUT HONOR OR HUMANITY

THE SA SAID THAT BLUE HADES HAVE ENTRUSTED RAMONA WITH some sort of exotic high-tech transportation device—but silly me, I wasn't expecting a stealth, supersonic, vertical take-off submarine fueled by the eerily whistling ghosts of necromantically murdered dolphins.

I take the lift down to the basement with Ramona and Mhari, where we find a near-featureless blue-black lozenge squatting on the concrete floor of the car park. It looms out of the shadows, and I see that its top nearly touches the ceiling—there's no obvious way for it to have gotten in here. As we approach, I get an unaccountable conviction that it's bigger on the inside than the outside; also, that bits of it change shape whenever I look away. But the real problem I have is that I walk through this garage daily on my way to violin practice in the storeroom, and I've never seen this thing in here before. The implications of its subtle presence are as disquieting as the SA's office window vista.

Ramona drives her wheelchair up to the side of the darkling hull and touches it. An oval orifice dilates, rim pulling back like a squid's siphon. "Follow me," she says, cheerily. "To the fish-mobile!"

A short tunnel leads towards a cramped passenger compartment fitted with not-entirely-humanoid seats at the front of the vehicle. There's some sort of glass cockpit affair at the apex of the narrowing compartment, a wraparound glassy curve that pulses with a dim glow. Ramona drives straight into it and parks her chair in the niche: four clusters of short tentacles sprout from the floor and twine around her wheels. "Make yourselves at home, and strap in," she says over her shoulder. "We're just waiting for Jim now."

"The window—" Mhari sounds as tense as I feel.

"Relax. It isn't glass, it's a projection of what the hull sensors can see, downsampled and filtered to block out blindfire or basilisk attacks. It won't burn you if your sunblock is compromised."

I look around nervously. The seats look as if they came out of a stealth-fighter cockpit design exercise by H. R. Giger: clearly they share an aesthetic with our office furniture suppliers. I secure my violin in a storage bin against the wall beside my own chair, then sit down and try to work out the intricate five-point restraint system.

Mhari slides into the seat beside me, clips herself in, then takes a mask out of her handbag and pulls it on. "Like it?" she asks. Behind us Officer Friendly climbs into his chair, fully suited up: it creaks under his armored weight. The hatch contracts and my ears pop very slightly.

I'm watching Ramona over the back of her chair; she's stroking and squeezing some disquietingly biomorphic controls—I hesitate to call them *knobs* or a *joystick*: the Boy's Own Freudian symbolism with which aviation technology is freighted is bad enough as it is— but the way they change shape and pulse as she fondles them is truly disturbing. A hatch in the ceiling above her opens and a helmet drops down, dangling from a fat umbilical tentacle. (I'll swear it has suckers.) She pulls it down over her head.

"What do you think of—" Mhari says, then: "*Oh.*"

We begin to move.

The motion is fluid and silent at first, utterly unlike any vehicle I've ever been in before (except for a brief hovercraft trip in my childhood, and that was tooth-rattlingly noisy). We glide forward between the concrete pillars of the car park, then turn smoothly towards the exit ramp. Faint ghostly whistles and pops accompany every change of direction. The hair on the back of my neck feels abruptly cold, and my ward burns against my skin. This is necromancy, but not the sort that starts with the destruction of *human* souls. Some other sapient species—a person, but not in human skin—was sacrificed and bound to power the engine behind us. It twists the computational geometry of spacetime around this capsule so that it changes position: entropy, information, and energy are all interconvertible sides of the same multidimensional coinage, one paid for in blood and agony. I shudder as Ramona drives our eerie vehicle up the exit ramp, pauses to check for cross-traffic, then turns into a street leading to Essex Road.

"From the outside, we look just like a white Mercedes Sprinter van," she tells us. "Same bounding-box, same physics model, all simulated. In reality, we're sitting inside a quasi-biological construct powered by necromantic information decay in a pocket universe—but try not to let that get to you."

I look at Mhari, at a loss for mundane conversational gambits with which to defy the eerie twist to our reality. "Nice mask," I say after a while.

She nods, expressionless. I can't tell if she's pleased: that's probably the idea. Her face is concealed by a white lacquered shell with mirror-glass inserts where the eyes belong, and a pair of tiny silver fangs protruding from the ruby-painted upper lip. She's bonded it to the front of a black silk balaclava, the neck of which is tucked inside the high collar of her blouse. With her black trouser-suit and gloves her skin is completely covered, protecting her from the lethal radiation of the day-star. And she actually looks—well, I'm not sure how to describe her. Scary is such an inadequate word, don't you think?

"I thought if we were actually expected to kick ass in person we ought to look the part. So you can call me"—she pauses for dramatic effect—"*White Mask*."

"You know, that's actually quite a good name," I agree, and pull my smartphone out to make a note of her alias.

"First law of vampire school," she reminds me.

"What's your creation story going to be?"

"It's an *origin* story, and I haven't thought of one yet. The truth is far too banal."

"What do you think Ramona should—"

Ramona steers us onto the northbound carriageway of the A1 and hits the gas—or piles further torments upon the undead souls of the slaughtered porpoises, or whatever it takes to cause us to accelerate. We gather speed. I try to ignore the high-pitched whistling and sonar ticks as Mhari thinks about my question: "Ramona's a fucking *mermaid*, Mo, all she has to do is drop her regular glamour and nobody will recognize her. That leaves Jim and you—"

"Don't look round," says Jim, so I look round.

"I said not to look," Officer Friendly says reproachfully. He's changed into a somewhat more compact version of his armor: the riot-van-friendly version. His face is invisible behind the mirrored visor of his helmet, and the blue light at its pointy apex is dimmed, pulsing like a sleeping laptop. As for the rest, it looks as if someone commissioned Stark Enterprises to design power-assisted battle armor for Judge Dredd. Or maybe it's just the Territorial Support Group's new model riot gear.

"Right," I say faintly.

"Don't worry," Mhari reassures me, "you can just be Scary Violin Lady." True enough, that pigeon's already flown—and taken a crap all over Trafalgar Square in front of the BBC News 24 cameras.

"I'm worried about our lack of forward intelligence—" I start to say when Ramona interrupts.

"Going invisible in three, two, one, *now*," she announces. "And going vertical, *now*."

The undead cetacean ghosts scream in existential agony as our vehicle tips back and shudders, very slightly. Then a couple of virtual me's of acceleration land heavily on my lap. I hope she knows what she's doing, and cleared restricted airspace before she pulled that stunt. It would be worse than embarrassing to trigger an airprox investigation: London is slap bang in the middle of some of the densest air traffic in the world, and the Civil Aviation Authority is a sister agency of ours. The shuddering diminishes slightly, the roar of wind just beyond the edge of the hull rises, and the sky outside the not-windows slowly darkens as the metropolis drops away beneath us.

"Above flight level six hundred we're out of controlled airspace," our pilot explains. "There's nothing to butt heads with except drones and the odd RAF Typhoon, and we can outrun them all."

"Please tell me you're not going to go supersonic?"

"Too late." She sounds smug.

Shit. "The paperwork's all yours, then." The moaning and clicking from the ghost engine behind us is threatening to give me a headache. I can feel Lecter stirring in his case, irritated and disturbed. "Last time the RAF scrambled to intercept an airliner they broke windows across three counties—"

"Relax, we're way too high for that. All they'll hear is distant summer thunder. Beginning descent and deceleration in six minutes."

Six minutes? But Manchester is nearly three hundred kilometers north of London! I glance around the interior of the shiny trade bauble that BLUE HADES have loaned us, along with a chauffeur to put it through its paces, then I think back to the diplomatic reception on the oil platform in the North Sea. *Right.* I'm just a woman from a tribe of Neolithic dug-out canoe builders, being given her first ride in an outboard motor boat. Maybe there is a message here? Perhaps BLUE HADES simply thought we were getting slightly too cocky and needed a low-key reminder of who owns 75 percent of our planet's surface area . . .

"I'm not getting a satphone signal." Officer Friendly speaks through a voice filter: it lends him a robotic, slightly menacing tone.

"Can't punch radio waves through the plasma sheath while we're hypersonic. Don't worry, we'll be down at street level again in just a few minutes." Ramona sounds distracted.

"What are we walking into?" I ask, trying to keep a lid on my anxiety. We're cut off from base, our analysts don't have full access to the Police National Computer network anyway, and we didn't have time for a full briefing; after what happened at the Library I'm feeling *very* twitchy. "Jim, what do you know?"

"The Deputy Chief said it was kicking off in Oldham. It started with a previously scheduled EDL demonstration and an Anti-Fascist Action counter-demo; nothing unusual, but it brewed up larger than expected, then turned ugly. Then the Major Incident kicked off—confirmed superpower involvement. Officers injured, extensive property damage, civilian demonstrators injured, an ambulance crew hurt and their vehicle destroyed."

"Shit," says Mhari. My thought exactly.

Jim continues: "We need more intel. We can't go in blind in a situation like this, we could easily make things much worse. So the first thing to do is to go find the incident commander and get briefed."

"Yes, absolutely," I agree. "Ramona, we need to set down somewhere so we can get a sitrep. How long—"

"I'm hauling ass to get us there as fast as I can," she says, just slightly reproachfully. "I can land us within a mile of Oldham center. Hmm. There's a good-looking football ground not far from there, and it's a weekday so the car park shouldn't be full . . ."

Oh God. I can just see the headlines: *Superhero team touches down between goal posts at Old Trafford: Pitch ruined.* I take a white-knuckled grip on my armrests as the doleful wailing of doomed dolphins lowers in pitch and the straps tighten around my torso. We're going in: un-trained, un-drilled, un-practiced, un-briefed, *and we're not even the right team.* We don't have a catchy name, an origin story, or matching underwear. The probability of this turning into an utter, irremediable clusterfuck approaches unity.

I close my eyes and hope the others don't pick up on my nerves. Because I have a terrible premonition that things are going to get a *lot* worse, before there's any chance whatsoever of them getting better.

EIGHT MINUTES AFTER DEPARTURE WE LAND IN THE CAR PARK of the Werneth mosque, just across Manchester Street from Werneth Park in Oldham. The sky is slate gray, a cold drizzle is falling, and a pall of smoke rises above the houses and shops to our north. The car park is littered with half-bricks and broken bottles; the only reason the mosque's windows aren't smashed is the bars protecting them. A convoy of police vans are parked nose-to-tail on the main road, sliding doors open and mesh screens deployed across their windshields. The distant roar of an angry crowd drifts across from further up the road, in the direction of the city center: they're chanting loud slogans, something ugly about Muslims. Other voices rise against them in counterpoint with another chant. Two tribes, trying to drown each other out. Or, given the weather, trying to provoke the other side into opening their mouths wide enough to drown in the rain.

A mobile police command center is parked in front of the mosque, obviously positioned to send a message to any hotheads who get too carried away—and also because the mosque is surrounded by high spiked railings and brick walls. Neighborhood relations here clearly leave something to be desired.

When we arrive, the incident commander (a regular Superintendent) is calmly speaking into a Tetra headset while the staff of the command center direct mobile units around the high-detail maps on their computer screens. There are other screens displaying the camera feed from the helicopter overhead and a handful of camera vans. "Where is he now?" asks the Super. "Good. Try to keep him there. I'll have more resources for you shortly." She ends the call and stares at us. "What took you so long?"

I clear my throat. "We were in London when we got the call, then in communications blackout during travel."

"Understood. So let me make this clear up front: *I'm* running this show. I point you and pull the trigger, and you do what I say. As long as you bear that in mind, we'll get along fine. Who are you?"

"I'm Dr. O'Brien, Transhuman Policy Coordination director." I pull out my warrant card. "This is my team: Officer Friendly, Ramona Random, and the White Mask. Your turf, your show, understood. But who are *you*, ma'am?"

"Superintendent Alice Christie, Greater Manchester Police." She unfreezes: "Okay, I've heard a lot about you," she tells Officer Friendly. "This should be right up your street."

I put myself forward: I don't want her bypassing me and going straight to Jim. "What's the situation on the ground?"

"Bad." She has a cop's roving eyes. From her expression as she gives us a second once-over she isn't sure she likes what she's seeing. "The EDL filed a 3175 two weeks ago. About 250 supporters were due to assemble on Railway Road at one p.m. and march down Manchester Road to Copster Hill—right past this mosque—then disperse. They started in the pub and got a bit rowdy, as usual, but that's when AFA sprang an illegal lightning counter-demo on us—they organized a flash mob, converged on St Thomas's Church, then headed on course to collide with the EDL right here. The Anti-Fascists got a turnout of about 100 to 150 bodies, and the locals aren't exactly EDL supporters either."

The English Defense League—self-named—are the knuckle-dragging wing of the British neo-Nazi racist fringe. They claim to want to defend England for the English, defined as anyone who's white working class. They hate immigrants, the police, and anyone who can count without using their fingers; they like football, cheap beer and curry, and trouble. (Don't ask me how they square the curry/immigrant circle.) Any time they march in a dirt-poor neighborhood that's 25 percent Muslim (like Oldham) you can guarantee they generate a robust response from the locals and produce a huge headache for the Police.

Officer Friendly rotates his helmet in my direction, then back to Christie: the nearest thing to a glance his robo-suit will let him make. "Who escalated first?" he asks.

"At first we had the EDL nicely boxed, but when AFA jumped us we had to call in all our support units. We were getting ready to kettle the illegals when the Fash got wind there was a counter-demo and about a dozen of them broke through our line and headed for Wellington Road. Which is a bit of a slog, frankly—you might have noticed the landscape hereabouts is a bit steep—and the officers on the ground didn't manage to head them off in time. So then we had the charming prospect of a dozen idiots with baseball bats charging at a much larger group who were looking for trouble.

"Then somebody set fire to one of our vans and everything went to hell." She shakes her head. "Lucky there was nobody in it at the time. We thought at first it was terrorism-related, but no, intel from ground level says it looks like the Fash have a super-skinhead who is flying, throwing lightning bolts, and shouting 'fuck off back to Pakistan or I'll stick a pig up your ass' at the AFA. *Charming.*" Her irony is leaden. "I'd have him under a section 4 if I had the firepower to make it stick. Anyway, that's when I asked the Chief to send up the bat-signal for you people—but it gets worse.

"Right in the middle of me trying to contain two different demos the sky turned funny. Forward Intel says there's a *Djinn* upstairs fucking with the weather! So there's a Nazi Übermensch on a beer-fueled rampage, some kind of supernatural maniac throwing lightning bolts upstairs, and there's not a *damned* thing I can do except keep the mundane demonstrators kettled up where they can't cause any collateral damage." She doesn't sound happy.

"Well," I say, "Officer Friendly is sworn in with the London Met, on secondment to ACPO; he's also an authorizing officer for firearms and other weapons. I, myself, and my other colleagues, are not police officers—my unit isn't fully operational yet. However, we're affiliated with the Security Service and can provide backup for Officer Friendly. If you point us at this, uh, Übermensch and his pal and pull the trigger, we can try to take him down. So I suggest we"—I gesture to include myself, Ramona, and Mhari—"handle communications and coordination while the Tin Man here does the heavy lifting."

"Right, that sounds like a reasonable plan. As long as you stick to a supporting role." She waves over a PC who's waiting by the screens at the back: "You, take these specials to Inspector Cho. He can direct them at the scene."

THERE IS NOTHING HEROIC OR NOBLE ABOUT THE WAKE OF A

riot. Broken glass and dog shit on the pavements, the choking smells of burning plastic and petrol, damp-streaked red-brick terrace houses with their windows smashed. The ferocious barking of chained pit bulls defending their yards mingles with the off-key team chants of hatred keeping time with the stamping of feet from up the steep, pot-holed street. The sky is as gray as the roads and the grass, and the rain just keeps on coming.

"The EDL are kettled two streets over," says Inspector Cho, pointing. He is in full riot gear, which tells me at once that I'm underdressed for this dance.

"Understood," blats Officer Friendly. "The superpowered one?"

"He was over there"—he gestures at the end of Monmouth Street, where two fire engines are hesitantly probing for a way past an over-turned van towards an ominous column of rising smoke—"throwing cars at the other one." He winces. "That stopped about a minute be-fore you turned up—"

A white Transit van, bonnet flopping open, rises above the sway-backed roofline of a row of back-to-back terraces, and crashes into the road just in front of the fire engines. I flinch at the bang. So does Inspector Cho, as do the other cops who form a loose line across the other side of the street. "Jesus!"

"Incoming," Ramona says tonelessly. An iridescent bubble appears around her motorized wheelchair. I dry-swallow, then open my violin case. I don't know what exactly I can do with Lecter if they're throw-ing two-ton vans at each other, but it feels better to have my sly mon-ster in hand. I turn him upside down to shield his strings from the rain, wishing I'd brought an umbrella.

"Let me handle this," says Officer Friendly. He takes two steps forward, gathers himself, and jumps. Unlike you or me, he soars above the houses on the other side of the main road, where he hovers briefly—until a violet-white spark of lightning flashes down from the clouds, and he plummets.

"*Fuck*," says the White Mask. She blurs forward. One of the riot cops turns towards her and she vaults over him, using his shoulders as a platform: he goes sprawling as she sprints into a side alley be-tween two terraced houses.

I'm in the process of raising my violin when there's a tooth-grating crashing sound. Officer Friendly wobbles into the air on the far side of the terrace and I gasp with relief.

But then there's a shout: "C'mere if yer think yer 'ard enough!"

I catch Ramona's eye. "Mhari needs backup."

She nods and begins to roll forward. I trot alongside her wheelchair. The cops take one look at us and make way. We head for the same backyard that the White Mask vanished into, the one Officer Friendly came down in.

The streets are narrow and cling to the steeply sloping sides of the valleys where they were built to provide cheap housing for mid-nineteenth-century mill workers. The houses are built back-to-back and shoulder-to-shoulder so that they each have only one exterior wall. Each row is pierced at intervals by dank tunnels that lead into the yards at the rear, giving access to the back of the row. They're cramped and cold and prone to rising damp, and the only reason they still exist is that the people who live in them don't have the money to live anywhere better. This part of the world has been living in an economic downturn since the early 1980s, like a never-ending bad dream.

The alley Mhari ducked into is slimy with lichen, cobblestoned, and piled half-high with domestic trash along one wall. It stinks of decaying cabbage overlaid by a tang of more exotic spices, cumin and tamarind and methi. Something feels wrong to me but I don't have time to pay attention to that right now. The yard at the end is partitioned by rotting wooden fences to either side, terminated by a brick wall at the back. "Where—" I begin to say, then Ramona waves for silence.

"Aaaah! Aah! Aaah!"

It's a wheezing gasp, from the far side of one fence. It sounds human and repetitive: someone is panting for breath. The gasping trails off into a hoarse whine, as if they're in so much pain they can't scream anymore.

A shadow overhead: it's Officer Friendly. He lands beyond the wall with a rattling crash.

Another shadow passes over us, and I look up into a swirling cloud with the face of a man, snarling hatred at something that crawls across the ground below.

"Bastard motherfucker!" someone beyond the wall screams. My hair is trying to stand on end, my scalp prickling with a gathering premonition of thunder. I raise my violin and witness the scene around me through Lecter's senses: hollow stone skulls lie in rows up and down the spine of a drowning world that teems with unclean verminous human life, crackling and hissing with imbecile thoughts, easily stilled by my will. Overhead, a slowly whirling vortex of power gathers its force to strike at a mantis-like presence of pure energy wearing the body of a wiry man with tattooed skin and swastikas on his knuckles who stands and shrieks defiance at the sky. "Fookin' immigrant Paki! Fook off back to raghead land or I'll fookin stab you in the fookin' balls!"

I snap back into my own head as the cloud above us begins to swirl faster. That's not good. I move my fingers into position and set bow to string, pulling in a note, and then changing key and shifting, looking for the right harmonic to drain the life-energy out of the thing in the sky.

You want me to do *what*? Lecter is surprised.

There's a loud crunch as Ramona rams her wheelchair into a rotting gate. She pulls back, rams again, and the gate collapses. She rides over it like a tank fording a river—then she screams. A pale green glow suffuses everything, the gathering energy of a lightning strike. *We shouldn't even be here,* I think distantly as I raise my weapon and take aim, *we're management, not heroes.*

There is a pink-blue flash so intense that it blinds me, followed instantaneously by an explosion. I stagger and my feet go out from under me on the wet cobblestones and I fall over, but whatever the lightning bolt struck it wasn't me: I'm deafened and dazzled but I'm still alive. I hear distant screams, then a repetitive thudding. It reminds me of distant rocketry over the Beqaa valley. I try to stand, shivering with suppressed panic: *If you can hear them, they're not coming your way,* I remember.

"Are you all right?" It's Officer Friendly. He lifts me to my feet and I lean against him for a moment.

"Well *that* didn't work too well," I manage.

"Are you all right?" he repeats, then peers at me: "I'm going after Ramona. Wait here?"

I nod dizzily, and manage to step back while he turns and darts through the broken gate where Ramona vanished. The sobbing, hoarse-voiced moaning from inside the house is back and it sets my teeth on edge. *Fuck this,* I think, and strike up a lullaby for monsters. Going after the *Djinn* didn't work too well, but he's not my only target today.

The strings begin to glow as I hit the simple melody; I play faster, fingertips sore. I know how to hit the right frequency to captivate minds, soothe them into sleep. All my people have wards, but I'm betting the random superstrong idiot shouting imprecations at the sky doesn't. I don't need to overdrive this, I just need to make him fall asleep as if he's had one tinnie of Special Brew too many. As for the angry face in the sky, I have a theory about that.

I hear a hammering crash from the yard where Ramona, Officer Friendly, and Mhari have gone to make their arrest. The shouting and sobbing and screaming—none of it theirs—slowly fades to the tune of rock-a-bye baby.

Suddenly I'm nose-to-nose with Mhari's expressionless white mask. "You can stop that now," she says tensely. "Jim's got his man. It's a real mess in there, we have injured civilians."

I look up at the whirling clouds above. Is it my imagination or do they seem to be trying to form a funnel? "It's not over. Let's get backup."

I trot after Mhari as she zips back in the direction of the Police line. I catch up with her as she delivers the news to Cho: "Two civilian casualties need medical attention urgently, Officer Friendly is also requesting a shielded heavy custody vehicle for the super he's restraining—"

I clear my throat. "No time, M—White Mask. We have to get back to the mosque right now."

Cho turns on me: "Why? What's so—"

I point a finger straight up: "One down, one to go."

"Shit," Mhari says succinctly. "You're sure—"

Look in the classrooms behind the prayer hall, Lecter whispers in the back of my head. He sounds drily amused. His ghostly laughter echoes in my head like the papery rustling of mummified hands raised in applause.

"Come on!" The clouds are still turning, gray-purple and ominously engorged. "We've got to move right now."

The broken sky tries to murder me as I cross the road. I keep Lecter raised, fingering a C sharp like an arrow held against a taut bowstring. When the brilliant pink flash hammers down at me and splashes off across the cobblestones all around, I feel a distant tingling, but nothing more. Lecter can eat more types of energy than souls. The sky thunders its rage and disapproval, mouthing imprecations at the tiny figures below.

Superintendent Christie barrels out of the command center, followed by a pair of bobbies: "Why are you back again?" she demands.

I point at the front door of the mosque. "You need to search the classrooms in back. You're looking for a man with a book, ritual trappings, and a sacrifice." A black goat would be standard, if they can rustle one up at this kind of notice, otherwise a chicken. I'm pretty sure it's considered *haram* to do that ritual at all, let alone in the grounds of a mosque, but then—

"What for? We can't just storm a mosque!"

"There's your reasonable grounds for suspicion," I say. I point up at the circling clouds which briefly form the visage of a scowling man's face: "You're looking at a weather control invocation. Officer Friendly is busy pacifying your Übermensch and the rest of us don't have your legal authority."

Christie follows my finger, then nods jerkily. "You'd better be right." The implicit *or else* hangs in the air as she turns to her two escorts: "Follow me!" Then she storms up the steps to the front door of the mosque and hammers on it. "Police!"

The door opens. I take the steps two at a time behind her. The caretaker—or possibly imam—falls back. "You can't come in here," he says half-heartedly.

"Yes, I can. I've been informed that a crime may be in progress on these premises." Christie glances over her shoulder at me: I don't need to be a telepath to know she's thinking, *If you're wrong about this, it's your ass.* "Which way are your classrooms?"

"Round the corridor, but miss, you can't—" He falls back in front of her, protesting all the way.

She's polite but firm, *very* firm, taking no shit. "How many classrooms do you have here? Are there fire exits? Which way are they? Where—okay. You have two seconds to open this door or I'm going to do it myself, don't make me wait—"

Our unwilling guide opens the door and walks in. He does a double take: "Hey, Anwar, what are you do*ing*—"

There is a crimson flash of light and a deafening bang from across the room, then it's raining indoors and Lecter's strings flare the light electric. I take two steps forward, shoes slipping on the suddenly wet floor as I pass a cop in riot gear who is standing in place, smearing the blood around on his visor in a desperate attempt to see what's happening. I pluck notes from my instrument, notes that absorb the thunder and fall flat and oppressive on my ears like atonal anti-music. Lecter nimbly drives my fingertips as I raise the blood-spattered bow and draw it across electric-blue strings that leave purple after-images in my vision, after-images like warped and melted prison bars that wrap around the silhouette of the man who stands chanting in the center of the summoning grid, holding a knife and the bleeding body of a black cockerel.

****Fun!**** sings my instrument as the perp brings the knife to bear, pointing it at us and chanting the lightning down. There are green worms spinning in his eyes because of course you don't get to run this kind of summoning without shielding and still keep your soul intact: this is classic suicide-cultist territory and Anwar isn't alone in his head anymore.

There's another pink-blue flicker-*bang* and I am dazzled and deafened, nearly thrown off my feet as Lecter absorbs a direct lightning strike at point-blank range.

"Police! Drop it!" yells the other officer—the one who hasn't lost his lunch all over what's left of the caretaker. He's drawn his Glock and he's given warning and he's about to double-tap the summoner, which would be fine by me if he was dealing with a regular armed lunatic. Unfortunately he isn't. The revenant in the grid is still chanting, and now he turns his knife in a circle, waving it in all the cardinal directions. My skin tries to crawl off my body with the intensity of the thaum field he's gathering around him.

May I? pleads Lecter.

Yes, I say, and he takes full control of my hands and—

Hiatus.

The next thing I am aware of is Alice Christie speaking rapidly into her Tetra mike. "We're in the back of the mosque, entry with probable cause. Two confirmed dead, one officer down needs urgent medical support, dead include prime suspect in earlier lightning-induced fatalities—"

Someone takes my elbow. "Ooh, tasty. Come on, Mo, let's get you out of here." They tug insistently, and I turn, mind fogged and numb. "*Damn,* I really need a drink. What a waste. Come on, walk, dammit." Mhari shoves me towards the door. "That looks nasty, I hope you've got a change of clothes back at the office. I guess now we know why real superheroes wear artificial fibers." I slip and slither across the caretaker's intestines, which have somehow untangled into a complicated gray-pink maze between the upper and lower halves of his torso. Mhari steers me around the Tactical Ted who, having lost it, is now shivering by the door. The smell of blood and feces is a sullen reek in my nostrils, nauseating and fierce.

"Let's go home," I mumble. It's funny: now I'm no longer in play, trying to hold on to my own stomach contents is turning out to be a real chore. I *hate* wet work. It triggers hideous flashbacks, and I can't get the mental taste of Lecter's gloating satisfaction out of my mouth. *Not* letting him off the leash whenever he feels like it is about 80 percent of my job. It's small consolation that the feeder animating Anwar's body was gearing up to zap us repeatedly until crispy, or that the man himself had died some time before we got here. Why does this stuff always have to happen to *me?*

We stumble out into the daylight, blinking (and cringing, in Mhari's case). The clouds are thinning rapidly, the rain has stopped, and I can see a blue patch of sailor's pants beyond the rooftops across the road. Ramona's not-so-yellow submarine is parked beside the command truck, still disguised as a white Mercedes van. I stumble straight towards it, when there's a thunder of rotors directly overhead, and I look straight up into a big telephoto lens poking through the open door of a helicopter.

"Don't say anything compromising," Mhari reminds me, "we're on candid camera." She pushes me back towards the mosque doorway, then pauses, body language telegraphing distaste: "And you're *really* going to have to bin that suit before the press conference, dear. Those bloodstains will *never* come out."

"Wonderful," I manage. Trying to match her mordant humor seems to help with the chore of holding things together: "This day just keeps on getting better."

"Yes, it does," says Superintendent Christie, her grim reaper voice just behind my right ear. "Because you do *not* get to bugger off back to London and leave me carrying the can. Once I get that bloody chopper out of the picture, *you and I*"—she pokes me in the small of my back—"are going to have a little chat about what happened in there. Because my boss is going to ask me for an explanation, and it had better be one which won't set this whole city on fire by nightfall. *Is that clear?*"

WE END UP IN A BRIEFING ROOM IN A POLICE STATION ON BARN Street. At least it's not a cell: that's a hopeful sign.

We are not, it seems, expected to shoulder the blame for Übermensch going off his trolley, throwing six assorted vehicles around, upending an ambulance, severely injuring half a dozen Anti-Fascist Action members, and nailing a middle-aged taxi driver to the back wall of his home for the crimes of having been born in Peshawar and dyeing his beard with henna. In fact Officer Friendly is quite popular with the force hereabouts, having saved any number of his nonsuperpowered colleagues the trouble of having to tackle the afore-mentioned juiced-up thug themselves.

However, we're getting rather less love for how we dealt with Anwar Kadir, a regular at the mosque and all around good egg—until he pulled out the extremely dodgy textbook, inscribed a summoning grid in the number two classroom, sacrificed a rooster, and got himself taken over by a class four manifestation (commonly known by the locals hereabouts as a *Djinn*).

The death of Mohammed Nasir, the unfortunate mosque committee member who let us in, is not going to be easily brushed under the carpet. Neither is that of Mr. Kadir, although the fact that he was throwing lightning bolts around at the time and threatening a Superintendent weighs in our favor.

But the steaming turd in the soup tureen is the fact that we *went inside a mosque in hot pursuit and killed him*. This is not good. In fact, it is extraordinarily bad. It would be bad enough if we'd done it in a church or a synagogue, but doing it in a predominantly Muslim neighborhood in the middle of a race riot . . .

Paradoxically, what saves the day turns out to be the TV news cameras showing me stumbling out into the daylight with my arm over White Mask's shoulders, both of us absolutely covered in gore. Mhari was right—my suit's utterly ruined—but it takes very little effort to imply that I've been injured in the course of taking down a superpowered monster. Superintendent Christie simply arranges for an ambulance to back up to the front door and for me to be taken away on a stretcher. Mr. Nasir was not the only member of the mosque committee to be sheltering on the premises. When the Super invited them to examine Kadir's little pentacle, there were many sharp intakes of breath. Then the imam picked up the book Mr. Kadir was working with—disturbing the crime scene, but we'll let that pass—and started swearing loudly in Pashtun. It was not a copy of the Koran; it was not a holy book at all. In fact, it was very, very unholy indeed, positively unclean—and he wanted it removed from his mosque as fast as possible.

We (I am using the corporate "we" here: I, personally, wasn't involved at this point in time) were happy to make it go away. The Laundry is always happy to expand its archives.

But this leaves us dealing with the unpalatable task of explaining our role in a multiple fatality police incident involving two separate riots and a superhero dust-up. If I was an authorized firearms officer and I'd just shot someone—hell, if I'd so much as drawn my gun and pointed it, never mind discharging it—I'd be facing a lengthy period of suspension on pay pending an IPCC enquiry to determine if in fact I had behaved lawfully, with possible prosecution at the end of the process if I hadn't. I'm not a police officer and I didn't use a firearm and I'm actually supposed to be running a new type of quick reaction force with backing from the Home Office, and the procedures we're supposed to follow start out murky, then drive off a legal cliff.

Which makes it a very good thing indeed that the only witnesses were Mhari, me, Superintendent Alice Christie, Constable Ed Carter (hospitalized for shock: under heavy sedation, may never work again), and Sergeant Barry Samson, who had actually drawn on Mr. Kadir and was about to pull the trigger when I beat him to it and maybe saved his life.

And which also explains why at ten o'clock at night I'm sitting in a briefing room, wearing a set of exercise sweats borrowed from the GMP ladies' basketball team and drinking a bottle of Coke Zero while Alice, who has spent the last four hours on damage control, explains what's going to happen in words of one syllable. Mhari— who escaped the worst of the mess when Mr. Nasir exploded because she was standing behind me—is also present: she's removed her mask and is looking surprisingly subdued.

"I am not going to charge you with manslaughter, Dr. O'Brien, because it is patently obvious that you were acting in self-defense and, indeed, in defense of myself and my officers. Personally, I would like to thank you for what you did back there. Nevertheless, I and my force commander would be *extremely pleased* if your team could refrain from visiting us again in an active front-line role until *all* your people are officially on the books as sworn-in constables. If the Met would see fit to discover that they've misplaced the paperwork and you simply forgot to tell me that your attestation was held the day before yesterday, that would be *amazingly* helpful. Oh, and if you could remind your friend from ACPO that he designated you as an Authorized Firearms Officer as well? You will need to talk to the IPCC about establishing due procedures for investigating fatalities resulting from the actions of officers on your, ah, force, and for controlling the use of potentially lethal weapons. I assume you have no objection to my division filing the preliminary paperwork to refer Mr. Kadir's death to the IPCC, and will supply your own sworn testimony in due course."

"I understand," I say woodenly. There's no credit to be gained by pointing out that in my parent organization we regularly use lethal force with minimal oversight: quite the contrary. I'm not in Kansas anymore, and the Security Service is supposed to leave this kind of head-banging to SCO19 and, in extremis, the Army.

Alice rolls her eyes. "You would not *believe* the shit-storm that's going to land on my head tomorrow, and on yours the day after. IPCC fatal incident investigations rattle on for years; they don't terminate until the weight of paperwork exceeds the fully loaded coffin and the gravestone on top. Sometimes they result in a manslaughter prosecution. I'm pretty sure this one won't, but your delayed or misfiled paperwork is absolutely not going to make things better. You can expect a dressing-down from Professional Standards, at the very least. And I'm serious about not coming back here until you've got your ducks in a row."

"Believe me, I'd like nothing more than to do that," I tell her. *Yes, a three- to six-month paid vacation would be just fine right now.* I instinctively nudge my violin case with one foot. I spent a couple of hours cleaning it, but there are still patches of dried blood that will take specialist attention. "I'm not sure we've got time, though. My unit didn't even exist until last Tuesday—"

"You'd better *make* time. If this was your organization's first outing, you *might* be able to roll over it, or not: but it all depends on whether the Home Secretary is feeling merciful and how the press spin things in tomorrow's broadsheets. At least Officer Friendly is on the books, and tackling that tanked-up chav is going to earn credit in the right places."

"We'd better head back for London," I say tiredly.

Mhari sniffs. "Ramona can drive. Officer Friendly took off a couple of hours ago under his own power."

"You go." Alice shakes her head. "I'll walk you to the car park. Oh, and we haven't had this conversation. Understand?"

"Absolutely," I say.

"Yes," agrees Mhari.

"Good. Because if we had accidentally discussed ways of working around an Independent Police Complaints Commission investigation, that would be very bad indeed—for all of us."

And that's how our superhero team's first clash with the forces of evil comes to an end.

IT'S AFTER ELEVEN AT NIGHT BY THE TIME RAMONA, HAVING driven out of town in her white van camouflage, takes us up into the starry vastness of the stratosphere while the abyssal ghosts hoot and trill in existential pain behind us. We blaze a cometary course southeast before descending somewhere north of the M25 to drive back into town along the A1 in dug-out canoe mode. Consequently, we don't slither and slide into the car park until shortly after midnight.

As soon as the hatch dilates, my smartphone beeps repeatedly, announcing a slew of messages. "Wait," I say. The very first one I glance at is an SMS from Dr. Armstrong. *See me in your office as soon as you arrive. Bring everyone who is traveling with you.* "Damn."

"What?" says Mhari.

"We're meeting the Auditors, upstairs, right now."

"Shit." It occurs to me that Mhari is getting just a tad repetitive: I resolve to find a way to tackle her about her language—but not right now.

"Do they want me, too?" Ramona sounds mildly anxious. It occurs to me to wonder if she's made the Auditors' acquaintance yet.

"Yes, they want all of us. Follow me," I say, and I stumble tiredly towards the lift. I'm still wearing the borrowed sweats, violin in one hand and bagged-up remains of my second-best work suit in the other. I don't so much feel like I've been dragged backwards through a hedge as I feel like I've been stomped flat, chewed up, and spat out by the Cape buffalo that lives on the other side.

The lift door opens onto the twilit lobby. There is a trail of light leaking along the corridor from the boardroom doorway. My mouth tastes of ashes and I'm exhausted: I really don't feel up to another grilling today, but needs must. I slowly walk towards the inevitable reckoning.

I'm about to touch the door handle when someone opens it from the other side. "Ah, Dominique," says the SA. His smile is polite but strained. "Do come in. And you, Ms. Murphy, Ms. Random." He looks past us. "Chief Superintendent Grey is elsewhere? Excellent. Do make yourselves comfortable—"

"Yes, do," echoes the silver-haired elder from the Audit Committee who confronted me the week before. "Please seal the room, Dr. Armstrong."

They've brought food. My nostrils flare: the odor of pizza drifts from a stack of square boxes in the middle of the table. They've even brought drinks, or at least bottles of mineral water. I'm instantly on edge, scenting a setup. "I expect you've missed your tea," says the Mouse Lady from the Audit Committee. (The only one who's not here is the woman named Persephone.) "Do sit down, ladies." Her attempt at emulating domestic hospitality is a washout, I'm afraid: she's even less good at doing motherly than I am.

The SA paces the perimeter of the room, sprinkling white powder from a silvery Thermos flask. Mhari looks at me apprehensively, then takes a seat; Ramona rolls up beside her. "I don't understand," I say, glancing at Dr. Armstrong.

"He's establishing a field-expedient grid," says Silver-Hair. "Total privacy is required. In the meantime, feel free to tuck in; you must be famished. Oh, I nearly forgot." He picks up a different thermally insulated container, decorated with biohazard symbols. "This is for you, Ms. Murphy. I suggest you consume it within the next hour; it will be nonviable by tomorrow."

I shudder and look away, suddenly nauseous. *Oh God, they did it. They went and* did *it.* PHANGs need a blood meal at least once every two weeks or their V-parasite runs wild. The trouble is, it has to be blood from another living human being. The commensal parasites that give them their superpowers, by way of the law of contagion, use the blood as a bridge into the brain of their victims—which they chew holes in. Blood is just a communications channel, not the meal itself, and V syndrome is a horrible neurodegenerative affliction I wouldn't wish on my worst enemy—similar to K syndrome, except at one remove. Hideous and terminal, and—

Mouse Woman notices me staring: "The donor is in a hospice, Dr. O'Brien, in the end stages of malignant melanoma. In this instance, she is already unconscious and will be dead of natural causes within twenty-four hours—she won't have time to suffer from V syndrome."

Mhari gives me a guilty sidelong look, her shoulders hunched. I look away and swallow. My stomach rumbles and the pizza smells wonderful, but I don't feel right about dining at this table.

"Please go ahead and eat," Mouse Woman tells me, a note of iron creeping into her voice. "This meeting is going to take some time."

Damned if I do, damned if I don't. I can still taste the metallic strangeness of Mohammed Nasir's blood on my lips. (I spat and rinsed with bottled water but it doesn't seem to go away.) I pull the nearest box towards me and open it. Pineapple and mushroom and ham: doubly damned I am. I nibble on the edge of a slice as Dr. Armstrong repeats his circuit of the room, chanting quiet mnemonics in Old Enochian. He sketches a ward on the boardroom door, then connects a crude-looking black box to the salt trail using a ribbon cable, takes his seat at the table, and switches on an LED camping lantern. "Is everybody ready?" he asks.

I nod, mouth full. Mhari is sucking liquid through an opaque straw. Ramona shakes her head. "Not really," she says quietly. She's been unusually subdued since we came up here. I wonder if she knows how she's been set up?

"Tough." The SA smiles humorlessly as he bends down and presses a button on the black box.

The office, and the faint traffic noises from outside, vanish.

We sit around a boardroom table floating atop a circle of carpet surrounded by total blackness, eating pizza and drinking blood. The only illumination is the SA's camping lantern.

"We have some questions for you," says Dr. Armstrong. "One at a time. Starting with, precisely what happened between the time you left the car park below this building and the time you returned. In your own words, without compulsion. Mo, you first." He raises his fingers and the quality of sound in the ward deadens until the only things I can hear are the Auditors and my own voice. (Great: they've put the others in a cone of silence.)

Fever-chills run up and down my spine. "What about Jim?" I ask.

"You have no need to know." Mouse Woman's eyes are shadowed.

Oh dear. "Well then." I lick my lips. "Ramona led us to her vehicle, and then . . ."

It seems to take forever to tell the tale, but the Auditors listen patiently. Then they release Mhari from the cone of silence and ask her to recount her version of events. I'm allowed to listen in but not contribute: as their manager I may have to defend them later if they say anything inadvisable.

I cringe when she gets to the sequence where Officer Friendly broke into the taxi driver's backyard and found what Übermensch had done there. Disgusting doesn't begin to describe it. Stomach-churning? Yes. But his sadism was constrained in the end by his lack of imagination: it was vile but petty.

Mhari describes the events in the classroom at the mosque and our subsequent discussions with Superintendent Christie. She makes no attempt to dissemble or self-censor, which surprises me: I didn't know she'd encountered Dr. Armstrong and his colleagues in their professional capacity before, but her body language is totally cowed, submissive. *Not* what one would expect from one of the self-identified lords and ladies who rule humanity from the shadows, setting interest rates and offering credit—not even what you'd expect from a vampire.

Finally it's Ramona's turn, but at this point she's pretty much just confirming what Mhari and I told the auditors. At the end, the Mouse Lady nods. "I believe your accounts are consistent," she says. "Michael?"

"Yes," the SA says slowly. "Yes, indeed. Dr. O'Brien"—he leans forward—"did you at any time see Chief Superintendent Grey? From the time you entered the basement to the time you arrived back here?"

Wait, what? "Of course," I say, confused. "He was sitting right behind me in the flying submarine—"

"I'm sorry, but I believe I have not made myself sufficiently clear. You have said that you saw Officer Friendly sitting behind you. Did you *at any point* see James Grey's face?"

"Whu-well!" I sit back, and glance at Ramona. She looks bewildered. "Well no, but he had his armor on the whole time. Why would I see his face?"

"Ms. Random, Ms. Murphy—did either of you see Chief Superintendent Grey? Or just a suit of armor?"

"Ulp." Mhari pushes her biohazard container aside and licks her lips. They glisten black in the dim glow of the lantern. "I don't believe so," she says hesitantly.

"It was definitely Jim in there!" Ramona insists. "I mean, he may use a voice distorter but his diction and body language . . . ?" She looks around the table uncertainly. "You're serious," she says in a small voice.

"Didn't he say he couldn't get a satellite signal inside the flying sub?" asks Mhari.

"We only have his word for it," I remind her. I look at the SA. "Are you serious?" I ask. "Do you really believe Jim wasn't inside that suit of armor?"

"I have heard no conclusive testimony to the effect that he *was*," says Dr. Armstrong, "merely conjecture based on diction and body language."

Oh god. Officer Friendly was sitting behind me for the whole flight out. *Standing* behind me. Whoever was in that suit could have leaned forward and garroted me and I wouldn't have stood a chance.

"I do not believe you were in immediate danger," the SA says calmly.

"We are merely investigating one low-probability contingency," echoes the Mouse Woman. "That information received from a sister agency is of questionable accuracy."

Silver-Hair leans back from the table and makes a steeple with his fingertips. "There are lessons to be learned," he says.

I can't help myself: "What lessons?" I demand. "Which agency? Are the police lying to us? Do you think Jim Grey is a plant?"

"He's not—" begins Ramona.

"*Chief Superintendent Grey* is very definitely what he appears to be," Dr. Armstrong interrupts. "The question is whether Officer Friendly is likewise."

"But Officer Friendly is Jim Grey's superhero persona!" I protest.

"That's what Chief Superintendent Grey says," agrees the Mouse Woman. "Certainly Chief Superintendent Grey wears Officer Friendly armor. Whether it is the only such suit of armor, however . . ."

"We think you should investigate further," says the SA. He smiles. "What else?"

Silver-Hair clears his throat. "Your attestation ceremony as officers of the law was held in front of Woolwich Magistrates yesterday morning and noted accordingly by the clerk of court. The paperwork is on its way to you: try not to lose it. Ahem. An order in privy council will be issued tomorrow formally re-designating this organization as the Transhuman Police Coordination Force—there is common law precedent, and an amendment to the Serious Organized Crime and Police Act (2005) will be tabled in the next Parliamentary session to regularize it. This leaves the, ah, IPCC enquiry. I believe we can head it off at the pass once you can demonstrate that you were acting lawfully to stop an imminent threat to life."

"Thank you for clarifying that," I say tiredly. So the Auditors have an onside lawyer? What a surprise. "What else should we be doing?"

"Generally, we want you to keep on doing what you're already doing. With, perhaps, a little more structure." The SA folds his arms. "Continue to solicit interviews with suitably solid citizens, and supervise their training and deployment. Collect forward intelligence on potentially disruptive superpower threats of three-sigma level and above." He pauses. "You need to work out what story you're going to feed the public and media to explain where you came from, sooner rather than later. It'll need to be compatible with the global superpower origin cover we're developing, of course, but that shouldn't be too hard." He pauses again. "And you might also want to investigate some sort of uniform or team costume."

"Now wait a minute," says Mhari, a gravelly snarl creeping into her voice, "if you think you're going to get me to wear spangly fishnets—"

"Not at all!" says the SA. "But"—he gestures at my bagged-up suit—"next time your clothes are ruined, you'll find it much easier to indent for a replacement if it's a uniform item rather than personal office attire."

"Are we done here?" asks the Mouse Woman.

"Not quite." Dr. Armstrong spares us a long look. "I want you to know that I'm proud of you; despite being inadequately briefed, not to mention trained, you did far better than we could reasonably have expected today. But in future"—he momentarily looks as if he's sucking on a lemon—"expect the worst. I'm afraid you won't be disappointed."

12.

END OF THE LINE

IT'S EIGHT FORTY ON A RAINY MONDAY MORNING A WEEK LATER, and I am already on the phone. "They stole a *what*?"

The voice on the other end is terse to the point of obscurity: "A tube station."

"A station. Not a train . . . ?"

I arrived at work ten minutes ago to find my voicemail was already backed up like a blocked drain. The contents smell nearly as bad, too: five calls from the British Transport Police, three from officials at Transport for London, one from the office of the Mayor, and two silent calls from blocked numbers. The latter I can ignore, but the BTP calls are worrying so I start at the top and work down.

"Aldwych is missing," Inspector Hoare explains in the slightly stunned tones of someone who woke up this morning to see lions lying down with lambs, rivers flowing uphill, and the sun rising in the west. "The G4S security guard phoned it in when he visited on his rounds at six a.m. I thought he was on drugs at first, but no, it's gone."

I hesitate to tell the inspector at the other end of the line that *I* think *he* sounds as if he's on drugs. Instead: "Who else knows?" I ask.

"Us, obviously—BTP London situation room, that is. Also TfL, equally obviously—they're responsible for station premises even when the stations are closed—"

"Derelict?" I interrupt.

"No, just closed. Aldwych was the only station on a branch of the Piccadilly Line that they officially closed in 1994. It used to be Strand Station when it opened, because it's on the Strand; there were plans to extend the spur to Waterloo but they were canned ages ago. The building's still used for filming, but trains don't run there anymore—a security guard checks it a couple of times a day to make sure it's not squatted. This morning he entered through the side entrance but couldn't gain access to the underground sections of the station. I sent an officer to Holborn to take a look and they reported back that the entrance to the spur tunnel's missing. Blocked off as if it was never there in the first place. Really spooked him when he saw it, I can tell you."

I think for a moment. "What do you mean by *can't gain access*? From the surface, I mean."

"The structure's been *modified*," the Inspector says darkly. "Best if you see for yourself."

"Okay. One more question before I come over: Why did you think of us? I mean, what makes you think it's a job for the Transhuman Police Coordination Force?"

"I asked around and was advised to talk to you people by our liaison at the Met. If you could have your man meet me there, it's near the corner of the Strand and Surrey Street—about a five-minute walk from Temple on the District and Circle Line."

"I'll be along in about forty minutes," I tell him, and hang up. Then I go for a little walk. My first stop is with Sam and Nick in the analysts' hole. They've added pale green cubicle walls and two more desks in anticipation of some new recruits, but otherwise it looks nearly the same as it did on their first day. Spartan. They're at their desks, but both look up when I enter. "I have an extra special rush job for you this morning. I need everything you can dig up on Aldwych tube station, anything at all in the past two or so years."

"Anything?" Nick looks surprised.

"Yes. It's been closed for more than twenty years, but suddenly—"
I shrug. "Email it to me, I've got to go pay a call."

"How do you spell Aldwych?" asks Sam.

My next destination takes some thought. Ramona is wheelchair
bound, which wouldn't normally be a problem, but I'm planning on
visiting a century-old station that closed around the time the Disability Discrimination Act came in: the chances of it being wheelchair-
friendly are approximately zero. Mhari is not unreasonably reluctant
to venture outside in daylight. The analysts are needed at their computers, and we *still* don't have any superpowered recruits—our most
promising candidates are stuck in the middle of their enhanced criminal background checks. That leaves me with a choice of Jim or Jim
for backup.

He answers his mobile at once. "Grey speaking."

"I've got to go out of the office to look into something, and I could
do with a second pair of eyeballs," I tell him. "What I really need is
the paranormal equivalent of a detective constable, but as I don't have
one, that leaves you. Can you spare a couple of hours this morning?
Or find a body you can send along to hold my hand through the finer
points of examining a possible crime scene?"

"Let me see—" I hear him typing on an old rattly desktop keyboard. His calendar is probably as full as mine: he may have an office
here but he's still spending half his time in the ACPO suite on Victoria
Street and another quarter at the Yard. "I'm finishing my weekly activity report for my boss and his executive, then there's a meeting at
eleven this morning, but I'm not a key stakeholder. I'll send my apologies and come along. Are you sure about this?"

"Not entirely, but the British Transport Police seem to think it's a
job for us."

"Well, if *they* say so, it *must* be true." He camps it up just a little
and I stifle a laugh.

"Personally I think it's a job for *Fortean Times*, but BTP seem to
think we're some kind of official Bizarro-World division. So unless we
can shrug this one off on the missing property office . . ."

"Missing property? Why would they be involved?"

I tell him about the missing tube station and we agree to meet there at nine thirty. I pause just long enough to grab my coat and violin case, and then it's out onto the uncharacteristically sodden pavement to do a job I don't have the staff to delegate to, which in turn gets in the way of my recruiting the warm bodies I need in order to do this kind of thing without getting my feet wet. *Wonderful.*

I'VE SPENT THE PAST DECADE WORKING FOR AN INTELLIGENCE organization rather than the Police. The rules are, shall we say, *different* over there.

The Auditors have fed me just enough uncertainty about Jim to alarm me, but not enough to give me any preconceptions about the cause for their concern. In the absence of evidence against him, he's still a vital part of my team. I hate the word *indispensable* because it's a sign that you don't have a working organization, just a bunch of temporarily cooperating individuals: but the sad fact is, I *don't* have an organization, I have a superhero team. Maybe in another couple of months I'll have Teams Alpha through Delta and a duty superhero roster and a training budget and a sickness/leave chart to track. But right now my team has all the logistical flexibility of a strip of balsa wood. So I can't wrap Jim up in cotton wool and run him through a loyalty test maze: I've got to depend on him to get the job done, despite not being able to fully trust him.

As if that's not bad enough, I can't even talk this over with Bob. For one thing, I don't have a life of my own anymore: I'm spending a day and a half a week at the Police college in Hendon, being given my very own accelerated catch-up course in being a really wet-behind-the-ears rookie trainee policewoman, with the added twist that I'm on MI5's management org chart, on payroll with a department of an organization (SOE) that was officially wound up in 1945, and I'm supposed to command a small and very weird police force all of my very own, with a Chief Superintendent working under me. If you want to map out my management matrix without getting hopelessly tangled up, you'll need to draw it on the surface of a Klein bottle. The homework alone keeps me up until midnight on those days when the job doesn't. I've lost track of my friends: I don't even know how Sandy's baby-bump is progressing this month, and (trust me on this) when one of your friends is pregnant, not getting daily or at least weekly updates is a sign that you're *really* out of the loop.

Finally, Bob isn't even in London most of the time. It turns out that Angleton left little piles of metaphysical unexploded ordnance all over the country, and Bob's being kept busy scurrying all over the map itemizing, neutralizing, and containerizing them. It's not that Angleton was particularly untidy: he just got to work in a lot of offices over nearly eight decades of service.

So about all I see of my husband is his name on my phone when he has time to call, which is maybe twice a week. And vice versa.

Believe me, this does *not* make me happy. A house cat is no adequate substitute for a life partner, even when she isn't trying to kill me in my sleep.

But let's get back to the enigma inside a conundrum that is Jim Grey/Officer Friendly: if he was inside the Laundry, the Auditors could carpet him and ask some extremely pointed questions under sanction of his oath of loyalty. Our take on internal security is that if we secure the soul, the flesh will obey.*

But Jim isn't in the Laundry. He's a senior police officer who has lately and semi-publicly acquired superpowers. The Laundry can't recruit him and hush everything up, the way we used to do with adepts who showed signs of occult talent or computer science geeks who tripped over the Turing theses. All the Auditors can do is nudge him into this neither-fish-nor-fowl unit I'm running, then get me to poke him and see if he jumps in a self-incriminating direction—and hope that if he does, I can bring him down before he does any damage.

---

* There are some disturbing exceptions—I'm still not privy to the analysis of how Iris Carpenter perverted her geas to the point where she could survive questioning—but in general we have a lower level of internal threats than other security organizations. And *no* whistle-blowers. Even though the existence of the Iris loophole means there is no room for complacency.

That's assuming the SA's suspicions are justified, of course. I like Jim: he seems to be a genuine straight arrow who is also a deep enough thinker to regularly surprise me with his insights. The SA is usually rock-solid, but the idea that Jim could be some kind of criminal seems so misguided as to be laughable.

But as Jim himself pointed out, the most effective criminals are the ones who move the fenceposts of the law to protect their activities: the ones you can't even build a case against. Treason never prospers . . .

I APPROACH THE BARRED AND BOARDED FRONTAGE OF ALDWYCH station along the Strand, past the front of King's College. A steady rain falls beneath a slate-colored overcast that suggests it has set in for the day. Buses and taxis rumble past, spraying water across the pavement whenever they plough through a puddle by a blocked drain. I walk as close to the buildings as possible. The station itself presents a narrow frontage to the road, red tiles framing a wide double doorway (closed off by a security grille) beneath a semicircular window. One side of the security mesh is drawn back, and one door stands ajar: a policeman stands inside, waiting just out of the rain.

"Mo?" calls a voice behind me. I turn just in time to see Jim hurrying along the pavement. He's in working uniform, with a high-vis waterproof on top.

"Good to see you; I was just about to—" I gesture at the entrance.

The officer in the doorway raises a hand. "You can't come in—"

I hold up my warrant card. "O'Brien, TPCF. I'm here to see Inspector Hoare." I show him my teeth: "My colleague here is Chief Superintendent Grey."

"Ah, right." He takes in Jim and his eyes widen as he falls back, retreating into the shadowed station lobby. "Please wait here, sir, ma'am, I'll be right back." He scampers away hastily.

I glance at Jim. "Shall we?"

Jim gestures: "After you."

The interior of the disused tube station is a bit grubby but otherwise in remarkably good repair. The floor tiles are uncracked and the wood panels on the walls are still solid, there's no rubbish, no sign of peeling paint or graffiti. But the frames for information posters and advertisements are empty, the ticket barriers are archaic—there isn't a single Oyster Card reader in sight—and I haven't seen that style of glass-fronted booth in ages. It takes me all the way back to nostalgia-tinged memories of childhood, a school trip to the big city many years before I came to make my home here.

It's hard to see into the station beyond the ticket barriers. I can just about make out a broad corridor with shadowed openings to either side, but I see no sign of escalators. The Piccadilly line runs deep and land prices in this part of London are high. This must have been one of the stations designed to be served by lifts.

The constable who was on door duty comes hurrying back, leading Inspector Hoare, a bluff-looking guy who eyeballs us briefly and straightens his back at the sight of Jim's shoulder flashes. He looks as if he's just swallowed a frog. *You expected the monkey; you shouldn't be surprised when she brings the organ-grinder along.* "This is Chief Super Jim Grey, from TPCF," I tell him. "I'm Dr. O'Brien, TPCF Director." I show him just enough of a smile to draw the sting. "Now, suppose you show us what's wrong?"

"Yes, absolutely. This way." He waves us through the dead ticket barriers. "Watch your footing, there's been a leak in here recently and the floor can be slippery." He lifts up a torch and points it at a pitch-black tunnel behind the barriers. "That's the passage to the passenger lifts down to the platform. They're missing."

I follow Jim forward, keeping my eyes peeled. It's a not-dissimilar layout to the other lift-only Underground stations—a stubby corridor terminating in a dead end, lift doors to either side. Except, where the doors should be, there are solid stainless steel panels. They glint dully in Jim's torch beam. "These panels aren't supposed to be here?"

"Definitely not: they're supposed to be sliding doors opening onto functioning lifts. And there's more." Hoare walks past us in the direction of a door at the end of the passage, labelled STAFF ONLY. He produces a huge bunch of battered-looking keys and unlocks it. "This is a spiral staircase. Emergency exit, you really do not want to have to use it—there are over two hundred steps. At least there were yesterday." He pulls the door open, to reveal another stainless steel panel.

"These aren't some kind of regular barrier?" asks Jim. "Fitted during maintenance? Maybe TfL have some work scheduled?"

"Sorry, sir." Hoare sounds anything but sorry. "Already excluded. That was the first thing we looked into."

Jim steps close to the sheet of metal. He twists the head of his torch until the beam is dazzlingly sharp, then slowly directs it around the edges of the frame. "I see no prints or tracks."

"No, sir. Looks like it was installed from the rear side. It's the same with the lift shafts."

How do you take over a disused tube station? Well, if you can come in from below you can move heavy equipment into place without anyone noticing up top. The trouble is in the *from below* bit. The tube network is one of the most heavily traveled railway systems in the UK. Yes, it shuts down for four to five hours every night while they kill the traction power and carry out cleaning and maintenance work, but that doesn't mean it's deserted. Quite the opposite: it should be crawling with staff and contractors.

"We should take a look at the blocked tunnel entrance." I say aloud.

"I can sort that out," says Hoare. "But I'm not saying you'll find it useful."

"And look up everyone who's had maintenance access to the branch line in the past year."

Hoare twitches. "Now *that* is an interesting question . . ."

LATER, STANDING JUST BACK FROM THE ODD EXPERIMENTAL warning signs at the end of Platform 5 under Holborn, I check my watch. It's pushing eleven. "I'm keeping you from your meeting," I tell Jim. "This doesn't need both of us. Frankly, I think it's a wild goose chase and I'd just as soon throw it back at—"

"I already cancelled." Jim is dismissive. "While I should, strictly speaking, be flying a desk, it does me good to get out once in a while and stick my nose into the real world—even if it's a less productive use of my time than organizing people and issuing policy directives. Which this isn't, by the way—unproductive use of time, I mean, mine *or* yours. The more experience of routine investigations you get, the better you'll understand the needs of the police units you're supporting."

There is something wrong with Jim's analysis, something very slightly off-kilter, but it takes me a few seconds to put my finger on it: he's looking at my responsibilities purely from a policing point of view. He's put me in a frame and moved it sideways, obscuring part of the big picture of what the Home Office needs, much less what the Laundry is trying to accomplish here, and focusing on his own preoccupations. Does he expect me to go native? But then again, he *is* a cop. It would be weird if he didn't view everything in terms of his own organization's needs.

I'm about to mention this to him when the tracks beside the deserted platform begin to rattle and hum. A bright yellow locomotive comes rolling out of the tunnel at the opposite end of the platform at walking pace. It's a battery-electric locomotive: one of the maintenance machines that can operate in the tube tunnels when the traction current is switched off.

It grates to a halt just before it reaches us, the ventilation fans on the panels covering its immense lead-acid battery packs humming. The driver opens his door. "O'Brien and Grey?" he asks.

"That's us," Jim says. He climbs aboard, and I follow him. The cab is surprisingly cramped. It's short enough that there isn't room for me to lay Lecter's case on the floor in a straight line from front to back; the seats are padded flaps that fold down from the rear wall.

Our driver is a short, wiry guy in TfL uniform and Sikh turban. "What do you want to see today?" he asks.

"I think we'd like to look at the Aldwych branch line," I say brightly.

To my irritation, he doesn't respond until Jim echoes me: "We hear it's been blocked off overnight and we want to take a look at the obstruction."

"Right, that's what I thought. Let me call Earl's Court and confirm." He picks up an antiquated-looking Bakelite phone handset and begins speaking in an oddly formal steam-powered dialect of air traffic control jargon. When he hangs up he looks at us, avoiding my eyes: "We'll be moving soon."

We wait. And we wait some more. And suddenly the red light we're staring at just outside the tunnel mouth goes out and a green light goes on above it, and we begin to move forward. I haul out my smartphone and point it out the windscreen, recording video.

"Eyes left," says Jim. I pan to take in the left-hand side of the tunnel. We slowly gather speed until we're rattling along at what seems like a terrific clip, but is probably no more than ten miles per hour. More signal lights appear in the tunnel ahead, green with a diagonal white slash illuminated above them. "That's us," says the driver. We begin to slow. I glance at the tachograph in front of the driver and see it's reading seven or eight miles per hour. So that's how fast we're going when we see the red light ahead and he throws on the brakes. We screech to a halt in plenty of time to see the bricked-up circle of the dead end ahead of us, the track ending at a pair of suspiciously shiny-looking buffers.

"That's not supposed to be there," our driver complains. "It wasn't there yesterday—" He sounds as if he's doubting his own sanity.

"What wasn't?" I ask.

"The buffers. That wall." He points: "There's supposed to be another half mile of track, then the western platform. With an old Northern Line train parked alongside it."

"You're telling me someone just walled off a tube tunnel, overnight?" Jim sounds as disbelieving as I feel.

"Oh yes." Our driver checks a couple of dials, then throws a big switch: "All righty, that's the end of the line. Now, if you'd care to follow me single file to the other cab, it's time to go back . . ."

* * *

I GET BACK TO THE OFFICE JUST AFTER LUNCHTIME, AND STEAL
ten minutes to type up a report on whatever the hell just ate my morning. I upload the video from my phone and email it to Sam for his urgent attention—then head for the first of what promises to be a lengthy
series of sessions with a pair of very sympathetic investigators from the
IPCC. My afternoon is then enriched immeasurably by an hour with a
senior body from Human Resources at SS HQ, then half an hour alone
with my homework (I am ploughing my way through *Butterworths
Police Law* in my spare time, wondering what I did in a previous life
to deserve this), and then a briefing by two amiable Health and Safety
folks who are here to give me a helpful orientation briefing on what
I can do to contribute to a healthy and safe workplace environment.

Not going head-to-head with neo-Nazi superpowered hooligans
or maniacs possessed by class four demons would be a good start; not
being trusted to carry around a necromantic occult artifact with a
taste for souls that talks to me in my sleep would be another. But, as
Bob would say, I digress.

Around five, I find myself in another meeting. This time it's with
Ramona and Mhari, who in the past few weeks have gone from triggering panic attacks to being among the more comfortingly predict-
able elements of my life. (Strange days indeed.)

"So, I got the CRB-enhanced checks through on The Torch and
Busy Bee," says Mhari, "and the good news is, they're clean enough
for our purposes. Busy Bee had a checkered childhood, but we're required to ignore anything prior to the eighteenth birthday except con-
victions in adult court for serious criminal offenses—and she was
basically an activist. Went on marches, not burglaries. From university onwards she's been politically engaged, but at the good-citizen
end of the spectrum. We might have a headache if we were vetting her
for the Laundry, but for the Home Office . . . well, we can kick this
up a level if necessary. It's not as if we're overflowing with candidates,
is it? As for The Torch, he's boringly clean."

"Good. If you have any doubts you should ask Jim about Bee's background and what it means. Do you want to invite them back for a second interview if the news is good?" I ask.

"We can do that," she says. She sounds pleased with herself. "Should Jim sit in on this round?"

"Yes, about that," I say, and give them a dump of my current thoughts on the subject. "It's not that I don't trust him because of"—I point at the ceiling—"but more a case of my not wanting him to hitch our little red wagon too tightly to his own special interests. We have to keep the big picture in mind. We operate with the privileges and duties of police officers, but we are not here solely to provide the Met or ACPO with backup. We need police powers because we have to operate in public, but we're not here to play cops and robbers with bad guys: there's a reason we've got the word Coordination in our name."

"As you say."

Mhari looks as if she's chewing it over. Meanwhile, Ramona has another issue to raise: "Are we on to any other business yet? Have you had any new thoughts about the uniform question?"

I twitch, remembering the fate of my #2 suit. "There's definitely a case for us to have protective gear available for field work; I'm less sure about the brief for us to play superhero dress-up. How far did you get to with that, anyway?"

"I put in a bit of time earlier in the week and came up with some ideas, yes." Ramona wakes her tablet, swipes a few times to bring up an image, and spins it around so Mhari and I can see it. "What do you think?"

"I think"—I pause—"it looks very Daft Punk." Or maybe Daft Punk goes Territorial Support Group/SWAT team.

"Part of our remit is to counter the cult of personality that goes with the whole public perception of superheroes," Ramona points out. "Nothing tilts the scale away from grandstanding individual and towards organization body like having a de-individualizing uniform. Any uniform you decide we should standardize on needs to define a corporate identity—unavoidably one that plays off existing police uniforms, because of the nature of the organization. It also needs to provide protection from hazards, and you said you wanted to avoid the cheesecake problem." By which she means the popular expectation that women with exotic powers should wear six-inch stilettos, fishnets, and implausible corsetry while courting hypothermia as they fight crime. (An expectation which has more to do with the historic age and gender distribution of the weekly comics consumer demographic than with, for example, a PHANG's desire to avoid exposure to sunlight or my own strong preference not to show off my impending middle-aged spread.)

I look at Ramona's proposed outfits. The chrome and silver motorcycle helmets with odd bumps for antennae and mirrored-glass faceplates—I can see why that would appeal to Mhari. The pointy top to the helmet, with the blue beacon, is an obvious shout-out to Officer Friendly's kit. The rest of the outfit reminds me of something else: "These are motorcycle leathers."

"Actually, they're Kevlar," Ramona explains. "With cervical airbags and extra padding around ankles, kneecaps, and elbows—just like high-end biker kit. But they're actually next-generation riot gear. It looks like motorcycle protective gear because it's designed to do much the same job—provide whole-body protection from blunt or sharp trauma and being thrown about. The cervical airbag is a biker thing, and bikers are taking to them to save their necks when they put down a ride at high speed; it seems to me that if we end up going hand-to-hand against someone with super-strength, they'll be a lifesaver. Or at least a spinal-injury preventer. I've also spec'd out earthed chainmail inserts in case of lightning or tasers, and heavy-duty wards in case of the usual."

"I take your point," I say carefully. "But isn't the overall effect a bit Darth Vader? I mean, all you need to add is a cape and a light saber. We're supposed to be operating as police, not imperial stormtroopers. What message does this look send?"

"I am the law, motherfucker, are you feeling lucky?" suggests Ramona.

"People." I pause for a moment. "Remind me of Peel's Principles of Policing, again?" Ramona looks blank. Mhari looks skeptical. "Policing by consent," I hint. "Come on, the basic rules we play by? Minimum use of force to achieve compliance, the performance of a police force is judged best by how little crime takes place on their watch rather than by how many heads they kick in, that kind of thing?"

"Since when do flying chavs with the ability to set fire to anything they look at consent to be policed?" Mhari crosses her arms. "We don't get called out until there's *already* a public order problem. At which point . . ." She looks to Ramona for support.

"If a little bit of pre-emptive intimidation saves us from having to fight, I'm all in favor of it," she agrees.

"Hmm." I stare at the blueprints for the Mark One Home Office Imperial Stormtrooper uniform some more. The male version comes over as distinctly Judge Dredd, but the female fitted variant is mercifully cleavage-free, doesn't show off the wearer's cellulite, and has boots that look like they'd be more at home kicking down doors than tottering around a bordello. "Need to sleep on this. Huh." Next item. "Mhari, did you get anywhere with the origin story?"

Mhari shakes her head tiredly. "I was talking to Jez Wilson, Gerry Lockhart, and Pete Russell—they've formed an ad-hoc committee to draw together a big lie suitable for public disclosure that remains consistent with everything that's already accidentally leaked. It's not just a front-page story, but a bunch of elaborate conspiracy theories to satisfy the tinfoil hat crowd. The headliner is that it's a mutant descendant of SARS, but the backup stories blame the Fukushima meltdowns, mercury preservatives in vaccines, and a rogue nanobiological warfare experiment by the US government."

"Well." I stare at Mhari. She stares back at me. "I take it you're not happy with these options."

"Are you?" she shoots right back.

"Dumb and dumber." I shake my head. "On the other hand, the kind of people who obsess at length about where superpowers come from . . ."

"We just need to distract them for a couple more years," Mhari reminds me. "Make them keep chasing after half-truths and lies. Sooner or later, CASE NIGHTMARE GREEN is going to leak—it's just a matter of time—and then we won't need an origin story anymore."

"Well." I resist the urge to clutch my head. "I suppose you're right, in the long term, but none of those are exactly helpful—"

"Why not?" asks Ramona.

"Because they all push epidemic or pollution narratives." I resist the urge to snap: "They paint us as *contaminated*. It's deeply unsettling to ordinary members of the public because it has echoes of ritual uncleanliness that go back a long way. The whole superhero narrative is flawed, anyway—it's a stand-in for the old-time Greek and Roman pantheons, ultra-powerful gods with dysfunctional emotional lives—we're going to be perceived as unstable by default, and now we've got some committee trying to convince us to play the part of contaminated untouchables?"

"You've got to admit, it's a step up from Dracula," Mhari says drily.

"Well." I try not to roll my eyes. Then I remember my early morning legwork. "Which reminds me: something new came up this morning." I tell them about Aldwych, then add the latest report from Sam. "The actual tunnel entrance has been blocked with brick backed with reinforced concrete; nobody's sure how thick it is, but it's a very professional job. TfL are looking into the maintenance contractors' logs to see who might have had access to the spur tunnel, but it's possible whoever decided to block it off ran an entire train load of cement, aggregate, and other construction materials inside before they did the deed."

"How much tunnel are we talking about?" Ramona asks.

I read my email, repeating the highlights aloud: "Two tunnels with platforms connected via an overhead walkway . . . we're looking at one kilometer of underground railway tunnel, and two platforms—one of which has been converted, with its track section replaced by offices, storage facilities, and a 1950s hostel for immigrant laborers which is said to be haunted. (I'm not making that up.)" I look up from my tablet. "Any suggestions?"

Mhari is skeptical. "Doesn't sound like superpowers to me. Sounds like the opposite, in fact—someone without superpowers. Like, oh, maybe another department that didn't tell TfL they were borrowing a semi-surplus tube station for something? Ministry of Defense? They used to use the deep tube tunnels for bomb-proof storage—"

"But why—"

"Wild goose chase, Mo," Ramona says firmly. "Just because the Transport Police thought it was flaky, it does not follow that it's *our* kind of flaky."

I really *do* roll my eyes this time. "You think they gulled me."

"I didn't say that." I notice Ramona's shared glance with Mhari. "You should consider taking some time off. I know you think you've got a lot of catching up to do, but you can only work seventy hours a week with homework on top for so long before you burn out."

"Yes!" says Mhari. "You're not a twenty-something, Mo. You don't have the stamina."

"And you do? You're a—" I catch myself just in time.

"*Yes,*" she snaps. "I can work a hundred hours a week if I have to. I just have to drink someone's, someone's—" She takes a deep breath. "It's not worth it. Not unless it's an *emergency*. Mo, we need you intact. You've been going at the job like a lunatic since we got back from Manchester: apart from that radio you listen to after everyone else clocks off, you've got no outlets. But it's business as usual. What happens if an emergency comes up and you've got no reserves? We don't have a fully formed management structure; we haven't in-processed the new recruits for training yet—we've been in business for barely a month. You're still a single point of failure for the unit, and you're actively damaging yourself."

"Mo, please"—Ramona joins in on her side before I can reply—"take some time off. If you're going to work weekends, at least give yourself three evenings a week when you clock off at six and don't come in until nine the next morning. Or start taking your weekends seriously. Or *something*."

I look between them, feeling bewildered by their betrayal. On a coldly rational level, they're absolutely right, but on a gut level it feels like a stab in the back. "You planned this!"

"Yes, Mo." Ramona gives me a look that suddenly makes me wonder how *I* look to *her* right now. "You're not going to slow down on your own, are you? You've been running with the brakes off ever since the treaty meeting—" She stops as Mhari looks away from me briefly, tension evident in the set of her neck. *Oh.*

Yes, I am probably working too hard; I've got a department to set up and insufficient staff and support. And besides, what is there waiting for me to go home to? A cat? A bed haunted by ghosts? Yes, I admit my dancing partner has been back for a few whirls around the nightmare, and has given me a pointed nudge or two in the direction of an evil dream opera score. But that's why I'm doing it, that's why I'm working every day until I drop: it's the only way to be sure I'll sleep soundly. "I'll think about it."

"You'll have to do better than that." Mhari winds up to badger me again. I'm not sure how she's doing this: her body language reads *scared/juggling live grenades.* Am I still that frightening? "It'll be nightfall in, oh, another hour. You can go home, but wouldn't you rather come out with us? Girls' night out, team-building exercise, whatever you want to call it."

"I don't feel much like dancing, thanks."

"You don't have to; you just have to let go of the job for a few hours! Can you even do that anymore? Because if not, you just proved my point."

"Oh hell." I surrender: she's got me bang to rights. "If you've got nothing better to do than drag me round wine bars for an evening, I shall just have to surrender gracefully." I force myself to smile. In truth, there's a knot of tension behind my sternum that does not dissolve in relief at the idea of spending an evening in the company of a vampire and a mermaid who both once upon a time had carnal relationships with my currently separated husband. It sounds dangerously like a mashup of *The Addams Family* with *Friends*, and if that doesn't have you reaching for the Gaviscon, your stomach is stronger than mine. But on the other hand, it's an excuse to avoid a certain textbook that's been gnawing at my brain of late—and we don't *have to* talk about Bob. "Let me wrap up in here and I'll see you at seven."

. . . AND THAT IS THE START OF A SLIPPERY SLOPE WHICH ENDS with me standing on a spotlit stage to give the performance of my life to an audience of thousands bewitched by a Mad Scientist, blood trickling from my fingertips as I struggle for control of the melody that will usher in the overture to the end of the world.

But that doesn't happen until much later . . .

PART 3

"GOOD HEAVENS, MISS SAKAMOTO! YOU'RE BEAUTIFUL!"

13.

CAPTIVATION

WE MEET IN THE LOBBY A WHISKER AFTER SEVEN AND FORM A post-work posse: one of those groups of hard-partying office ladies you see around central London after working hours. In our case the partying is relatively sedate. One of us is in a wheelchair, another can't go anywhere with black-light illumination, and I'm over forty and have been working so hard I'm feeling my age.

Luckily there's a nice little bistro round the corner that has a duck confit to die for, a shelf of fascinating artisanal London gins which they serve in ancient jam jars, and modern jazz background music that doesn't set my teeth on edge. So that's where we start, with the idea of working our way on from there.

We eat, and we talk, and Ramona and Mhari systematically steal the conversation whenever I try to steer it back towards work. To my horror, they want to talk about *personal* stuff. But not *my* personal stuff: *their* personal stuff. Ramona has been stuck in a very expensive hotel room since she arrived—she needs a whirlpool bath more than she needs a bed—and she's having difficulty looking for a flat to rent that is wheelchair-accessible and has a suitable bathroom but doesn't cost a bazillion pounds a week. On the other hand, she's commuting from the North Sea each weekend: "I just go home and head for the unthinking depths," she says, "where I school." You couldn't make it up.

Mhari looks at her enviously. "No strings on me," she says, uptight. Ramona, of course, takes this as a challenge and enlists my assistance in crowbarring Mhari open. By the third large glass of pinot I wish she hadn't; I've learned more than I ever wanted to about Mhari's problems hanging on to long-term boyfriends, even before she contracted her unfortunate condition. "'S funny: I should have gotten my fangs into him a lot harder, except I didn't *have* fangs back then," she says of her most recent ex. She chuckles unhappily at some personal joke that I don't get, then upends the last few drops from the bottle into her glass. "You don't know what you've got until it slips through your fingers."

This strikes uncomfortably close to home, so I ask them whether they're also wondering if these three-sigma and above superpowers are on a one-way trip to K syndrome city, thereby giving them an excuse to glare at me and change the subject. Derailing: three can play at that game.

We manage to hit another wine bar but it's only just past ten o'clock when I realize I'm yawning so furiously I have to excuse myself. I'm wobbling on my feet, and not just from three glasses of wine. The Japanese have a word for it, of course: *karoshi*, death through overwork.

I'm tired and tipsy, so instead of grappling with bus and tube I use an app to call a private hire cab. I pay cash and the driver drops me at my front door, where I stagger in, go straight upstairs, and face-plant on the bed. It's my first undisturbed and dreamless night of sleep in ages.

A week passes. I attend more meetings and training courses than seems humanly possible, get politely grilled by an Assistant Undersecretary to the Home Office (actually a terrifyingly senior civil servant, but I'm properly prepared for our session this time), get our proposed uniforms redesignated as "protective clothing" (which applies a whole different regulatory brush to them and *totally* gives me cover for banishing skintight Lycra from the picture forever—it's a fire risk, don't you know), then spend an inconclusive and somewhat lachrymose evening with Bob before he ships out to Belize to inspect a ruined temple in the jungle that Angleton vandalized thirty years ago for some reason.

I am failing to exercise properly, eating badly, and working too hard. I can't shake the feeling that I'm underqualified for this job and I'll be found out at any time; also, that it's not a role I'm temperamentally suited to. On the other hand, with M. and R. tag-teaming me I am keeping back three evenings a week for myself. I continue to play my instrument, periodically misuse Dr. Armstrong's office as a confessional, and maintain level flight rather than embarking on a downward spiral. Which is about the best I can hope for under the circumstances.

LATER IN THE WEEK AND TO EVERYBODY'S SURPRISE, TWO NEW analysts and a receptionist join the team—and then our first two actual card-carrying Home Office superheroes arrive: The Torch and Busy Bee.

The Torch is nineteen and comes from Macclesfield. He's about one-ninety centimeters tall, painfully skinny (but stronger than he looks), and not academically inclined. Descended from mill workers: Dad's a builder, Mum's a plumber, scraped a couple of GCSE passes, and left school at sixteen to follow Dad into the building trade. Ambition: to work his way all the way to the top, which is defined by the rarefied job description of "skilled bricklayer." Which, to his credit, he was on course to become—until three months ago, when he discovered that he could light cigarettes by snapping his fingers. Then bonfires. Then convert a fifty-quid B&Q barbecue into a blazing molten Dali sculpture, which is when the *Macclesfield Express* dubbed him The Torch and offered him a cape and a mask in return for an extremely silly front-page photo op. Prior to us inviting him down to the Big Smoke for an interview, his furthest excursion from home was via Manchester Airport for a package holiday in Marbella when he turned eighteen. The poor lad is utterly out of his depth and painfully naive, but he means well and seems to cotton to the idea of a higher calling in the Police. As long as I assign someone to wipe his nose and ensure he has a fresh change of underwear every morning, he ought to pull through the seething mass of culture shock that is his first exposure to London.

Busy Bee is going to be more of a handful, but I think I've got a grip on where she's coming from, if not where she's going. She's twenty-six and has a file with the Met's Forward Intelligence Unit that had me arguing back and forth with Jim for days before we agreed to see her. The file was opened in her late teens, back in the Bad Old Days when the Met were Doing Stuff We Don't Admit We Do Anymore Because It's Not Allowed. Stuff like Spying On ~~Domestic Terrorists~~ Political Activists. Or, in Bee's case, teenage feminists.

Some throwback in FIT was terrified that she might hurl herself under the King's racehorse at the Grand National—after all, if it could happen in 1913, surely it's still a clear and present danger? (Votes for Women still being a notoriously controversial political hot potato in the twenty-first century.) Consequently, her file is the Police equivalent of Green Kryptonite, except that she hasn't actually ever been charged with—much less convicted of—anything. So let's provisionally re-file her record under Movie Prop Kryptonite and move swiftly on.

It turns out that our *Apis agilis* comes from a long line (well, at least one generation) of *New Statesman*–reading bolshie teacher-activists of the kind the Education Secretary sees under every bed; Dad rose to the dizzy height of town councilor, while Mum continues to teach social sciences at a former polytechnic. Bee got involved in reproductive rights activism in her teens, went on counter-demos against anti-abortion activists, and generally made a bit of a buzz. Then she headed off to university to study political science and economics as a prelude to Taking Over the World, and lowered her sights to taking over one student society at a time (for course credits on the pol. sci. side of her degree).

That was before she acquired the ability to speed herself up by a factor of ten, which happened ten weeks ago when she darted into a busy road to rescue a runaway two-year-old from a runaway cement mixer, under the unblinking gaze of an experimental hi-def traffic camera. TV news coverage ensued, followed by the usual fifteen minutes of fame (condensed down, in her case, to a ninety-second feel-good slot at the end of the hourly cycle). She can only do it as long as she can hold her breath—she can't absorb oxygen or discharge carbon dioxide from the linings of her lungs while in super-speed mode—but what she can accomplish in that time is impressive. During our skills matrix review Ramona added "Can administer wedgies at a rate of five supervillains per second" to the checklist. I was tempted to leave it in, despite the HomeSec's notoriously unpredictable sense of humor—and though I cut it in the end, it's not far from the forefront of my thinking about how we could deploy her. Also, she's cute (in a petite black-with-yellow-stripes-and-dimples sort of way).

All we need is for our next pair of candidates to clear the Enhanced CRB checks and we might even be able to start training them for deployment.

ONE AFTERNOON, I'M IN A MEETING WITH JIM AND THE ANALYSTS (now augmented by Gillian and Karim, two new transfers from the Laundry) when the Met ECC phones me to pass on the unwelcome news that the elusive Professor Freudstein has struck again.

Ironically, it happens while we're sitting around a table brainstorming possible approaches to the nascent Mad Scientist Menace. Freudstein—and our signal lack of success in getting a lead on him, not to mention his stolen forty million pounds and rare musical score collection—is a persistent irritant, one of a growing list of problems that are on our collective to-do list, along with the likes of the Mandate. We'll get around to them just as soon as the agency is fully staffed and ready to move from setup to active operations, honest. Until then, all we can really do is map out the beat we're going to have to patrol.

For his part, Jim is convinced that the MSM is real: "Freudstein looks like a fairly plausible type specimen," he explains, "and that's disturbing, because the thing about criminals of a given type is that for every one we know about, there are usually four more we don't. Also, we haven't managed to collar him yet. Which is not a good sign."

"Yes, but our prior probabilities are—" I stop dead, realizing there's stuff I can't talk about with Jim. Sam and Nick are cleared. Gillian and Karim, coming from the Laundry, are also cleared: I could talk to them about Ellis Billington and JENNIFER MORGUE if necessary. But while Jim is cleared for joint operations that require police liaison, I'm not inclined to be loose-lipped about other operations around him as long as the SA isn't certain he's on the up-and-up. Even operations that are over and dead and buried. (Anyway, Billington wasn't exactly a Mad Scientist. Mad *Businessman*, maybe, but Scientist? I'm not so sure.) I clear my throat, then hesitantly finish my sentence with "—unclear."

"Not really!" Gillian volunteers brightly. "We've seen several three-sigma instances of intelligence enhancement in the past few months. For example there's Brainbox, who aced *Brain of Britain* last month and maxed out on Mensa's IQ test. There may be many more low-grade examples, but they don't stick out like a sore thumb. Intelligence isn't like flight or pyrokinesis—it's something all of us have."

"Anyway, you don't have to be terribly intelligent to complete a PhD," Karim grumps. "You just need to be stupidly persistent. If anything, being too smart gets in the way—"

"How would you proactively identify a Mad Scientist, anyway?" asks Sam, dragging the round-table back on-topic before Karim starts fulminating about the state of his student loans.

Jim responds. "Let's see. Traditional Mad Scientists aren't team players, are they? And science is very much a team sport, this century. You could probably go some way towards narrowing the field by looking for sudden resignations from research groups or by hunting for researchers who've suddenly stopped publishing." He makes it sound so easy. "Unfortunately the lead time on publishing a peer-reviewed paper is months to years, so there's a lot of lag in the system." He continues to undermine his own case: "And researchers quit for any number of reasons. They have babies, or they take a highly paid job offer from a bank, or they just get bored and take up martial arts. That happened to one really famous mathematician: these days she's the world's third-ranking female cage fighter."

Cage-fighting mathematicians; violin-playing philosophers. Now that I think about it, there's probably room in our unit for an epistemologist to work on Theory of Supervillains. I wonder idly if I could convince someone else to take over as director so I can step down and colonize that niche, then shake myself. "We're not here to discuss ex-scientists, we're here to figure out how to proactively identify mad ones with four- or five-sigma superpowers," I remind him. "Although it *does* seem to be a rather difficult project."

Karim speaks up again. "Rather than looking for signs of emergence, maybe we could look at their goals instead?" he asks diffidently. "Has Freudstein said what he wants?"

"No," says Jim. He frowns, looking as worried as I feel. "And if he did, could we trust him to tell the truth about his motivations? Mad Scientists aren't really a problem unless they're also brilliant. That's part of the problem space. Dumb Mad Scientists would be a bit pathetic: I think we can ignore them. Ditto the lazy variety. So we're looking for hyperintelligent, energetic Mad Scientists. And the brilliant ones are going to tell us whatever they think is most likely to cause us to do whatever they want us to do, rather than gloating about their real motivations."

"Like what?" I ask. "What would a Mad Scientist conceivably *want us to do* . . . ?" The question hangs in the air like an unexploded grenade.

"Um." Jim, so highly articulate most of the time, is actually unable to frame a reply. After a moment, he explains: "Freudstein has very efficiently raised hell while concealing his motivations. So I'd have to say, insufficient data."

"So we need to focus on gathering data." I smile at him to defuse the implied criticism, and continue: "It seems to me that Mad Science can't come cheap. They would obviously need a research center or lab of their own, and the money to pay for equipment and materials and electricity. Also, minions to do the legwork—install equipment, run experiments, keep records, do statistical analysis. And we *know* Freudstein has minions—unless he started by figuring out how to clone himself for the British Library robbery. So we're not looking for an Igor, we're hunting an entire team of disillusioned postdoc researchers whose parent institutions didn't renew their rolling annual employment contract and who think they're working for a respectable company doing research into whatever the Mad Scientist wants.

"The flip side . . . the flip side is that scientific research is a bottomless money pit. You can approximate Doing Science to standing on the Crack of Doom throwing banknotes down it by the double-handful, in the hope that if you choke the volcano with enough paper it will cough up the One Ring. Unless you're doing pure mathematics or philosophy, of course, in which case it's HB pencils and ruled A4 notepads all the way down. So where there's a Mad Scientist pursuing their hobby horse, even if it's something as innocuous as developing a new taxonomy of wood-boring beetles, I think we're likely to find some kind of low-input, high-output income stream, operating with questionable regard to legality. So we'd be looking for organizations that keep a low public profile, employ a fair number of high-powered staff who go about their tasks in secret, and which are headed by people who picked up a PhD or two by accident before they heard their true calling. Finally, they'd have an incredibly opaque income stream. Identifying such organizations is really a job for the National Crime Agency, who can distinguish a Mad Scientist Menace from a regular organized crime ring by profiling the folks at the top. Of course this breaks down if by a huge coincidence our Mad Scientist is the heir to the Duchy of Cornwall, or the alter-ego of the Duke of Westminster, in which case we're looking for a demented lord spending money like water. But that's a low probability, I believe." I look at Jim. "What do you think?"

Jim looks slightly taken aback. "Are you sure you're not a Mad Scientist yourself?" he asks. "You've certainly got a grip on the psychological profile, and your ability to monologue—"

That's when my phone rings.

"O'Brien speaking."

It's our new receptionist, Lizzie. "Dr. O'Brien? I've got a call for you from the Emergency Control Center at New Scotland Yard. Inspector Cooper on the line . . ."

"Thanks, put them through. Hello? Inspector? I'm Dr. O'Brien. You asked for me?"

"Yes, you're flagged on our alert list to be advised of any developments involving alias Professor Freudstein?"

"I am. Yes?" I sit up straight. Across the table I see everyone staring at me.

"We have just received a communication from Freudstein, or someone claiming to be them. The call originated with a previously inactive prepaid phone, bought in cash from a major supermarket chain six months ago, somewhere in Edgeware—we're trying to locate the phone and its carrier now, but it looks like the call was planned to minimize traceability. The caller said they were speaking on behalf of Professor Freudstein, specified that you, that is, Dr. Dominique O'Brien, Transhuman Police Coordination Force, were to be notified, and he gave a codeword previously associated with the perpetrators of a previously unattributed incident three days ago."

"What was the previous?" I ask.

"I'm sorry, I'm not at liberty to tell you. You need to take it up through channels—Superintendent Drummond at CNC Sellafield can brief you. The codeword Freudstein said to associate with your name is 'Infinity Concerto,' whatever that means."

I end the call hyperventilating: Freudstein coming to the attention of the Civil Nuclear Constabulary can't be good.

Jim gets there first. "I heard Freudstein . . . ?"

"Sellafield," I say bleakly. "Freudstein did something there *three days ago*. He's just claimed responsibility and given us a codeword—and he's hanging it on my neck."

"Sellafield?" That's Karim. He sounds shocked.

I look at Jim. "We need to get in touch with a Superintendent Drummond. Find out what the hell is going on and why Freudstein wants to talk." Because they never hand you a codeword unless they *want* to talk, from a position of strength. "Can you follow this up for me?"

"Yes." Jim stands up. "I'll go make some calls. Looks like Freudstein's decided to give us some actual insights into the Mad Scientist Menace. Let's just hope they're not misleading and deadly."

SIX O'CLOCK ROLLS AROUND AND I'M STILL IN THE OFFICE, ONE ear tuned to the radio—late summer is the Proms season, the mammoth sequence of standing-room-only concerts that are to classical music in London as Wimbledon is to tennis—so there's a new concert broadcast from the Albert Hall just about every night. I'm using it to try to distract myself from worrying about that call while I update my weekly situation report to the SA. There's a knock at my office door: "Come in," I say without looking up.

"Hello, Dominique. Do you have a few minutes?"

It's Jim. "Sure." I smile tiredly. "I was just about ready to wrap up. Did you get anywhere?"

"Yes—" He looks around my office. "Yes, I did." He sounds frustrated. "It's Freudstein's work, although they didn't know it at the time. Three days ago." He shakes his head, face unreadable.

"What did Freudstein do?"

"Tampered with the national plutonium stockpile."

"He— *What?*"

"He didn't steal anything: he just wanted to send us a message. A very scary one, in my opinion, but a nuanced one. Pretty much what you'd expect from a Mad Scientist with a genius-level IQ who wanted to rattle our cage. It might have been better in some ways if he *had* stolen something, frankly: at least we'd have a clear-cut idea of what was going on. The implications are still sinking in, which is why they're keeping a tight lid on it—DA-Notices on the news media, massive security panic, circular firing squad, the whole nine yards."

"He didn't steal anything—" I stop. "Oh, you said tampering. What *kind* of tampering?"

"They're not entirely certain yet: it's going to take a full audit of the contents of SPRS—the Sellafield Product and Residues Store—to rule out the possibility that the *obvious* tampering was a decoy to divert attention from some other nefarious activity. I mean, we know he messed up a bunch of archives at the BL to conceal the theft of manuscripts, but this is worse. Someone who is now tentatively identified as Freudstein or his accomplices broke into SPRS, got into part of the secure plutonium store, and left behind additional storage flasks containing approximately twelve kilograms of mixed-isotope metallic instant sunshine. Just in case nobody noticed, they painted them lime green and sprayed CND symbols and smiley faces on top." He sighs heavily. "*Needless* to say they had to get past razor-wire fences, cameras, dog patrols, an electric fence, more cameras, and into a heavily reinforced concrete building patrolled by trigger-happy officers of the Civil Nuclear Constabulary armed with fully automatic weapons and an Army surface-to-air missile battery on top—because when they finish building the annex, it's going to contain nearly a hundred tons of plutonium. Twelve kilos is enough to build two basic atom bombs . . . heads are going to roll."

"I'll say." I hit "save" and shove my keyboard away: the weekly sitrep suddenly seems trivial. "That's what he broke into? The secure plutonium store? Just to send us a card saying, *Hi, I baked you an atom bomb but I eated it*?" Butterflies take flight in my stomach. "Jesus."

"The first step is to make sure nothing else is missing. Freudstein could have played a shell-game on us, after all. Swapped storage flasks around . . . the second step is, I'm told you can usually identify the production source for these isotopes by looking at their relative abundance. There are several other nations who might take a keen interest in checking their deposits for unauthorized overdrafts. But to do that means confessing your sins to the IAEA, who leak like a garden sprinkler and who will go totally apeshit if they think someone got at the UK stockpile. I mean, we'll never hear the end of it. Questions in the UN Security Council, ambassadors being called in, that kind of thing. As soon as it hits the press—and it's too big to hush up—it's going to go nuclear, if you'll pardon the expression. And then there's the question of how Freudstein did it in the first place. On which subject they're going to want our input." Jim sounds gloomy.

"But we've barely got anything on him!" I feel like tearing my hair out.

"Yes, I told them that. But we're the Home Office supervillain experts. They're not happy. I reckon we can expect to be carpeted by Her Upstairs no later than Monday. Sooner, if it goes back to COBRA—they were briefed on the original break-in, but the Freudstein angle is new."

"Whoop-de-doo. Do we have a report on how he—no, they—got through the security perimeter?"

"That's going to be classified, but we can probably get hold of it if you really need it. But. Hmm. Why did you say 'they'?"

"Oh, come on. The profiling exercise we've been doing—if there *is* a real Mad Scientist Menace, then it's probably more accurate to call it a Mad Science Corporate Menace. You don't brew up pocket death rays in your basement all on your lonesome—"

"What about the Laundry's extradimensional summoning devices?" Jim leans forward. "I heard some of your devices are ultra-portable, compact. *Programmable.* We're talking laptop-sized, not particle accelerators."

"Maybe, maybe, but that stuff's *dangerous.* One misplaced semicolon in your program and an extradimensional amoeba shows up inside your brain and cores you from the inside out. Our researchers practice pair programming for a reason—there's more chance of one of them spotting a lethal bug before they find it the hard way." I shudder. *Leave that stuff to Bob.* "Our own equipment and materials are heavily classified and protected by our usual security geas—oath, that is, or maybe curse of obedience. It provides *slightly* more security than your regular oath to Queen and Country. Meanwhile, if you try to develop a nondeterministic invocation geometry engine from scratch, you run the risk of getting overconfident and finding out the hard way that there's a memory leak. That's why progress in the occult sciences was so slow until we developed digital computers *and* had a war-footing organization working on it."

But the thought has a certain nagging consistency. What if Freudstein is an insider? With some level of access to our standard code libraries and some theoretical background, a lone highly intelligent Mad Scientist could play catch-up surprisingly fast. Build a whiteroom clone of our core tools, working at home on their own time . . . Worse, what if Freudstein is a front for an entire insider team—a government department that's gone rogue? I can't see why such a group would want all the unwelcome publicity Freudstein is drawing down, but just because I can't see it doesn't mean there's no fire concealed behind all the smoke and tabloid headlines. I don't want to share this last insight with Jim, but it's definitely something to suggest to Internal Affairs via Dr. Armstrong.

"It's getting late," says Jim. "I was thinking about looking for something to eat. Do you have any plans for dinner?"

"No, I just need to finish this report and I'm done—"

"Let me rephrase: Are you hungry? If so, would you like to accompany me to a restaurant?"

I blink. This *is* one of my three-nights-off, and I've completely forgotten to make any plans. "I can do dinner, but I need to finish this report first. Give me ten minutes?"

"Happy to. Lobby in fifteen?" He rises smoothly to his feet and looks at me expectantly.

"That'll be great," I tell him, and I mean it. Then I go back into deep focus. I've got a weekly situation report to file, after all; and I can slip my theories about Freudstein in with the rest of it.

I MAKE MY WAY DOWN TO THE LOBBY AROUND SIX THIRTY AND find Jim cooling his heels there. His face lights up when he sees me. "Mind if I drive?" he asks. "It'll save me coming back here afterwards."

"Happily." I follow him down to the basement garage, past Ramona's lurking vehicle of the uncanny—maintaining its white van disguise for the time being—to a silver BMW Z4 roadster. It's parked with its soft top folded away. "Nice motor. Yours?"

"Mine," he confirms as he zaps it awake with his keyfob. "I have to do a lot of driving."

I slide my violin into the narrow gap behind the passenger seat, then climb in. I find it a snug fit; Jim wears his car like a glove. He glances over his shoulder and gooses it to life, backs out of his slot, then screeches up the exit ramp before giving way to pedestrians who are crossing the entrance. Clearly he's no Steve McQueen. The sky is gray and threatens us with rain, but he drives with the roof down. I hunch behind the windscreen, very glad I tied my hair back. He drives aggressively (*everyone* in London drives aggressively), but attentively, sticking to speed limits and paying a lot of attention to his mirrors. "Cyclists," he explains, while stopped at a traffic signal: "They're the biggest hazard right now, especially at dusk. Most drivers are blind to them, especially if they're running without lights. But if you don't spot one coming up in your blind spot . . ."

"I get it," I say. Bob and I don't own a car, although we both have driving licenses. "We didn't discuss where we were going."

He gives me a sidelong grin, then the lights change and his eyes go back to their hazard perception scan as he flings the sports car around a road pillow and a chicane and nails the needle to the speed limit. (Which is only thirty, but it feels a lot faster with wind in your hair and bugs in your teeth.) "Trust me?" he asks.

"Okay . . ."

It is an early autumn evening in London and for an instant I'm back in my early twenties again, a time when I was in love with a strong, witty man who had a sports car and wanted to impress me (that was a more innocently dangerous time, two decades ago). It was a time of naive pleasure, when all life's possibilities seemed open to me, before we married and subsequently divorced. I'm older now, but Jim is not only strong and witty, but a whole lot wiser than David ever was—and I suspect more dangerous in a fight (for all that David did military service in Israel). So the flash of déjà vu is not unwelcome. But I'm older now, and I recognize certain warning signs, starting with the pocket rocket whose passenger seat I'm now strapped into.

"So, Jim, I take it you're not paying your kids' university fees?" I prod.

"Nope." I wonder for a moment if he's being terse because he's looking for a narrow turnoff from Victoria Embankment, or because I struck an exposed nerve, but then he explains: "Sally lives with Liz, and Liz out-earns me—she's a QC. She got the house, I got what she calls the mid-life penis extension." He pats the steering wheel affectionately. "That was three years ago. Time flies." Then his head swivels rapidly as he stops and reverses rapidly into a snug parking space. "I'll worry about the university tuition when Sally gets a place—she's sixteen."

So my guess was right. "Was it the job?" I ask.

"Which one? We both took our chances in a relationship-eating profession." He looks morose for a moment, then his expression clears: "Come on, I need to put the hood up before we go eat. It'd be a shame if it rained."

The restaurant turns out to be a trattoria near Covent Garden Market, a short walk from our parking space. Jim holds the door open for me, a slightly old-fashioned gesture I wasn't expecting. "Reservation for two, name of Grey," he tells the maître d', and insists I go first as that worthy leads us to a table with a commanding view of the London Transport Museum. We're not far from the Strand, and the presence of the concrete-blocked Aldwych tube station nags at my attention like a loose tooth. "If you want wine, be my guest," he offers. "I'm strictly on the wagon when I'm driving."

"And I've got a meeting tomorrow at nine o'clock," I say, trying not to wince at the thought. "Maybe some other time." I pick up the menu. "Do you have any suggestions?" *Do you come here often?*

"I'm told it's all good, you can't go wrong." He studies his menu for a bit. "But I think I'll keep it simple: the bruschetta followed by the lasagne."

I roll the mental dice, decide to try the mozzarella and tomato salad, then the spaghetti aglio e olio. "I wish I could keep my life as simple as this menu."

A waiter turns up to take our order. After he's gone Jim starts up the conversation again, with a leading question: "I can't help noticing you spend an inordinate number of hours in the office." I can imagine him continuing: *And one of your colleagues mentioned a tense domestic situation.* Because offices leak.

I wrinkle my nose. "My husband and I both work for the Laundry. No children, not that it matters. Yes, things have been tense lately. He's, um, living elsewhere at the moment. Trial separation." The words somehow make it sound more final than it is.

"I'm sorry." His pro forma apology closes off that line of conversation before I can succumb to the temptation to use him as a shoulder to unload on—highly unprofessional, I know. "All I can say is, I hope it gets better for you."

"To tell the truth, I'm too busy to notice right now." Bob's bouncing all over the map, I've managed to cut back to working only seventy hours a week, and I don't have time to deal right now. "I've been walking the all-work-and-no-play treadmill for a while. I really ought to get out more."

"You're here, aren't you? It's a start."

"Yes, but I haven't been to a concert or a theater or the opera for months. I haven't even tried to score tickets to any of the Proms." Even before the current crisis I was withdrawing: the panic attacks I get in public places with no cover and too many people had been growing for a long time. If anything they're a little better these days, since Agent CANDID went on the shelf and Dr. O'Brien the Bureaucratic Functionary came out of the closet. And some of the mythological tropes . . . *they cut too close to the bone. The bone violin. The—*

"How about you?"

"Now that you mention it, hmm. I was spending too much time in Aberdeen and Fishguard earlier in the year. Wonderful places, but not exactly capital-city-grade cultural beacons," he says drily. (When he's thinking, he goes very still, I notice. Bob gets twitchy.) "Just as the whole three-sigma superpower thing blew up out of virtually nowhere, in a matter of months. Which ate all my spare time especially after I discovered I was . . ." He looks rueful. "I haven't been spending enough weekends with Sally. Liz has been nagging me to pull my weight, and I'm afraid she's right."

"I imagine looking after a sixteen-year-old must be a bit of a headache."

"Oh, it's mostly about building trust. She's still in the *ugh, parents, uncool* stage, but she's self-aware enough to know that it's just something she's going through. So I'm trying to give her enough space that she doesn't feel the need to burn bridges she might want to maintain later. The best thing you can do is provide them with a support framework rather than a cage. Don't try to micromanage and overprotect them, let them know they can come to you when they've got problems, and as long as they've got a reasonably level head, that's what they'll do." He pauses. "And I try to keep a poker face whenever she introduces me to a boyfriend."

His expression does something to me: I grin at him, then giggle, and he chuckles, and we end up laughing at each other. In my case it's at the vision of a typical teenage male's reaction at being invited home to meet the girlfriend's parents for the first time and discovering that Daddy is Robocop; I'm not so sure what Jim is laughing at.

"I try to go easy on them," he adds when the chuckles subside. "We were all young once."

"Oh, I know some people who weren't," I say carelessly, thinking of Angleton. It brings up an incongruous sense of absence, the missing-tooth outline of a vacated life. "Um." I pick up my water glass. "To absent friends."

"Absent friends," he echoes with a clink of glassware and a quizzical expression. "Someone close?"

"Co-worker," I say automatically. "Known him for nearly ten years. Died a couple of months ago."

"Oh, that incident . . . I'm sorry for your loss." And he does indeed look genuinely, respectfully concerned.

Food happens, and so does conversation that is amusing and intelligent and that steers clear of the two pitfalls of work (not safe for conversation in public) and messy personal entanglements (not safe for conversation in private). I actually enjoy myself, so I'm a little sad to see the dessert menu and realize that my eyes are larger than my stomach. "This isn't going to work," I sigh. "I can't stay here forever. And anyway, I've got that nine o'clock meeting tomorrow."

"Not to worry, I'll give you a ride home." Jim starts looking to catch the waiter's eye. I've been trying for a few minutes, fruitlessly—the invisibility thing is particularly infuriating in restaurants—but he has the middle-aged alpha male Gaze of Waiter Summoning down pat, and the maître d' is over in a split second. "My treat," Jim says, brandishing his plastic.

"Hey, not fair!"

"You can pay next time." His smile is bland.

"You're making assumptions," I accuse.

"I hope not." He looks suitably chastened, though. While the maître d' goes to fetch the chip and pin reader, he continues: "I've been thinking. You're feeling culturally deprived, and I've got a sixteen-year-old barbarian to educate. How would you like to go to a concert or two with me and Sally? She needs the exposure, and we both need to get out of the office more—"

"I'm assuming by 'concert' we're not talking about the latest reunion tour by Union J, right?"

"I was thinking more along the lines of *The Marriage of Figaro* myself. English National Opera are putting on a run starting this weekend and I was looking for an excuse to go and see it."

"Ah, *that* kind of education! I can provide the *Mystery Science Theater 3000* commentary, highlight all the rude bits if she gets bored." It sounds good to me. "Okay, deal. Let's keep our eyes open for fun stuff happening in town, hmm?"

"Deal." He nods.

A thought occurs to me: "But your car . . ."

"That's all right: Sally can ride on the roof rack." He guffaws. "Kidding, really and truly: just kidding. I'll get Liz to agree to a car swap in return for a Sally-free evening. She kept the Volvo but she's been making cow eyes at the Z4 ever since I bought it: she'll bite."

"Works for me." We push back our chairs and stand. I pull my jacket on and follow Jim out; we head back to his car. "Deal. Now you'll need to give me directions, if you want that lift home to go anywhere useful . . ."

So I do that, and he drops me at my front door. I do not invite him in, and he doesn't try to kiss me, because we are not dating. But at least I have something to look forward to next weekend.

14.

INFECTED

MY FIRST MEETING THE FOLLOWING MORNING IS IN THE NEW
Annex. The SA has organized a date for me with our tame superpower epidemiologist and his boss, Dr. Mike Ford, and intimated that
there are things here that I need to be briefed on urgently that are not
for general consumption. I am, as they say, agog.

Dr. Mike doesn't actually work at the New Annex: he's based at
one of our outlying R&D labs, disguised as a somewhat recondite
office in an engineering company south of the river. For this particular
briefing, the SA has actually *summoned* him—which is quite a feat.
Dr. Mike doesn't like to travel. He's seldom seen outside the building
he works in. There are rumors about a camp bed that lives under his
overflowing desk. To see him in the New Annex is distinctly unusual.

The meeting is on the fourth floor, in one of the Mahogany Row
briefing rooms that has been restored to regular use since the Code
Red incident. I can't suppress a cringe as I tiptoe past the boarded-up
doors of the offices above and to either side of Room 202—two floors
below—with fresh wards and THAUM HAZARD signs prominently
displayed. Angleton (and others: Judith, Andy . . .) died down there,
giving their lives for the nation in a senselessly bloody endgame

engineered by a master vampire who was already dead when it kicked off. And for what outcome? My husband, now estranged, possessed by or possessing the alien soul-thing that rode in his former boss's flesh. My own life, damaged and diverted. A breach of sanity and a plethora of endings. *I can do this,* I tell myself as I edge around the last of the off-limits rooms and walk swiftly towards 411, heels clacking on the scraped-bare floor. They have not yet replaced the thick wool carpet. Its woven-in wards sparked and burned during the battle two floors below, triggering the sprinkler system.

To get to Room 411 I have to pass through a vestibule with a blue-suiter on duty. I leave my handbag and phone with him on the way in; Lecter, as an occult device, is a special case, and after some discussion I'm allowed to keep him—but not my highly dangerous lipstick case and tissues.

The room itself is windowless and boardroom-sized, with chairs, a lectern, and a projection screen. Think in terms of a much older and somewhat more spartan version of COBRA, only set up as a miniature lecture theater rather than a committee room. The security we don't see is enforced by summoning grids embedded in walls, floor, and ceiling, alien Actors and Agents locked and programmed to strike out at certain classes of threat. Any information leakage while the doors are shut is sensed and traced, and if it's directional, active countermeasures may be deployed. It's a *really* bad idea to snoop on a high-security briefing in Mahogany Row.

Once inside I find myself among a select few. The SA himself is here, of course, as is Dr. Mike. Our paranormal epidemiologist, Julian Sanchez, is setting up a set of overhead projection slides (PowerPoint is strictly forbidden in these briefings, for obvious reasons: it supports Turing-complete macros), and we have some additional hangers-on. Colonel Lockhart is here from External Assets. The strikingly pretty young Auditor, Seph or Persephone or whatever she's called, sits beside a bloke whose body language screams Special Forces at me—I've seen enough of them in my time. (He's Special Forces, after the British—or maybe French—fashion: incredibly wiry, not a bulky bodybuilder the way the Americans make them. Emphasis on enormous stamina rather than sheer strength.) He's introduced simply as "Johnny," which leaves me wondering, but it's not my job to police the guest list. We're just taking our seats when the door from the vestibule opens again. Mhari slips inside and hastily sits down next to me. I manage not to flinch at the abrupt move. I'm getting better at it.

"Good morning," says the SA, smiling down at us from the lectern. "I'd like to start by asking Dr. Sanchez to give us a brief rundown on the epidemiology of the superpower outbreak as it has evolved over the past month. After his backgrounder, Dr. Mike will then discuss the implications."

"Er, hi," says Sanchez. He looks nervous at first, but sheds it rapidly as he gets into his stride. "Today I'm here to deliver an update on the three-sigma incident monitoring project that I reported on a month ago, along with additional data. This comes with good news and bad news attached.

"First, here's last month's graph of notifications of superpower incidents." A familiar slide showing an ominous hockey-stick curve appears on the screen. "Second, let me add the new items we've processed since then." The shocking exponential slope from last month, in blue, is extended, in red—and shows a dramatic off-ramp, tapering back towards a steady state. "As you can see, it seems to be a classic sigmoid curve—suddenly goes from a horizontal line to near-vertical increase, then just as suddenly tails off and goes flat again, albeit at a higher level. We're still working on the confidence limits here, and there's some scope for updating the curve as more low-grade incidents work their way through our reporting system, but it looks, for now, as if we have dodged the bullet. There is no super-hero singularity looming in our near future. Just a regular elevated rate at which ordinary people will suddenly acquire enhanced capabilities."

There's an audible relaxation of tension on all sides, a sudden rustling and shuffling and wheezing as we stop holding our collective breath. I wasn't consciously aware that I was doing it, like the rest of them: *We're not going to die just yet,* I realize. To say that my guts turn to water with relief is only a slight exaggeration. I try not to slump too obviously; beside me, Mhari lets out a tiny gasp.

"That's the good news," warns Sanchez. "There's bad news, too. Before I get into that, I've been asked to give a brief overview of the international situation. We are not tasked with assessing and evaluating extraterritorial events that do not represent direct threats"—because, *money and time*—"so this is based on secondary sources: reports from cooperating allies, public news reports in non-cooperating territories. Different cultures have different responses to paranormal phenomena. In sub-Saharan Africa we are tracking an upswing in reports of vigilante attacks on suspected witches. There may be some correlation with homophobic political rhetoric: moral panics frequently spread to adjacent targets by contagion. Certainly there has been an upswing in reports of *koro* from western Africa recently . . . In predominantly Islamic countries there have been increasing reports of *Djinn* and *ifrit*, and witchcraft trials have been reported in Saudi Arabia, Pakistan's tribal territories, and Afghanistan. However, they can't be ascribed directly to superpower manifestations: witchcraft accusations are often leveled at ordinary men and women as a pretext for settling grudges. There've also been outbreaks of miracles in Poland, Ireland, Mexico, and elsewhere in Central and South America. Statues of the Virgin crying tears of blood, that sort of thing. Religious manifestations in India, much speaking in tongues in Baptist churches in the Deep South.

"Overall, the incidence of religious anomalies worldwide—reported miracles, curses, incidents of successful imprecatory prayer—is up by roughly 150 to 200 percent over the past three months.

"As for superheroes, they've broken out all over. Japan has its own version of the paranormal-slash-superpowered individual in popular culture. Luckily the prevalent anime and manga media tend to emphasize social responsibility and teamwork, with even their fictional bad guys frequently working within a controlled framework. We understand that the Home Office is actively liaising with the National Police Agency under the auspices of the National Public Safety Commission"—I share a glance of mutual ignorance with Mhari:

nobody's told us about that—"and others to define best standards for co-opting and diverting transgressive behavior among the superpowered. There are also reports of *yokai*-related crime and disorder, but these are less clearly correlated with—"

"Yokai?" asks the SA.

"I'm sorry, I should have said: traditional Japanese folkloric and mythological monsters. *Neko-mata*, the two-tailed cat demon; *Nopperabo*, the faceless ones; *Kappa*, or water goblins. *Kitsune* and *Tanuki* and *Nurikabe*. They've got hundreds of the things—Japan is one of the most densely haunted territories on Earth if you believe the folklorists, and the plethora of Shinto *Kami* or spirits overlap with *Yokai*, monsters. When you first get paranormal bleed-through, it manifests via canalized pathways.

"Moving on. In the United States the tide seems to have been stemmed by two very successful initiatives: the big media franchises are proactively litigating for trademark violation against infringers—they've sued sixteen Supermen, twenty-one Batmen, eleven Iron Men, and nine Wonder Women so far—while the Nazgûl appear to have taken action to ensure that no four- or five-sigma instances reach the public eye. There's such a sharp cutoff point in the power spectrum of reported American superpower events that it's fairly clear somebody is suppressing the high-end individuals. Probably by a conscript or kill strategy, knowing how the Black Chamber operates.

"The American mainstream news media have so far steered well clear of the subject because the phenomenon has been enthusiastically embraced by the talk radio fringe, leading to a death spiral of diminishing credibility. So we see a situation over there where the visible superpower scene resembles a low-rent version of the World Wrestling Federation with added special effects and non-trademark-infringing suits, while in the background the Black Chamber are either icing or co-opting the high-power examples. This follows an emerging pattern among the G20 governments, whereby they appear to be splitting into two groups: those who adopt a strategy of co-option and positive leadership, as in our own case, and those who go for outright suppression, such as the Russian Federation and the United States."

Sanchez clears his throat and drinks from a water bottle. "As you can imagine, the likes of the FBI and the DEA take a very dim view of having to compete with Superman. And they've got the entrenched support and the corporate contractors with the lobbying muscle to make their preferences stick. We shouldn't be surprised, really. But anyway. I think I'm done here. It's time for the bad news. Dr. Mike?"

Dr. Mike stands up and slowly shuffles to the podium. He doesn't look well, I realize with a stab of concern—it's been too long since I dropped round for a cup of tea and a chat about the latest thinking on CASE NIGHTMARE GREEN, which is simultaneously his curse, his obsession, and his entire career.

"Yes, that," he says slowly. He looks at us. "The step-function in superpower outbreaks is good news," he says. "It means we don't have to worry about the entire population manifesting quasi-godlike powers—at least, not unless there's yet another step-function transition lurking unseen in our future. But it leaves us with a major problem. What you must understand is, we don't yet know the full spectrum of medical side effects of these emergent occult capabilities. However, there is reason for serious concern. I've been working with Dr. Wills at UCLH to try to determine an approach for dealing with this. Let me illustrate."

He shoves a slide showing four MRI brain scans onto the projector. *Oh dear.* I think I know what's coming up, and the only reason it's not my breakfast is because I didn't eat this morning.

"On the upper left, a cross-section through a healthy adult human brain. Here's the cerebral cortex, this is the cerebellum, here are the intraventricular foramina, channels filled with cerebrospinal fluid that perfuse the brain." He points them out. "Now, here on the top right is a similar view of the brain of a practitioner with advanced Krantzberg syndrome."

The difference is visible, even at this scale. The bright cerebral cortex still has a thin rind of white, but there are dark bubbles scattered through the interior. The foramina are larger, the cerebellum oddly withered-looking. "Note the classic signs of a neurodegenerative pathology," Dr. Mike says, pointing out the features to watch for.

"Feeders attracted by the subject's repeated introspection and visualization of summoning vectors have, over time, chewed microscopic chunks out of the cerebral cortex until the interior is a barely functional lacework. The human neocortex is structured as a sparsely connected network, and the feeders preferentially leave the long-range connections alone, not wanting to kill their host prematurely; but microvascular accidents associated with their activities have caused ischemic degradation here, here, and here—" He points to the largest patches of darkness. "The patient died three weeks after this MRI scan was taken; at post-mortem, after the CSF was drained, his brain was found to weigh about two-thirds as much as expected based on its exterior dimensions. The rest was scar tissue and fluid."

Mhari is making faint choking noises beside me: she holds a hand daintily in front of her mouth. *Tough*. Dr. Mike ploughs on indefatigably. "Now, moving on. Bottom left: this is the healthy brain of a three-sigma superpower who first came to our attention five weeks ago. As you can see, it looks superficially similar to that of the control case above. And now"—he points to the bottom right quadrant—"for something completely different!"

I squint at it dubiously. "This is a cross-section of the head of the three-sigma power known as Strip Jack Spratt. Spratt died of a subarachnoid hemorrhage while in police custody in the wake of the incident in Trafalgar Square. At the time of his demise the police surgeon had provisionally assigned him a diagnosis as an unmedicated paranoid schizophrenic with the controlling-machine delusional archetype *and* superpowers, the psychological impact of which we may assume to be destabilizing with respect to his grip on reality. As you can see, the left hemisphere is largely intact. And if you would like to compare it to the advanced K syndrome example above . . ."

The similarities are unmistakable. Enlarged foramina, dark bubbles, lacy cortex.

"In my opinion, Mr. Slaithwaite had less than two months to live at the time of his hemorrhage. In fact, the hemorrhage was almost certainly a side effect of his K syndrome: about ten percent of cases experience a cerebrovascular accident rather than dying of dementia.

Now, you must focus on this: examination of his medical and police records show *no sign* of paranormal capabilities more than four months prior to his arrest in Trafalgar Square. So the unpleasant conclusion is that he went from zero to advanced K syndrome in around three to four months. Total life expectancy post-superpower: six months, the last two of them with an advanced neurodegenerative condition. Being an uncontrolled, fully active three-sigma supervillain is about as lethal as contracting an inoperable diffuse astrocytoma or similar brain tumor."

Dr. Mike glances around at us. His eyes are tired and baggy. "This isn't universal," he says quietly. "We have some superpowers who have been confirmed for six months now. I managed to persuade two of them to undergo MRI scans and there is *no evidence* of active disease. You must understand that for the time being this remains a one-off—we don't have enough samples to confirm beyond reasonable doubt that the superpowered are subject to K syndrome or a related neuropathy." I feel a faint shaking through the seat of my pants: it's coming through Mhari's chair, which is hooked up with mine. She's shuddering. It's her personal nightmare: PHANGs need to drink blood from a living human or they succumb to a not-dissimilar degenerative condition, V syndrome. It's ugly, progressive, and ultimately fatal. Without thinking I reach for her hand. Her fingers close convulsively around mine, almost painfully tight.

Dr. Mike presses on. "Nevertheless, I believe there is sufficient evidence to strongly support the hypothesis that the superpowered are just as subject to K syndrome as occult practitioners. Superpowers all manifest a strong thaum field: it would be logical to anticipate that feeders are drawn to them—and unlike a ritual practitioner, or even a PHANG, they have no defenses. Finally, although the rate at which new superpowers emerge appears to have plateaued, they continue to do so. And we have no way of tracking the spread of low-level powers. The worst case now is not that we face a superhero singularity, but that we face a low-level pandemic of K syndrome affecting the wider—undiagnosed—population at a rate that could potentially be as high as one in ten thousand people per year. If this hypothesis is supported, we need to identify all superpowers as a matter of urgency and arrange for them to receive the same training and protective measures as our own practitioners. To do otherwise would be unconscionable and inhumane."

The SA stands, and walks to the podium. "Thank you," he says, his smile slightly strained in the face of the stunned silence that follows Dr. Sanchez's and Dr. Mike's presentations. "That was most thought-provoking!" His smile vanishes. "Now, as you can imagine, this presents us with something of a conundrum. So I'd like to devote the rest of this session to discussing ideas for monitoring, tracking, and if possible, remediating the problem of K syndrome parasites afflicting our three-sigma and higher superpowers. Not to mention dealing with public awareness of the risk of K syndrome to the lower-powered. Does anyone want to speak first? Ah, Johnny, I see you already have your hand up . . ."

"WHAT ABOUT BEE?" MHARI DEMANDS. HER VOICE IS SHRILL and grates on my nerves. "And Torch?"

We're walking along the fourth-floor corridor in the direction of the stairwell. I feel numb. I don't want to be having this conversation: "What about Jim?" I counter.

"What about"—she stops dead, blank-faced—"what?"

I keep going for a couple more steps, then turn on my heel to face her. "Officer Friendly," I say quietly, "is at least a three-sigma power. How much of what he does is down to the fancy armor, and how much is his own mojo?"

"I assume it's mostly him, but I really don't know." She pauses. "But I know who will."

I allow Mhari to lead me down the stairs to the third floor, then along the corridor leading to the HR hive. Strictly speaking the New Annex only houses Field Ops personnel and supporting specialties; there are a lot of outlying groups, including R&D, Training, Admin, Analysis, and HR, all of whom have their own offices elsewhere in the capital (and in some cases outside it). But Field Ops has its own rather

specialized HR requirements, and consequently HR has its own out-
post within Field Ops' territory. It's there to handle things like payroll
and pensions for Residual Human Resources,* disciplinary hearings
for chaos magicians, and new background identities for operatives
who have been declared dead. Mhari is clearly familiar with these
offices, for she heads straight towards one corner, knocks on a door,
and says, "Alison? It's me! Do you have a couple of minutes?"

"Sure! Come in!" Alison is a chirpily cheerful thirty-something in
a canary-yellow top and big bold spectacles with shoulder-length
brown hair. "You're looking good, Mhari! Who's this?"

"This is Dr. O'Brien, my director," Mhari says. I smile and do the
office-hello waggle-dance, and Alison buzzes right back: pretending
we're all worker bees together, got a hive to run, honey to store, pol-
len to collect. "We've come up with an unusually knotty HR problem,
and rather than go through channels I was hoping you could help us
sort it out here and now."

"A problem?" Alison looks suddenly wary.

I take a deep breath. "We've just been to a briefing that I can't
share with you in detail yet. It has some worrying implications for the
risk of medical disability"—I catch Mhari mouthing *K syndrome* out
of the side of my eye and send her a disapproving look—"and in
particular some of our staff are potentially at risk. Direct employees
I know how to deal with. The trouble is, one of the people in my
group is actually a designated liaison officer from another organization: the Metropolitan Police, by way of ACPO. His personnel file
here is probably no more than a placeholder—a record of him signing
Section Three and being approved for liaison. What I want to know
is, what can I legitimately get hold of?"

Alison looks puzzled. "He's a policeman? On the cleared list, am
I understanding this correctly? With the Met?"

"The Met have seconded him to the Association of Chief Police

---

* We do not use the Z-word; it's a violation of our group-wide policy on respect for diversity
and equality to refer to metabolic status.

Officers, who have assigned him to my unit, which is nominally part of the Security Service but staffed with a mixture of Laundry, SS, and ACPO bodies." Alison begins to look twitchy as I lay it all out before her. "In addition to this employee being a police officer, he's a three-sigma superpower. I need to know the precise date on which his powers began to manifest, and their scope, as tested—"

"Why don't you ask him?" Alison asks. Clearly she doesn't lip read.

I give up. "We think he's at risk of a neurodegenerative condition," I tell her. "One associated with his superpower. I will ask him directly if I absolutely have to, but I'd prefer to perform a preliminary risk assessment and identify our options before I talk to him and, if necessary, refer him for counseling. I don't have his full personnel file, and although he's working for me he's outside my reporting chain: I can't pull his records without cutting across at least two agencies, which will take time. *If* he's at risk, this would obviously be bad. If he's *not* at risk, I'd prefer to avoid alarming and upsetting him needlessly. So what can we do?"

"Oh, Mhari." Alison's expression is priceless. "You *do* find them, don't you?"

"I do my best." Mhari looks rueful. She leans forward, making eye contact: I hope she's not trying to roll someone in HR with her PHANG mind-control power, but no . . . "What do you think we should do?"

"I think you'd better give me Problem Child's full name and identifying details. And an email address"—she sends me a significant look—"where I can reach you. So you want to know about the scope of his superpowers?"

"Yes," I say. "And one other thing. In strictest confidence now: when he's not being a regular officer, he has a secret identity you might have heard of. He's Officer Friendly. Yes, he's working for me in both capacities. The thing is, I'm also curious about the capabilities of his special armor. If he's at risk of K syndrome whenever he exercises his superpowers, it may make a huge difference if he's relying on the armor for strength, flight, or other capabilities—or if he's doing it all himself via an unconscious invocation loop. Someone must have arranged for him to get his hands on it—my money is on ACPO—so there will be records in his professional training and development transcript pointing to when and who taught him to operate the thing."

Alison smiles. "I like the way you think. That'll be a big help, if I can find someone with access."

I stand. "If you can do this for me, it'd be more than a help: it might save his life."

She stands and waves us towards the door. "Message received." She nods at Mhari. "We must get together some time, eh?"

Mhari nods. "Been too long," she agrees. "Must fly! Until next time . . ."

I GO IN TO THE OFFICE EARLY ON WEDNESDAY, BECAUSE I'M meeting up with Jim and we're going off-site for the day. We have a dog and pony show to deliver, and I'm actually quite nervous because a lot of our future work will hinge on how it's received. I made sure to leave work early yesterday for a hair salon appointment, and today I'm wearing my sharpest suit so I'm looking my most presentable. It's not the Home Office: it's an even more secretive and powerful organization—the Association of Chief Police Officers.

It was Jim's idea, actually. He came up with it late last month: "The Manchester business with Alice Christie got me thinking," he said. "The Home Office has a clear view of what we're doing here, and the people at Hendon are aware of you—but I haven't seen much high-level chatter yet. I think it'd be a good idea to prepare a series of in-person briefings about the Transhuman Police Coordination Force and its work, to get the commissioners up to speed—otherwise there are going to be misconceptions, and they'll fester."

"Sounds good. We ought to do that, and sooner rather than later—I'll get Karim and Gillian, or whoever's available, to pull together a bunch of slides, then you and I can go over the raw material and see if we can turn it into a lunchtime presentation? Do you want to see if you can organize a session with an audience we can poll for feedback later?" The offer of free food ought to bribe at least a couple to sit still while we PowerPoint at them, then we can use their responses to refine the pitch.

"I can do better than that," Jim assures me. "ACPO has semiannual summit meetings attended by Chief Police Officers from just about every force in the UK, right here in London, and the next one is in two weeks. There's a day of briefings and presentations after the general meeting, and I think I can get us a speaking slot. It's a first-class opportunity for networking, too. I can introduce you to all the main players."

So fast-forward to this morning. I go up to my office to deposit Lecter in the safe I've had installed there, collect my laptop (with preloaded presentation and a backup memory stick for emergencies), check the morning email for unexploded administrative ordnance, panic when I see the time, and head for the lobby. Where I run into Jim as he comes in. "Good morning, Dr. O'Brien." He's all formality today, from his mirror-finished black DMs to the epaulettes and braid on his dress tunic. "Are you ready to go?"

I shrug, but my jacket shoulder pads are so stiff they barely move. "I'm as ready as I'll ever be. Let's call a cab."

ACPO headquarters occupies part of a gray concrete and glass slab of post-brutalist office space on Victoria Street, sandwiched between Boeing's London offices, the Department for Business Innovation & Skills, and the back side of New Scotland Yard. It's so anonymous it could be mistaken for a council office or a firm of accountants, if not for the trickle of extremely senior police men and women in dress uniforms arriving from the Yard. The cab drops us off by the front door, and Jim leads me inside to reception: "Chief Superintendent Grey and Director O'Brien from TPCF. We're giving an open briefing on the new Force's area of interest across the road later this morning."

"Yes, sir." The receptionist peers at his terminal: "I have your badges and kits for the breakout sessions here. If you'd like to go through the door to your left, Andrea will sort you out with your speakers' packs . . ." A minute later we're both wearing badges on lanyards and clutching printed schedules and a note telling us where to go and when. I follow Jim's lead, happy to be socially invisible in unfamiliar surroundings.

"We don't get to sit at the high table or attend the big meeting," Jim murmurs to me. "How about we go up the road and give things a last run-through over coffee?"

"That'd be great," I say fervently, and allow him to usher me along the covered walkway leading to the entrance, past the front desk, and up to the canteen. Where we drink enough coffee to wake the dead, go over our presentation one last time, double-check that the laptop's battery is up to the job, and cool our heels until it's time to go up to the eighth-floor briefing rooms that ACPO has booked for the breakout sessions after the principals finish with their main meeting.

The presentation:

About sixty Very Important Police Officers have converged on ACPO HQ and the Yard for the day. They're here to discuss important policy matters affecting multiple forces, to chat one-on-one about matters of professional concern with their peers from other forces, and to attend briefings from a variety of agencies and organizations: the Crown Prosecution Service, newly outsourced forensic laboratories, HM Revenue & Customs, the National Crime Agency . . . and us. Because these are Very Important Police Officers and their time is valuable, they have carefully planned which seminars and presentations to attend: consequently we get the undivided attention of just fourteen of them. The extra seats are filled by the folks from the CPS, outsourced forensic laboratories, HM Revenue & Customs, the NCA, and other agencies who aren't actually giving presentations of their own at the same time as us. It could be worse: they're not our core target audience but we're getting the message out, and that's what matters.

I'm not going to bore you with the presentation itself. You've probably sat through enough management PowerPoint pitches to write it yourself: open by defining a problem (the power curve showing the increasing frequency of superpowers over time), then introduce an organization to deal with the problem. Add a mission statement and an org chart, rhapsodize about your agency's values, describe the future rollout of services, outline a protocol whereby your audience may send up the bat-signal to request your assistance, and finally thank them for their attention and reassure them that as valued stakeholders you welcome their feedback. Credits and curtain call.

The audience, as always at this sort of off-site summit/miniconference, is far more interesting than the presentation itself. The front row is mostly middle-aged white men in senior police uniforms (one woman, one nonwhite: not even the most optimistic commissioner will deny that the UK's police forces have some catching up to do on diversity, especially at higher ranks). But appearances are deceptive. You don't get to Assistant Chief Constable or above without being a habitual overachiever with a razor-sharp mind. Half of them have doctorates; the other half had to work even harder to get there, whether at thief-taking or politics. We allowed five minutes for questions and I'm still answering them when one of the organizers pops in through the door to wave us out to make room for the next speakers.

"Well, *I* think that went well," Jim confides as we emerge into a hallway where our hosts have set up a table with coffee supplies.

"I hope so." I pull out my compact to check my hair's under control and my mascara isn't running. "They really had me sweating at the end."

"What, John's grilling about training and professional standards?" Jim is busy with the refreshments.

"Yes, that—no, all of them." My face having neither melted nor exploded, I put the mirror away and accept the cup of coffee Jim hands me. "John was right: it normally takes three months to train a PCSO, and two years for a probationary constable—and we're trying to rush through candidates who didn't originally want a career in policing?"

"It's not quite that bad." I can't tell whether Jim's speaking of the coffee or the training program. "We're running a specialist unit that gets called on as backup in response to specific events. The superpowered don't need training in everyday policing tasks that don't fall within their remit: they'll never be deployed in a situation where they don't have a responsible officer in charge. They just need to keep their noses clean and follow instructions. And I don't think anyone is ahead of us on the learning curve in our field, so there's nobody for us to look bad in comparison to." I take a cautious sip of coffee as I wince. Jim's perspective is blunter than usual: perhaps it's the uniforms on all sides making him open up. "That's probably what they're thinking, even if they're more polite to your face," he adds. "Join me for lunch after the next talk? I think I can promise you an eye-opener."

I sit through the next half-hour slot (a woman from the CPS discussing new procedures for handling cases involving serious financial malfeasance—not my thing *at all* although I can see it's useful to the intended audience), using the time to decompress. In due course I tag along with Jim behind a clot* of uniformed senior officers as they make their way towards the canteen at New Scotland Yard—because it's necessary for them to be seen there, canteen culture being what it is even today.

There's a side room waiting for the top brass, although the door's open so that everyone can see that they're just regular coppers who eat and drink the same food as everyone else. Even if it's a buffet and there are starched linen tablecloths waiting for them. Jim walks straight in—as an ACPO staffer it's his right—and I tag along, hoping nobody calls my bluff.

My middle-aged invisibility seems to come in handy—at least at first. I find myself sitting opposite Jim, sandwiched between an assistant chief from South Wales, Graham Walton, and his opposite number from Humberside, Chris Norton. They seem to know Jim (he's probably on their radar as young and ambitious, possible future competition for a top slot), but the conversation is friendly enough:

---

* What *is* the collective noun for a group of very senior police officers, anyway? In their uniform tunics and white shirts they remind me of magpies or crows, but referring to a murder of chief constables seems somehow inappropriate . . .

almost collegiate. So I do my best fly on the wall impersonation as they politely grill Jim about my organization.

". . . So we're particularly worried about the public order angle," Graham is telling Jim. He has a sausage impaled on the end of his fork and gestures with it while he speaks, knife poised ready to scoop a mashed potato shroud atop it when he finishes and has time to chew: "Not your outliers, but the low-end troublemakers who come out to play at chucking-out time on a Saturday in Cardiff. Your two-sigma tanked-up chav with a skin full of Bucky can raise Cain on the early watch, but what if we're not covered? Because you've only got the one team—"

"We're working on it." Jim's gaze flickers my way, then slides away as he looks at Chris Norton to see how his response is going down. "We're still working up to operational status from zero across the board, Graham"—a sidelong glance at his Welsh interrogator, who is now demolishing his plate—"but we have to get the back-office system in place first. Currently we're focusing on intelligence-led operations, starting by compiling a register of all known high-end offenders. We're also working up a team of PCSOs with three-sigma or higher capability who can be brought into play by field commanders who need backup—"

"But what about the leadership culture?" Chris pushes in. "I know you're overstretched already with your ACPO brief, but what other officers do you have on-force to provide mentorship in a progressive policing environment?" I clear my throat, but he doesn't stop: "There's just one of you, and from that org chart you showed us earlier the TPCF is already up to twenty staff and growing rapidly—too rapidly for organic promotion from within. Do you plan to advertise senior positions for recruitment from other forces?"

"Excuse me—" I try to cut in.

"No need for that," Jim replies, without giving me a chance to answer. It's really annoying: I expected better of him. "We have a management skeleton already in place: people drawn from the Security Service who are on loan to the Home Office. It turns out the MoD already has a lot of experience handling superpowers. The real issue is building a Police culture within the organization, not finding high-quality administrative support and management personnel."

"Excuse me—" I say, but as Graham finishes chewing, he leans towards Jim.

"But surely you'll be wanting training standards officers and cadre who already have front-line experience?"

It's as if I'm not even here. I give up and stir my salad listlessly with my fork. "Gentlemen," I say quietly, "don't mind me. Feel free to pretend I'm not here—"

"You'd have to ask my director," Jim replies to Graham. "She's in charge of all senior staffing decisions, although she defers on them to her head of HR." He doesn't look at me. It's like he's forgotten I'm here. He smiles ingratiatingly: "You could ask her."

"Maybe later." Graham goes back to ploughing through his lunch.

"The real problem, it seems to me"—Chris Norton speaks quietly, almost inaudible against the background chatter and the sound of canteen cutlery—"is the overall trajectory of the epidemic. We have to assert control now, before the structures we rely on for the reinforcement of societal consent break down."

"Which structures in particular?" Jim asks, in a mild tone of voice I've come to recognize as his Socratic sucker-bait.

"Authority," Chris states. "Yes, yes, Peelian principles are all very well. We police by consent, the public are the police and the police are the public, and so forth. But that growth curve you showed us is troubling. It seems to me that if we have a major ongoing outbreak of superpowers, the entire structure of public consent may be dangerously weakened. We rely on most people obeying the law of the land most of the time because it's the right thing to do—and when that fails, we rely on them obeying because they must, because we can always out-escalate them. But superpowers will undermine that. If it's just a handful, we can muddle through with backup from TPCF and good intelligence. But heaven help us if it hits ten percent of the population and the hard core of regular troublemakers cut loose."

"We're going to need a bigger stick," Graham agrees, dabbing at his lips with a napkin.

"So where's the bigger stick?" Chris asks Jim, disarmingly candidly. "One team of extraordinary PCSOs isn't going to cut it, if you don't mind me saying. We really need something better. The Met should provide leadership on this one."

"We're working on it," Jim says defensively. "There are plans afoot." His gaze flickers past me as if he's forgotten I'm here. "But nothing I can really discuss in public yet."

Chris puts his knife and fork down. His plate is as spotless as his uniform. "Well, I just hope it's ready when we need it." He smiles. "Well, gentlemen: we have fifteen minutes until the next session starts. If you'll excuse me?" He rises to leave; Graham Walton follows his example. Jim watches them leave.

"Well, that was illuminating," I mutter.

Jim glances at me, then suddenly twitches as if seeing me for the first time. "What?" he asks, eyebrows raised in surprise.

"What indeed?" I look at him. He looks slightly flustered. Embarrassed, even.

"Uh, Dr. O'Brien, I'm sorry, I didn't—"

"Oh, don't mind me." I smile, thin-lipped. "I can handle it. Canteen culture, eh?"

He nods. "Canteen culture." But I have an inkling that it's something more than that.

I BARELY NOTICE THE REST OF THE WEEK, I'M SO BUSY. I'M bogged down in a sea of minutiae, fully occupied juggling a huge brief: team recruitment operations, budget estimates, our continuing research into individual cases and general superpower threat projections. I don't have time to be upset or angry about the way the ACPO delegates virtually ignored me, as if I were invisible. Developing invisibility as my superpower: wouldn't *that* be something? (Something *hellishly annoying*, if you couldn't control it . . .)

Our failure to find Freudstein is eating away at me. I've also got a horrible feeling of near futility, coupled with a sense that I'm spinning my wheels, that however hard I run I'm not gaining on our workload, that CASE NIGHTMARE GREEN is closing in, and that a tidal wave of horror is surging towards us, still unseen, just beyond the horizon—

Let's just say I'm not sleeping very well.

I continue to hope HR will deliver something more about Jim's background. I try to be patient, but if Alison can't get results within a week, I'm going to have to escalate my enquiries. I put this to Dr. Armstrong at our Friday morning confessional in the New Annex, and he gives me absolution. "I understand your concerns, Mo. I believe you've taken the correct action with respect to Jim. Under the circumstances, it would be indiscreet to enquire too openly about his capabilities. As for Bee, Torch, and the others—"

"They're a known quantity," I point out. "I can refer them to Dr. Wills directly, get them checked out weekly if necessary. We've got protocols for dealing with K syndrome. My real concern is that Jim is a special case. As you yourself said. Anyway, where *did* that armor come from?"

The SA is imperturbable. "You might as well ask where Ramona's vessel came from."

"BLUE HADES, but—" I stop dead. "I first met Jim at the reception during the treaty negotiation sessions up north."

"Jolly good." The SA nods.

"Is that why you're suspicious of him? You think BLUE HADES gave him the armor? Why would they do that?"

"Why would they loan us Ramona and her chariot?" He raises an eyebrow expectantly.

"Somebody asked?"

"Yes, somebody asked. In the case of Ramona, somebody asked if they knew anything about the superpower problem: that's when they offered to send us a liaison officer and some specialized equipment. The trouble with dealing with the Deep Ones is that sometimes something is lost in translation . . ."

"So they sent Ramona as a message. A very clear one: 'Mess with us and we have the capability to make you very sorry indeed. Meanwhile, have a nice day fighting crime.' But Officer Friendly . . ."

"Also fights crime," the SA reminds me gently. "And works for ACPO. But please remember that it's a mistake to base an analysis on insufficient data."

"Or on *a posteriori* reasoning, don't teach your grandmother to—sorry. But. Why Jim?" I take a deep breath. "Null hypothesis: Jim was just *there*. Assigned to Fisheries and cleared to liaise with our people so he was probably a Person Of Interest to whatever passes for BLUE HADES' HUMINT people—Ramona's employers—when his superpowers manifested themselves. Either BLUE HADES gave him the suit, or someone else did, or he made it himself—but he's a cop, not a Mad Science Corporate Executive!"

"That's a reasonable assumption. In the absence of evidence that there's anything more to it, Occam's razor suggests it's the most likely explanation. But it's a bad idea to rely on the razor for too close a shave: sometimes you get cut." Dr. Armstrong unlocks a drawer in his desk. "You haven't seen these." He pulls out a slim display folio and hands it to me. "I am not showing you this because it does not exist. Officially."

"What—"

The cover bears the BAe Systems logo, subtitled Computational Invocation Applications Group. I open it. It contains a bunch of presentation folders, with glossy promotional renderings. I blink a couple of times to clear my eyes because I'm not entirely sure what I'm looking at. The first few pages look like Mhari's proposed "protective overalls," complete with helmets, except they're in British Army Brown and the wearers are carrying L85 rifles with Very Scary Electronic Sights bolted on top and choppers hovering menacingly in the background. Then I flip a page and come face to face with something familiar. Take Officer Friendly's outfit, swap out the frankly theatrical helmet for something that looks like a cross between a praying mantis's head and a gas mask, and color it Army: you get something called the Future Battle Environment Suit. *This* time the L85 is just a carrier for a pair of side-by-side ruggedized cameras, a Joint Line-Of-Sight Vitrification Weapon according to the caption. A basilisk gun, in other words.

"Jesus," I mutter.

Dr. Armstrong removes the promotional brochure from my nerveless fingers. "Power-assisted chameleon suits with tactical displays, mesh networking, armor, and strength amplification," he says. "A triumph of our new strategic technology transfer program. Some of this stuff *did* come from BLUE HADES, in return for certain . . . services. Chicken feed by their standards, but highly useful to us nevertheless. Their approach to CASE NIGHTMARE GREEN seems to be to give the natives muskets while keeping the Gatling guns for themselves." His expression is disapproving. "The Army think it's just the ticket for when the stars come right. It's not as revolutionary as you think: the Americans have been working on something similar since the late 1980s, the Future Force Warrior program. It's all a bit pricey in today's austere climate, though. One might consider the possibility that a certain large corporation has chosen to demonstrate some of the less sensitive aspects of their new toy chest by painting it blue and loaning it to ACPO as cover for one of their less well-understood capabilities."

"Ah." It would certainly explain a lot. ACPO suddenly acquire a super-cop: How to protect his identity and make best use of his capabilities? Throw in a serendipitous marketing approach . . . "Tell me they weren't also looking into selling this as next-generation riot kit?"

"I'm disappointed in you, Mo: How could you imagine that the militarization of the police might be seen as a huge potential growth market by defense contractors?"

"How indeed." A thought strikes me. "Can I get my hands on some of this stuff for my team? Not the basilisk gear, but the power-assisted armor? So far, Mhari's come up with unpowered body armor with helmet-mounted communications kit, but the strength amplification . . ."

"Would you trust your trainee team with it?" askss the SA. "That's a serious question."

"If I can't trust them with it, they don't belong on the team."

"That's the right answer." He nods thoughtfully. "Tell Mhari to talk to me directly. I'll point her at someone who may be able to help."

And that's another Friday morning confessional over: stick a fork in me, I'm done.

THAT FRIDAY AFTERNOON'S HIGHLIGHT IS A PERSONNEL REVIEW with Mhari and Ramona. Our next two recruits have *finally* been cleared by CRB, and we are on course to induct them next Monday. They're a bit mundane if you stack them up against Officer Friendly, but they're squeaky-clean role models, and that's actually more important in my opinion. Mhari delivers the HR smackdown:

"First up: Lollipop Bill. Aged sixty-four, former ambulance paramedic, retired at sixty. For the past few years he's been working part-time as a school crossing attendant." Wearing a hi-vis coat and wielding a fluorescent sign, he's one of the army of unsung heroes and heroines whose very important job is to walk out into a main road and bring the traffic to a screeching halt when the primary school kids are chucking out, in order to stop the oblivious yummy mummies and white-van men from mowing down bairns like ninepins. "He came to our attention two months ago when he had an argument over right of way with a courier firm Ford Transit—and won. Bill saved a bunch of six-year-olds from being maimed or killed, and incidentally discovered that he's got lightning reflexes and super-strength. He's not as fast as Bee and not as strong as Jim, but he used to be fully certificated in first aid, and we could do with a paramedic on the team. Oh, and the guy behind the wheel was charged with texting while driving."

Bill is an affable-looking sixty-something in good shape—he could pass for a decade younger—with a salt-and-pepper beard and neatly trimmed hair. Born in Jamaica, emigrated with his parents when he was three, naturalized citizen, three kids and six grandchildren, he's a genuine good-natured public servant and all around British hero with an ethnic spin: *exactly* what we need.

"Okay." I nod. "And the other, Captain Mahvelous—"

Mhari pulls up his file. "Eric Talbot. Aged thirty-eight, software developer, civil partnership, works in banking."

"Why isn't he one of yours?"

She sniffs. "Obviously he isn't bright enough." Ramona clears her throat. Mhari shakes her head. "Want me to continue?"

"Sure, let's get this over."

She gives me a tight little smile. Smug, even. "Origin story: He and his hubby were on their annual boys' day out for London Pride this year and decided to head over to Old Compton Street for some clubbing after the march. Halfway there they ran into a group of gangbangers who were looking for trouble, or maybe some easy wallets to lift: your traditional queer-bashing ensued. Or rather, your traditional queer-bashing was *attempted*. That's when Captain Mahvelous discovered his hitherto unknown talent for telekinesis, and his affinity for dumpsters. And then, in short order, the joy of introducing would-be queer-bashers to said dumpsters. He hospitalized two of them—broken ribs—but the entire incident was captured on CCTV, and as it was six against two and the bad guys had knives, it was an open-and-shut case of self-defense."

"Okay. Any history of violent affray?"

"He's clean—his total police record prior to the incident consisted of two speeding tickets."

Ramona clears her throat again. "So, let's see. We have a three-to-one gender profile, which is bad, but balanced against it we have one LGBT and one feminist activist, one ethnic minority, one pensioner, two youths. Which makes it almost but not exactly off-target for the team makeup you were handed by head office, but at least the poor oppressed male trolls won't have an excuse to go all rage face because it has too many girl cooties. If we can downplay the LGBT, ethnic, and pensioner angles, it's *almost* what we've been told to procure . . . are we missing anything?"

"No—sorry—no wheelchairs or missing limbs. No religious minorities either."

"I don't believe your current Home Secretary will care too much about that," she says drily.

"Your?"

"Okay, our." She shrugs. "While I'm on land: after all, you people were good enough to give me a passport, so I suppose that means I've got dual nationality . . ."

Mhari makes a cutting gesture. "Ancient history. The point is, they meet our brief for a team, and we can probably tap-dance our way around the diversity angle: it's hard to form a group as badly balanced as the brief we were given without actually practicing illegal discrimination. At least this bunch look reasonably tractable, leaving us to get on with the heavy lifting in the background. Two super-speed, two super-strength, one pyro, one telekinetic. Can we work with that?"

I lean back and think. "We need to get them into Hendon ASAP," I say finally. "And devise some training-wheel exercises. Sorting out uniforms is now a higher priority—Ramona, can you take your latest spec and get us some provisional costings on it? Budget to equip eight in the field, three sets of protective kit per person, we'll worry about some kind of dress uniform later. Then it's time to get our public relations hat on and work on a media relations strategy."

"You think?" Mhari asks, with wholly unnecessary (in my opinion) ironic emphasis.

I sit up. "We're management. Finally we've got a superhero team to manage!" *Just as long as the job doesn't nibble their brains into lethal lacework,* my inner conscience nags me. "So all we need to do now is sort out training and medical support, then brief the PR firm and the scriptwriters you've got lined up and see what they can come up with."

"Indeed." Mhari mirrors my mannerism, sitting up and looking attentive.

I can't always tell when she's taking the piss, and it's mildly upsetting—but not enough to justify reprimanding her. "Just remember the first law of management," I tell them.

"What's that?" asks Ramona, walking straight into it.

"Being management means having to hold your hands behind your back while your inexperienced junior staff crap all over a job you could have done in five seconds—and then taking their mess right on the chin."

* * *

MAYBE IT'S A FULL STOMACH AND AN EMOTIONAL UNWIND AFTER a week of attempted *karoshi*, or possibly it's because I park Lecter's case too damned close to the bed, or perhaps it's just the phase of the moon: but I go to sleep, perchance to dream, and what I dream is this:

I'm dancing through the ruins of an ancient city.

Two moons ride high and full above me in a cloudless night sky, drenching the scene around me with blue-gray twilight. Beneath my feet, the lime flagstones are worn smooth by the passage of time; to either side, decaying classical frontages and columns rise roofless amidst piles of rubble, like the bones of Whitehall a thousand years after the extinction of London. There are few trees here and less grass, but rose bushes curl thorny tendrils around the tombstone relics of the city. Their flowers are black as velvet night in the gloaming.

I'm wearing a long white tunic, not unlike an ancient Greek chiton; my feet aren't bare, but my sandals are so thin that I can feel every crack and abrasion on the stones. The music—

—It's ghostly, it's wild, and it teeters on the edge of arrhythmia: a skirling mournful howl of tormented strings, the distant moaning of a tied-down giant whose vocal cords are being bowed by malign Lilliputian tormentors, intent on turning his every attempt at spoken communication into a vehicle for an inhuman melody. It keeps me on my toes against my will, even though my muscles are burning and tired—for I anticipate the imminent arrival of the soprano and baritone leads.

As I spin past a half-tumbled wall, I spy a milestone. The word Carcosa is engraved on it in Roman letters, but the number below is indistinct.

I look up, glancing away from the alien moons (one seemingly larger than Earth's, the other smaller but still showing a visible disk). The stars are bright, but there are too many of them, harsh and pitiless and untwinkling—a smear splashed halfway across the sky like the Milky Way, only far denser and brighter. This isn't the world of the Sleeper in the Pyramid, unless it's a view of an earlier time: but that's no cause for celebration. My feet carry me along a broad curving boulevard. There are side streets through the rubble and wreckage of this magnificent city, and as I pass them I catch glimpses in the distance of a lake, of terraced hillsides looming in the darkness at the edge of town. There is motion on the other boulevards, a swirling of bone-white dancing bodies making their processional way towards a common destination where all roads converge.

Voices rise in unearthly harmony, singing lyrics that blend with the god-voice of the distant strings towards which I am now running:

Along the shore the cloud waves break,
The twin suns sink behind the lake,
The shadows lengthen
In Carcosa.

Strange is the night where black stars rise,
And strange moons circle through the skies,
But stranger still is
Lost Carcosa.

Songs that the Hyades shall sing,
Where flap the tatters of the King,
Must die unheard in
Dim Carcosa.

My avenue of the dead terminates at a huge circular plaza, dominated by the shattered segments of a fallen column of vast proportions. Four plinths surround it, much like Trafalgar Square, but surmounted by unfamiliar statues: heraldic alien monsters, a dragon with a beard (or tentacles?), a cephalopod with baroque spines sprouting from the edges of its shell. The dancers, all clad in white chitons and with skin as pale as chalk or bone, converge on the stage at the bottom of the semicircular amphitheater that lies at the feet of the ruined column. The music comes from a hidden pit at the side of the stage—

Come quickly! We shall be late for the chorus.

My hitherto-unseen bone-white dance partner takes my hands and swings me around, redirects me on a breakneck scramble down the worn stone seats of the amphitheater towards the orchestra—the stage—towards which the other dancers are racing. He's muscular and tall, overlooking me, and when he pulls me tight and lifts me across a huge segment of the column that has crushed half a row of seats into rubble, I seem to recognize his face. "Jim, we can't—"

That's not my name in this place. Quickly! There's no time to lose!

We arrive on the stage as the white-draped singers form up in two rows across the middle, standing before the audience of ghosts and memories that overflow the seats. But my partner doesn't stop and pull me into one of the lines: instead he redirects me towards the side. "Wait, what do you want?" I demand.

There is no time! Quickly, you must play!

He picks me up and carries me into the shadows at the edge of the orchestra, then lowers me down into the pit of shadows. The bone-shapes of the half-glimpsed players shift and rattle, making space for me upon a shelf-like bench. Claw-hands tug and worry me into place, fencing me in and handing me a familiar instrument that glimmers in the darkness.

"But I don't know the score!" I cry as Lecter settles into my hands like a long-lost bloody secret.

Yes you do, says my dancing partner, wrapping his arms around me from behind. I look round in terror—the kind of terror that wakes one shuddering from a nightmare—and find myself in his arms, for now he is seated and I am straddling my demon lover, legs spread for his bone-white body. Because this is a dream I am simultaneously drawing my bow across his glowing violin strings and riding atop his all-too-human manhood: grasping the instrument, gripped by the instrumentalist.

I feel him pulse in rhythm as the notes flood through him, rising from my crotch to my blood-dripping fingertips in a wave of ecstasy and horror. I can do this, I realize, I *can* play these fingerings, I *can* draw *sul tasto* and bring these notes into existence and soar all the way to heaven—but the music is *wrong*, corrupting, the implications of its inexorable logic leading to a concluding nightmare. *I do not want to play this piece,* I realize. "No," I say, the horror winning out in a race against ecstasy, "no, *no*—"

I wake up.

I wake up.

Those words are prosaic, inadequate to describe the experience of emerging from that dream: I feel as if I've been hit by a truck. I lie atop the sheets, drenched in sweat, and feel shaky and very, *very* horny. I am simultaneously repelled by my own sensuality and furiously angry.

I roll over to the side of the bed and grab Lecter's case. "Listen, you fucker," I hiss: "You will not ever, *ever*, do that to me again, do you understand?" I shake him: "If you ever try that again I will put you in a weighted box and dump you in the English Channel. Or maybe I will just pick up this crowbar and smash you to pieces. Oversight and Internal Assets can piss up a rope: you will not *ever* force yourself into my head again or I will *destroy* you."

There is a contrite, dread-filled silence in my head, where once might be heard the echo of a sly titter.

Good, I think. I scared the bastard.

I'm still horny. I need a distraction; it's late, but . . . I open the case, unlocking its evidently ineffective wards. In the real-world moonlight coming through the Velux window overhead, my bone-white violin is still a thing of beauty. Passive, lying still, just an instrument. I'm angry *and* horny. I pick up bow and body, my grip harsh, over-controlling: let's see, let me improvise around a theme . . . how about *no means no?* I make up a harsh little ditty, a discipline song, and work out my anger with a fiddle and a snarl of concentration, sawing and shuddering as I work my will on him, letting him know exactly who's on top in this relationship. He's very submissive, very contrite, very compliant. Offering to make good. But I don't want that: I just want him to know that my dreams are my own, and he has no right to invade and pervert my most intimate fantasies.

Silence is not consent.

When I'm done with my harsh music lesson I put him away, and this time I store him in the wardrobe, sketch reinforcement wards across the violin case, and for good measure seal the major containment ward on the door. Then I go to the bathroom and hunt in the medicine cabinet for a sleeping pill. I take one, head back to bed, and eventually fall into a deep, solitary sleep.

And this time, I do not dream of the King in Yellow.

15.

FRESH MEAT

I AVOID THE OFFICE ON SATURDAY. INSTEAD, I SPEND THE morning trying to catch up on the housework. I manage to put in two hours before I give up in despair: at least I vacuumed the carpets, and the dishes are all clean. Then I goof off for an hour of not-entirely-fruitful internet research on a subject that is close to my heart: ways and means of destroying human bones. But my heart isn't in it, and I keep checking the clock. Finally I go upstairs and prepare a suitable outfit, something artfully bohemian-casual and utterly *not* office-appropriate, and go back downstairs to pretend I'm not waiting.

At ten minutes to two the doorbell chimes. I check the peephole, then open it. "Hello?" I ask.

A gawky teenager with skin to die for and inexpertly applied eyeliner looks up at me. "Are you Mo?" she asks, sizing me up with a judgmental eye.

"Yes." I glance past her and see a Volvo Estate sitting double-parked like a self-propelled roadblock, engine idling. There's a familiar profile at the wheel, and as I glance back at the girl, I recognize echoes of Jim's bone structure. "You must be Sally?"

"That's right," she says. "Dad says he can't find anywhere to park—you coming?"

"One minute," I promise, and retreat back inside to grab my shoulder bag. Then I vacillate violently for a minute over what to do about my violin case. It's still upstairs in the wardrobe: I *ought* to take it, I'm responsible for the instrument—but I'm still several steps beyond pissed off at Lecter. I'm furious and not entirely rational, and anyway, from a safety perspective this is a secured safe house, with an alarm system and wards up to the eaves. Lecter is locked in an anonymous-looking wardrobe behind a particularly vicious containment ward, and anyone who breaks in and takes him while I'm gone will regret it for about as long as a cable thief gets to regret grabbing hold of a live high-tension bearer in an electricity substation.

Lecter can look after himself for a few hours. And I really don't want to touch him right now. What is usually a comforting security reflex currently sets my skin a-crawl. I feel naked without him, but feeling naked in public is less uncomfortable than having to pick up his case and haul him around with me. I was well on my way to learning how to look after myself before they offered me the custody of a really special instrument; I can still look after myself: all I need is to find a new and suitably qualified custodian and I can be done with the White Violin for good.

I suddenly realize that I have turned a hitherto-unseen corner in my own mind.

I lock up, set the alarm, and follow Sally out to the car. After a brief no-you-go-first tap dance she slips into the back, leaving me the front passenger seat. "Afternoon," Jim says breezily. "Mo, this is Sally. Sally, this is Mo. Please don't kill each other. Have we got everything?"

"I've got my Nexus," Sally says with the long-suffering air of a teenager who is used to adults trying to organize her, "and my phone and my pen and my class notes," she adds. *Oh dear: do I detect an attitude?*

"Forget the notes," I advise her. "I don't know what he's been telling you, but we're going to see a farce. Slapstick comedy with music, eighteenth-century style. It has a chunk of romance that was so smutty they had to censor it back in the day, and a sprinkling of pointed political satire that also nearly got it banned—and the music's by Mozart, which might not be your thing but which is *generally* considered to be not half bad, which is why they're still performing it more than two hundred years later. My advice is to sit back and enjoy the music and the costumes and the farce, or whatever takes your fancy, and ignore the notes unless you get hopelessly lost."

"So it's a musical," she says, chin on fist, elbow propped on knee, telegraphing boredom. "The last musical Mum took me to was *Chicago*."

"Do you think they'll still be performing *Chicago* in the twenty-third century?" I ask lightly.

Jim drives the urban tank sedately, but I'm pretty sure I feel his wince through the steering rack when Sally drops her Broadway bombshell. Or maybe I'm projecting. I glance at him. He's in weekend casual, chinos and open-necked shirt with a sports jacket—this is an afternoon matinee performance. When he's not in uniform or a business suit, he looks younger and free-er than the Jim I know from the office; also older and more mature in a family-guy-with-teenage-daughter-in-tow kind of way. "Liz and I have, shall we say, different tastes in music," he says.

"Yeah, he likes all kinds of crap eighties rock, like Devo and The Fall," Sally warns me.

"Are we not human?" he asks rhetorically.

"No, we are Devo," I answer. Devo is fun. Musically unpolished and simple but conceptually ironic fun.

"You see?" Jim says to his daughter.

"No fair!"

There ensues the usual parking-in-central-London ritual, a walk to the Coliseum, soft drinks and strictly no popcorn for Sally, and then a cracking performance of Mozart's adaptation of Beaumarchais's stage masterpiece. Sally seems bored at first, or at least expects to be bored, until midway through the first act between the dueling insults and the start of the cross-dressing comedy of mistaken identities. By the end of the first act she's paying attention, and by the end of the second she's agog.

After nearly three hours Sally is clearly flagging, but from what I can see out of the corner of my eye, when she looks at her tablet she's checking up on the plot rather than goofing off on Facebook—a good sign. Jim is clearly enjoying himself, which is also good. As for me, I'm immersed in Mozart's complexity and richness, with a lush visual extravaganza to keep my eyeballs occupied as I follow the music. A pall of existential fatigue actually seems to fall away from me during the performance: by the Count's final plea for forgiveness I'm as relaxed as I've been in weeks.

Afterwards we take a wander and end up in Wagamama, which is clattery and white and stark, a complete antithesis to the opera. "Did you enjoy that?" Jim asks Sally as she tackles a bowl of yaki udon. She nods, wide-eyed.

"It was different," she says. "Not stuffy, like I'd imagined."

"We could do it again some other weekend," I say. "Some operas *are* stuffy and boring"—Bob would say, *up their own arse*—"but I know which to avoid."

Sally fixes me with a Look that stacks at least three years on top of her notional age and asks, "What's in it for you?"

Jim looks at her sharply but I shake my head and smile at her. "I need to get out more. Your dad can tell you about what I do, but I've been working too hard lately, putting in regular seventy-hour weeks. This is me attempting to redress the balance."

"Are you married? I mean, do you have a partner? What do they think?"

"I don't know what he thinks," I say truthfully. "We're going through a bad patch, and he's moved out. Like I said, too much work. For both of us, I think."

"Hah." She lowers her eyes back to her soup bowl, worst suspicions evidently confirmed.

"I'm not dating your father," I tell her. "We just agreed we both needed to get out of the office some more."

When we finish our food, it becomes apparent that Sally has plans for the evening. "Thanks for the show, it was great. I want to go shopping now," she says. "The shops don't shut for another hour."

"But your mother's—" Jim is obviously thinking of feeding the parking meter.

"I can get the tube home," she says artlessly. "You two need to talk."

"Wait—" he begins to say, but she's already walking away.

"That one sees more than she lets on," I warn him as his eyes follow her retreating back. "Don't worry, she's got a phone."

"I know," he says, sounding anything but confident. "I mean, I know *in theory*. But it still feels like she only learned to walk last month."

"What were you telling me the other night about not helicoptering?"

His shoulders slowly relax.

"Maybe you're right. Want a lift home? I'm afraid I'd rather stay out of pubs or wine bars—it being Saturday night."

"A lift would be good." I shudder slightly at a passing shadow, reach for a hard case that isn't slung over the back of my chair, then check myself. "I'm quite tired, to tell the truth. I slept really badly last night."

We head back to the urban tank and climb in. "By the way," he says, "there's a run of *La traviata* at the Royal Opera House, ending next week. Can I interest you in it? Just the two of us, perhaps?"

"I'm—hmm." Suspicion and skepticism set up a train wreck clangor in my head: Has he been cold-bloodedly stalking me, using his daughter as a human shield? Or am I seeing ulterior motives where none exist? "Why not take Sally?"

"She's got exams the week after next. Resits, I'm afraid. Culture's all very well, but not at the expense of grades." Both his hands are on the steering wheel as he checks for cross-traffic. I can only see his face in side profile, but he seems more intent on driving safely than on slyly checking me out. As excuses go, it has the ring of truth to it.

"Okay, then yes"—*tentatively*, I warn myself—"you may indeed consider me interested. How about, oh, Saturday, if we can score tickets?"

"You'll be lucky. Would you like me to try and shake some loose?"

"That'd be great," I tell him. Saturday evenings hit me hardest when Bob's away exorcising sacrifice pits in Yucatán or something. Tonight I'll be okay—even if I'm stuck at the kitchen table with a mug of Horlicks and a stack of purchase orders to approve—but often those evenings seem to stretch out endlessly.

"Deal," he says, looking pleased: his expression makes me feel happy.

JIM TAKES ME HOME, AND I RESUME MY MACABRE RESEARCH with a light heart and a mug of the aforementioned Horlicks. My social appetite is sated for the time being, and I'm happy to be back in my comfort zone with the front door locked.

To tell the truth, I just about managed to forget about Lecter while we were at the opera—but I felt a nagging sense of unease as we braved the crowds on New Oxford Street on our way to the restaurant, and it didn't go away even when I reminded myself that I was on a date with Officer Friendly and his daughter, that the bracelet on my left wrist was a beefed-up ward strong enough to stop the Mandate dead in his tracks should I run into him again by accident, and that even without the violin I am a certificated combat practitioner with the ability to cause an unholy amount of collateral damage if I cut loose by accident. I've become accustomed to relying on my singular instrument to an unhealthy degree. I've *got* to stop using Lecter as a crutch, if only because I can't start to sort things out with Bob if I don't.

I take a break from the purchase orders to go back to my macabre (and ultimately futile) research project. Destroying the bone violin would be quite easy if he was merely made of mundane scrimshaw. Bone is a somewhat more rigid material than the spruce and maple of a conventional instrument, but Lecter's body is thinner in places, to impart the flexibility required by a resonant instrument. If he was inanimate, a wood axe would suffice to dismember him, and a kitchen waste disposal unit would crunch the debris. You might wreck the kitchen unit, but the violin would come off worse.

The trouble with trying to do away with him using mechanical tools—the problem that renders this entire project an exercise in futile wish-fulfillment fantasy, if I'm perfectly honest—is that Lecter is an occult instrument. To destroy him, I would first have to reverse and unwind the bindings that anchor his soul, or what passes for one, to his body. They weren't designed to be unwound, and to make matters worse I could reasonably expect Lecter to put up a fight.

Your sidekick Mr. Grenade stops being your friend the moment you pull his pin out: just so with the violins Erich Zahn created at the behest of Dr. Mabuse. Lecter has steadily grown more powerful ever since we entered the opening stages of CASE NIGHTMARE GREEN. He's now alarmingly strong; if I'd met him for the first time as he is now, he'd have eaten me alive. I expect any attempt at exorcism will result in him making an all-out bid to suck my soul out through my eyeballs, and I suspect the only entity I've met who could possibly hold him in check is the Eater of Souls.

Lecter is bound by geas to serve the Laundry, and my superiors have entrusted him to me because they think I'm a safe pair of hands. I'm responsible unless and until I can find a new bearer to hand him over to, and I can't in all good conscience condemn someone else to what he'll inevitably do to their mind. So I'm stuck with him unless I can find a legitimate reason to destroy him. But one does not go cap-in-hand to the Board of Directors to request the destruction of an irreplaceable offensive artifact just because of a spot of relationship trouble. Short of obtaining clear evidence that Lecter has become a danger to the organization, getting the SA to agree to sign off on a formal request for his destruction, and running it up the chain to the board, I don't see any permanent way out of my present fix.

On the other hand, a nice relaxing swim in the Channel doesn't *have* to be permanent.

Thinking these thoughts I walk upstairs, unseal the ward on the wardrobe, remove the violin case, and carry it back down to the kitchen table. Then I open the lid and stare at the thing inside.

"Do you know what I'm thinking?" I ask.

The violin lies still, quiescent and inert in its coffin lined with ivory silk.

"I went to the opera today," I tell him. "I went outside without you. For the second time this week." It's true: the meeting at ACPO and my afternoon with Jim and Sally are the only times this year that I've allowed myself to get more than a hundred meters away from him. "I'm still mad at you. But now I know something else: I can live without you." *Modulo some withdrawal symptoms, but . . .* "What do you think of that?" I'm not sure that I can live without my instrument, but I'm not prepared to live *with* him if we can't establish exactly who's in charge of our relationship. "What do you say?"

Sorry.

"I've been thinking," I muse aloud: "Destroying you, unbinding you, would be difficult. Not to mention extremely hard to obtain authorization for. I can send you to sleep with the fishes for a while, but that wouldn't stop you finding a new host, would it? Maybe the best thing would be if I just admit defeat and surrender you. I can tell Dr. Armstrong I can't carry you any longer. I can tell him why, and I can tell him, warn him that you're growing stronger. They'll need a more powerful player to control you. And those don't come along very often, do they? So they'll carry you back to that humidity-controlled safe in the basement of Dansey House and seal you up alone in the dark again, and this time it'll be for months or years. Maybe decades. All alone in the dark."

Please don't do that.

"So it's please *now*, is it?" I shout, thumping the kitchen table so that the violin case bounces. "Well, *tough!*" I take a deep breath. "Here's what's going to happen. I am going to get a warded gun locker installed here and another at the office. You're going to live in them when I don't need you. At night, for example, when I'm sleeping. You'll come out of your box when I need to practice and when I need to deploy you and for transport. That's all. If you try to escape or slither into my dreams, that's *it*. It's the safe for you. I'm through with this. You've had your chance. You tried to kill Mhari, you tried to kill Bob, you tried to force me to play you. No more. No more chances, no more apologies. That stuff is over for good. Do you understand?"

Yes.

"Good." I close the violin case. "Back in your box." I carry him back upstairs and stash him in the wardrobe again.

So hungry, I hear him whisper in my head as I close the door and then turn the key in the lock. His voice is like contaminated engine oil floating on the surface of a river at night. A sharp stab of anxiety grips me: *Is he lying to me?* Something about his supine display of remorse rings false. *Well, fuck you,* I think. "Sleep tight."

Need food— I activate the ward: blissful silence descends.

The rest of the weekend is uneventful. If only I could relax and enjoy it.

IT'S TUESDAY, AND PIGEONS RELEASED WEEKS AGO ARE COMING home to roost.

Monday started with an all-hands meeting to introduce our four new hires to the analysts, HR, and support folks. That kind of event is *always* risky, teetering on the edge of embarrassment. For quiet, gawky Billy, aka The Torch, it's his first-ever job in a workplace with carpet, much less indoor plumbing and co-workers who wear suits. There's a 150 percent pay rise hanging over him like the Sword of Damocles: What is he supposed to do to earn it? He's silently terrified, even though he has enough firepower in his right index finger to take out a main battle tank. For my part I'm just glad that his hoodie, combats, and trainers are clean enough he doesn't look as if he's walked in off a construction site. Bee, aka Lucy Teller, is infinitely more mature—if by mature you mean sassy: with her dark hair gathered in pigtails and wearing a '50s style yellow dress with black horizontal stripes, she could pass for a hipster on speed, if hipsters had a permanent caffeine buzz and metaphorical stingers. She's excited, energized, eager to make a difference. This poise has Billy, unsurprisingly, caught somewhere between fascination and terror, so he's pointedly ignoring her. *Great* way to start building a team, team.

Our two other new hires aren't here yet, but I can at least show everyone their mugshots and order that they be made welcome on arrival. Speaking of which:

"I'd like you all to welcome Billy and Lucy to the Transhuman Police Coordination Force. They've got a steep learning curve ahead of them and lots of training courses before they can represent the Force in public—along with our two other front-line superpowers, Lollipop Bill and Captain Mahvelous, who will be arriving next week. Billy and Lucy: Mhari Murphy will start you on your basic orientation today and introduce you to everyone this afternoon so you don't need to memorize their names right now. I know this is all a lot to take in at once"—I suddenly realize that even though Jim's elsewhere and Sam is visiting a sick relative, there are nearly a dozen people present—"but don't worry, you'll get used to it in no time."

The formal introductions done, I beat a hasty retreat into my office. There's plaster dust on the carpet and an unpleasant oily smell in the air, courtesy of the hulking gun safe in the corner.[*] I check my chair carefully for plaster dust before I sit down—I'm wearing my smart suit today, in anticipation of spending the afternoon at a Home Office briefing session—and am about to bury myself in prep for the anticipated grilling (on anything we can contribute to the Freudstein problem) when Ramona motors in.

"Hi, Mo," she says. "I've got a surprise for you!"

"What kind?" I ask cautiously.

"Nothing bad." She smiles gleefully as she whirrs forward, holding up a USB key.

"What's that?"

---

[*] It arrived early last week. When I phoned Harry the Horse at the New Annex and he said it couldn't be fitted before next month, I snarled semi-politely and referred him to the Senior Auditor: it's *amazing* what taking God's name in vain can accomplish, when you've got God on speed dial and he considers your needs to be an urgent priority.

"First cut at a promo video. Want to watch it together?"

I suppress my first reflexive response (a groan), force a smile, and say, "Can do." Then I shove the memory stick into the front of my newly chained-to-the-desk PC. We've recently acquired new software that locks everything down, only lets data in (not out) when you plug in a dongle, and refuses to run software that hasn't been installed and authorized centrally by IT Support. In my opinion (and everyone else's) it turns our PCs into single-function boat anchors, but two months and ten employees on, our organizational threat surface has expanded until it's too dangerous for us to risk laptops. Also, we now have to play by civil service regs, not Laundry rules. "Let's see what they've come up with."

"Move over."

I shove my chair sideways to make room for Ramona. There is indeed a movie file on the stick. I double-click, wait for the obligatory three virus scanners to do their stuff, then sit back while the video player fills the screen with the first thing the organizational PR agency's collective subconscious has come up with.

START ANIMATION SHOWREEL:

> **THE SCENE:** A boringly normal-looking suburban street in Anytown, England. Dogs bark, children shout, a delivery van drives slowly past.
>
> **CUT TO:** A different street, more densely urban: houses on one side, a big new charter school campus on the other. Uniformed kids hang around outside the gates and in the playground . . .
>
> **VOICE-OVER:** Keeping our schools and homes safe.
>
> **PAN RIGHT:** A street corner adjacent to the school. Just round the corner, past more buildings, the camera zooms in to frame a man in a lime-green PERVERT SUIT and cloak, crouching in front of a house. He brandishes a teddy bear at the camera.
>
> **PERVERT SUIT:** *Arr*, I am NONCE-BOY! I hang out on street

corners near schools and 'ipnotize your kids! 'Oo knows what hideous perversions I fantasize about perpetrating on their smooth underage flesh, what nightmarish pedobear-related fantasies I intend to corrupt their innocent little souls with—

ZOOM OUT: A posse of SUPERHEROES are racing down the side street towards PERVERT SUIT.

SUPERHERO 1: It's NONCE-BOY! Get 'im!

SUPERHERO 2: On my way!

SUPERHERO 3 (FEMALE): Flying scissor kick! *Oh Piroge* jump!

THEY FIGHT.

CUT TO: NONCE-BOY lying prone on the pavement with his hands and feet hog-tied in elaborate Japanese rope bondage style. The SUPERHEROES stand over him. He grins horribly at the camera.

NONCE-BOY: They're making a big mistake.

CUT-TO: A Police interview room. TWO INSPECTORS are cross-examining NONCE-BOY.

INSPECTOR 1: And what exactly did SUPERHERO 1 say?

NONCE-BOY: I heard him distinctly say, "It's NONCE-BOY! Get 'im!" Then he attacked me without provocation.

INSPECTOR 2: Are you denying your previous? You've done time for *hideous crimes of hideousness*! He obviously thought you were about to get up to your old tricks again.

NONCE-BOY: Nevertheless, I has my Human Rights! Including the right not to be beaten up by random vigilantes! (*Confidingly*): And there's more.

INSPECTOR 1: What else?

NONCE-BOY: SUPERHERO 3 used her *Oh Piroge* jump on me. That's sexual assault, that is!

CUT-TO: A Police briefing room with the TWO INSPECTORS.

INSPECTOR 2: It's no good. He's got us bang to rights.

INSPECTOR 1: We can't let him go! He's a pervert—

INSPECTOR 2: But he's right about one thing. The SUPERHEROES who took him down are vigilantes. They didn't observe due process, they didn't identify a suspect in the process of committing or preparing a crime, they aren't sworn officers of the law like you and me, they used dubious or outright illegal methods, and they inadvertently handed his defense a watertight case. In fact, they'll be lucky if he doesn't sue them.

INSPECTOR 1: All we can do is let him go and hope he falls downstairs on his way out of the cell block.

INSPECTOR 2: And this is a one-story-high police station, so that's not terribly likely.

INSPECTOR 1: (*Addresses the camera*): So NONCE-BOY walks free, all because those SUPERHEROES acted like idiots.

ZOOM IN: INSPECTOR 1

INSPECTOR 1: Want to be a SUPERHERO? Don't be like these numpties! Join up with TPCF. Get wise, get trained, get your villain.

FADE TO: Home Office Logo, Transhuman Policy Coordination Force contact information.

"WELL, WHAT DO YOU THINK?"

"Hmm. I think that was pretty good, actually. It compared favorably with *Plan 9 from Outer Space*. Three rotten tomatoes?"

"I was thinking *Surf Nazis Must Die*."

"Actually, if they ham it up a bit more, say if they turn the dial from nine to eleven and switch from animation to human actors, it might hit Adam West Batman values of kitsch. Who knows? We might be on course to be the first government agency to win a Golden Oyster award."

"But it got the key points across, didn't it?"

"I know it's meant to be funny, but there's a fine line between being laughed *with* and being laughed *at*. If we go public with this, we'll be a laughing stock."

"So that's a no, Mo?"

"Remember the search for the HomeSec's sense of humor? They had to ground the rescue choppers for maintenance checks, they'd been airborne so long. If we take this to the Home Office, someone's going to have to explain all the jokes to her, and I don't want that someone to be me. I'm pretty sure she's got Medusa DNA." Pause. "Unless, hmm. Unless we make it look like a leak. What if we let it show up on YouTube with a disclaimer saying it's an unreleased rough treatment?"

"You mean it's kitsch enough it might just go viral? But we could disclaim it if it backfires? Holy Batman, that's brilliant, Mo!"

"Who knows? It's a long shot, but it *just might* work."

16.

DEMOCRACY IN ACTION

THE AMUSEMENT AFFORDED ME BY THE FIRST OF OUR PROMO
video treatments is short-lived, because after a lunchtime raid on Pret
A Manger I have to return to Marsham Street and the Home Office
for the long-dreaded grilling about, well, everything.

This session is somewhat smaller than the previous one: but it will
be chaired by the Right Honorable Jessica Greene herself. Luckily Jim
is coming along, fancy uniform and all, so I'm not the only sacrificial
rodent entering the snake pit. But I confess to feeling some trepidation—
almost enough to make me dial in the combination on my safe and
remove Lecter. (But not quite. If it's a really hostile session and I get
upset, there is a very remote chance that I will undergo a stress reaction, and if Lecter is present the potential for certain defensive reflexes
to cut in is *also* present, and it would be a *very bad idea* to eat the soul
of the fourth ranking minister in the cabinet—even though some of
her harsher detractors would laugh in disbelief at the very idea that
she has a soul in the first place).

I meet Jim in the concourse outside. He looks the very model of a
modern police major-general. "Afternoon, Mo. How do you want to
play this?"

I shrug. "I think we should be blunt but honest. Aside from operational work-up, our biggest priority is the search for Freudstein. Message is: we are working on building a profile of him, but we are handicapped by a lack of resources and information. Freudstein is a canny opponent and he is clearly attempting to manipulate us. We intend to get inside his decision loop and outmaneuver him, but so far we have very little data upon which to build a predictive model of his activities because they are cunningly arranged to be maximally flashy but effectively random."

Jim nods but looks withdrawn. "She's not going to like that."

"No, but what else—"

The door opens and a Junior Undersecretary beckons us forward.

"Remember it's not all about Freudstein," Jim warns me quietly, and then we go in.

This conference room has natural light, courtesy of a row of high windows opposite the doorway. There's a U-shaped set of tables for the Home Secretary and her staff, and a table set across the end for people giving evidence or testimony or confessions. That would be us, I guess from the semicircle of a dozen faces opposite. Mrs. Greene sits at the far end of the U, chatting affably to a senior departmental secretary to her right. Our usher directs us to the seats in the hot spot, then closes the door, and we're off.

"Dr. O'Brien. It has been nearly eight weeks since the individual or group identifying themselves as Professor Freudstein first came to our attention. Why haven't you caught him? Or her?"

Mrs. Greene is as direct and friendly as the business end of a machine gun. But it's not personal, and I know how to handle this sort of interrogation. Years of performing in front of the Auditors have hardened me.

"With all due respect, one might ask why the security guards at the Bank of England, SCO19 at the British Library on Euston Road, or the Civil Nuclear Police at Sellafield all failed to capture him. I don't want to play the blame game, but they were on-site during his previous appearances; my unit was not, and furthermore, we're still working up towards an operational capability which we have not yet achieved. Let me emphasize that: we're not fully operational yet. We're still recruiting and training personnel. The real problem with Freudstein is that we're not dealing with a normal criminal here.

"As I said, I don't want to play the blame game. Freudstein doesn't fit any of the threat profiles those forces are designed to deal with. In fact, from the planning he's demonstrated so far, he's operating more at the level of a hostile government agency rather than a criminal gang or terrorist cell. He—or they: I think there's a very high probability that we're dealing with an organization here—have access to trained special forces people, automatic weapons, helicopters, vehicles, and inside intelligence on some of the nation's most tightly guarded facilities. That's before we mention enough plutonium to credibly threaten us with multiple nuclear weapons. What we *don't* have is any kind of clue about his identity, real or purported, nor do we know what he wants." *Although,* I fail to say aloud, *there's probably a clue buried in what he stole from the library. If only we knew what he was really after and what were the decoy thefts!*

"Freudstein is our number one priority, and if we develop a source, or if a sister agency can give us a lead in time to deploy, we will engage him immediately. My analysts are currently creating a database of all known superpowers in the UK, and we are developing a profile for Freudstein and looking for possible leads on his real-world identity if he is indeed a five-sigma evil genius—but we're still dependent on leads from other forces. Nobody saw fit to inform us of the Sellafield incident until three days after it took place: that's typical of the level of cooperation we're currently getting. Again, I do not want to attribute any blame for this. In many cases the forces concerned don't even officially know we exist, much less have a set of criteria for referring incidents to us. But it's not helping us do our job."

"Why not?" Mrs. Greene is typically blunt.

"Because we were only formally established as a police force by order in privy council *four weeks ago,* and while we've sent out briefing packs to all the other forces, they're still working their way through the system. Jim and I briefed as many ACPO chiefs as we could reach at their summit last week, but it takes time for new information to get from the head office down to the feet on the beat."

Greene shares a brief whispered exchange with the woman on her left—a parliamentary private secretary, if my nose serves me right: an MP on the first rung of the ladder to ministerial rank, essentially a political gopher assigned to the HomeSec—then turns back to me. "Dr. O'Brien, I notice a pronounced defensiveness in your responses and a lack of proactive engagement with your primary objectives." Her eyes narrow. "You've been up and running for eight weeks: What *have* you accomplished?"

Oh shit. I think on my feet: "Let me start from the top. I've assembled a core management team of *experienced* superpowers, able to provide an austere—basic—response in event of a notified incident while our operational team is in training. We were active in time to be on-site during the Euston robbery. We subsequently established transport and logistic capabilities that support deployment anywhere in the UK, and have already deployed operationally in response to a support call from Greater Manchester Police." *Please don't ask how it went.* "We have created an analysis department, which is, as I said, currently working up a database of all known superpowers in the UK of three-sigma or higher capability. We have established liaison protocols with ACPO and are in the process of bringing all the territorial forces up to speed. We have recruited—after enhanced CRB checks and interviews—a core superpower team suitable for deployment with backup and oversight from the management team once they are fully trained. We are undergoing intensive training in police procedures and operations, because it's necessary for our superhero team to be sworn-in officers of the law—I should note that training for a probationary constable is normally two years, but we're working with Hendon to get them through the essentials in less than six months. We've been working with a Home Office–approved PR organization to produce a range of public information materials in support of our core function of diverting potential vigilantes into working within a lawful framework—"

Mrs. Greene is rubbing her forehead. Am I giving her a headache?
Oh dear.

"Dr. O'Brien," she says, icily polite, "this is all very well, but it's
not helping to catch Freudstein. In case you hadn't noticed, this country is facing a general election in nine months' time. Freudstein is
currently setting the paranormal policing agenda by default, and if
your organization hasn't caught him by then, *it isn't going to exist.*
You might not have been paying attention, but my Right Honorable
opponent, the Shadow Home Secretary, is making hay with the superpower issue. He's publicly saying that your Force is a boondoggle and
that when he's in my office he will start with a blank sheet review.
And I should remind you that the only reason Freudstein's escapades
are not yet public knowledge is because Freudstein hasn't publicized
them and we have managed to keep the lid on everything except the
British Library robbery due to the potential for public panic. But the
blackout isn't going to last forever, and your failure to apprehend
Freudstein could become the sensational lead story across *all* media
at any moment. If that happens, it will make this government look
bad. I need a concrete achievement to point to within the next month.
Get me one." She raises a hand: "Without shooting up any more
mosques." Her tone is dry enough to parch the Sahara.

Her gaze slides away from me to look at Jim. "Chief Superintendent. What is the state of readiness of the TPC Force, in terms of the
Police Service Readiness Criteria?"

Jim doesn't miss a beat. "Working up, ma'am. That is to say, it's
simply not fully operational yet and won't be for at least four months,
as my director said. Our key bottleneck is that there is only one identified three-sigma-plus police officer in the country, and he's already
working for TPCF. Everyone else has to pass through basic training.
TPCF is actually *ahead* of where I would expect a new organization
to be at this early stage. Its lean staffing level and austere budget mean
there's no room for featherbedding, and it's agile and responsive.
Also, we've been able to import management with existing experience
of dealing with extraordinary threats from the MoD. The downside
of that stance is that it's brittle—we're reliant on highly skilled indi-

viduals rather than functioning as a resilient organization. Dr. O'Brien is addressing this, but as she noted, it will take time."

Mrs. Greene nods. I keep a poker face as I realize that she'll accept it coming from a man in a uniform, but not from a woman. She fixes Jim with the unblinking basilisk stare she learned from her idol, the Iron Lady. I seem to be beneath her notice. "Get me something. *Anything* newsworthy and positive will do at a pinch, but what I really want is Freudstein's hide. I expect weekly updates in the meantime."

We are dismissed: the pit bull releases its chew-toy and we limp away to nurse our wounds.

I'M GOING TO FAST-FORWARD PAST THE INEVITABLE SHOCK-waves that fan out from my collision with Mrs. Greene. If you've ever been carpeted by the Boss and found wanting, you know how it goes. Let's just say that I spend the rest of the day (and early evening) in a council of war with the entire executive team—being me, Jim, Mhari, Ramona, and by special invitation, Dr. Armstrong himself—while we hammer out a highly unofficial hit list and a bunch of itemized deliverables that might meet the HomeSec's political requirements rather than our official (and bewilderingly useless) terms of reference. There is no point in prioritizing *doing your job* when your organization faces being defunded in less than three months' time if you don't do something else: you do what's necessary in order to ensure your organization survives, *then* you get back to work.

(This is how the iron law of bureaucracy installs itself at the heart of an institution. Most of the activities of any bureaucracy are devoted not to the organization's ostensible goals, but to ensuring that the organization survives: because if they aren't, the bureaucracy has a life expectancy measured in days before some idiot decision maker decides that if it's no use to them they can make political hay by destroying it. It's no consolation that some time later someone will realize that an organization was needed to carry out the original organization's task, so a replacement is created: you still lost your job and the task went undone. The only sure way forward is to build an agency that looks to its own survival before it looks to its mission statement. Just another example of evolution in action.)

When we break up around seven, I un-mute my phone and check for messages. There's a text from Bob: *Mind if I drop round this evening? Need to collect some stuff.* My heart bumps up against my breastbone. *Sure,* I text back. He sent it a couple of hours ago. I didn't know he was even in town this week: last time I heard from him he was in Western Australia, visiting a very peculiar First Nations site in the outback.

I collect my instrument case and head home, bone-tired and somewhat depressed. When I get there, the hall light is shining through the window above the porch. As I didn't leave it switched on, I assume that means Bob's home. So I unlock the door, check the alarm (it's switched off), and go inside. "Bob?" I call.

"Here." The reply comes from upstairs.

I close the door and open the safe in the under-stairs cupboard and shove Lecter inside. But I do not lock it—not just yet. I head for the kitchen, where I smell something delicious in the convection oven and see the table is laid for two. A flash of gratitude is followed by a stab of resentment: then a moment of self-interrogation—why am I resentful of my husband for making assumptions about my desire to dine with him? I shake my head, then go to the cupboard and haul out the cafetière and the jar of decaf.

A few seconds later I hear Bob's footsteps on the stairs. He gets as far as the kitchen doorway, then stops. "Who died?" he asks, looking me up and down.

"My career, if I'm not lucky." I pour hot water over the coffee grounds. "We were ambushed by the Home Secretary this afternoon. Be a dear and keep an eye on this while I change?"

"Sure." He takes over while I head upstairs and replace my suit in its carrier and pull on jeans and a tee shirt. Wearing office formal at home is too much like surrendering to the job. And it was making Bob uncomfortable—he's in his usual, which this decade is combat pants and casual shirt.

I find him downstairs in the kitchen, stabbing a roast chicken to death with a meat thermometer. "You could have mentioned you had dinner plans," I chide.

"Sorry, I didn't think you—" Double take. "You have alternatives?"

"Yes." I sit down. "Ramona and Mhari ganged up on me, so I'm taking three nights a week off. Going to the opera, eating out with co-workers, anything at all really: just as long as it stops me burning the candle at both ends every day."

"Oh, well: that sounds like a good idea." He nods ruefully. "Next time I'll check in advance."

"Sorry, I should have warned you." Apologies are the keystone of an enduring relationship. Failing to apologize for mistakes, or getting onto a treadmill of belittling insults, is a bad warning sign. So far we've avoided it, but . . . "I thought you were in Australia this week?"

"That was *last* week." (I rummage in the wine rack while he talks.) "You wouldn't believe how many sites Angleton worked at during his career. Even if he only left behind one a year that needs checking out, if it takes me an average of a week to handle each of them, I'll be running around with my tail on fire for the next eighteen months. Week before last, it was the sealed collection of a library in Cardiff that held the foul papers of a guy who wrote mathematical puzzle books in the sixties—it's got all the stuff Angleton made him leave out of the published editions. He was an ex–Bletchley Park analyst, nothing to do with our mob, but it had to be inspected. Angleton didn't confiscate his notes—he just put the frighteners on him and told him not to do it again. So now *I* have to check them out, and either confiscate them and fend off the angry librarians or write a memo explaining why potentially hazardous papers are lying around in a library we don't control . . . And *last* week I had to go check the cleanup on an Aboriginal site in Western Australia, two hundred miles east of Perth, south of the big mining complex. Angleton got all over the map."

I plant a bottle of sauvignon blanc on the table. It's from a New Zealand vineyard—extravagant, but I've got my husband back for the evening so what the hell. I attack the screw cap and pour two glasses. "How long are you in town for?" I ask.

"I've got three days, mostly for filing reports and catch-up meetings.

Then they're sending me to Leeds for a week to poke around a proposed new headquarters site for buried hazards." He shudders. "That's why I'm raiding my side of the wardrobe. What are we going to *do?*"

"Eat," I say. It comes out sounding like either a promise or a threat or something. To tell the truth I have no idea what we're going to do, or even if we're still a *we*.

Bob dishes up slices of roast chicken breast and drumstick, roast potatoes, carrots, and swede on the side. For all that it comes in supermarket pre-packs, it's welcome. We eat in companionable silence for a while.

"You've got a lot of travel going on," I say eventually, "but when things quieten down . . . do you want to see if we can make things work again?"

Bob chews mechanically, eyes staring right through me. Man-boy, thoughtful. He swallows. "I don't know if that's even possible anymore."

"Go look under the stairs."

Suddenly he looks round. "Where's your violin?"

"Go look under the stairs."

He stands and walks through into the hall. A minute later he comes back and sits down again, then takes a mouthful of wine. "Is that what I think it is?"

"Yes." I nerve myself for the next step. "It's warded, Bob. The violin lives there . . . for the time being."

He puts his glass down. "You're trying to give it up?" He sounds appalled and hopeful all at the same time.

The words come in a rush: "It's too strong for me, Bob! It's getting more powerful all the time, and I'm getting older, and there's going to come a time when I can't control it anymore. Michael—the SA—says I'm now the second-longest carrier it's ever had. We're looking for someone new, someone it can't Renfield. But if we can't find someone to replace me, it's going to have to go back in the inactive inventory."

He stares at me, clearly surprised. "What changed, love?"

"You did. I did." I grab my glass and take a gulp of wine and then set it down hastily because my hands are shaking. "If you can, can do something, I'll meet you halfway." I don't know if it's a promise or a plea, but either way I mean it.

He takes a deep breath. "I can't give up the Eater of Souls, Mo. Not, *don't want to*—I mean, I *can't*."

"Can you make it safe?" I ask. "I mean, safe enough to be around me without, without . . ."

He stands and walks around the table: I stand, lean against him, let him hug me. "I really need to talk to someone about applied containment theory," he says. "When I get time." Which would be a diplomatic way of saying *no*.

"You're very busy," I tell him, trying not to sound as broken as I feel.

"I'm sorry," he says. Letting go of me he repeats: "When I get time."

"We've got all the time in the world." I sniff, determined not to get teary.

"I don't think so." He looks at me, anxious and needy. We make a dismal pairing: barely treading water on our own, so weighed down by our personalized curses that we're each looking to the other as a life raft. "It's been well over a month already. Please don't let this become the new normal, Mo. Please?"

But all I can do is mutely shake my head. It's not up to me anymore. I've given up a lot to be here: if Bob can't meet me halfway, I don't see what possible future we've got.

ON FRIDAY MORNING I GO TO MY WEEKLY WITH DR. ARMSTRONG. I tell him about last Saturday's dream, and my subsequent dealings with my instrument.

"That's a rather worrying development," he says after I wind down.

"The violin intruding in my dreams? Do you think it's time for me to—"

"No, you're still perfectly able to control him if you set your mind to it. I meant the *location*."

"What? The ruined city?"

"The King in Yellow." The SA closes his eyes for a few seconds. "I haven't heard that name in a while. It's disturbing."

"What is it?" I did some digging, of course: there's a thick file on it in the Stacks, but I didn't have time to trudge round to Dansey House and sign myself in for an afternoon of reading dusty archives: I'm too busy fighting administrative fires. I told the analysts to follow it up for me, along with all the other manuscripts Freudstein stole, and it's somewhere in their work queue.

The SA opens his eyes. "Carcosa is one of the legendary lost cities. Or rather, a legendary lost Neolithic civilization, nearly pre-agricultural, drowned like Doggerland and the great cities of the Nile delta and the Arabian Gulf when the sea levels rose after the last ice age. They had elaborate court rituals centered around the worship of the King in Yellow. Subsequently the foundational material for some not inconsiderable occultist foofaraw in the late nineteenth century. It's a rite of binding, Dominique. Not unlike the ritual that certain meddling fools—who should have known better—tried to use to bind the Eater of Souls a couple of years ago." His unblinking stare makes me feel very small. "They wrote an opera around one of the invocations. One of the solos—I do not know which; it's too dangerous to read the score—installs a very small execution loop in the auditory cortex of anyone who hears it. If warded, one is safe, but if not, well, the first invocation anyone feeds you starts executing on your brain. *Not* nice. Carcosa is lost, and it is widely believed that it is lost because the King in Yellow bound his subjects in that manner, and unintentionally carried them all to a hell of his own conception or fed them to a god of his own devising or some such."

"That particular manuscript was part of the British Library heist." I don't like where this train of thought is going.

The SA turns his lizard-heavy gaze on me for a moment. "Do you suppose it was Freudstein's real target?"

"It would make sense." Played on a non-occult instrument the loop would just be an earworm: a short melody, very hard to dislodge from one's head. But played on a device able to perform polydimensional chromatic transforms, it'd leave the audience vulnerable to demonic possession by the first trivial feeder to come along. "But they'd need something like my instrument to, to install the loop."

"Yes." Dr. Armstrong is thoughtful. "There are certain disturbing rumors about the reason Dr. Mabuse commissioned the white violins—rumors along those lines."

"Mabuse?" He was a man of whom many stories are told, none of them good. "But surely he didn't actually stage a performance of *The King in Yellow*?"

"I don't believe he had the opportunity to do so. Then all known copies of the score were destroyed during the war, or collected by institutions that were, shall we say, uninterested in sponsoring a performance."

"It'd be grossly irresponsible to play it without working a protective ward into the refrain—"

My phone rings. Before I entered his office I set it to do-not-disturb: only a very short list of people can get through.

"'Scuse me," I say.

The SA swallows whatever he was going to say. "Certainly," he says, slightly stiffly, as I pull the smartphone out.

"Ah. It's important," I tell him as I glance at the screen. "O'Brien here. Speak."

"Mo?" It's Mhari. "We have an incident call-out."

"Where?"

"Downing Street. It's the Mandate." She fills me in quickly. He's somehow penetrated the security cordon, and is visiting the Government Chief Whip for tea and a chat in that worthy's official residence. What he didn't reckon with was the face recognition software running on the computers fed by the CCTV cameras around Whitehall. He can beguile a human watcher, but not a database system.

I get hot and cold and shivery with adrenaline, reflexively reaching for a violin case that isn't at my feet. "How long has he been there?" I ask.

"Only ten minutes so far," Mhari says eagerly. "We can get there if we hurry. Jim's in the office with Torch and Bee—"

"Okay. Tell them to go ahead and deploy around the area, don't wait for me. Don't let the Mandate leave the scene but don't interfere with him until I give the go-ahead. I'm coming back to the office to— no. Scrub that. Mhari, you know what's in the safe in my office?"

"Ye-e-s . . ." She doesn't sound happy.

"Tell Ramona to open the safe and bring the violin, in its case, then deploy. I'll give her the combination over the phone. If there's any trouble or if it tries to resist, don't bother; I'll swing by the office to collect it myself. Main thing is, I want everyone, and the violin, on deployment: I'll meet you there directly. Can you do that?"

"Let me get this straight? You're deploying without your—"

"No! I'm relying on security-cleared personnel to bring it to me: I'll collect it at the incident scene. You, Ramona, and Jim are all aware of its capabilities. I trust you know better than to mess with it."

She laughs, slightly shaky. "No shit! It's sunny outside."

"So go as White Mask." *The Home Secretary wants a show? Let's give her one.*

"Yes, Mo."

I end the call. The SA is watching me patiently. "Yes?" he asks.

"It's the Mandate," I tell him. "He's gone too far this time. I've got to go—"

"I'm coming with you," he says, unfolding himself from his chair. "You said it's happening at the Chief Whip's residence, didn't you?" He rummages in his desk drawer and pulls out a bunch of ancient-looking keys.

"Yes—"

"Follow me." He walks towards the curtained windows at the far end of his office. I stand and follow him, and he pulls back one of the ceiling-to-floor drapes at the side to reveal a narrow wooden case-ment, paneled, in which is set a keyhole. "Now let me see . . ." He works his way around the bunch of keys until he finds one to his lik-ing. He inserts it in the keyhole, turns it, and the casement hinges open like a very narrow doorway. Beyond lies utter darkness. "Follow me," he repeats, and slips sideways into the night.

I take a deep breath. "Where does this go?" I ask, tiptoeing after him.

"Sideways." I can feel a smooth surface in front of my nose, and there's another wall behind me: it's so narrow I have to turn sideways, hoping I won't get stuck. The air is cool and fresh, and for some reason I know in my guts that there's no ceiling overhead, just an infinite expanse of not-sky. I glance over my left shoulder and see the rectangular column of light from the SA's office dwindling with each crabwise shuffle. "Not far now," he reassures me.

"*What* is this?" I ask.

"You know about the ley lines and bike paths. The shadow roads aren't so different. Think of it as the institutional equivalent of hotel-space . . ."

He's clearly been listening to Bob too much: *So we're taking an extradimensional shortcut.* I don't want to think about it. Extradimensional geodesics are wonderful until you run into someone or something else that's coming the other way. Bob once ran into some shotgun-toting cultists on a shortcut: it's why he has a ten-centimeter-long scar on his upper right arm. He got off lightly, though. Not all the users of such routes are human. Sometimes someone you know uses one to save a little time and you never see them again. I shudder and hurry after the SA's receding shoulder. I can just see a twilight rectangle beyond him.

Most democracies have legislatures that meet in some sort of a parliament or senate building. The UK's House of Commons meets in the Palace of Westminster, a gothic pile on the banks of the Thames, near the middle of the cluster of neoclassical government offices known collectively as Whitehall. (The Palace of Westminster isn't as old as it looks: the original burned down by accident in the 1830s and this one is a replacement. It also got rebuilt in the 1940s, after it burned down for entirely non-accidental reasons.)

About a third of a kilometer away from Parliament there's an unassuming little stretch of road called Downing Street, lined with eighteenth-century town houses that have gradually been hollowed out and turned into a warren of offices and residences for the three highest politicians in the government: the Prime Minister, the Chancellor of the Exchequer, and the one nobody's ever heard of—the Chief Whip.

The Chief Whip is the Prime Minister's personal representative to individual MPs, telling them how they are expected to vote. And to give you some idea of how important the Chief Whip is in the British parliamentary system of government, that worthy lives at Number Nine Downing Street, next door to the Prime Minister. While my boss, the Home Secretary, as number four on the totem pole, doesn't rate a residence on the street.

The SA steps out of a panel in the wall of a side corridor and into a marble-floored entrance lobby. I follow on his heels as he marches straight towards the front door, and I hurry to catch up with him. "Where are we?" I ask.

"Foreign and Commonwealth Office." There are metal turnstiles and a security barrier ahead: he nods affably at the guard and slips through. I follow him, doing my best to look as if I belong here. We're both dressed for the part, which helps: the SA in dark gray pin-stripe and me in a black trouser suit.

Out on the street, my phone vibrates. It's Mhari. "Mo here. I'm with the SA on King Charles Street at the FCO building. Where are you?"

"We're northbound on Whitehall, just pulling over beside the entrance to Downing Street. Ramona's putting the flashers on."

"Okay, we'll be with you in two minutes." I hang up and tug the SA's sleeve. "They're at the east entrance, round the block."

"Poor timing on my part," he says tightly, quickening his pace.

Downing Street is not open to the public. There are anti-vehicle defenses and electrically operated gates at either end, not to mention armed officers from the Diplomatic Protection Group. You do *not* park within spitting distance of those gates unless you're the Police and it's an emergency. Luckily we *are* the Police (technically) and it *is* an emergency (even if they don't know it yet); also, my people have a uniformed Chief Superintendent to wave at the guards. But it's still going to be a little bit tense.

When Dr. Armstrong and I come round the corner, we see Jim

standing beside the van, head to head with a uniformed Inspector from SO17. Ramona's watery chariot has sprouted high-vis markings and a strobing light bar; a red DPG car has drawn up behind the van and its officers are standing alongside, but they're not pointing their assault rifles at anyone in particular yet. I take this to be a good omen.

We walk up towards the cluster and I pull my warrant card in readiness, but the SA beats me to the punch. As an armed officer moves to intercept, he gives the man a saintly smile and says, "I'm with him," nodding at Jim. The constable staggers slightly, then recovers and steps aside.

"Sorry," I say as we shoulder past: "Transhuman Force."

Jim seems to be having a little problem with the officer in charge of the Downing Street watch. "We haven't been notified of any problem—"

"You won't be. A four-sigma supervillain has gained access to the Chief Whip's office. Anyone capable of calling for help has already been disabled."

There is a whirr from the direction of the van: Ramona is lowering herself from a side door using some sort of wheelchair lift. "Dr. O'Brien," she calls.

I join her, leaving the SA to assist Jim in giving the creditably tenacious Inspector a backgrounder. "Thanks," I say as she hands me my instrument case. Is it my imagination or is Lecter unusually quiet? I walk back over, just in time to hear the SA calmly deliver what should be the definitive smackdown.

"The gentleman who the Chief Whip is currently playing involuntary host to walked right in because your men were unable to see him. Luckily, his ability to cloud minds is not so effective on CCTV cameras: Why don't you ask the control room for confirmation?" Dr. Armstrong smiles his saintly but subtly terrifying smile, then speaks, head tilted to one side as if he's listening to an invisible earpiece: "It is now 11:58. Ask them to confirm that at 11:43 a gentleman in a three-piece suit and a bowler hat walked up to the gate and was admitted, then proceeded to the door of Number Nine, where he was also admitted by the officers on door duty. That's our man."

"But that's impossible—" begins the Inspector, as I notice a blur of motion behind him. It's Bee; she jumps right over the two-meter-high spiky steel gate, then flashes along the street, covering the distance to the Chief Whip's front door in under a second.

"You appear to have another intruder," Jim tells the Inspector. "Good thing this one's a trainee constable, isn't it?"

"Back off!" The Inspector is so focused on the threat under his nose that he doesn't take his eyes off Jim, even though the Diplomatic Protection Group constables on the other side of the barrier are making a beeline for—

"Can we leave this for later?" I butt in, doing my best to be visible: "We have to apprehend the Mandate immediately!" I hold out my warrant card in front of the Inspector's nose and shove every gram of willpower I've got into it. He recoils in alarm. I don't dare look away from him: if my suspicion about what's happening to me is right, it's quite possible that if I break eye contact he'll suddenly forget I'm even standing in front of him. It's always more pronounced when I'm stressed: people seem to stop being able to see me, as if I'm not just socially invisible . . . "Torch, I want you to trip the fire alarms in Number Nine just as soon as you see Bee's in position. Try not to set the building alight, it's Grade One Listed and there are people inside. Jim, Ramona, get those officers to safety if the Mandate kicks off. I'll cover if it turns hairy." Mhari is hiding in the van, but I can't blame her: it's a bit bright out here today. I heft my violin case, finger on the quick-release button, and wish I'd had time to pick up some noise-cancelling headphones to hook into Lecter's pre-amp. They degrade the sound quality, but given who we're up against . . .

"You c-can't—" the Inspector stutters: I'm impressed. He has *real* willpower. "You'll answer to the Home Secretary!"

"I certainly hope so. Now let us in, otherwise I promise you that *you'll* be the one who's up in front of Professional Standards to-morrow."

A thin plume of white smoke begins to trickle from an attic window at Number Nine. "Oops," someone says aloud. An alarm siren keens. In the street, four or five officers are somehow tying themselves in knots. Bee let them get just close enough to think they'd got her, did the I'm-just-a-petite-and-harmless-girl thing to avoid provoking a restraint hold; then before they can get the cuffs on she's behind them, in front of them, performing cartwheels in the street—then she vanishes just as the door to Number Nine opens and everybody inside begins crowding out.

Inspector Diligent talks urgently into his Airwave. The Downing Street gate draws back and the Keystone Cops performance changes to something more sinister, as officers dash for cover and bring weapons to bear on the doorway.

Men and women stumble around in front of the Number Ten railings. They don't look as if they've left the office due to a fire alarm: they look dazed and confused, as if they've awakened from a disturbing dream to find that the dream was real. There's a blur of motion, and suddenly one of them sprouts a black cloth hood and takes a dive, feet swept out from under him. A moment later Bee is sitting triumphantly on his back, locking handcuffs around his wrists. He twitches and tries to say something: instead of listening she pulls out a taser and zaps him in the arse.

Jim, the SA, and I move forward into the crowd of evacuees. A very distinguished-looking senior politician nearly runs headlong into me as I sling my violin case over my shoulder. "You can't arrest him!" he's shouting at Jim. "He's going to be our next Prime Minister! He's going to save the Party!"

I look the Chief Whip in the eye. "You have got to be kidding." He doesn't seem to hear me. I reach into my handbag and grab the spare heavy-duty ward bracelet. "Wear this, you'll feel better."

"But you can't—"

He's still raving as I slither past him. The Mandate is having his rights read to him by a very smug-looking Chief Superintendent Grey. There's chaos on all sides, but I put my hand on Bee's shoulder and lean close to her ear. She tenses as I say, "Come with me. Don't say anything."

"All right—Dr. O'Brien?"

"Over here." I lead her away from the throng of confused staffers and agitated cops. "Did he—"

"Boss? I can't see you!"

I draw a deep shuddering breath. *Okay, so it's really happening to me.* "Never mind that right now. I was just going to say, good job. And now let's get you out of here before those nice officers from SO17 remember you and realize that you're still missing."

"Thanks." Bee is still buzzing with adrenaline. I guide her towards the front gate. "But how are you doing this, boss? I didn't know you had a superpower!"

I force myself to keep going. "Neither did I, Bee. But it seems to work, and if it works, don't knock it."

CATCHING THE MANDATE RED-HANDED IN THE ACT OF TRYING TO suborn one of the Home Secretary's most senior colleagues is about the best possible way to end a week that began with the HomeSec effectively demanding that we prove our worth or be shut down. But it's no cause for complacency.

The good news is, we've nailed the Mandate. He's going to be charged with aggravated trespass, abduction (of the Chief Whip), and attempted electoral fraud. He'll get his vote, all right—but it's going to come from twelve jurors, the count is going to be read out to him over a CCTV link from a courtroom, and he's going to win a seat in a high-security prison cell, not Parliament.

The bad news is that half the afternoon is soaked up by all the paperwork involved in wrapping up the incident, including the necessary handling guidelines once we've booked him into the secure lock-up at Belgravia nick. As I tell the custody officer: "You will need earplugs and high-power wards—my people will provide them. Do not speak to him, do not listen to him under any circumstances. Communicate in writing only, no more than one sentence at a time. If you've got any hearing-impaired custody officers, now would be a great time to offer them some overtime. Oh, and your front desk staff need to monitor the behavior of the custody officers in direct contact with the subject by CCTV *at all times*. External vault door control, not internal."

The list goes on, seemingly endless. I'm still half convinced they'll slip up and let him walk away by the end of the weekend.

The rest of the afternoon and early evening I spend writing a report, eyes-only, for Mrs. Jessica Greene. I explain in words of one syllable exactly what the Mandate is capable of and why he was able to walk right into the door next to the Prime Minister's residence, and what the consequences would have been if we hadn't stopped him: a new PM and then a new Home Secretary before the election.*

Thankfully there are no currently scheduled by-elections, so we don't have to add a murder investigation to the Mandate's account. (It's pretty hard to prove murder to a jury who are mesmerized by the accused, especially when the alleged victim—whichever MP the Mandate had decided to replace—will almost certainly turn out to have left a suicide note.) I'm pretty sure that trying the Mandate is going to present the Ministry of Justice with a huge headache as it is— maybe a tribunal of judges wearing wards and earplugs?—but that's not our problem to worry about.

The expected summons arrives in my email inbox around seven o'clock. *See Me, Monday, 9:30 a.m.* It comes directly from the Head Mistress's appointments secretary. This is the first Home Office meeting I'm actually looking forward to, I realize. Even though I'm pretty sure that the reward for a job well done will be a royal bollocking for still not having found Freudstein.

As I'm about to go home, I get a final email, this time from Jim: "Scored tickets for the final night of *La traviata* at Covent Garden tomorrow at eight p.m. Invitations to a reception afterwards. Want to eat first? We could make an evening of it."

---

* It's not as if MPs don't die at random intervals during a parliamentary session—or even commit suicide—and if that happens, a by-election is called to fill the empty seat. Nor is it likely that a promising candidate with a golden tongue and high-level backing won't get elected if he stands in a safe seat, weeping crocodile tears for the MP who killed himself . . .

Ooh, sounds like fun. I smile to myself and send back: "Yes, and yes." I pause. "What's the party dress code?"

"Black tie," he replies. "Our host is a sheikh. The hospitality will be something special."

"Ok," I send. And just like that, I have a date.

17.

A NIGHT AT THE OPERA

SO, SATURDAY.

I wake up early, stung by the realization that I said *yes* when Jim escalated to formal, but the only suitable outfit I've got that's not five years out of date is a bit risqué. So I brave the autumnal clouds and the weekend shoppers, and head for Peter James and competitors. In the end, I do not buy a new dress, because everything that looks good doesn't fit, and vice versa. On the other hand, once I've spent hours fruitlessly wandering department store floors, my existing gown doesn't look so extreme. So I end up buying something much more useful: a calf-length black coat with silver detailing. It's cheaper than a posh frock, and I can get a lot more mileage out of it. I then blow what's left of my budget on a frivolous sequined clutch, opera gloves, and a new pair of court shoes with heels just tall enough to help me look Jim in the eyes without crippling me.

I get home at two in the afternoon: hungry, tired, and suffering from just a little ennui at the frivolity of it all. I'm old enough to know better than to play dress-up party doll for a man, especially one I'm not married to and need to be able to look in the eye next week at work. Or to blow a ton of cash on shoes and a handbag and a ticket to the opera, when I could just as easily rent it on DVD. Never mind the whole dating in the workplace thing—*that* can go horribly wrong in so many ways that it's not even funny. On the other hand, there hasn't been a lot of frivolity in my life these past few years, has there? Let alone fun. And Jim and I are both grown-ups, I tell myself. I can handle this, as long as it doesn't go too far. So I chow down on a very austere edamame salad I bought on my way home, then go upstairs to shower and begin preparing myself for the ritual of a formal night out—a kind of formal that Bob and I haven't done in longer than I care to remember.

Around four, my phone buzzes. I pull it out of the evening clutch; it's a message from Jim: *Want me to pick you up at 5:30?*

Yes, I send back. Then I go into panic mode. I've showered and done my hair and I'm half-dressed, but I'm not ready. The next hour passes in a blur. Finally, I look in a mirror. A stranger looks back at me: sleepily sophisticated, all lip gloss and crimson nails. She doesn't look like me *at all.* Her red hair (the gray stragglers dyed into compliance) hangs loose in a waterfall over the shoulders of her lace-topped black gown: she's a striking stranger, my princess-world twin sister. There is jewelry: a silver chain supporting a discreet silver bangle, earrings, bracelets that contain heavy-duty wards. It's as if I'm looking into a magic mirror that shows me who I might have grown up to be if I'd settled on "trophy wife" as my life's ambition in secondary school. (All *look at me* rather than *look at what I do.*) I wouldn't want to be her every day, but it's an interesting role to try on for an evening. I pull my new shoes on, wiggle my toes to make sure they still fit as well as they did in the shop, go downstairs (proving I can walk in them without breaking my neck), and pull on my coat. Just in time for my phone to ring.

"Hello?"

"It's me. We're parked outside. Want to come out and meet me?"

"Sure," I say. I check that Lecter's asleep in the safe, energize the wards, arm the burglar alarm, and let myself out.

There is a stretch limo sitting in front of the house. It's not huge—

you'd never fit a full-length one through London's twisty suburban streets—but for our purposes it counts. Jim stands beside the door, holding it open for me. He wears a tux well: I suddenly no longer feel overdressed. He takes my hand with a smile. "I hope this meets with your approval, ma'am?" he asks as I climb in. There are wide leather seats and a minibar in front of us with a bottle of sparkling wine sitting in a silver tub. Jim climbs in next to me, fastens his seat belt, and leans forward: "We're ready," he tells the driver.

The opaque divider in front of us whirrs up, then the car begins to move. The suspension is very soft, and a good thing, too: Jim fills two champagne flutes and hands one to me. "You look marvelous," he says quietly. "I almost didn't recognize you."

Slightly star-struck, I take the glass: "And you've outdone yourself, you smooth mover!"

"I thought we should start as we mean to go on." He looks quietly smug. "Might as well celebrate our success."

"To success," I say. Chink of glassware. I take a sip: bubbles in my nose. "Past *and* future."

It takes half an hour for the limo to rock and sway across the bridge and into the heart of the theater district, by which time our glasses are running dry—but rather than offering a refill, Jim raises a finger. "Nearly there," he says.

"Nearly where?" I ask.

"Surprise."

The car pulls in beside a slightly grubby red carpet that runs out to the curb. Then I see the restaurant awning: "Oh my." I'm not used to dining in restaurants owned by chefs with their own TV show.

"Don't worry, the pre-theater option is very reasonably priced. We have"—he pushes back his cuff to reveal an antique Rolex Oyster—"seventy-five minutes. And we have a reservation. They'll be ready for us."

He hands me out of the car, and we walk together to the door, which a uniformed doorman opens before us. I feel very self-conscious, but not in my usual bad, vulnerable, cross-hairs-on-the-small-of-my-back way. Once inside, an attendant takes my coat; Jim's pupils dilate as he sees my dress properly for the first time. "Good golly, Miss Sakamoto, you're beautiful!" he misquotes.

"*Science!*" I whisper, with emphasis, and grin at him. His answering smile is qualitatively different from anything I've seen on his face before, and for a moment the part of me responsible for self-restraint hopes that I haven't gone too far.

Dinner is a blur. Small portions, designed not to inconvenience the stomach of the theatergoer: it's beautifully laid out but not terribly filling. Jim's conversation is witty and entertaining and we skirt around work delicately. "If only we could organize the whole planet as well as you've organized your department," Jim says wistfully. "You could bring about world peace and abolish poverty and crime! Except we'd have to elect you planetary overlord first."

"Nah, I'm really not up to that job," I tell him. "Anyone who could do it well is sane enough not to want it. Anyone who wants it is by definition unsuitable. Anyway, it's a committee job—even being head of state for one country is too big a job for a single person to do without a whole team working behind the scenes. What do you say?"

"At ACPO team-building sessions we have this discussion on days with a Y in their name." He pauses to eat a mouthful. "It's called the setting-the-world-to-rights session. You can probably imagine the direction it takes when you get a room full of twenty mildly inebriated senior police officers with PhDs in sociology or criminology."

"It's probably a good thing they don't have their hands on the levers of power, then. When your tool is a hammer, every problem looks like a nail. They run the Police: QED."

"They're not quite as simple-minded as that," he says, mildly.

"No, of course not." I reach across the table and touch his hand reassuringly. "But. 'Rules are rules,' and their career path has conditioned them for decades to believe that laws should always be enforced even-handedly. Rule of law and all that. It's not their job to ask how the laws are made, and who benefits from them. Rules are fine for machines, but human beings aren't perfect spheres of uniform density and negligible frictional coefficient."

"Ah, the spooks viewpoint." His lips purse in good-natured amusement. "Any number of shades of gray."

We finish up in the restaurant. I go to powder my nose and while I'm gone, Jim summons the limo: as we reach the front door, it's at the end of the red carpet, waiting for us. *He booked it for the whole evening,* I realize with a frisson of doubt and secret excitement. I'm conflicted: unsure how to react. Bob moved out a couple of months ago, but I'm not ready to put a dot at the end of that sentence and move on: it's all a bit fast. On the other hand, it's fun and magical and an excuse for escapism: romance, even. Bob is many things, but there is not a single romantic bone in his body. Whereas Jim, who one might expect to be a stolid, plodding policeman, has a barely submerged romantic streak as wide as a motorway. Setting the world to rights indeed!

The opera itself is almost an anticlimax. Verdi, doomed lovers, romantic tragedy: What more is there to say? It is, needless to say, a solid, reliable performance with one or two call-outs. Jim has found us seats at the front of a large box, but it's also home for the evening to other groups—corporate executives and their WAGs (and in some cases, HABs). They're all dressed to the nines so we don't stand out. It makes for an odd combination of intimacy and anonymity, and so we sit knee to knee for two and a half hours.

The final curtain call is over; the lights come up. Conversation rises around us. "The evening is still young," Jim murmurs, "and the magic carriage won't turn into a pumpkin until one o'clock. What do you say?"

"I say, hello evening . . ." He offers me his arm: I take it, and we return to the limo (one of several queuing patiently outside the crush in front of the Royal Opera House). I slide into it gratefully. "Where to next?" I ask.

"I have something in mind." His eyes twinkle wickedly. He knocks on the partition: "Destination four, please."

"Wait, where—" The car begins to move.

"It's a surprise," he says. Quietly: "Do you trust me?"

"I—" I look him in the eye. "This is all a bit fast."

"I'm sorry. If you want, I'll give you a lift home immediately—"

"No, that won't be necessary." I relax. He's fast, but smooth—and he knows when to back off. He's a grown-up: more grown-up than Bob will ever be. Is that what I've been missing? A real grown-up man in my life? I'm not sure. I'm not sure I'll ever *be* sure, frankly. His attention is flattering, *very* flattering. I'm absolutely dead certain he's been working up to this for some time. But he's given no hint of it before now. "Surprise me," I tell him, stretching luxuriously.

"Happily. It'll take about twenty minutes to get there. Would you care for a top-up?"

And so we get through our second champagne flute of the evening.

SOME TIME LATER WE PULL UP ALONGSIDE ANOTHER RED CARPET. "You can leave your coat in the car," Jim tells me, "he'll pick us up when we're ready to go." So I shed my heavy outer shell and Jim helps me out of the limo, and we walk along the runner. There are *reporters* here, paparazzi: one or two flashes go off and I almost flinch before I realize that they're not aimed at me.

"What *is* this?" I hiss in his ear, a rictus smile baring my teeth at the world as I lean on his arm.

"Look up."

I look up. "Wow, it's Minas Tirith!" Yes: the red carpet leads to a glass entrance and an atrium with a ceiling high enough that our office building could fit comfortably under it. We're at the foot of the London Shard, the tallest building in the European Union. It's pretty small beer by Chinese or American standards—it doesn't even make the top fifty skyscrapers worldwide—but it's the tallest *here*. And Jim is leading me across the lobby red carpet towards a bank of express elevators.

"I scored two tickets to a very exclusive party," Jim confides in me. "I'm afraid this qualifies as work, not pleasure: hope you don't mind."

I tighten my grip on his arm. *Dammit.* "Why?"

"I thought you ought to be here to see it."

"To see what?"

"I got wind of it yesterday afternoon from a source at the Yard, via the Integrated Intelligence System. It's a meet-and-greet for persons of interest to our host, his eminence, Sheikh Ammar Al Nuaimi. I very much doubt he'll be seen in public here tonight, but there may be some discreet invitations to his apartments downstairs from the observatory level. Most of the guest list are investment bankers and political lobbyists, but word is that he is extremely interested in meeting three-sigma powers: I barely had to express interest . . . ah, here we are."

The spacious glass-walled lift to the observation deck is stunningly fast and smooth, and my ears pop on the way up. We don't have it to ourselves, mind you: the other passengers are a mix of middle-aged couples and younger and more glamorous hangers-on, all in evening dress. Nobody I recognize. At the top, the doors open and white-gloved attendants direct us out onto a floor which serves as an open-air viewing platform. It's surrounded on four sides by giant triangular glass walls and support trusses that extend several stories above us. We're sheltered from the wind, but it feels light and airy and a little bit chilly: a harbinger of early autumn. Waiters with drinks trays and bottles circulate discreetly. Jim and I both accept glasses of white wine. "Do you recognize anyone here?" I ask.

Jim scans the room slowly. "Not yet." There are about forty people present so far, with more arriving steadily. I think I recognize one: she looks vaguely like Persephone the Auditor, if I squint and try to imagine how she would look in a couture gown with her hair scraped back and lacquered until it gleams.

"I'm not sure," I say. "Got one possible, but she's one of ours."

"I've got another," Jim says quietly. "Not a POI, I'm afraid: she's an Assistant Commissioner in the Met. And my boss's boss."

That rank might sound junior, but it actually puts her three levels above Jim, a Brigadier to his Colonel. I briefly wonder if we've blundered into a black tie version of *The Man Who Was Thursday*, updated for a new century. "Might be best to avoid her," I propose, gently steering him away from the direction he was scanning. Arm in arm, we slowly pace the length of a stupefyingly high glass wall. "This whole meet-and-greet for superpowers thing might have worked out a lot better if the Sheikh hadn't specified black tie. They don't exactly stand out when they're not wearing skintight Lycra with capes, do they?"

"Indeed not." We reach the corner and turn. "Uh-oh." Approaching us from the other wall is the woman Jim zeroed in on, in conversation with a distinguished-looking fellow with a white goatee and thick glasses. She looks to be about my age, wearing a rather plain dark blue evening dress.

"Ah, I thought I recognized you!" she says to Jim. To me, a brief pro forma smile. "Hello. I'm Jim's boss's boss. Laura Stanwick." She extends a hand.

We shake. "This must be matrix management central then, because Jim is working part-time for me," I tell her.

"Oh?" She suddenly focuses on me like a hawk. "Then you must be Dr. O'Brien." I let go of her hand. "I've read a lot of reports about you," she says drily, "not much of it negative."

"Thank you . . ."

"Shame they've thrown you in the piranha tank at the deep end," she says. Another brief smile. "Good show yesterday." She turns to Jim, implicitly dismissing me: "Jim, we need to talk about implementation of the plan some time next week. It's imperative that we move forward with all due speed."

"Um, yes, ma'am." Jim casts me a worried glance. "Can this wait until Monday?"

"I suppose it'll have to." She glances at me. "See you around! Can't stay, must circulate. Toodle-pip." She collects White Goatee, who is swaying slightly and contemplating his nearly empty wine glass. "Come along, dear."

Jim stares after her. "Well, I never."

"Never what?" I take his arm. "Surprised to learn that Assistant Commissioners are married?"

"No . . ." He trails off. "But I hope she hasn't gotten the wrong end of the stick about us. Here, let's circulate. We'll never know if anyone interesting is here if we pretend to be wallflowers."

Suddenly I realize that I am standing far too close to the glass, and I am backlit, making me a perfect sniper target. I take three long steps sideways, then look round furtively as I tug my gown back into place. "Sorry," I say.

Jim looks concerned. "You're very twitchy tonight."

"I left my violin in the safe. Old security reflexes . . . let's stay away from the walls from now on?"

We circulate for what feels like the best part of an hour, while we drain our wine glasses. We pass the woman I suspect of being an Auditor once more, but she's so elaborately made-up that it might be her evil twin, and in any case she gives no sign of recognizing me. Nobody is casting fireballs or levitating or crushing coal into diamonds. It's just a very boring reception for the sorts of movers and shakers that a moderately anglophile Sheikh might invite round for a Saturday night's entertainment.

"This is crap," I confide in Jim's ear around the time my glass is empty and my feet are beginning to ache from the hardwood floor.

"Want to split?" he whispers back.

"Yes." I lean on his arm. "If we'd got the database up and running and had a contact sheet memorized, this might have been useful, but as it is we're a couple of weeks too early . . . get me out of here?"

Jim sends a text, and the long black beetle-shiny limo is waiting for us at the end of the red runner when we arrive at the bottom of the lift shaft. Everything about the Shard is calculated to make you feel bug-on-a-microscope-slide small: the celebrity perp walk down the carpet seems to take forever, and for some reason—too many glossy magazines, I suppose—I keep a fixed grin on my face the whole way. I'm falling into an acting role again, rather than being myself as I was for a few hours in Jim's presence. Then I feel his strength through his arm and I snap back into my own head: only now I have an impulse to lift my shoulders and stick my chest out and tap my heels as I walk, because Jim is magnificent and he needs a glamorous catwalk companion, and I want to be the sort of glittering woman who belongs on his arm, because this sort of setting comes with a natural magical glamor of its own. *Look at me!* The smile feels natural as I tighten my grip on him. Then he opens the car door and hands me in.

Once the door is closed, the car begins to move. "Where to?" he asks quietly. "I can take you home if you want."

I am intensely aware that we're in the back of a limo together, on a slippery leather seat that slides half-flat. I'm still holding his hand, and I'm keeping myself from sliding down the seat mainly by digging in one heel and bending my knee so that it pushes into view. I'm not wearing the lace stockings I picked for Bob: no, I chose sheer black silk for tonight. Suddenly I feel very wicked. "I want you to take me home," I tell him, taking his hand and tugging it across to rest on my knee. "But you choose the route—fast or slow." Then I lean towards him and he kisses me.

I DON'T KNOW HOW LONG WE SPEND IN THE BACK OF THE LIMO. Time flies by when you're having fun. On the other hand: we're in a car. And kissing and cuddling is all very well, but I'm still a bundle of unresolved internal conflict and zinging energy. I haven't *completely* lost my grip on myself. I want to have fun, damn it: I've had precious little in the past month. But an icy-cold part of me also wants to be able to go to work on Monday and look my co-workers in the eye. Nor am I quite certain I'm ready to give up on Bob for good. The self-doubt finally prompts me to cool things a little: Jim follows my lead because, I suspect, he, too, is mature enough to realize the consequences if we take this to its logical end point. One-night stands with co-workers are *so* not my thing—so we pause on the threshold, and I don't invite him in with me when the car pulls up outside my front door.

"Thank you for a wonderful evening," I tell him with heartfelt gratitude as I pull my shoes on.

"No, thank *you*." He pauses. "I was not expecting this turn of events. I mean it." He sounds slightly shaky. "I'm touched."

"Well," I say awkwardly. We kiss again. "I need to get my head around it, Jim. It's been a wonderful evening but I don't know if it will still be wonderful if we go too fast—"

"Well then, we shouldn't do that," he says, as level-headed as I could hope for. "Talk tomorrow?"

"Definitely," I say, then before I'm tempted to change my mind and invite him in I climb out of the car and walk to my house alone. Part of me is kicking myself for not throwing caution to the winds, but I've got a lot of questions to answer before our next date, up to and including whether I want to try and salvage my marriage first. And something tells me I won't have very long to think about it.

I GO UPSTAIRS AND SHED MY GLAMOROUS MIRROR-WORLD SKIN, then crawl into bed alone—except for Spooky, who parks herself precariously on the footboard and stares at me with huge dark eyes. Bloody cat, trying to psych me out.

I fall asleep and dream, of course. And it should come as no surprise at all that it's a classic anxiety dream, bubbling up from my conflicted lonely subconscious. I dream that I'm walking through the darkened streets of London, some time in the early hours of the morning. It's cool and it's been raining recently and a chill wind raises gooseflesh on my bare skin—naked because this is the *classic* anxiety dream, the one where you're in the nude and everyone else is wearing clothes.

A voice I know only I can hear is calling me, telling me to catch the tube: if I don't, I'll be late home, late reaching safety and security. (Which is silly because the tube shuts down at 1 a.m. and the traction power stays off until the first trains start running again shortly before 6 a.m., but dreams don't have to make logical sense.)

So I scuttle between darkened doorways, avoiding masses of wind-strewn litter and the odd sleeping homeless person: heart-in-mouth I cross Whetstone Park, tiptoe up Gate Street in the dark. Two police officers on foot patrol walk past on the opposite side, certain to see the naked woman crouched in the doorway—but they look right past me and keep on going. In this dream I am naked but I have the middle-aged woman's unwanted superpower of social invisibility. What kind of sense does that make? Dream logic.

This is definitely a dream, because in real life you would not catch me walking the streets naked after dark. Nor would I carefully descend the dozen or so steps to the gates of a locked tube station. I slip through the barrier, then chain the gate shut behind me. The escalators are stilled for the night: their metal steps are sharp and cold under my feet as I descend in near darkness. I've got a feeling, an urge, that the compass in my skull is telling me to proceed to a familiar platform. Platform Five. Aldwych branch, the other nagging strand of my unsolved-cases anxiety. I walk along the short platform until I come to the end. The signals are set to red and the track power turned off, but I still shudder. Something scuttles and moves in the tunnel entrance: tube mice.

I cross the warning barrier at the end of the platform and climb down onto the track bed. My feet ache continuously now, for I've been abusing them constantly for hours—shiny new heels, then bare-foot on the street. I walk into the tunnel.

Help. It's the still, small voice of my demon lover, my muse, my curse, my destiny, floating in the darkness in front of me. It's Lecter: abducted and abused, held hostage by strange powers that want to tie him to a new bearer.

I stumble and shuffle along through the darkened tunnel for an infinitely long time. Track ballast scratches at my feet; when I slip, I catch myself on the cold, rough brick and cast-iron lining of the wall. I walk past rows of arched recesses, survival trenches for tube work-ers. In my dream they serve as niches in an ossuary, each one filled by the on-end coffin of a plague pit burial, open to reveal their occupant's final deathly grimace. Heavy cables snake alongside at ankle level, secured to racks bolted to the walls. Anxiety dream redux: my subconscious couldn't frighten me with naked-on-the-streets-of-London, so it's iterated through loss-anxiety to a healthy dose of siderodromophobia.

****Beware.****

For some time now the tunnel has been descending and curving to the right. It's dark as a night with the new moon riding low, only the odd emergency light and signal showing me the way forward—the relatively bright platform is lost in the distance behind me. But I have walked past a points signal repeater, and can just make out something irregular and metallic at ground level. I touch the wall. It feels different, smoother. I run my finger along it, walking slowly forward until it roughens again perhaps ten meters further along the tunnel.

Back up, says the voice in my head.

I back up obediently, and then I trip over something hard and cold at ankle level. I catch myself as I tumble, and then I am no longer walking along a tube tunnel. This is a wider corridor, with a wooden floor and scuffed tan-painted walls, doors opening off to either side. It's clearly backstage at a theater or performing venue of some kind: it curves, and—

I am in one of the side rooms. It's an instrument store, with stands and piles of cases full of orchestral equipment—the instruments that don't usually go home with their owners. Here a row of kettle drums, there a wooden cabinet full of tambourines, triangles, and other minor items.

Over here! calls the quiet voice, and behind a row of stacked wooden chairs I find a familiar battered white violin case. My heart pounds as I reach out and take it, and then I am clutching his case in front of me (as if it's adequate concealment!) while I shiver on a floodlit stage in front of a full house, a very *familiar* house. It's the Royal Albert Hall, and I'm on stage wearing only my gooseflesh-raised skin, and every seat is full, the audience staring at me accusingly. Their faces are pale, indistinguishable blobs that seem to hover in the twilight, somewhere between the collars of their uniform shirts and the brims of their custody helmets.

* * *If the lead violin would care to take her seat?* * * The conductor is gently sarcastic as he chides me in Lecter's borrowed tones. There is a throne—no other word is fit to describe it—at the center of the stage, below the organ, where the soloist would normally stand. This being Lecter's dream I might have expected monstrous charnel furniture assembled from interlocking bones: but as I shuffle backwards towards it (violin case still clutched defensively between my body and the silently staring disapproval of the audience of faceless officers), I realize it is made of thousands of stacked police notebooks. * * *We are waiting for the lead violin,* * * the conductor explains to the audience.

I am nearly at the throne of evidence when I realize that the violin is no longer in his case: I'm carrying him in one hand and the bow in the other, and there's something *wrong*. A body in blue steps forward, shadows skeletally grinning under his helmet as with bony hands he positions a manuscript on the monstrous music stand that sits before the violin soloist's throne. I know that score: I've performed it a dozen times in my dreams over the weeks since the British Library robbery.

I see the conductor's face for the first time: or rather, I don't, because I recognize him from his absence, and he's in the high security lock-up at Belgravia where we put him after the takedown on Downing Street, isn't he?

"You can't make me do it!" I shout as I throw Lecter's bow at the Mandate.

Lights snap on overhead, a concussive blast of photons that scorch the back of my eyelids. I cower and cover my face with one arm. Figures step forward out of the photorhodopsin-stained backdrop: two in front, two closing in behind me. Daft Punk Territorial Support Group Judge Dredd Empty Uniforms—the uniforms Ramona had designed for my people—close in around me, raising power-assisted gloves that contain no human fingers. The Naked Woman versus the Empty Suits.

"You're nicked!" The uniforms chant in unison as they grab me and twist my arms painfully behind my back. I can't breathe. They ratchet a pair of handcuffs closed around my wrists, zip-lock my ankles together, drop a bag over my head, and lift me to shoulder level. I'm suffocating as I open my mouth to scream: but there is no air here, just a tongueful of warm fur.

With an angry chirrup, Spooky plants a surprisingly cold pad on my cheek and stands up, flexing her claws. I realize I'm lying alone between damp, chilly sheets, breathless and heart pounding in the wake of a suffocation nightmare. I resolve never to complain about Spooky sleeping on my face again, then I get out of bed and go downstairs to check the wards on Lecter's safe.

Because you can never be too careful.

SUNDAY IS AS SUNDAY DOES: I SPEND IT PROSAICALLY, CATCHing up on housework chores and trying not to ask myself whether what I feel for Jim has the potential to turn serious. This is, of course, like trying not to think about green elephants: once you start consciously trying to avoid it, it becomes impossible. So I pop a sleeping pill at bedtime, and it is a distinct relief when Monday morning rolls around and I can dive back into a distracting office.

The first thing I do when I get to my room is to park Lecter in the securely warded safe. Then I fire off an email to Dr. Armstrong, asking if he has a spare hour. To my surprise, he gets back to me right away: this lunchtime is available. So that corner of my diary is penciled in for a chat about these dreams I've been having—and by extension, about Lecter—and other, more worrying things.

Last week I decreed that from today we'd be starting up regular Monday morning management meetings, just to keep all department heads in the loop. The Unit—with an effort I remind myself that we're now officially a Force—is big enough that we have to crawl out of the

Precambrian jellyfish swamp of bottom-up organizational structure and grow a management backbone. I don't know everything that's going on anymore, and although I know all the names and faces of the people working under me, there's no way I can stay in touch with what they do. Ergo, delegation, and the bane of management that ensues: endless meetings.

For now the meeting team consists of Ramona, Mhari, Jim, and myself: so we hold it in my office over coffee and it's blessedly short. It's going to change soon enough, though—I can see the writing on the wall.

I get my first surprise of the day when I ask, "Do we have any other business?"

Jim nods: "Yes, I got a memo via the Home Office. It's about the inaccessible tube station—BTP got a resolution, it turns out there's some other agency involved. Aldwych has been shut for years anyway, and apparently TfL agreed to transfer it to this other agency on a five-year lease without telling anyone, including the on-site guards." His cheek twitches.

"That's—" Mhari shakes her head.

"Crazy?" I ask. "Do you know who the agency in question is?"

Jim's frown deepens. "As it happens, I do." He glances at Ramona, then Mhari, then back at me. "Promise this won't go any further?"

"Promise—" I stop dead just as Ramona nods slowly.

"I think I see where this is going," she says tonelessly.

Mhari's eyes narrow. "Spill it," she tells Jim.

Jim nods, very slightly, then glances at me. "I'll thank you for not spreading this any further," he tells us, "but you know full well that most police officers have not been briefed about the existence and true purpose of the organization you people really belong to."

The Laundry's *true* purpose? I shrug. "Yes, but—" I stop. "You're not telling me—" I begin.

"It's the Specialist Crime and Operations Department." He clears his throat, a worry frown forming at the corners of his lips, his eyes. "Very few of them—almost none of them—are cleared for Laundry-related material. And someone up top, high enough to have tons of clout but nevertheless not on the briefing list, decided that in view of the rising tide of supervandalism it would be a good idea to have a deep bunker for incident command and containment of dangerous individuals. I mean, you saw how small and under-equipped the cells at Belgravia nick are?"

I nod. "Carry on."

"It came from the top down a while ago, and I didn't get the memo because I was on secondment: it was while we were on that fisheries jaunt. Aldwych is being rented until the CrossRail TBMs can be redeployed to build us a proper facility—if we get the budget for it, of course. So the first element of the rebuild was to shut off street-level access. Once construction has finished, they'll partly reopen the stairwell, but as an oubliette so that villains can be sent down but can't get back up. They're going to run it like an ICBM silo, with watch crews on duty and underground access only via special trains." He looks disapproving. "The next Criminal Justice Act will make changes to our ability to detain suspects for questioning without charge just to make this work."

"Well, that's—" I hesitate to say *nice*.

"How good of them to keep us fully informed!" Ramona chirps pointedly. Jim avoids her gaze.

I roll my eyes. "People, please let's try not to get into the habit of saying what we think *all* the time?" Ramona is actually right: the Met setting up a secure supervillain nick *without telling us* stinks like a month-old fish. It reeks of maneuvering under false colors. Someone in the executive suite is trying to cut us out of the action on our own turf. What else might they be hiding from us? But it's impolitic to say that sort of thing aloud, especially on the record.

"I'm very sorry." Jim finishes his coffee. "But it's strictly hands-off. There's some kind of pissing match going on in the executive suite at the Yard—at a guess they've got a couple of Deputy Commissioners squabbling for who gets to run the new specialist command. You don't get to that level without being a *political* officer, if you follow my drift. Doubtless they'll end up making a bid for *our* unit in due course." He sounds disgusted. "Save me from empire builders." He pauses. "It's probably worth my skin if word gets out that I told you this."

"Well, that's just peachy," I manage. "Don't worry, your secret is safe with us, Officer Friendly. So, um, do we have anything else to talk about this morning?"

It turns out that there is nothing else to discuss, which is probably a good thing. They say if you start each day by swallowing a live toad nothing can possibly make it worse, but after that piece of news I'm not so sure.

And then my day *really* begins to turn to shit.

I'm shutting down my laptop to go and do lunch with the Senior Auditor when I get a voice call from Alison in HR. "Dr. O'Brien?" She sounds worried.

"Hi! You caught me on the way out of the office. Is there anything I can—" I do a double take and nearly facepalm. "Is this about Jim Grey?"

"Yes, yes it is."

I'm on edge immediately because there's a brief pause between her words that doesn't feel right. "What's the problem?"

"Well, you asked me to look into his medical background and the details of his armor, and, um, it puts me in a sticky position. I'm afraid I can't help you. I mean, I *can't*. Medical files are legally privileged information. But you mentioned his armor? I can confirm that it's definitely unpowered. If you've seen him walking through walls in it, that's entirely due to his own powers. It's also tailored closely to fit. I *am* allowed to say that he first manifested superhuman abilities nearly fourteen months ago. Um. Doctor? I know this isn't my field, but if he *isn't* being screened for K syndrome on an ongoing basis, he could be heading for big medical trouble."

I put the phone down with an *oh-shit* sensation in the pit of my stomach: not just the usual headache of sending one of my staff for a bunch of tiresome medical tests and juggling rotas to cover for him, but a nauseous sense of dread. Good news: Jim's armor isn't haunted. If I see Officer Friendly flying around, then he's Jim, which means he isn't holding out on me—isn't a sock puppet for Freudstein. Bad news, though: Jim's vulnerable, just like any other occult practitioner. And something in me balks at the idea of exposing him to threats that force him to use his powers in ways that make his gray matter a tempting tidbit for the feeders. But that's the sort of threat I'm supposed to expose him to, daily, as part of our job! It hasn't been a problem with Bob, for ages—his entanglement with the Eater of Souls protects him, just as Lecter insulates me from their attentions. But Jim is vulnerable, and I can't be detached about it anymore: I've fallen into a conflict of interest.

So I'm feeling particularly fragile as I catch the tube across London, feeling naked again in the absence of my instrument. Being out and about on business without a violin case slung over my shoulder simply feels *wrong*. Try to imagine James Bond without a gun or a Martini in sight: It's incongruous, isn't it? But I have to leave Lecter behind in a secure storage lock-up because I'm on my way to have lunch with Dr. Armstrong to talk about the white violin. I'm not sure Lecter can hear, exactly, but he can tap into my senses eerily well at times, and I have a feeling that having him listening to the conversation I intend to have would be a really bad idea.

And so, to the office with the disturbing dimensions and the secret stash of really rather good single malt—not that I plan on consuming any: I need my wits about me.

"Ah, Mo! Come in, come in." Most people do office casual only on Friday, if at all, so I'm slightly taken aback to be confronted by the SA in a knitted wool cardigan and tartan bedroom slippers. I enter anyway. "Is something the matter?" he asks, focusing over my shoulder.

"Yes, I think so." I let the door shut, then sit down in his visitor's chair without waiting to be invited. "It's about Lec—I'm sorry, it's about the white violin. And it's about Officer Friendly as well, but mostly the violin."

"Ah. So it's time for *that* conversation," he mutters as he sits behind his desk, takes his spectacles off, and polishes them with a microfiber cloth. He glances at me, his gaze startlingly intimate without the intervening crystal barrier that normally screens him. "How far has he pushed: speaking to you in your dreams, sending you entirely new dreams, or actual possession?"

"All of the above," I admit. "Although the only incident of possession so far was when"—bleeding on the fretboard as the bow drags my fingers across blue-glowing strings, a terrified pale figure crouching before me in the living room—"in a moment of extreme emotional stress and exhaustion I was confronted by what I perceived to be a threat."

"And?" he prompts gently.

I shudder. "Bob was there: he managed to talk me down before anything too bad happened."

"Well." He picks up his half-moon reading glasses and puts them on, then carefully adjusts them before he looks at me. His delay doesn't inspire confidence. "How long ago did that happen?"

"The morning after the Code Red."

The SA nods thoughtfully. Is it just my overactive imagination, or is he really disturbed? "It would have been good to have known the full scope of your reasons for misgivings earlier," he says, slowly, choosing his words with the care of a man walking across an uneven icy pavement. "I think I may have underestimated the urgency of your earlier concerns, Doctor. Are you sure you can continue to control the white violin? What do you call him?"

"Lecter." It slips out before my internal censor can block it, and he winces visibly. I carry on, feeling distinctly reckless: "And no, I'm not sure I can hold him in check at all times. When I took down Strip Jack Spratt, Lecter nearly weaseled me into strangling him. I had a big fight with him a couple of weeks ago and threatened to chuck him in the English Channel if he didn't stay out of my dreams—he backed off, then—but it's only a matter of time before an incident crops up where . . . well. As long as he gets his blood, I think he'll do what I want; the problem is what happens if I have to stand down before he's fed."

I stare at the backs of my hands. I feel as if I just confessed to personal inadequacy. *Get it off your chest,* they say: but nothing about the hollow dread, the unanswered question, *what happens next,* that fills your mind after confession. Somehow while I've been carrying the bone violin, the veins and tendons have risen to the surface: flesh falling away from the metacarpals, skin loosening and losing its elasticity, thinning, becoming almost transparent: it's been years, and I'm growing older, and I'm just too tired to arm-wrestle with dream-demons whenever I need to do my job. I look up at the SA. "I can keep him under lockdown and only bring him along on major incidents; I can probably continue to do the job on that basis for a while longer . . . but I'm losing fine control, and sooner or later there'll be an accident."

Dr. Armstrong stares at my eyes. Then he nods, just a slight inclination of the chin. I don't need to tell him what "an accident" means, for which I am profoundly grateful—I can tell he's imagining the writing on the wall, sprayed in the arterial blood of innocent victims.

"I understand," he says softly. An ambiguously pensive expression tugs a curtain of worry lines down across his forehead, gathered in swags by the corners of his eyes. "You've reached the limit of your ability to control the white violin, and if you continue to do so, the risk of an unacceptable incident will rise sharply."

I nod, unable to trust my voice.

"Very well, then." He pauses. "Mo. What I am going to say next is in strictest confidence and must go no further. In particular, you must not share this with your staff. *Any* of them. Do you understand?"

What the hell? I nod again, utterly taken aback.

"The Police and Home Office rely on police intelligence assets for their situational awareness." His diction is fussily precise, as if he's repeating a briefing paper he read and memorized for just this contingency. "In particular, police intelligence is oriented towards supporting police operations. It has to deliver evidence that will stand up in court: it is constrained by rules that do not necessarily apply to defense intelligence organizations." (*Like us,* I interpret.) "Defense intel organizations, in contrast, operate under rules of compartmentaliza-tion that might seem excessively onerous to the police, who take a more collegiate approach to apprehending bad actors.

"So. I'm going to ask you to take it on trust when I assure you that it is *utterly essential* to the agenda of OPERATION INCORRIGIBLE that you continue to act as the white violin's custodian until the end of this month—for another three weeks. You can and must take steps to minimize the risk of collateral damage: keep the instrument in a warded safe at all times, only remove it in response to an emergency, cease regular practice with it. I can arrange a prescription for strong sleeping pills if necessary. But I need you to continue in your current role until the end of the month."

I lick my lips. "Why? What agenda? What happens then?"

"Then?" He smiles humorlessly as he ignores my first two ques-tions and evades the third: "Then you can set down your burden. The violin will either go to a new carrier"—he's bluffing, we've got no-body else remotely strong enough to pick up the instrument: Lecter would eat their soul and turn them into a pithed zombie within an hour—"or be consigned to a secure repository until such time as we are forced to revisit the balance of risk versus safety. You will be re-tired from that particular duty, but in any case I believe we are due to review your career development path in preparation for your forth-coming promotion: you'll have plenty to keep you busy."

Forthcoming promotion? What forthcoming promotion? He said we. *That means the Auditors . . .* I'm still puzzling it over when he continues: "The real purpose behind OPERATION INCORRIGIBLE is that we have reason to believe that the organization operating behind the cover identity of Professor Freudstein is fully aware of the white violin and intends to make a play for it."

It's like a punch to the guts. As Bob would say in one of his more annoying Reddit moments: *Wait, what is this, I don't even.* The violin is a seriously classified asset: most of our sister agencies don't know about it, much less random Mad Science villains. I manage to restrain my reaction to a terse, "You cannot be serious!"

"Oh, but I am." At some point in the past minute his smile warped into a grimace. "And that's all I can tell you, other than to point out the obvious: if the white violin is locked down in a secure vault, either Freudstein will be thwarted—in which case, they'll come up with some other mischief before we can smoke them out—or they'll attack the vault, in which case there will be a horrible mess. In the worst case, Freudstein will take the violin and we'll take the blame. Unthinkable. I believe an active defense—you—will do a better job than any passive defense we can organize. Especially after the Code Red incident demonstrated certain shortcomings in our ability to manage our institutional threat surface."

"You're setting me up as a target," I hear myself saying, as if from a great distance.

"Yes. Wasn't that obvious?"

He waits for an explosion: I don't think I want to give him one, but I am so *very* tempted. Duty, however, wins out. I nod, trying not to clench my jaw. "Until the end of the month."

"Yes."

"You're sure about this? There's nothing else you can give me about Freudstein? No other way of drawing him—them—out?"

"I am very much afraid so." He pauses. "We dropped the ball on this one before we even knew it was rolling. We were distracted by the other crises in train—mistakes were made."

Mistakes were made. There's a story here, but I'm effectively on the outside of the organization now, trying to peer in through the one-way mirror: "Do I get to hear the full story when the situation is, ah, resolved?"

"Yes." He looks at me bleakly. "I know how hard this is, Dominique. I hope . . . I hope and trust you'll agree with me that it was necessary, when you have the full facts." He pause, then adds: "There is one thing. You must take pains to avoid tipping your staff off—but I am going to authorize the release of tracking wards for your team. Ostensibly to ensure your executives are reachable 24x7. You know what to do."

I stand. "Yes, I do," I say tightly.

"Was there anything else?" he asks.

I don't trust myself to talk about Jim. "No, nothing important right now. Good-bye." Then I walk out of his office feeling as if I've just been date-raped by my best friend.

18.

CASSILDA'S SONG

I GO BACK TO MY SHINY OFFICE WITH A BROWN-BAG LUNCH AND I sit at my desk, trying to eat despite my suddenly leaden stomach. I manage to choke down half a low-calorie Mexican chicken wrap before a wave of nausea grips me and I quick-march to the bathroom, where I throw up as quietly as I can. Afterwards I lean on the wash-basin until the dry heaves are definitely under control, then I brush out my hair and carefully check my face for makeup damage.

It's not like I haven't been staked out as a tethered goat before now. In fact, it's how I ended up auditioning for the white violin in the first place: after the incident in Amsterdam with Bob and the museum archive and the tentacles, I went looking for some way of protecting myself. Because *never again* sounds pretty good if you've ever been grabbed by a halfway-sentient monster and used as a fishing lure: the phrase *I'd rather die than do that again* springs to mind, and I'm not exaggerating. If it happens again, going quietly into that dark night is my Plan B: Plan A is to fight like a rabid bobcat.

Anyway, the point is that Dr. Armstrong is thoroughly aware of my service record. If anyone should be expected to know better than to put me in such a position, it'd be him (or if not him, Bob: but Bob is not my line manager, for which, praise the Lord). And that's why I'm throwing up in the bathroom (and trying not to let any sound escape: I don't want to frighten everyone). I trust the SA would not do this to me unless in his professional opinion *there was absolutely no alternative.* Freudstein has run rings around the Police and backed the SA into a corner so tight that the only way out entails a risk of civilian collateral damage—no, let's not be euphemistic here: scores of civilian deaths—and a senior agent's sanity.

So he's hung it on me like a fucking dead albatross. And there's nobody to vent on, because he's my regular workplace confessor— and Bob is unavailable. Worse, Bob is unreliable. (I know *exactly* what Bob would say if I told him about this—he'd tell me to spit in Dr. Armstrong's eye, and I love him for it—but I can't turn this assignment down because . . . *you'll agree with me that it was necessary, when you have the full facts.*) Nor can I reasonably vent on anyone else: Jim, for example. Right. So be it resolved: at the end of the month Lecter *is* going to check in with Internal Assets for secure storage. And if I don't agree that the ends justify the means in the case of this assignment, Dr. Armstrong will have my resignation.

I go back to my desk, pale and sick with fear, and sit like a sack of potatoes for the next hour while I try to mentally digest. At which point it gets to be too much, so I hang out a DO NOT DISTURB sign, lock my office door, and give myself a timed crying jag. Another makeup refresh, and I feel well enough to unlock the door and resume the robotic semblance of business as usual. But I still feel as if I've been mugged, or discovered Bob was cheating on me, or something like that.

Later that afternoon I manage to sit through a meeting without losing it, and although Mhari gives me a few strange glances I don't think anyone else really notices. When it's time to go home, I collect Lecter from my office safe, and I manage to navigate my way via bus and tube without jumping at shadows more than three or four times: anyone who notices it probably puts it down to one triple-shot latte too many (or to my nonexistent nose candy habit). I shovel the violin case into the safe, lock the front door, then inspect the wards on all the walls and windows twice over before I can relax enough to take my jacket and shoes off and make a pot of tea. The sleeping pills get a workout that night, despite Spooky's best attempts to wake me up so I can play with her at four in the morning, and I'm still a little groggy when the alarm wakes me at six thirty. But at least I don't have any more horrible dreams about performing naked in front of the Police Federation at the Albert Hall or dancing with Lecter in doomed Carcosa; and with sleep comes a sense of normality resuming, or at least the routinization of fear.

The fearful takes another step towards becoming the new normal when I return to the office that morning, violin slung over my shoulder. I deliberately vary my routine: leave at a different time, walk to a different bus stop, catch the tube between two different stations, and cover the last mile by taxi (and damn the expense). I stow Lecter in my office safe, neither opening the case nor trying to talk to him in my own head: let sleeping curses lie. And I get on with my life, pointedly paying no attention to the Damocletian sword the SA so helpfully drew to my attention.

The SA is not so easily ignored. We still have some paper mail to process, and a small padded envelope arrives via my in tray. When I open it a plain-looking metal band falls out: silver, I think, like a very plain wedding ring. I recognize his fussily old-fashioned handwriting on the note that is spindled through it like a treacherous promise.

Dominique, this is the sympathetic link ring I mentioned yesterday. I requisitioned it from its previous holder; Ms. Murphy already wears the counterpart. It will enable you to contact her in event of the emergency I mentioned. I have requested the preparation of a set of four linked rings for your entire team, but they will take at least ten days to arrive.

I scowl at the ring, then on impulse raise it to my nose and sniff it. My fingertips prickle slightly: I get a sense of Mhari's presence from it, but why is there someone else, someone familiar? *Damn Dr. Armstrong, damn him to hell.* I slide the ring onto my right ring finger, where it fits snugly, despite having been sized for a male hand when I shook it out of the bag.

Barely thirty seconds pass before my desk phone rings. I pick it up.

"Dr. O'Brien." It's Mhari. She's using my surname, which is unusual these days: the weeks of after-work drinks have, if nothing else, put us on a first-name basis.

"Yes, Mhari?" My finger twitches. "Is it the ring with the sympathetic link?"

"The—" I hear her sharp intake of breath. "Yes. Where did you get it?"

I chew my lip for a moment. "The SA gave it to me. He's concerned about our ability to coordinate in an emergency—if one of us was on the tube, for example, unreachable by phone. He's getting us a complete set, for the entire team, but it'll be a couple of weeks. He said in the meantime I should get used to this one . . ."

"I, uh, I see." She sounds slightly taken aback. "Why me?"

"Why not?" I reply, with forced levity. "We're where the buck stops."

"I suppose so." But she sounds doubtful—suspicious, even—as she puts the phone down. Yet another item to add to the list of questions I'd really like to put to Mhari but can't justify asking for fear of wrecking our working relationship.

Around ten o'clock, Ramona whirrs gleefully into my office. "They've arrived!" she cries.

"What have arrived?"

"Our uniforms! Come on, come on, don't you want to see how you look in skintight Lycra?"

I really don't—I really, *really* don't—but I go anyway because staff morale trumps personal body-image issues: when you're the chief exec, you can't afford to balk at superficially innocuous activities that you've prescribed to your staff. So I follow Ramona out to her office, where Mhari is unpacking a big brown cardboard box full of plastic-wrapped stuff. "What," she says, "am I expected to wear—"

"Mo? This is yours!" Ramona nudges her wheelchair towards another shipping carton. "We've got another four for the B-team—this is for sizing; if they don't fit properly, I'll send them back for adjustments before we put through the full order. You can change in the bathroom stalls."

I bridle at that: "Excuse me, but I have an office of my own!" I pick up the box Ramona's pointing at and head for the door. Best get the indignity over in private. The box is surprisingly heavy. "You and Mhari can meet me in my outer office in half an hour," I tell her. "In uniform."

I will say this for Ramona: her prototype uniform for the Transhuman Police Coordination Force resembles a police assault uniform much more than the G-cup-bustier-with-mini-skirt that I'd been dreading. It is not skintight, apart from the fireproof rip-stop leggings that go under the cargo pants and gear belt. It protects vital assets with anti-stab ceramic inserts rather than letting them all hang out on display. The gloves are nice and flexible, and the helmet is full of exceptionally expensive-looking milspec Google Glass work-alike electronics, although you can take them out and wear them strapped to your face, Borg-style. The boots are sourced from one of the suppliers where the cool Special Forces kids go to spend their pocket money when they're unhappy with their Army-issue combat boots. I pull it on without undue difficulty, fasten everything up, and discover to my surprise that it actually makes me *feel* like I'm ready to kick down doors and arrest supervillains. It's got GPS and Airwave radio and built-in cellular digital and even supports a bolt-on night vision monocular.

There's just one problem with it, as I tell my executive team (aside from Jim, who is at ACPO headquarters for some kind of meeting today): "The HomeSec's focus group will take one look at this and tell you to sex it up."

Ramona's version of the uniform is tailored to her anatomy: hers *is* skintight in places, but it's the skintight fit of thick layered neoprene rather than nylon or Lycra, because it doubles as a wetsuit for a mermaid. Mhari raises an eyebrow at me. "Why do you think that'll be a priority?" she asks.

"You know perfectly well why—" I only recognize her ironically raised eyebrow once I've opened my mouth, so I bull on just in case I'm misinterpreting her. "For the same reason they want a *balanced* team rather than a competent one. It doesn't fit the cultural agenda they're trying to impose. We look like police officers trialing some kind of experimental next-generation tactical uniform—"

"Because we are—" Ramona interrupts.

"Thank you! . . . But the point is, we're supposed to look like we stepped out of a superhero movie. We don't even have capes. Which is good, but it's not what they ordered so it's a lever to use against us." I cross my arms defensively: "I can pull the Health and Safety defense but I'm not sure I can make it stick."

"So don't tell them just yet," Mhari suggests. "I mean, let's at least see if they're workable on operational deployment? If it works in the field, they'll have a much harder job spiking it. And"—she shrugs, sleekly statuesque, and for a moment I almost see her as some kind of far future space marine—"I for one really *don't* want to be told my uniform needs to show more bare skin for the teen gamer demographic."

"Oka-a-y . . ." I think for a moment. "How about you try this on the B-team and get their feedback, Ramona? I'm going to wear mine around the office today and see if there are any obvious adjustments needed for chafing or wear. If we get called on active deployment, we'll trial it. Otherwise, though, we keep it under wraps. Just in case."

"Just in case," Mhari echoes, nodding her approval. I feel a flash of gratitude, then annoyance: I don't *need* her approval. It's still pleasant, though. "How about I go and roust out Bee and Torch? I'll send them up to your office, Ramona. Then we can go and have a fashion parade and scare all the analysts!"

JIM IS BACK IN THE FORCE ON WEDNESDAY. AFTER WE TESTED the uniforms around the office all Tuesday, Ramona packaged them up and sent them for dry-cleaning (and in some cases, alteration or replacement)—so I invite Jim into my office to show him the video

Nick recorded of our impromptu fashion show. His reaction isn't what I expected.

"HM Inspector of Constabulary will have to approve these," he says bluntly, "and I can tell you up front that the Uniform Committee will probably reject them, or ask for big changes."

"Wait what?" I stop dead. "But we need—"

"Item: opaque face masks are *right out*, even for riot gear. Forbidden by policy, it makes it hard to identify officers from CCTV footage. Item: I see no badge numbers on display—ditto on identification. Ramona didn't ask for the standards for uniforms, did she? Nowhere to show rank insignia, those equipment belts are all wrong, and there's a standing directive to avoid looking like imperial stormtroopers."

"Jim." I try not to sigh: "I'm supposed to be running a *superhero team*. They're *supposed* to look like they're capable of lifting you by the throat and snarling *you have failed me for the last time*." I minimize the window and stare at him. "What's eating you?"

"Sorry: yesterday left a bad taste in my mouth." He shakes his head as if trying to dislodge an annoying fly that's buzzing around. "Our dog-and-pony show the other week made bigger waves than I realized, apparently. Several chiefs went home and started asking about civil contingency planning, and now they've got their knickers in a twist because we're making them look as if they're unprepared. So the first order of their day, after helping themselves to all the reports I've written on the subject for the past nine months, was to spread a little gloom around, which means making all this"—his sweeping hand gesture takes in the entire building—"redundant. So they've set up a working group on responding to extralegal paranormal activity, staffed entirely from within existing forces rather than borrowing from the Ministry of Defense."

"Oh, for—" I bite my tongue, furious with myself for the sudden stab of relief at knowing I'm going to be off the hook if this goes through. "What's *that* supposed to mean?"

"It means there's going to be a ministerial-level pissing match, and I for one have technically been caught offside. Which may actually work out in your favor, Mo, but only if you want to really make this fly as a police support organization rather than a stalking horse for your own department."

"Well." I fall silent, unable to think of anything else to say that won't come across as bitter and cynical. After the SA's bombshell on Monday this is exactly what I least needed. I've got a meeting in half an hour to discuss a deployment roster for the junior supervillain busters once they've finished their training period, but I'd rather just cancel and go home and hide under the bed, crying. (Not that that's possible.) I look at Jim. "Is there *any* good news?"

"Oh, well, I was hoping you'd ask." Suddenly he looks smug, as if he's been plotting something.

"Come on. Spill it."

"I, ah, acquired a pair of concert tickets." *Now* he smiles. "For this Saturday evening. I know it's short notice . . . but would you like to accompany me to the Last Night of the Proms?"

My jaw drops. "What. How . . . ?"

"I asked around and these two dress circle seat tickets sort of fell into my pocket." He looks innocent, the kind of innocent you get when you collar a pickpocket.

"Fell into your pocket my ass! Um. Pardon my French." (Do I want to go to the highlight of the Proms season with Jim? *Do bears defecate in sylvanian ecosystems?* as my husband once put it.)

"Yes or no?" he presses.

"I'm trying to decide between *yes* and *hell, yes*. You're not making it easy!" I take a deep breath. "Of course I'll go. Assuming. Um. You didn't have to bribe or murder anyone to get the tickets, did you? There were no witnesses and you buried the bodies properly?"

The BBC Proms are not some kind of high school dance, but a century-old season of orchestral classical music concerts held every late summer around the UK—but mostly in the Royal Albert Hall in London. These days they're the biggest classical music festival in the world, with over a hundred concerts and spin-off events in a variety of other cities.

I've been to plenty of concerts at the Albert Hall before, and even to Proms concerts, but haven't had time to do so this year due to the pressure of work—and I've *never* got into the last night, the climax of the season. There are queues for tickets at the best of times and no guarantees: and you can't buy tickets for the Last Night *at all*, unless you can present ticket stubs from five earlier concerts. (See "pressure of work" above.) People *with* tickets—standing tickets at that—often queue overnight just to make sure they can get in. Dress code: anything goes, but fancy dress is recommended. There's a lot of patriotic flag-waving, especially at the close when they play "Rule, Britannia!" Music: aside from the regular playlist there are pieces courtesy of everyone from the Pet Shop Boys to Prokofiev by way of Benjamin Britten and Beethoven.

Oh, and the Last Night of the Proms gets broadcast live on national TV and radio, with big-screen video repeaters at satellite concerts in other cities. As I said, it's the biggest classical music cultural event of the year in London and has been so ever since the 1890s: in terms of excitement it's the musical equivalent of a major Apple product release. For Jim to suddenly produce a pair of reserved seats is only marginally more plausible than for him to reach into his tunic breast pocket and pull out three live rabbits and a partridge in a pear tree.

So when he reaches into the aforementioned pocket and produces two familiar-looking concert tickets, I can't help myself: I gape at him.

"I had to pull some strings," he says, slightly smugly, "but I didn't have to kill anybody or even blackmail anyone, honest. Actually, what happens is that a bunch of tickets get allocated every year to various London organizations—fire service, ambulance, you get the picture. Some of the private box holders donate them, or sell them and donate the proceeds to charity." (Many of the boxes at the Royal Albert Hall are privately owned; I gather the leasehold on a box costs anything up to half a million pounds.) "The Met regularly gets about a dozen, most of which go in the charity raffle. I owe some favors if we take these, so if you *don't* want them, I need to know right now so I can give them back and apologize—"

"You didn't raid a raffle pot?" I stare at him, eyes narrowing. "Because if you—"

"No!" He sounds shocked. "I'd never do something like that. But between you and me, the Commish's rather more fond of the Sex Pistols and the Clash than he is of Elgar. He's a 'Police and Thieves' man." Suddenly his eyes widen: "Please, for the love of all that's holy, don't *ever* mention that in front of any journalists? It's really not the image he wants to project. If word got out . . ."

I manage to shut my mouth. Gaping is unseemly, and anyway, if I gape any wider, I'll dislocate my jaw. London's top cop has a secret fondness for punk rock? The timing fits: punk is forty-something these days, and the Boss would have been a teenager, bopping to 45s and spiking his hair with soap back in the day. "His secret is safe with me," I manage, making a fist and holding it to my heart, "it will accompany me to the grave!" Then I succumb to a quiet fit of the giggles.

"So you wouldn't mind accompanying me to the Last Night of the Proms, using a ticket rejected by a superannuated old punk?"

I hesitate momentarily. The SA is setting me up as bait: but whoever he's stalking wouldn't dare do anything at such a public event, would they? Besides, I'll have Jim at my side, and as bodyguards go, Officer Friendly is pretty hardcore. "It's a date."

THE REST OF THE WEEK PASSES. I DO MEETINGS: BACK TO THE Home Office on Thursday for a relatively gentle anal probing by the aliens from Professional Standards, followed by a brisk session with a pair of auditors who, while far more innocuous than our own, are still capable of putting me in a very uncomfortable spot while reviewing my budget projections. I carry on reading my homework, remember to go to the gym, and order up a supermarket food delivery. I keep procrastinating and finding reasons not to pull Jim aside for That Talk, the one about K syndrome and wards and brain scans and not overdoing the superpowers; on the other hand, we're not punching villains right now so it's less urgent than it might otherwise be. And as the matter's now on the radar, it occurs to me that Jim isn't the only one at risk, so I add to my overflowing to-do list: *institute regular K syndrome medical screening for all personnel*. I even find time to go out for drinks with the girls on Thursday evening, although I keep my date with Jim to myself for the time being.

Friday: a big meeting with the analysts and the B-team. We're working up that list of three-sigma and better supernormals, and my people have begun to launder them past the PNC database to see if any of them may be persons of interest from a criminal point of view. (I'm not so much concerned about teenage drinking exploits as a long record of armed robbery followed by the development of superpowers: if we can find the next Catwoman wannabe before she starts knocking over banks, that'd be a generally all-around good idea.)

But we're still no closer than before to identifying possible candidates for Professor Freudstein, which leaves me walking around with the skin of the small of my back crawling as if there's a cross hairs painted there. I can't shake the SA's worrying implication that Freudstein is a front for an organization, that they are inside our institutional decision loop, and that the raid on the British Library rare music manuscripts store and Dr. Armstrong's unhealthy concern for me and my instrument are connected. I am developing a nervous habit of checking whichever warded safe Lecter is stashed in—whether at home or at work—every couple of hours, even when I haven't been out of the room: I can't see this ending well for anyone, even though the sleeping pills are working and I'm free from intrusive dreams for the time being.

Other stuff happens, of course. The (cleaned, altered) uniforms are delivered, complete with kit bags so we can take them home in case of an out-of-hours call-out. (Whoopee.) Mhari and I test our rings, until I get the hang of inconspicuously getting her attention. They're basically magical pagers, able to run without a power source and work in places where there's no cellular coverage. Finally, there's an afternoon training review with the junior mythosbusters, as Sam has christened the B-team—Bee, Torch, Lollipop Bill, and Captain

Mahvelous—then a bunch of routine budget approval forms to fill out. And that's my working week done.

I collect the violin from my office safe and the uniform kit bag from under my desk, then lock my office door. It's nearly eight o'clock. The sky is darkening towards twilight as I nod at Marek, our shaven-headed evening shift door guard, and head for home. Lecter is a presence at my back, his case slung over the small of my back like a reliquary holding the unclean remains of a perverted saint: he feels oddly heavy and quiescent, as if waiting for something. The sky overhead is the sickly orange-red of street lights reflecting off clouds and my forehead feels tight, a premonition of a thunderstorm hanging fire. My unease as I walk towards the nearest bus stop is not the normal one I've become accustomed to since the SA sprang his unwelcome surprise on Monday—and in any case, if anyone or anything thinks they can take *me* on the streets of London, they're making a very big mistake—but something is nagging at the edges of my attention, like a specter scratching at the decaying lychgate of a graveyard—

Oh, that. "Yes?" I ask coldly.

Can we talk? I swear if a raw head and bloody bones could whine like a hungry dog begging for liver and intestines to swallow—

"*What's there to talk about?*" I realize responding's a mistake as soon as I let the thought out, capering madly through the empty chambers of my skull, but by then it's too late: I've admitted that Lecter is calling me, even though the wards and chains and bindings of his case. And, silly me, I've walked right past the bus stop. So I keep on walking.

I'm lonely.

I stumble on a loose paving stone and nearly go over on one heel, so shocked that my surroundings barely register. *You have got to be kidding me. Lecter is* lonely? "*Why is that my problem?*"

The host is my eyes. The host is my ears. Without the host I am trapped forever in the red/warm pulsing darkness.

This is just too creepy for words.

For a long time now I've had an internal argument with myself about whether Lecter is sentient in his own right or just a passenger that stimulates his host's brain to fulfill his basic need for sustenance, like one of those hideous isopod parasites Bob told me about. Or like Mhari's V-parasite, the thing that lends her various powers in return for the curse of a peculiar thirst. In which case, my conversations with Lecter are just me talking to myself under the influence of a brain-controlling parasite, which is pretty bad.

But *this* implies that Lecter is sentient and aware when I'm not around. That when I lock him in the safe and go somewhere, I'm placing an intelligent being in a sensory deprivation cell, deaf and blind. When we do this to people, we call it torture. Lecter isn't a person—whatever he may be, he's far too dangerous to set free—but he's at least a class four agency, and if he's fully sentient in the absence of his host . . .

I know you fear my hunger. It is my nature: I cannot be otherwise. But must you torment me so?

"I'm not tormenting you," I reply automatically.

These past days/alone in the warm darkness/you leave me . . . The words decay into an incoherent impression of oceanic vastness and a sense of longing. ***Parted so long from my greater self, I seek reunion. Denied reunion, I crave experience.***

My skin crawls. Just how much of my life has Lecter been experiencing vicariously? Too much, I get it. The question is, can I turn this craving for experience to my advantage? *"What do you want from me?"* I ask.

Bear me. Be my eyes and see for me. Be my ears and hear for me. Don't leave me alone in the warm/red darkness.

I shake myself out of my conversational reverie, look round. It's beginning to rain. I hold out my arm: "Taxi!" For a moment I'm afraid that my still-only-intermittent invisibility superpower is going to cut in, but then a black cab swerves towards me and I give it my address, and the hell with the cost: I'm not going to get caught out in a late summer thunderstorm with a haunted violin whispering to me.

"If I carry you around, will you stay the hell out of my dreams?" I ask.

Yes! Lecter feels *eager*. But he shuts up. And that night, for the first time in weeks, instead of locking him in the warded safe in the hall I place his case beside me on the other side of the bed when I sleep.

DATE NIGHT.

Saturday is a bit of a blur, to be honest. I sleep sinfully late, not rising until well after eight. The morning goes on housekeeping chores, neglected during the week. Lecter watches (in his case) while I vacuum and iron and run the washing machine, a strangely passive voyeurism. (And what must it be like, to be an alien spirit bound into an instrument carved from the agonized bones of dying men and women, immobile and helplessly dependent on a human host, hungry for experience and thirsty for blood—watching while the human host irons the next week's workwear?)

Around lunchtime I go for a brisk walk around the park in lieu of the gym—I'd have to leave Lecter in a locker, and I have a most peculiar feeling that he'd consider it a breach of trust—then back home in mid-afternoon. Whereupon it's time to get ready for the concert, and I suddenly realize I don't know what to wear. Last time out, Jim said "black tie"—but this is the Last Night of the Proms. The *real* tradition at the Last Night is fancy dress: the more outrageous the better. I've got one halfway current evening gown, or the little black dress I wore to the reception on the oil rig—but I'm not really into costuming. In fact, I don't think I've worn any kind of costume since—

—Since last Monday, now that I think about it—

Bingo. Jim was going to pick me up around six, so I grab my phone and text him, *It's the Last Night: going to wear fancy dress.* So, while the imp of the perverse has my attention, I pick up the uniform kit bag from where I left it in the hall and take it through to the kitchen.

Playing dress-up really isn't like me: but nothing that's happened since that horrible morning when I woke up to the phone ringing and the empty bed and answered a call to Trafalgar Square has really been *me*. At least, not the me I've been trying to become for the past decade. Once upon a time, there was a me who wouldn't have blinked twice at the idea of going on a date in fancy dress: once upon a time, I had room for frivolity. What happened?

I've been so busy running in circles, being the responsible adult in a madhouse as the world slowly comes apart at the seams, that I've pretty much forgotten what it's like to have fun. Now that I've got my very own superhero kindergarten to run, I'm even busier being a responsible adult than when I was simply wearing Agent CANDID's shoes—but there's not much fun in that life, not very much frivolity, not very much *Mo* as opposed to *Dr. O'Brien*. I've been shoveling the bits of me that don't fit the sharp-edged requirements of the workday week into a mental closet—an overstuffed closet, now bulging at the edges. Well, damn it, there's still *some* space for fun in my life. I can, too, go to the Last Night of the Proms on the arm of a superhero! And there's only one way to do it.

When the bell rings at six on the dot, I am ready and waiting. "Come in," I call, unlocking the door to find Jim on the front step. "Well? What do you think?"

Jim's eyes widen. He swallows. "Fancy dress. Right." He removes his uniform cap and holds it as he inspects me from head to toe. "Right."

Jim is immaculately turned out in a Police Chief Superintendent's full dress uniform, complete with white gloves and an inordinate quantity of medal ribbons on his chest. I suppose it makes sense: we're going to the Proms on tickets liberated from the Commissioner's own office, after all. And as for me . . .

Ramona delivered on the alterations we'd discussed on Monday. In addition to the sinister-looking helmet and the Borg-style head-up display and comms headset, the kit bag contained a classic black half-mask that hooks over the ears—and a half-length cape, clearly modeled on the rain capes coppers on the beat used to wear back during Jack the Ripper's days. By leaving off the cargo pants, helmet, and anti-stab vest, but keeping the leggings, cape, and mask, I managed to assemble a passable comic book superheroine outfit. With the cape slung across Lecter's case, I only look slightly hunchbacked. And if it all goes horribly wrong, well, I can turn invisible and die of embarrassment in private, right? "What do you think?" I repeat, still uncertain. (I'm more worried about my makeup than the outfit itself: nothing washes out your cheeks and lips like a velvet half-mask, but I'm worried that I overcompensated on the theatrical side.)

"I think you look great!" Jim says with that desperately fervent tone some men affect when they're trying to think their way through the social minefield of commenting on their date's attire half an hour after it's too late to do anything about it. Then his brain finally catches up with where he wants it to be. He slowly smiles. "You know what? They're going to think we're *both* in fancy dress!"

I grin at him, trying for impish, and he offers me his arm, which necessitates him putting his hat back on. His BMW is waiting at the side of the road: he opens the door for me, and we roar off *very slowly* into the London evening traffic.

JIM FINDS A PARKING SLOT JUST OFF BAYSWATER ROAD. IT'S A big concert, with overflow screens and a huge crowd in the park. The weather has improved since yesterday's overcast and rain, and we stroll—or rather, promenade—along Broad Walk, past the Round Pond, mingling with the crowds who are here for the outdoor event. Big repeater screens are set up behind the sound stage, and the orchestra for the Prom in the Park concert are tuning up as we hang a left in the direction of the Albert Memorial and then head across the road to the hall itself. Where, despite the hour, there is still a huge queue of Prom-goers.

Patriotic excess is the rule rather than the exception in this crowd: there are balloons and Union Jack flags galore and immensely silly costumes. We take our place in the queue behind a man dressed as John Bull, complete with Union Jack waistcoat—Steampunk seems to be the thing this year among the dedicated costumers—and in front of a couple in full evening dress. Behind them, a group of flag-waving younger concert-goers seem to have decided that Tweed is the New Black: students, I think, too painfully earnest to be true hipsters. (Behind *them* I spot a Dalek accompanied by two Cybermen, presumably there to help their legless exterminatory friend up the entrance steps.)

As the queue moves, people are chatting. "I hear there are some last-minute changes to the program," John Bull tells us: he has an iPhone in a brass-and-leather case connected to his fob chain.

"What's happening?" I ask.

"Well, the guest conductor is still Sakari Oramo, but word is that they're replacing Henry Wood's *Fantasia* in the second half with something special!" He looks perturbed, and well he might: the *Fantasia on British Sea Songs* is a classic staple for the Last Night concerts, and any true Proms geek is bound to be intrigued by a mysterious substitute.

A gap has opened up ahead of us while we've been talking. *"Exterminate,"* grates a pointed electronic rasp from behind me. Jim casts the Dalek a stony-eyed copper's stare, then clears his throat and, taking my arm, steps forward.

The queue is moving again: "Excited?" I ask him.

"I—" Jim pauses, nonplussed. "I think so." He doesn't *sound* very excited.

"Well." I squeeze his hand. "I am!" And, I realize, it's true: it's a great big party, with a party atmosphere and excellent music and a mystery symphony to come! After the past week it's a huge relief, an excuse to forget all about work for a few hours. And then—

Look, it's a concert hall. Not huge by modern standards (but it was *enormous* when it first opened in 1871). If you've been to classical concerts or rock gigs or even theatrical performances or musicals, you know the drill. You queue, and the ticket staff check your tickets and direct you to another queue, past the cloak rooms (where I deposit neither cloak nor violin case), then up stairs and through fire doors and along a dark-walled tunnel (in this case, lined with wooden panels), then through another door into the auditorium. In our case, we go up an extra flight of stairs instead, then along a curving corridor with many doors until Jim finds the door that matches our ticket numbers, and opens it for me. And we're in a box. It's our own little walled-off segment of the dress circle, off to the left of the stage and very dim inside, but with an unobstructed view out over the floor of the hall.

Now, if you are thinking "classical music concert," you are probably thinking of a polite, middle-aged audience seated in orderly rows before a stage with an orchestra on it. But this is the Proms. Indeed, this is the Last Night of the Proms. While there *are* seats (and we have some), the Proms are famously standing concerts. The floor of the Albert Hall is basically a Victorian mosh pit populated by Daleks, Cybermen, women in steampunk dresses, and men in Union Jack waistcoats and bowler hats. There are balloons. There are flags. There is a steady crackle of party poppers and a nostril-tickling peppery smell of gunpowder. The audience are excited, the air heavy with anticipation. Jim and I take our seats in the front row of the box, and I unsling my violin case and lean it against the front wall. We don't have it to ourselves: we're sharing the darkened box with a gaggle of fifty-something men and women, their faces somehow vaguely familiar. (Perhaps I've seen them on TV?) As I lean forward to take in the vista, I half expect the conductor to abseil down from the rafters in white tie and tails. I can feel Lecter at the back of my mind, soaking it all in: the sounds, the sights, the buzz of quiet anticipation rising from the audience like steam from a simmering pot. "When is it going to kick off—" Jim asks, just as the lights dim and the conductor walks onto the stage from the rear.

I shush him and sit back, expectantly, and a woman sits beside me and clears her throat. "That's Sakari Oramo, isn't it, Dr. O'Brien?" I startle and glance at her.

"Assistant Commissioner Stanwick?" Yes, it is: even if I didn't recognize her from the party on the Shard, her uniform would be a big clue.

She half smiles. "I'm glad to see Derek's tickets are getting put to use by someone who can appreciate them," she assures me, touching my wrist briefly to defuse any implied criticism: "I hope you're enjoying yourself! I'm sure you can tell us all about the program afterwards!"

Beside me, Jim sits rigidly upright, his face expressionless. As my eyes adjust to the darkness, I realize we're sitting in a pack of Police top brass—Jim is the knave and I'm the joker. I wonder what *that* means?

But I don't have long to wonder because the concert gets under way almost immediately. It opens with a special piece by a contemporary British composer, commissioned by the BBC, then Arnold's *Peterloo Overture*, with new lyrics, then a couple of songs by middling-familiar composers, and next a first: Richard Strauss's *Taillefer*, in a recital by the guest soprano—

Look, it's a *concert*: and I am here to enjoy myself. If you're that interested, you can look up the running order on the web or stream the broadcast via BBC iPlayer. Most of you won't be, though, so I'm not going to bore you with it: let's just say, big symphony orchestra, famous guest conductor, violin soloist, soprano, tenor, and baritone, and a medley of old favorites and innovative new compositions performed to an appreciative standing audience of thousands with an atmosphere more like a big stadium rock gig than a normal classical event.

I open my ears and eyes wide, soaking it all in. A little part of my brain is watching the soloist's technique, observing the conductor's cueing and execution—that bit of your brain that you simply can't switch off when you're observing a virtuoso performance in a field you know something about. And another part of me is distantly aware that Lecter is listening eagerly, vicariously marinating in my emotional responses, but I don't have enough concentration to spare on irritation—and anyway, isn't that why I agreed to bring him?

All too soon the crescendo of applause and the rising lights signal the intermission. Jim claps enthusiastically; around us, our temporary companions are only slightly more restrained. "That was really rather good," Laura Stanwick confides in me. To her partner: "Don't you think so, Alan?"

Alan, whoever he is—sixtyish, distinguished salt-and-pepper hair—agrees. "Quite special . . ." The hall public address system announces a twenty-minute break, drowning out the rest of his response.

"Would you like anything from the bar?" Jim asks, framing his question to take in both myself and his proximate superior: "A glass of wine?"

Stanwick accepts his offer: "A G&T would be marvelous—"

"And mine's a Sauv. blanc," I tell him, with a smile.

"Be right back." He taps two fingers to his forehead briefly, as if saluting, then slips out of his seat. A moment later, Stanwick lays a hand on my wrist. I tense involuntarily, a premonition sending chills up my spine.

"Director, would you walk with me?" She nods towards the front of the box: "Bring your instrument, please."

I pick up Lecter as she stands, then follow her towards the door. I know a setup when I see one: The only question is, how deep does this go? I should have known Jim didn't get those tickets by accident. As I follow Stanwick out, I reach for my phone—it's in the utility pouch on my belt. One glance tells me there are plenty of notifications. "Just a moment," I say, glancing at the screen.

Stanwick doesn't bother with her own phone: "There's no signal in here," she tells me. "These booths were redecorated recently with shielded wallpaper to cut down on interruptions."

"I see." I put the phone away and swallow, trying to work up some saliva. My heart pounds unevenly as I tighten my grip on the violin case's quick-release button. The notifications all came from the OFCUT suite running on the device—there's a strong thaum field here. *Too* strong. "Where are we going?"

"There's someone I'd like you to meet, backstage." She glances over her shoulder. "We don't have much time if we want to be ready for the second half." I look round, following her gaze: her companion, Alan, is following us. Now there's enough light I can see that he's *another* Deputy Commissioner.

"What exactly is going on?" I ask as my feet carry me after her.

"Later," she says tensely. There are other concert-goers in the corridor. Stanwick leads me to the staircase, then heads down them briskly. We go with the flow for the time being, but once we reach the ground floor, there's another staircase going down—and very little traffic. The corridors here have scuff guards on the walls and uncarpeted floors, and I find myself curiously unsurprised when, as we turn into one, another two cops fall into step behind us—these two wearing street patrol gear, stabbies and hi-vis jackets over black combats, pistols discreetly holstered on their hips.

Well, that tears it. The skin-crawling sensation that I've been aware of for the past week, that there's a target pinned between my shoulders, is back in full strength: I can feel Lecter coming to full alertness, coiling and writhing slowly in the smoky velvet-lined void in his case. The adversary surely has me in his sights. But . . . *the Police?*

We come to an office; just past it there's a staircase leading up to the doors in back of the stage. It's cluttered with desks and papered with posters announcing past performances. Stanwick makes a beeline for the director's desk and sits down behind it. There's a folio in the middle of the desk, and she opens it and begins to sort through papers. "Go ahead, Alan," she says. "I'll take it from here."

"If you're sure—"

"Yeah." She looks straight at me. "Dr. O'Brien. Sit down." There is no *please*. I sit opposite her, acutely aware of the two armed officers flanking the only exit.

I lick my lips. "What's going on?" I ask.

"I think you know what's going on." Stanwick looks at me sharply. "But we don't have time to tango right now. I'm going to have to ask you to read this, please."

"Read—"

She slides a letter from the folio across the desk towards me. I take it with nerveless fingers.

It's on Home Office letterhead. And in one brief paragraph it sets out my worst nightmare.

It identifies Freudstein. It tells me what to do. And it puts me in a terrible quandary.

* * *

FOR THE PAST FEW MONTHS, THE BIGGEST SOURCE OF STRESS in my working life has been our lack of progress in identifying our Mad Science villain.

The obvious answer, so obvious it has been our main avenue of investigation, is that the pseudonym *Professor Freudstein* is the front for an organization. Why is it obviously an organization? Because there might be an evil genius somewhere in the picture, or even a Mad Scientist, but in this century, you don't do science without teamwork. Neither do you break into the Bank of England on your own, or the Sellafield Product and Residues Store, much less the British Library. Each of those incidents has to have involved one or more insiders, or someone with privileged information and the ability to suborn a high-level security system. So: Freudstein is a group of people able to stage remarkable coordinated operations with virtual impunity, a group with access to fissile nuclear materials, a team who are able to stay inside my unit's observation/decision loop, able to plan the most so-phisticated schemes—

These are not the activities of a rogue genius or a loose cannon. These are the coldly calculated actions of a sophisticated organization that has huge resources and understands criminality too well for it to actually *be* a criminal.

And now I know what that organization is.

"YOU ARE *ABSOLUTELY* OUT OF YOUR FUCKING MIND," I TELL THE Assistant Commissioner in charge of the Specialist Operations Directorate of the London Metropolitan Police, "and if you think I am going to cooperate with *this,* you have another think coming."

I push the letter back across the table at her, then cross my arms. "Not. Going. To. Happen."

Laura's face goes still, in a peculiarly over-controlled way that suggests she's bottling everything up tight. She pauses for a couple of seconds before she speaks again, this time in the distant tones of a copper reading a charge sheet to a petty criminal she's just nicked.

"Dr. O'Brien, you have just been presented with a written order signed by the Home Secretary, under Part Two of the Civil Contingencies Act (2004), declaring a large-scale civil emergency and ordering you to support special operations as directed by my command. In case it has escaped your attention, *you swore an oath before a magistrate* not very many months ago. This is all by the book." Her smile is thin and utterly lacking in humor. "Are you rejecting a lawful order?"

I try to center myself. "May I suggest that running a false-flag supervillain operation is one thing, but ordering the deployment of a class six quasi-sentient occult invocation engine is another matter entirely?"

"You can suggest it, but I'm not listening." She mimes hear-no-evil. "This is a crisis, Dr. O'Brien. You don't get to say *no*. You're part of Operation Freudstein now, and you're going to play the violin sonata from the second act of that manuscript."

You have got to be kidding. "Convince me." *Play for time.* I fidget with the ring on my right hand, desperately aware that if Mhari mistakes it for a routine itch or is sleeping or otherwise distracted—

Stanwick gestures at the glass wall separating us from the ops room. "You've got all the pieces: five minutes' time out won't hurt. Tell me what your hypotheses are and I'll set you straight."

"Hypotheses?" I shrug. "You're part of a working group within ACPO, the Association of Chief Police Officers. A clearing house and information exchange between territorial forces, operating at the very highest level, with some staff seconded from other forces, that also undertakes operations directly on behalf of the Home Office. Your command has responsibility for a bunch of major security briefs— you run the counter-terrorism command, what used to be Special Branch, among other things. You're therefore the logical person to put in charge of responding to the imminent threat to law and order posed by a, a"—I check with my internal censor: it grants permission for me to continue, which is in itself worrying—"sudden sharp spike in the prevalence of both ritual magic and informal paranormal powers, commonly interpreted by those on the receiving end as making them superheroes."

She nods minutely, so I continue, listening for the caution of a still, small inner voice. "You plotted the same graphs that *my* employers have been sweating over for the past few months. You saw the sudden upswing and worried that before long *everyone* would be casting fireballs, levitating, building space stations, and generally getting in the way of community policing. So you began looking for a solution to the problem, framed tightly as a superpowered public order issue. Then my people came along. Have you signed section three?"

She nods. "I know who you are," she says, with a surprising level of quiet vehemence. "SOE. Another wartime relic." Her cheek twitches. "We are out of the unlawful activities business, Dr. O'Brien. We're part of the Home Office, not the Ministry of Defense. Unlike *your* employers we attempt to do everything by the book. Sometimes we fail, and then it's time for Professional Standards and the IPCC to work out what went wrong, but the point is, *we don't cut corners.*"

I roll my eyes. "Sure. And we deal with threats you can't handle. *Existential* threats. Your job is to enforce the law, but the law in question applies to human beings here on this Earth. It doesn't work so well after a nuclear war, which is the only sane comparison for what my organization is responsible for heading off—"

"That's where you're wrong." She gives me a brief, feral smile and taps the disastrous letter again. It's lawful, it's signed by the Home Secretary herself, and I'm not willing to bet that my Laundry warrant card can trump it: short of getting it countersigned by the Queen, it doesn't go much higher than this. "Civil Contingencies Act, Dr. O'Brien. It was drafted to govern *exactly* that sort of situation."

Shit. She is, of course, technically correct: the CCA is the overarching piece of civil defense and disaster preparedness legislation that governs how the United Kingdom would be ruled in the aftermath of a nuclear war or an invasion by undead alien gods. She's got me bang to rights. And she continues, remorselessly: "You agree that it's my organization's job to enforce the law, don't you?"

Where is she going with this? "Yes."

"Well, we consider the outbreak of three- to five-sigma superpowers to be a critical problem. An out of context problem for the practice of policing, if you're familiar with the term." *Oh God.* "We have to take preventative action to stop it from turning into a tidal wave of lawlessness. And we have to do it as soon as possible, before disasters like the EDL march in Oldham become daily occurrences. Your sock-puppet public relations superhero team isn't going to provide a constructive role model for our superpowered youth—it's just going to be the butt of their jokes. Don't think it hasn't been tried before any number of times, during various panics over juvenile delinquency. We're facing Armageddon, Dr. O'Brien; we've got to head it off before it happens. A nightmare of lawless rioting lumpenproletariat with superpowers is just around the corner. *You* may be concerned with the defense of the realm, but *I'm* concerned with ensuring there's a realm left to defend."

"Aren't you exaggerating a bit?" I ask.

That's a mistake. Laura proceeds to deliver the smackdown, in the shape of a canned three-minute lecture on Law And Disorder In The Big City: "Our total overall detection rate is just twenty-four percent, Dr. O'Brien. Less than a *quarter* of reported crimes for which we get a confirmed clear-up. In some areas—offenses against vehicles, burglary, theft, and criminal damage—we're under fifteen percent. In reality most of those crimes are the work of a hard core of serial offenders, so we get them eventually—but in the meantime it creates a chilling climate. It creates the impression that we are institutionally incapable of preventing crime. Law-abiding citizens like yourself go about in a state of fear out of all proportion to the scale of the problem, fanned by the tabloid media. Meanwhile, real criminals feel empowered and invulnerable. If some of them subsequently become invulnerable *in reality*, we will have a desperately serious problem. Bad enough if they were to be robbing sleepy banks who pay insufficient attention to securing their vaults—" She reaches into the folio and produces a Police evidence baggie containing a pair of DLT tapes. "Think of the climate of fear! We can't afford to let go for a split second, Doctor. We're all that stands between you and anarchy red in tooth and claw."

I know where Laura is coming from, now: she's a member of the *you couldn't handle the truth/thin blue line saving you from drowning in a sea of filth* school of police opinion. Which is all very well, but better policing and more powers to stop and search isn't going to protect us when the Sleeper in the Pyramid wakes up. "That's not going to happen," I point out. "I don't know if you've been briefed yet, but the superpowered are at risk of K-type dementia. The more power they use, the faster they're going to come down with—"

"Doesn't matter, Doctor. A malevolent five sigma who succumbs to a neurodegenerative condition after two weeks is still a disaster." Her eyes widen slightly. "Is Jim Grey at risk?" I nod. "Oh dear." "We—the Laundry—have some experience in managing this condition. There are techniques that can reduce an occult practitioner's susceptibility: they may work for superpowers, too. After all, they're just informal ritual practitioners with an intuitive/somatic interface . . . But. But. If you want to tackle the superpowered, you need to build hospitals, not super-dungeons."

"Nevertheless." She swallows, looking appalled: she's genuinely rattled, if I'm any judge of character at all. "If I give full credit to what you're telling me, that just makes your willing participation in Operation Freudstein all the more important."

Tell me more: I'm fascinated. "Why the name?"

"It's a portmanteau: the twentieth century was book-ended by the nightmares of Freud and Einstein. Freudstein is a high-profile awareness-raising exercise, to show everyone just how dangerous a five-sigma criminal can be: we can point to his activities and say, that's why we need these special contingency powers. *Before it's too late.* For a project simulating a Mad Scientist, whose goal is to provide the impetus and the mechanism for performing surgery on the collective subconscious of a nation, what could be more appropriate?"

I nod encouragement. "Let me guess. This sonata you want me to play. It's from *The King in Yellow*, isn't it? The second act? Or the third?"

"Yes." The Assistant Commissioner looks past me, at something happening in the control room. "You know the Last Night is being broadcast live: audio on Radio Three and television on BBC One? We can push this broadcast a bit further—we can tie in to the backbone routers at Telehouse Docklands using the same interconnect GCHQ use for their MTI surveillance. And we can transparently redirect the DNS queries from any computer in the UK to point wherever we want them to. In a nutshell, we're going to piggyback your solo on every YouTube video session in the country. At the same time, we will push a Playout update to Sky and Virgin." The satellite and cable monopolists for the UK. "We won't get everyone, but a good thirty percent of the population should receive saturation coverage. Maybe even half." She smiles encouragingly: "Just think, you'll have the biggest audience of any live event in Britain since the Royal Wedding."

I frown; her smile goes away. "What's the payload?" I ask.

She leans forward. "Peel's Nine Principles of Policing." The lightning grin comes out again: "We're not stupid, you know. We know about the risks of installing a firmware upgrade in somebody's brain. So the core message is very simple: *The police are the public and the public are the police.* I can hardly believe you've—I mean, your organization—been sitting on such an incredibly powerful tool for decades and nobody's thought of doing this before? We're facing a crisis of law enforcement: just getting a third of the population to work with us, including a third of the superpowered, is going to go a huge way towards mitigating the—"

She keeps on wittering away, but I am half past listening. I make pleasant face contortions and nod occasionally while I try and work out what to do. In the distance I hear Lecter crying out, single-stringed moans of hunger and need. There's been no response from my ring: for all I can tell it's a piece of inert jewelry. I can tell her the instrument is cursed until I go blue in the face: it won't help. The Assistant Commissioner has a PhD in Criminology and runs on Home Office–dictated rails. She doesn't hold with antiquated beliefs in curses or intrinsically evil instruments, and I doubt she can sight-read sheet music well enough to know what *The King in Yellow* is all about. Hand her a tool that can install a rootkit in twenty million brains and she doesn't see any risk that isn't outweighed by the promise of installing a Police state machine in those heads.

She's running out of exhortations and starting to look at me askance, as if wondering why I'm not agreeing with her more enthusiastically. I'm out of time. "It's feasible in principle," I admit reluctantly. "The trouble is, the violin is very hard to control—"

"I don't think so." She stands up. "I've read your personnel file. You're the most powerful wielder that instrument has had in decades: You've outlasted all but one of your predecessors, haven't you? You can sight-read; I'm assured it's not a very complicated piece. For its impact it depends as much on the instrument as on the score."

"But I can't—"

"Can't, or don't want to?" she demands sharply. "Dr. O'Brien, I'm not *asking* you to play that sonata; I'm *ordering* you to."

"But—"

"Keith, Martin, get her on stage—" She addresses the armed cops on the door. "Interval's nearly over and she's on next." To me: "You *will* do as I say," she says, holding up the letter, the words on the page crawling before my eyes as with blue fire: "By the power vested in me, I command and compel you." And as the geas on the page gets its fingers into my head, I feel myself standing involuntarily, grip tightening on my violin case. I turn towards the door, unable to help myself.

"Jim will hold the score for you," she tells me. "Now get up there and do your job, *Officer*."

I can't stop myself: and as my feet carry me towards the steps leading up to the back of the stage in the Albert Hall, unready and unwilling to give the performance of my life, I work out why. The geas working against me is my own oath of office. I was lawfully assigned to the Security Service and thence to the Home Office: so Deputy Commissioner Stanwick is *lawfully* able to order me to do this, with authority right from the top of my secondment! It'd take the SA himself suspending me from active duty to break me out of this trap, and in the meantime—

—I'm climbing the stairs with Lecter crooning tuneless alien phrases in the back of my mind, and then the spotlight leads my unwilling feet towards the violin soloist's podium. And I'm out of time.

19.

THE KING IN YELLOW

THAT NIGHTMARE I HAD, WEEKS AGO, ABOUT PERFORMING NAKED
on stage at the Albert Hall in front of an audience of empty police
uniforms?

Too realistic for comfort: the nascent sense of panic is chokingly
familiar, but there's no escape through waking up this time around.

As I walk out onto the stage, past the percussion, then forward to
the strings, I can't see the audience. We're lit brightly from above, but
the whistles and chatter and applause and the crackle of party poppers all take place beyond the footlights. There's a burst of clapping
as I walk towards the front, and the odd appreciative wolf whistle.
The other musicians are in formal concert black, the soloists in
evening gowns and tuxes, our conductor in white tie and tails; my
superhero drag marks me out as if I was naked—

There is a music stand waiting for me. Jim stands stiffly beside it,
perspiration glistening on his forehead. The other violinists look at
me with ill-concealed incredulity as an announcer hurries up to the
conductor and they confer quietly.

I can't break out of this walking nightmare however hard I try. I
find my hands are full, busily unlocking my violin case and extracting

the bow and body without my conscious volition getting a look-in. *Fuck it, Mhari, where* are *you? Why aren't you here?* I glance at Jim. Maybe I can talk to him: "Jim?" He doesn't make eye contact. He looks slightly glassy, swaying in place as if anchored to the ocean floor in the grip of a watery current: *Another geas?* "Jim? Snap out of it!"

His hand reaches out towards the music stand, adjusts the somewhat tattered, brown-covered score that waits for me, and Lecter *snarls,* triumphant.

The young, incredibly pretty, and astonishingly talented soloist who carried me away with her brilliance during the first half—she's barely twenty and she's already better than I'll ever be—leans towards me and peers at my instrument in perplexity. "Who made this?" she asks, raising one perfectly threaded eyebrow. "I haven't seen one of these before—"

I manage to tear my eyes away from the cover of the score and stare at her. "If you value your life, *run,*" I hiss at her, and she recoils, eyes wide. "I mean it! Get out now, before it's too late!" I raise my bow and lay it across Lecter's strings, and he responds, just a faint ripple of lightning blue running up and down the fingerboard, which is incredibly sensitive tonight.

"Who *are* you?" she asks.

"Trafalgar Square. The Mayor, remember? Things are going to break bad. Get as many people out as you can—"

The lights are going down on the audience, and the background of noise changes. Jim is still swaying slightly, and after a moment I realize he isn't blinking: faint tear tracks run down his cheeks, but that's an autonomic reflex. *"If you've done anything to him,"* I warn Lecter, *"I'll—"*

Not me. Lecter sounds awfully smug. ***Play now?*** His anticipation fills me with an awful, dull foreboding.

Beside the conductor, the announcer clears his throat, then raises a cordless microphone. "Ladies and gentlemen, I'd like to announce a change of program for the second half."

He pauses. You could hear a pin drop. Changes of program are *not* normal during the Last Night of the Proms. "We will, of course, be concluding the evening as usual with a round of 'Rule, Britannia!' then Elgar's *Pomp and Circumstance March No. 1* in D major, 'Jerusalem,' and the national anthem. But first—

"First, we have something very special for you tonight. It has never been played before in a concert hall: indeed, the score of this piece was thought to have been lost until, barely a month ago, a copy came to light in the rare manuscripts archive during the clean-up after the Mad Scientist Professor Freudstein's robbery of the British Library! Some of you may have heard of a famously obscure play called *The King in Yellow*—it was in part the subject of a television crime drama last year. *The King in Yellow* was converted to an opera but never performed in full; Franz Kafka prepared the libretto and a score was subsequently written by his collaborator, the violinist Erich Zahn, for performance on specially adapted instruments of his own devising, but the rise of fascism put an end to all attempts to perform it until after the war. During the early 1960s, Delia Derbyshire of the BBC Radiophonic Workshop attempted to rescore the concerto for electronic instruments, but the controversial nature of the piece resisted attempts to bring it to a mainstream audience.

"Until now, that is. With the recovery of the original score we are delighted to present, for the first time, the extraordinary violin sonata from the second act that marked the zenith of Erich Zahn's career. Our special guest soloist for tonight is Dr. Dominique O'Brien, lecturer in music at Birkbeck College, who is not only a leading authority on atonality in modernist composition during the Weimar period, but a talented soloist in her own right and one of the few musicians who performs with an original Zahn instrument. Accompanying her on percussion, wind, and brass is the BBC Philharmonic orchestra, while elements of the text will be narrated as prose by . . ."

Jim reaches out jerkily, as if not in control of his own arm muscles, and turns back the cover to reveal the first page. My nerveless feet shuffle sideways, positioning me before the stand. I turn to face the invisible audience, wishing that my own superpower would manifest right now and vanish me from their purview—wishing the very earth would open up beneath my feet and swallow me. My guts are loose with fear; this is not stage fright but something far, far worse: the sum of all my nightmares.

I can't stop myself: I read the bracketed staves of the first line, see how the movement begins with the wind section, and where I'm supposed to come in. A will not my own compels me to seat my instrument properly between shoulder and chin, and pushing past my terror, brushing my pathetic resistance aside, Lecter takes control of my wrists and fingertips. My traitor hands begin to play.

I HAVE BEEN PLAYING THE VIOLIN SINCE I WAS EIGHT YEARS old, and I've practiced virtually every day with Lecter for the past decade. I've published papers on the intersection of music theory and occult inference systems; I came to the attention of the Laundry for my research—and the Black Chamber, too—so I know whereof I speak when I say that music has power. I also know what I'm on about when I assert, with some certainty, that while I am a reasonably proficient musician, I am in no way up to the standard of a guest soloist performing before the Last Night audience at the Albert Hall. (Third violin, maybe—at a pinch, if I really worked at it and the orchestra director was hard up for talent.)

On the other hand, I'm probably the only violinist in the country who can both sight-read the particular score in front of me and understand what it's saying on *all* levels—the musical phrasing and the deeper expressions it invokes. The first page is light enough, an introduction in a minor key that gives me time to warm up; but soon enough Jim turns the page before me and we're into a much stronger exposition, two themes alternating from F-minor to D-flat major . . . with a subtext that makes my skin crawl and itch as if tiny insects are burrowing beneath the surface, for I recognize the pattern of an invocation when I see one. My instrument's strings glow almost invisibly in the spotlight glare, but I can feel Lecter's power gathering in a rush as he awakens. From the corner of one eye I can just see the soprano soloist taking breath as she prepares to give voice to Cassilda's lament, beside the turbid waters of the Lake of Hali—

My turn, Lecter hums, overwhelmingly satisfied, like a gigantic predator that is gathering himself to pounce on the fattest, juiciest prey—

"What will this do?" I can't stop reading, my fingers refuse to still themselves—the geas has me enchained—but sight-reading doesn't quite take all my attention.

I return to myself thuswise.

I glimpse a vision through the eyes of Lecter's interior space, and it is truly frightening. The stony amphitheater of my earlier dream is superimposed over the stage of the Royal Albert Hall. The ceiling has disappeared, revealing a clear sky pierced by the lights of a thousand alien stars. Around me an orchestra of the dead plays for an audience of the damned.

"Who are *you?"*

Lecter laughs, the madness of strings: ***I am an echo of an echo, ripped from yellowing bones enrobed in shrouds to dance within this rigid body: Do you know me yet?***

The violin in my hands feels alive by proxy. As the piece moves back to the major theme, I feel him, warm and pulsing with stolen life, all the lives he's drunk down over the years and decades since the mad luthier of Munich bound a summoned demon into an instrument carved from the still-raw bones of human sacrifices: *"Are* you *the King in Yellow?"* I demand as Jim, somnambulant, turns the page and our little songbird at the podium raises her voice in song.

I am no more the King in Yellow than your littlest fingernail is the bearer of the white violin! But *soon* . . .

Then the development steps up a level, and I can't spare any attention for horrified contemplation: my fingers and hands and arms and upper body are all caught up in the progression as the chorus join in song, chanting lyrics increasingly mutilated and warped to serve the ends of Freudstein:

Strange is the night where black stars rise,
And strange moons circle through the skies,

But stranger still is
Lost Carcosa.

Songs of law the Hyades shall sing,
Where flap the tatters of the King,
Must die unheard in
Dim Carcosa.

Bind those who hear these words,
To love the law though death itself shall die,
Unquestioning, obedient in
Dim Carcosa—

—The Albert Hall has completely disappeared.

I seem to stand amidst a frozen orchestra as the music dies away around us. Jim is frozen beside the music stand, a puppet in the hands of a tired master: his eyes glow faintly with the spiraling wormsign of feeders in night. The audience on the stone steps of the amphitheater are familiar, Prom-goers transported bodily to the alien place, immobile in the grip of some force that has stopped time itself. I look up at where the ceiling should be and see moons—two of them, shining down like symbols of merciless alienation.

My hands are empty. I jerk round, half-panicked, a sense of helpless vulnerability—I know in retrospect this sounds laughable—gripping me, because the violin is my most powerful defense and Lecter vanished just as I found myself on this stony stage. But then I realize what's going on.

Looking for me?

I dry-swallow, looking up at Lecter's true form. "Not really," I say in a very small voice, trembling slightly.

Too bad.

In this place Lecter doesn't wear the body of a bone-white violin. He doesn't need to. I know where we are: previously he's invaded my dreams, but now, flushed with the power of a major summoning, he's dragged *me* into *his* dream. Now I know what to look for I can feel ghost fingers moving, the tension of neck and shoulder betraying a performance still in progress.

I couldn't risk you refusing to cooperate further with my little joke. The gaunt figure floating in mid-air before me seems to smirk, even though its face is hidden from my perception by a veil of palest golden lace. ***So I thought I'd invite you backstage with me, while your body plays on without you.***

"This is where you live, isn't it?" I glance away. Around us the frozen figures stand, row upon row, eyes flickering with tainted phosphorescence. "This is where you've always been."

I'm the last one, you know. The last surviving key. All the other violins are lost, destroyed or locked away—all but me.

"Yes." I turn back to face him. It. Him. The avatar of that which the pale violins were created to summon, when the stars were right. Lecter's shadow: the King in Yellow, released from captivity within the body of the bone violin. "There are people who really don't think you should exist anymore, did you know that?"

I am aware. His amusement is icy. ***But once the key turns in the lock, I shall come into my full birthright, and they will cease to be of concern . . .***

HERE I STAND, TRAPPED TIMELESS IN THE GAP BETWEEN TWO beats of a measure in a work of transcendental melodic magic that has been perverted into a summoning. Here I stand, caught inside the dreamscape of my own cursed musical instrument, while it seeks to pervert the perversion, to turn Operation Freudstein's insanely dangerous attempt at a mass geas of compulsion into an invocation instead, a summoning for the King in Yellow. Here I stand outside of time and space, and I notice that I'm shaking.

I'm not in shock, and I am not cold, for there is no temperature in Lecter's dream. I am, I slowly realize, livid with anger and just barely bottling it in. Anger? *Rage*, actually.

Let me enumerate the roots of my rage:

I'm furious with Bob for deserting me to become the new Eater of

Souls. I'm mortified and angry with myself for falling for Jim's charms while failing to realize that he'd been placed in my organization—whether or not he knew it—by our adversary, to provide them with a continuous stream of intelligence about us via his weekly reports. Even before we come to my abduction into this waking nightmare, I was furious at my instrument for daring to tiptoe around my dreams and hopes and fears, resentful of the way it manipulated me with Mhari.

I'm pissed off at Dr. Armstrong for dumping me into the Directorship at INCORRIGIBLE, also known as the Transhuman Police Coordination Force, a job for which I am absolutely inadequate and unqualified; but above and beyond that I am *disgusted* with him for knowingly putting me in a position of assumed helplessness in hope that it would lead our enemy to play their hand, despite being fully aware of my history, of what unquiet ghosts it would dredge up.

I'm upset at myself for being afraid of standing backlit against windows and for spooking at loud noises in crowds. I'm angry with all the waiters and shop assistants and police foot patrols who can look right at me and fail to see me as I slowly drown in the oceanic waters of social irrelevance, succumbing to the invisibility of the middle-aged woman until it gradually becomes a three- or four-sigma superpower, an expression of my own not inconsiderable strength as a practitioner feeding on my sense of self-doubt and inadequacy. (The invisible man is a Wellsian supervillain, but the invisible women are all around us, anxious and unseen.)

I lack the words to adequately express how incensed I am by the activities of Deputy Commissioner Laura Stanwick of the Metropolitan Police and her cronies within ACPO, who have decided on their own initiative that nanny knows best, and that creating a nightmare supervillain as a stalking horse to justify raping twenty million minds in parallel is a *perfectly acceptable* price to pay, if it improves cooperation with the police in a time of national crisis—a crisis that they barely understand and are in no small measure unintentionally contributing to, by diverting our scarce resources.

That the culmination of Operation Freudstein is an attempt to compel millions of people to obey the rules of policing is bad enough. That they've recklessly chosen to ignore my urgent warnings about the risks of overfeeding the white violin is worse. That the instrument in question sees this as an opportunity to become the undead avatar of the King in Yellow (and is well on the way to doing just that, if I'm any judge of demonic summonings gone wrong) is just unspeakable.

But all of this is displacement.

The harsh fact is, I don't much like who I've become or what I've done with my life since I followed Bob down the rabbit hole of the Laundry all those years ago. I have, admittedly, had all those extra years of life and even some stretches of something approximating marital bliss; I can't forget the way Bob rescued me twice from fates that don't bear thinking about. (Admittedly, I returned the favor: we've played a hair-raisingly extreme version of "for better or for worse" over the years.) But it's been crumbling for ages now, as I was sent on one nightmarish job after another, culminating in Vakilabad and then the nonsense in Trafalgar Square—history repeats itself, first as tragedy and then as farce. I've sacrificed a lot to the Laundry. I allowed my academic career to wither, marking time in a teaching niche. Kids—well, they were a nonstarter once I understood the horrifying implications of CASE NIGHTMARE GREEN. Salary . . . don't get me started. I'm in my forties now, my best years behind me, marriage coming unraveled, career tanking spectacularly, and when the chips were down, the oath of office I swore rendered me unable to say "no" to the most heinously immoral order anyone has ever given me.

My self-respect has taken a battering from these successive betrayals of trust. But I'm still angry: and as long as I'm not numb, I've got something to work with.

And more to the point, I think Lecter has inadvertently given me a way out.

THERE IS THIS THING ABOUT MY OATH OF OFFICE: I'M SWORN TO the defense of the realm, and I'm sworn to obey lawful orders.

That's the horrible thing about Laura Stanwick's having served me with notice under Part 2 of the Civil Contingencies Act, signed by the Home Secretary, after the SA helpfully seconded me to the Home Office. It's entirely lawful, because the CCA is essentially an enabling act that allows designated emergency commanders to make it up as they go along. It was designed to ensure continuity of operations in event of a major catastrophe, such as a nuclear war. And I'm helpless to refuse it, because the geas built into my oath of office requires me to obey lawful orders.

But the sorcerers who devised the geas weren't stupid. I have some latitude in how I interpret an order.

Laura Stanwick ordered me to go on stage with the white violin and play the sonata from *The King in Yellow* before a live audience.

But she didn't order me to help Lecter unlock the astral gate and summon his master. That's the instrument's agenda, not the Home Office at work.

And, more prosaically, she forgot to order me *not to do anything else.*

IN THAT FROZEN MOMENT, STANDING IN THE MIDDLE OF THE amphitheater of dreams in Lecter's memory of long-lost Carcosa, I realize what I have to do.

I draw on what willpower I have and slip sideways, away from even this shadow of reality. Lecter's spectral outline shifts, drifting towards me: I take a step back, then another.

Where have you gone?

I can *feel* my invisibility, like a cloak I can tug around myself. I take a step sideways, towards Jim's frozen image. The glowing eyes—he's not possessed yet, not quite: he's just open *to* possession, if Lecter comes into his full power and erupts, unleashing a tidal wave of hunger across the stage. I reach around his shoulders and shroud him in my imaginary cloak.

What are you doing? Reveal yourself at once!

A voice of thunder rattles from the stone steps around us, hammering my ears. Jim's body is rigid as stone, stiff, unbreathing in this place—an instant between heartbeats—

The thing that is Lecter pounds away across the stage, bowling through the oboes and clarinets like a vengeful fury, scattering mannequin musicians in all directions.

Come back! he howls, distracted. *Good.*

I can't feel my fingers properly. That's *also* a good sign. It means the illusion he's woven to trap me here is slipping slightly.

I lean in close towards Jim's face. "Jim. Jim! Wake up! Snap out of it!"

Something changes. He doesn't move, doesn't respond—but after a moment I realize he's *breathing.* Trapped in this place with me, outside time.

"Jim!" If this were a fairy tale, I'd have to kiss him or something, but unfortunately the real world is a whole lot more complicated—and I am not going there until Officer Friendly and I have had a free and frank exchange of opinions about loyalty—

So instead, I kick him on the right shin, hard.

"Ow!" Jim staggers, the luminosity fading from his eyes. "Ah, ow! Mo, where are—"

"Get *down*!" I grab him again, stretching my shroud, and drag him to the ground as Lecter howls and shrieks overhead, blotting out the moons as he flies across the arena.

"Where are—"

"*Shut up,*" I hiss. It takes concentration to extend my imaginary cloak around others, but I've done it before. I did it for Busy Bee in Downing Street; I can do it for Jim here. "Listen, we're awake in Lecter's dreamscape. Stanwick thinks if I play this sonata with the modified lyrics, she can turn a third of the population into obedient little constables. Lecter has other ideas, and if I finish it, we're in a world of hurt. *That*"—there is a pale silver ovoid glimmering in the air at the far side of the stage, a portal of a kind I've seen before and really don't want to be seeing here—"is Lecter attempting to summon his superior avatar, the King in Yellow—"

"Oh shit, is that—"

"*Yes, shut up*—in a moment you're going to wake up on stage again and *you've got to stop me playing*. Do you understand?" I grab his shoulders, wrap my arms around him.

I stare into his eyes and see the confusion bleed away, replaced by worried concern: "Mo, can't you—"

"Laura hit me with a geas! Do you know the story, the red shoes? *Someone else* has to stop me."

"But I—" He looks sick. "I'm *really* sorry, I had no idea she was planning—" Another mournful howl splits the air: Lecter soars high above the ruins of Carcosa, searching for his runaway host. "You want me to stop you playing?"

"Got it," I say. "And try not to use your superpowers. If you use them here, it could be *really bad*." That would attract the feeders, like sending up an occult signal saying *K syndrome fast food buffet here*. He's hugging me back, and because we're trapped between ticks of the clock in a dream of desolate ruins, I lean close to him and kiss him on the lips once, by way of a good-bye, and as I feel him respond we—

—Fade to standing spotlit on a stage, wrists and shoulders feeling pierced by hot wires and blood trickling down my stinging fingertips to lubricate the blue-humming strings of the white violin as I face the music in the Albert Hall, the bow dragging my hand back and forth as the tempo increases and the chorus raise their voices in an unearthly counterpoint—

****Found you!**** Lecter shrieks inside my head, as my right ring finger buzzes emphatically and I sense rather than see a great tattered bat shape flapping towards me out of the darkness beyond the lights.

Then Jim makes his move and all hell breaks loose.

FOR A SPLIT SECOND JIM STANDS BESIDE ME, WHITE-GLOVED hand hovering over the corner of the score from which my bleeding hands are compelled to play. Then he grabs the manuscript and *jumps*. I told him not to: but of course, silly me, my mojo is all about *being ignored*.

I gape, following his leap. Any lingering doubt that Jim is indeed Officer Friendly vanishes after him as I follow his trajectory towards the dress circle boxes.

COME BACK! Lecter howls in my head, deafening me, but the geas is broken: with no musical score I *can't* continue the performance. I slowly turn towards the orchestra, lowering my bow as a steady trickle of blood runs down the fingerboard of my instrument and splatters to the floor.

There's something wrong with the bow, I realize dimly. My finger vibrates again, an urgent imperative. Faces look at me, and these eyes are indeed glowing, writhing blue-green worms twirling within the heads of people who no longer exist in any human sense of the word. The instrument feels *dead*. It feels like, like a violin made of bone. The anima that gave it such a vibrant sense of life has departed.

No, it's not dead. Rather, I'm keeping an iron grip on my own visibility because something in the back of my head is *terrified* that Lecter will notice me again. I've blocked him out completely. As long as he can't see me, his attention will be turned elsewhere. But that might not be a good thing.

All around me stand the bodies of orchestra and Proms-goers, occupied by the lesser feeders in the night for whom the recital has opened the way: mindless processes of contagion and possession that swirl in the wake of the greater summonings and seek living bodies to run on, allowed to swarm in because Laura Stanwick wouldn't take no for an answer and didn't let me fully explain the risks of a recital with the white violin so close to breaking loose—and in a moment they're going to realize that I'm not one of them—

The words *oh* and *dear* spring to mind.

I often find myself wishing for my husband, most frequently for trivial reasons ranging from mere comforting conversation to kitchen sink-side assistance—but right now I could *really* use him. If Bob was here, putting down an incursion of a few thousand hungry feeders in the night would be a non-problem: that's the sort of thing the Eater of Souls *does*.

Again, if things stood as they did six months ago, when I was still in control of my instrument and Lecter damned well did as he was told, this would be a non-problem.

But not only am I no longer with my husband, I am hiding from my instrument's attention (because he seems intent on turning me into a tool of his own will). So I appear to be stranded in the middle of a zombie mosh pit with a thousand or more feeder-possessed bodies, a numb violin, a dysfunctional superhero costume, and only my own talent to fall back on. I just hope the feeders *aren't* paying attention to the bat-signal right now, because if they are, I'm done for.

Tightening my invisibility around me like a cloak, I carefully step sideways towards the soloist's seat—I'm really glad to see that she listened to me and left. I think I can do this: the possessed are still focused on where I stood a moment ago. And they're not actually moving. Maybe they can't see me—no, they're tracking me. Or rather, they're tracking the thing I'm carrying. They're tracking *Lecter*.

This goes beyond an *oh dear* moment. I analyze my options, and this is what I get:

I can get out of here on my own. They can't see me, any more than anyone else who I don't want to be seen by can see me. But if I scuttle away, I'll be leaving several thousand Prom-goers in thrall to whatever brain-eating parasites Lecter has invited to the party. I'll also be leaving a truly hideous mess for the first responders when they arrive on scene. What I *should* do is try to banish them—but I can't do that without my instrument's cooperation.

Or can I?

I look up at the shadowy recesses of the ceiling. Jim's up there somewhere, isn't he? He took the score. I can only hope he's got the sense to run away, that the feeders didn't notice him, and that the high-power ward I upgraded him to is strong enough to protect him as long as Lecter can't see him directly—

(My belt pouch vibrates. A moment later the ring on my right hand contracts painfully, pulsing twice.)

—*This had better be important.* I reach into my pouch and quickly glance at my phone. There's a text message, from Mhari. My knees go weak. *We're coming in. Can you distract them?*

I tap out a reply with shaking fingers: *will try*. I hit "send," then shove my phone back in the pouch and look around. The second violin sits slumped forward, eyes glowing—her instrument has fallen at her feet, unnoticed. I pick up her stand and score. My fingertips feel as if they've been burned, and I leave a reddish smear on everything I touch, especially the papers. Careful not to brush up against any of the possessed, I pick my way past the immobile players and walk towards the concert grand parked at the side of the stage. I'm in luck: the lid is down, the pianist not yet on stage to play his part of the program. I climb onto the stool, then boost myself up onto the top of the horribly expensive instrument, trying not to think about what my boots are doing to its finish—but for what I'm going to do next, I need a raised platform with a good view in all directions, the better to see my audience.

I set up the stand, open the score, and raise my instrument. *Mine*, not Lecter's. It's still the same bone-white body, made from materials nobody in their right mind would enquire too closely about, but there's no sense of his attention hovering around it. Lecter, the entity bound into the body, is elsewhere right now. No time to check whether this is safe, I've just got to hope that it works—

I flip through the score, looking for what I need.

Stanwick's inadvisable editing of the second half of the night's program replaced a medley of popular pieces with *The King in Yellow*, but she didn't touch the traditional closing sequence: even to a manipulative philistine like her, rearranging the traditional end of the Last Night concert qualifies as sacrilege or treason or both. So I cut straight to the climax. First up in the sequence is Ansell's *Plymouth Hoe*, a nautical overture, but there's precious little I can do with it with just one violin—I could run through the main theme, but it's light on strings and heavy on the brass and winds. So I flip past it and go straight to "Rule, Britannia!" Now *that's* scored for strings. I'll have to improvise a bit, and I can't count on any support from the chorus (who are peering, green-eyed and silent, in the direction of Lecter's body), but it's really hard to mess up something so deeply ingrained in anyone who learned violin in a British secondary school. It's traditionally followed by Elgar's *Pomp and Circumstance March No. 1* in D minor—better known as "Land of Hope and Glory"— then "Jerusalem" (the Proms are *really big* on Elgar), finishing with the national anthem.

"This had better be worth it, Mhari," I mutter. I'm terrified that I'm going to get this wrong: that's what comes of paying too much attention to my own fear and self-doubt. I've *got* to do this, got to get it right the first time. I take a deep breath and I start to play, my fingertips sore and bleeding across strings that remain stubbornly dark.

The sound of one violin playing in a concert venue the size of the Albert Hall is a lonely thing, but there is none of the usual quiet side chat, shuffling, and laughter you'd expect from a regular audience: as I begin, you could hear a pin drop. Normally the audience would be on their feet, brandishing banners and singing along with the lead soloist and the BBC chorus: it's the nearest thing you'll get to an American-style display of hyper-patriotic flag-waving from the normally reticent British. But this isn't a normal concert audience. As I play, I look around at my audience. They're cold, cold as the grave: thousands of pairs of pale green-glowing eyes focus on the thing in my hands, their bodies standing immobile, trapped within shells of flesh. I can't even tell if they're still alive or if their souls have already been eaten. Part of me is still concentrating on my invisibility, fearful that if I relax my focus, Lecter will notice me. If he wins again, I'll have to play, and I won't be able to stop until my hands are bleeding stumps no longer able to hold bow to string—

Heads begin to turn, one by one at first, then in a wave of iridescence that flashes across the floor of the hall. Something is happening behind me, but I don't dare look round: I have to keep the music flowing. But it's hard to concentrate on playing and to withhold myself from visibility at the same time. The need to remain unseen is the antithesis of the performative impulse.

Stop it. Stop it now!

Lecter has finally noticed me. My fingertips burn as the strings and bow light up with blue-green fire, spiraling whorls of light that echo the gaze of the possessed. Is it my imagination or does he sound frightened, querulous?

"*Not going to stop,*" I hum quietly along to the score.

You must not do this! Where is the score? Where has he taken it?

"*Don't know, don't care. We're going to finish this, Lecter. We're going to bring this back to the Last Night of the Proms, and you're going to make all your little friends go away.*"

Somehow I manage to flip the page without smearing blood all over it.

I've won, you know. The voice in my head bleeds menace. ***Eat them all.***

"*If you eat the audience, I can promise you an eternity of torment. The Auditors won't stop me: you can go too far, you know.*"

Before me, the audience sway gently. One by one, they begin to raise their arms. I don't dare to hope: they're possessed, after all. This might just be Lecter directing them to act in unison. But I feel his attention drifting from me; no, something is wrong. Something I didn't anticipate. But what?

At first I think the stage lights are coming up. But then I realize the shadow of my legs stretching out before me is being cast from a single source, directly behind me rather than overhead. I turn to face the light and falter, recover, then force myself to keep playing even though I desperately want to flee.

Carcosa, Lecter tells me. ***Where the King in Yellow waits.***

It's a gate; circular, perhaps five meters in diameter, its rim burning with a pale limelight fire as it stretches across the stage in front of the organist's pit. Beyond it I see a shadowy stage, dreadfully familiar rows of cracked stone seats rising up in the amphitheater beyond, other performers on stage, white-shrouded, their features invisible as they dance and sway to inaudible music performed at the command of one who has not yet come.

With a barely audible sigh, the first rank of the possessed audience collapse in windrows, their glowing eyes simultaneously extinguished. The ward I wear around my neck stings my skin, heating up painfully. The gate ripples, then firms up—

"Mo!" A shrill voice shouts behind me. "Hold on!"

I stare at the gate, horrified, as the bubbling laughter and triumph of the strings rises from between my fingers and my nerveless hands continue to pull notes from the white violin without any conscious volition on my part. All I can do is watch as Lecter rips the life from bodies by the thousand, pouring it into the opening he's carved in spacetime. I can feel something else on the other side of the gate respond, a dreadful sense of recognition as an echo of Lecter's attention turns my way. I want to stop my hands moving, but they won't do what I command. *Is this my fault?* Part of me wonders as I fail to make the music stop before the thing on the other side answers the call of its smallest part, the fingernail scraping bound in bone that is Lecter—

Something slams into me from behind, throwing me bodily off the top of the piano. For a split second I'm falling, but then I land and someone cushions my collapse. In a blurring moment I'm surrounded by Bee, interposing her hands between my elbows, knees, head, and floor. Somehow I'm still holding the violin in one hand and the bow in the other: still glowing blue-green, so intense that they leave after-images when I glance at them.

"What," I manage to say, then my arms are trying to raise the instrument and set bow to string, but it's really hard to play the fiddle when your shoulders give a painful wrench and your wrists are suddenly handcuffed.

"Don't fight," Bee pants in my ear. There's a huge weight on my back, and after a moment I realize it's Captain Mahvelous. I'm being sat on by my own minion. Wonderful.

"Mhari—"

"Here, Mo." She jumps across fallen chairs and lands beside me, the two halves of the violin case in her hands. "Can you put it in—"

"Too strong," I gasp. "Won't hold it. Also—" I nod towards the gate.

"Well, all the same—" Mhari cringes back from the fiddle, which is trying to poke her. "Who can—"

"Coming!" calls Ramona. "Wait for me!" The whine of her wheelchair sets my teeth on edge like a dentist's drill as she rises and flies above the field of bodies. For a moment the glamour slips and I see it as it is, and wish I hadn't: those aren't wheels, and her chariot is disturbingly alive. But then it descends to the stage and I blink and it's a wheelchair again.

You can't stop me! Lecter roars. I try to let go again, but all that happens is my hands twitch helplessly.

"Wrong." Ramona throws something to Mhari. "Warded gloves. Bee, go and help Lollipop and Torch. Eric, see if you can work that thing out of her hands; Mhari, hold the case while Eric closes it, then shove it over here while I—"

Slaves! To me!

I've been dreading this moment. All around us, the possessed are rising—those who haven't already been life-drained by Lecter. But they're not going to human-wave us: rather, they're bunching up, opening corridors to the back of the floor where I see other bodies with green-glowing eyes that almost match the luminosity of their high-vis vests. Of course: Lecter's had over an hour to work on Laura's people, hasn't he?

"Get off me," I gasp.

"Soz, not going to happen until you let go, boss." Some unseen force tugs at my fingers as Eric—Captain Mahvelous—shifts his weight. My ribs creak. Then suddenly my fingertips close on air. "Great! Is it in—"

There's a loud clatter as the bone violin and its bow skitter into the case that Mhari holds warily at arm's length. She slams it shut, then fumbles the catches closed. "In the bag." Mhari sounds exhausted. "You can let her up now. Sorry, Mo." She turns and shoves the case across the stage. I can still feel Lecter in my head, buzzing furiously, but he's curiously muffled.

Eric rolls off me and apologetically produces a handcuff key. I raise my wrists. "Jesus, boss, what happened to your hands?" he asks.

I look past his shoulder as he unlocks the cuffs. "Behind you!"

Because I'm watching the approaching cops with the green-glowing eyes and their raised batons, I am looking away at the moment when Ramona runs her chair at the violin case and sends it skidding across the stage and through the gate to Carcosa. Even though I know it's for the best, the memory of losing my instrument forever fills me with an unrelieved sense of gray anguish even now. Decades ago I read *The Lord of the Rings*; I believe Tolkien understood something of that sense of loss, from his description of the ringbearer's torment at the edge of the Crack of Doom. It's the anguish born of losing a part of your body, or a chunk of your soul, and like all amputations it is best for the subject not to watch it with their eyes open. I don't see the violin case skitter across the threshold, but I feel it, a bone-deep ache in my hands and heart that spreads rapidly.

Come back! The voice is muffled but I can still hear him, from a great distance.

The officers are closing in. There are at least half a dozen of them in crowd-control gear; behind them, another four uniforms, Laura Stanwick among them. The glowing eyes—is that my perception of them? Or is this something else? They move too normally, too fluidly, to be truly possessed, but—

"You *idiot*," Stanwick swears, glaring at me. "You had just *one* job and you still managed to make a balls-up of it."

"Was *that* part of your so-called job?" I ask, waving a bloody thumb behind me at the rippling portal. "Because—"

"You're under arrest," she tells me, ignoring the gate floating at the back of the stage. It's as if she can't see it. And yes, her eyes *are* faintly luminous: What's gotten to her? Backwash from the payload she tried to install in everyone? "We'll work out the charges later, but disobeying orders issued under a CCA note will do for starters. Also, destruction of—"

Soon.

My skin crawls as I hear Lecter's call in the distance, and an answering echo. Something is approaching the other side of the gate: I can feel it. So, from their behavior, do the rest of my team—but Stanwick and her people seem blind to the sense of immanent dread. "Close the fucking gate," I call, not caring who responds. "Close it down *now*."

Mhari: "On it—"

"*Not yet*," an amplified voice booms out. A moment later, the floor beneath me vibrates. I register shock on Stanwick's face for a split instant before I look round and see Officer Friendly standing before the gate. In the ghostly moonlight streaming through the portal the blue strobe light on top of his helmet looks almost washed out, a flickering sapphire of doubt against the forces of night. He's holding a tube of some kind in one hand: I recognize it just as he throws it through the gate, rippling pages unfurling and flapping. "*Close it now!*" he booms, as I feel something lurch closer, the focus of a malevolence a thousand times vaster than Lecter searching for—

Mhari throws something small and dense at the wall of light. "Down!" she shouts, taking a dive towards the floor at one side. I look away and begin to raise my arms to shield my face, then the high-end banishment ward hits the gate and slices it to shreds, severing my final link with my instrument.

And that's all I remember.

"SO," ASKS THE SENIOR AUDITOR, "WHAT HAPPENED NEXT?"

We're in his office. He's seated behind his desk, chair reclined, a half-full crystal tumbler of smoky amber anesthesia sitting to hand. I'm standing with my back to him, in front of the curtained window, inspecting the weave of the fabric: an expensive, heavy brocade, quite capable of blacking out whatever lies beyond. I'm wearing a cardigan over a baggy dress I can put on and take off without using my fingertips—I'm still on sick leave.

"I woke up in hospital. Unlike many others." I shove my gloved hands deeper into my dress's pockets. "Slept again. Woke up once for Bob, told him to take the damned cat. Another time, Jim was there. He wanted to apologize. Said he didn't know about the Freudstein conspiracy. Did you know about him?"

"Let's keep to your story for now." He's gentle but ruthless. "What else?"

"Well. After three days they let Mhari in to brief me. Or maybe she just walked past the nursing station: it's hard to keep her out of somewhere. She told me about Jim's call. She told me what Jim told her, about Assistant Commissioner Stanwick's operation—"

"*Ex*–Assistant Commissioner Stanwick," he interrupts. "I'm sorry, please continue."

"Operation Freudstein was the Met's official undercover operation to justify their acquisition of unlimited powers under the Civil Contingencies Act for policing supernormal powers. Coordinating with like-minded chief constables in other forces, with a nod and a wink from the Home Office, although I think the HomeSec was careful to ensure that she wasn't personally briefed on exactly what they were doing. *We* were set up to fail, thereby demonstrating that an agency with *our* background couldn't possibly do the job. Incidentally, if I were you, I'd be really worried about that. Someone in HMG really doesn't love us and want us to be happy—"

I take a deep breath, then turn round and stare at Dr. Armstrong. He nods mildly, looking utterly unperturbed.

"I lost an irreplaceable asset—the violin," I remind him. I wish he'd be angry, so I could be angry right back at him. "I trusted a man who was planted on me as a spy." And I nearly allowed it to become a personal betrayal: but the SA doesn't need to know about that side of things. "I failed to stop Stanwick subverting the geas in my oath of office, and as a result, I failed to prevent a horrific civilian mass fatality—" The death toll at the Royal Albert Hall was lower than I feared at the time, but still well over two thousand. It made news headlines around the world: blaming it on a deranged supervillain seems somehow inadequate. National trauma ensued: there's popular support for Parliament banning all superpowers, and who could blame them? Even if we know it's really not possible, any more than a law banning drowning would prevent riptides. "The spin-out organization I set up is almost certainly going to be wound up, or in-sourced within the Met as part of the Specialist Operations Directorate, once they finish cleaning house. Oh, and if I'm really lucky, I may regain enough sensation in my fingertips to play the violin again some day." I allow some tension to creep into my voice as I get to that part. My fingers still ache dully, four weeks later: my pain control consultant is gradually tapering off the opiates.

"Sit down, please, Dr. O'Brien." He gestures at the padded armchair alongside the desk. "What do you expect me to say?"

"I expect you to say you're sorry," I say coldly.

"Well, yes, and you may take that as a given." He glances away, as if embarrassed. I take *that* as my cue to sit down. "Do you understand why—"

"Yes."

"But you—"

"You knew what it would do to me." He knows about my trust issues. He knows what happened last time someone used me as bait in a trap. Chewed up and spat out, damaged goods. "I know you thought the ends justified the means in this case, Michael. And I can't refute your case. That a major ministry was trying to colonize our turf, using recklessly inappropriate methods. That a very senior police officer was, with approval from the top table, running a rogue paranormal operation. That they'd gotten delusions of omniscience and decided that *their* ends justified *their* chosen means, regardless of collateral damage, including nearly summoning the King in Yellow. Oh, and they were working with a senior police liaison organization known for having employed covert intelligence assets to infiltrate other groups—admittedly this was at a rather higher level than the usual run of the mill Forward Intelligence Team asset. And Jim wasn't exactly *hiding* the fact that he was a cop, was he? Nevertheless."

I chew my lower lip as he looks at me. The next sentence will be the hardest.

"I want to tender my resignation," I say, very careful to keep my voice as even as possible. "Effective immediately." Then I cross my arms and wait.

"Um." Dr. Armstrong slides his half-moon glasses off and fumbles on his desk for a cloth. "Excuse me?"

"I want to quit," I explain. "It's too much. I can't. Can't do it. Anymore." My throat doesn't want to obey me. "Every time I go back and try harder it gets worse. It's eaten my life and my friends and my marriage and my hands. And I'm not making things any better." I sniff. I am determined not to cry, but my control is wearing thin.

The SA finishes polishing his glasses and puts them back on, then peers at me over their rims. "Have you ever had a nervous breakdown before, Mo?"

"I have never—!"

"No? I should think not." He glances at a paper file on his blotter, then reaches into a recess in his desk and pulls out a bottle and an empty glass. "Will you at least join me in a glass?"

"I—I—" I stare at the bottle. I don't know what to say, but I shudder violently, and he seems to mistake it for a nod.

"You've been driving towards the precipice for the past eighteen months," he says as matter-of-factly as if he's discussing the weather, while he pours me a glass of Laphroaig. "To be honest I wasn't sure you'd make it this far: you've been burning the candle at both ends for too long." He nudges the tumbler towards me. It's so full it nearly slops over. "Cheers."

"Cheers—" The whisky is a decent enough single malt, but my sinuses are so clogged with unshed tears that all I can taste is fire water and wood smoke. "What?"

"Nervous breakdowns," he says, very seriously, "have a lot in common with acute PTSD. You've been courting it for a while: relationship trouble, overwork, burn-out, sleep deprivation, acute stress, and the added burden of"—he swallows—"carrying the white instrument. That's how almost all of us get out of it, incidentally: the violin bleeds you until you can't handle it anymore. Got out of it, I should say."

"But it's gone!" I raise my voice. "I lost it!"

"No, Dr. O'Brien, *your team* made a joint determination that it had become dangerously unstable and decommissioned it before it could kill any more civilians. It nearly killed you, in case you've for-gotten? It overpowered *you*, the second-longest standing bearer, the only one to have custody of it during the active conjunction of CASE NIGHTMARE GREEN."

"Who was the longest-standing bearer?" I ask before I can stifle my morbid curiosity. "And what happened to him or her?"

"Judy Carroll carried the violin for nine years, back in the 1980s and early 1990s." I nearly spit single malt across the room: Grandmo-therly Dr. Carroll, in her twinset and pearls? "Back before the unfor-tunate incident at Dansey House she and I were discussing what to do with the instrument when you could no longer carry it. We had already determined that there were no suitable candidate successors; I believe our biggest dilemma was how to decommission it safely, without provoking an incident along the lines that eventuated at the Albert Hall."

"Well." I swallow. "I still want to resign."

"I know you do." Dr. Armstrong sips his whisky and frowns at some passing thought as he watches me. "Naturally enough: you feel betrayed and let down right now. And I can't say you're unjustified. You're right about your organization, by the way: I gather they're already opening up a slot on the org chart at the Yard, tentatively labelled SCO20—serious paranormal crime. They'll purge the man-agement team except for Jim Grey, and keep the rank and file on as cadre for the new unit. But that need not concern you."

"The HomeSec probably wants my head on a plate," I mumble.

"She's not getting it." He leans forward. "Oh, she may have to receive your written pro forma resignation, but that's not the same *at all*."

"I told you, I want to quit."

"Yes well, we can't always get what we want, can we, Mo?"

"What's *that* supposed to mean?"

"It's supposed to mean that we owe you a lengthy stretch of sick leave while you get your head back together. We also owe you a pro-motion and a performance bonus, or as much of one as we can scrape together—this isn't the private sector, alas, or you'd be down at Earl's

Court pricing up your next luxury yacht. And if it will set your mind at ease, we *won't* be putting you back into field operations as Agent CANDID, or anything remotely similar. There's a statute of limitations on field ops, and eight years of carrying the bone violin means you're fully paid up: after you come back, you won't be punching tentacle monsters anymore.

"But that doesn't mean the organization is through with you. Quite the contrary, in fact." His smile is avuncular, warm, friendly, and utterly terrifying. "Your attempt to resign while in the grip of an acute stress reaction is noted and declined. Go home, Mo. Play with the cat, write up your report, take a break. Now that the white violin is out of the picture, why don't you see if you can sort things out with your husband? Take a month; take two.

"But sooner or later you'll feel better, and when that happens, you should drop in and see me. There are a lot of things we need to talk about, once you've calmed down and regained your center. For one thing, Judith's seat on the Board of Auditors is waiting for you. And for another, you know what they say about the traditional reward for a job well done . . ."